DISTRACTION

SOUL SEER CHRONICLES, BOOK 4

S.J. CAIRNS

Cover design by Getcovers
Logo created by S.J. Cairns
Logo image by CNuisin depositphotos.com ID 265803116
Tree vector by alepdaru@gmail.com depositphotos.com ID546365346

ISBN 978-1-7782426-9-4 (Ebook)
ISBN 978-1-7782611-0-7 (Paperback)
ISBN 978-1-7782611-1-4 (Hardcover)

Previous editions printed 2019

Black Thumb Publishing
Ontario, Canada
www.sjcairns.com

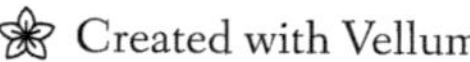 Created with Vellum

ACKNOWLEDGMENTS

It's amazing the difference support can make.

I ramble on in each book in my acknowledgements about my online writing group—The Quillies—and how lucky I am to have them, but it's true. I would still be a hunched back hobbyist in front of my computer if it weren't for them. From one introvert to a bunch of others and peppered in with those extroverts who help us shine, I love you guys.

The name of this book was apt, considering the deadlines I missed. I thank you all for getting me back on track with some tough love.

Dad,
Even though you won't read my books for fear of catching a glimpse
into your daughter's sex life, your passive support gives me strength.
Thank you.

1

LOCATION, LOCATION

Power sprung from the deepest part of me, riding a surge of fury. Donovan called my name. When a blip of control returned, Ranlyn was flat on his back beneath me. Raw rage drained from me as I looked down into the wide-eyed surprise of my Elder. The fabric of his sweater was dust in my fist. I stared at my hand, opened it, and watched the remaining ash fall to the ground. Rough hardwood floors scraped my palms as I scrambled off him. I hit something and looked back to see Kim's sneaker. She lay beside our other Elder, Miklos, both still unconscious. Their soul glows were so wrong, mixed up between their bodies—hers too bright, his not bright enough.

A lightning strike of pain clenched my teeth and cranked my body backward into a painful arch, gripping me tight. My muscles contracted to the brink of tearing. The pain railing through me stopped and left me a moaning heap on the floor. I tried to move, but all I managed was a slight rocking. A throbbing tingle pulsed through me as I pushed up onto my hands, muffled voices echoing in my skull.

When the throbbing subsided, Ranlyn's screaming at the only conscious or unpossessed Elder bounced off the walls. He insisted he could have handled the situation without injury. Hinapouri claimed self-defence. He didn't argue, but I knew her enough to know she understood her attack against me was overkill.

Donovan was pushing up from the floor onto all fours, Hinapouri's assault impacting him just as much as it did me. He started the healing process, fixing us both in a snap as his power worked its way across our connection.

Ranlyn knelt in front of me. I took his outstretched hand and sat on the edge of the couch, only then seeing the hand-sized chunk of missing sweater on his chest.

He followed my line of sight. "A shirt can be replaced."

"Maybe. Kim can't be."

He exhaled but didn't say anything.

Donovan sat next to me. "There has to be a spell or ritual to fix Kim and Miklos's souls."

"Does there?" Hinapouri glared at Donovan.

He responded in kind.

Ranlyn looked at Kim and Miklos in front of the brick fireplace. "This is why we travel through the veil alone."

I stood. "If you've seen this before, then wave your magic wand and do whatever they did the last time."

Ranlyn stood in front of me. "We don't have magic wands."

"They are all dead. Or wished they were." At a questioning look from me, Hinapouri added, "The people who didn't travel alone through the veil." Hinapouri sat on one of the couches and began nonchalantly fixing her braid.

Ranlyn glared at his co-Elder, who continued to fix her hair without care for how she was pissing me off.

My power rushed to the surface again. "I'm not leaving her like this! You told Miklos to bring her through the veil with him, knowing she was hurt. If you thought she was a goner anyway, you would've left her behind and saved yourself an Elder."

Ranlyn crossed his arms, his thumb grazing his bottom lip. "You refused to go through without her."

"Wha—? You don't pin a donkey tail on a zebra. This isn't my fault."

"Correct, Soul Seer." Hinapouri's scathing glare focused on her co-Elder. "Ranlyn's priorities are clear."

Ranlyn turned to me. "Our duty as Elders is to put the Coven before ourselves. I needed to be conscious to get through my wards or I would've sacrificed myself by taking Kim through the veil. Miklos knew his duty. The Puppeteer may not have killed you right away, but you would have died. We would lose two members—one a Soul Seer, another a Sect Leader—since recent incidents prove you and Donovan die together. Leaving Kim behind with you meant the loss of another member and Sect Leader. My choice was clear." He looked around me at Hinapouri. "As are my priorities."

The Maori Warrior continued to braid her hair without outward concern for Ranlyn's opinions of her, either ignorant or uncaring of his insinuations.

Not that I was surprised, she would never sacrifice herself for Kim, me, or anyone else. Above all, Hinapouri was a survivor.

Donovan went on to troubleshoot with Ranlyn, but everything he said was shot down.

I couldn't stop looking at Kim and Miklos. Finding her inner mojo to wield the power of a true Magic was mission priority for Kim, but this energy transference caused by her going through the veil with Miklos wasn't right. If getting rid of parts of his power now stuck in Kim meant she went back to the lower wattage of her Kitchen Witch powers, it beat dying. We had to figure out how, and soon. I had no clue how long they could stay like this.

I sat next to her. Blood had dried in streaks on her skin from her eyes, nose, and ears. If it wasn't for the pink in her skin and the fact that her chest rose and fell, she would look dead.

"Here." Ranlyn handed me a bowl of warm water and a tea towel, then returned to the kitchen.

I looked around to see Hinapouri and Donovan were missing, and then registered the unmistakable sensation of being hit by a stream of water, my body temperature higher than normal as he was doing what Kim couldn't and enjoying a hot shower to get rid of the blood and grime from the attack by the Puppeteer and the Eradicators.

As I did my best to wash off as much blood, dirt, and grass stains from Kim's skin, I was lost in thought about what we had run from. I couldn't believe the Woodland of Energies was gone. Could the trees regrow? They were made from the ashes of dead Magics. Powerful ones. I would hope they weren't so easy to get rid of. Though they were put into the Creation for safe keeping, so maybe.

Was Aunt Lacey gone for good? Seeing her spirit put a damper on my atheist thoughts regarding the afterlife and posed too many questions for my tired brain to flit through right now.

Kim wasn't dead. Her heart still beat—maybe too fast, but it kept her going. Did she know she was unconscious? Did she feel it when Miklos took her through the veil? Caine heard nothing from his hospital room while he was in his sleeping curse, but his condition was so different. I didn't know what to expect of Kim.

Blood mixed into Kim's vibrant red hair. I washed away enough of the gruesome reminder of the Human Engineer's macabre invention to get her looking half-way decent, so she wouldn't be scared shitless by what she saw when she woke up.

I would no doubt scare myself if I checked a mirror right now. Vampire Ball attendant's walk of shame or zombie movie extra wasn't selfie-worthy when the blood was real.

I couldn't imagine what was happening with Kim and Miklos's souls, but I needed to try. She had saved my ass so many times, I should get her name tattooed on my left cheek. I owed her.

Bringing my power to the surface was easy. As was letting it simmer as I laid one hand on Kim's head and the other on her chest and forced healing strength into her body. Besides the closing gash on her forehead, persistent unconsciousness meant no further proof of success.

I sat back on my heels.

Hoping my bestie would spring up and make a snappy lesbian porn remark, I laid my hands on her again. Once more, nadda, zilch. She was a red-headed sleeping beauty with a macabre twist and my lips weren't the secret weapon to saving the kingdom.

If healing won't work, I wondered if something else in my arsenal would. It was risky, but worth it.

Eyes closed and concentrating, I was sucked into a soul read without forcing it. Shit! I was hoping for a coy soul when the power crammed within Kim twitched to attention-whore level desperate and grabbed hold of me. It pulled me down into her without permission. Instinct raged in response and had me fighting back. In a place with no access to my limbs, traction was impossible and pointless. I was dragged deeper, blinded by a fit of memories showcasing Kim and Miklos's lives in a jumble. Miklos was winning over Kim as his strength outweighed hers tenfold.

A faint, pulsing light—the shimmer of Kim's soul glow—was cowered into a crevice as Miklos's energy flew around like a pissed off wasp, trying to breakthrough her body manually. I didn't want to deal with him and went to her.

A blip of light was tucked away in a tiny space away from Miklos's crazed energy. I got in close and sensed her confusion, frustration, fear, and the overall feeling of being invaded. Conversation was far from girl-talk over mojitos and nachos, experienced through sensation and interpretation of unseen nuance rather than words.

A desperation of impending doom was clear. Kim's soul knew life like this would be short. They weren't compatible, weren't meant for this fusion of energies. Maybe they could survive on a host of feeding tubes and medical equipment, but Miklos would drive Kim insane the longer he terrorized her. He continued to rush into me and the surrounding area. Me being here drew attention to Kim's hiding spot.

Damn. I was a heat-score instead of a wingman and Miklos was relentless. I bet if I attempted the same soul reading on Miklos, he would be pissed pieces of Kim's soul were squatting within him and would be aggressive in his tactic to evict her. Either way, one Magic would win and the other would die. I had no faith Kim would come out the winner.

I had learned all I could and wanted out. Miklos somehow knew this and ramped up his frantic buzzing around me. Unable to stand another second of him, I promised Kim I would find a way to return and get them back to working order, and then tried to find my way back.

I bypassed the mix of their memories to where I began but couldn't get out. I panicked and became a spinning mass of energy bashing into a doorway I couldn't see. A frantic, non-verbal plea to "Let me the fuck go" resulted in a sudden release.

I caught myself on the couch behind me as I panted and tried to run my fingers through my blood-caked hair.

Ranlyn sat on the couch across from me, steam rising from the mug in his hand. "What was that?"

Slapping footsteps on the upstairs floorboards preceded Donovan leaning over the railing. "Yeah, Sophie. What was that?" He rushed down the stairs, ripping his stained shirt over his wet hair and shoving in his arms.

I pushed up from the floor to sit on the couch. "I don't need your permission to do anything."

A flaring reaction flooded me across Donovan and I's connection. He plunked down on the opposite couch, his dark eyes unblinking in unspoken challenge.

I knew exactly what rumbled around in his brain and he knew it.

Considering he placed my welfare in the forefront, hitting me with the selfish card was fair, but it didn't mean I was going to cow down at being called out. The mix of "you're right, but you still piss me off" boomeranged through the connection until Ranlyn stepped in.

"What's going on here?"

"Sophie's being an irresponsible brat."

I made a throaty sound. "If me being a brat helps Kim, it's worth the risk. I'm not apologizing."

Ranlyn put his mug on the floor between his feet. "What were you doing to her?"

"She was reading Kim's soul. Alone. Something dangerous to both her and myself considering she nearly killed us the last time."

"That's what defibrillators are for. Soooo sorry I thought of Kim and Miklos, the two most fucked up souls in this room, before ourselves. How selfish of me." I turned my whole body to Ranlyn, implying an A-B conversation. "We discovered that I can not only see souls but can channel a soul's memories and get down into the root of their power. A couple accidental mishaps caused some seizures— once because I read back into Caine's past and then Gareth's since Caine is also the vessel for Gareth's power." Ranlyn's eyebrows rose at this. "Again, accidental, but what the fuck is a healing ability good for, if not healing?"

He nodded. "But you can't heal yourself if you're dead."

"Thank you."

I ignored Donovan's 'I told you so' attitude. "I was reading Kim's soul, hoping I could understand why her soul glow is so bright and why Miklos's isn't bright enough."

"And?"

"Miklos and Kim's souls and power are inside her body, vessel, whatever you want to call it. I'm assuming that applies to Miklos as well, though I'd rather blow a feisty rhino then read his soul. He's super pissed and terrifying Kim. I don't totally blame him. He's an immortal Elder partially trapped in a Kitchen Witch. Both want this over ASAP. I don't know how much longer they can handle it."

Nodding while he seemed to be processing my explanation, Ranlyn sat back into the couch. "Can you extract souls?"

"Ewww. I hope not. Sounds gooey."

He shrugged. "I know of some who can. None with beginnings in Soul Seeing that I'm aware of, but Soul Extractors can remove a soul from its vessel. Usually in its entirety, for various purposes."

I raised my hand at him. "You don't need to explain for me to get the gruesome picture. Maybe I'm supposed to be able to soul extract.

Who knows? I'm not about to experiment on Kim. Olive didn't know about the Soul Reading, so I don't have anyone else to ask. Use your Elder contacts to find one of these Extractors. Can't imagine they advertise a power like that. Besides, how is removing someone's soul a gift?"

"You can kill people with the same gift used to save them." Donovan's deadpanned reminder of the horrific times I had used my disintegration power, accidentally or in one instance of coercion, didn't make me want to speak to him.

"If you know one, dial them up. I'll help if I can, but no way I'll do it without one of them next to me with the 'Extracting a Soul Handbook' memorized word for word."

"They may be difficult to track down. I'll work on it."

"Where'd Hinapouri go? She should be helping."

"And the Apporter? And Jheri?" Donovan's tone prickled.

I hadn't seen the Apporter since the clearing outside Diluculo and had forgotten the pixie of a Summoner who brought Aunt Lacey's spirit to us inside the Creation. I hadn't had the chance to thank her. Could she have slipped by the Eradicators?

"Hinapouri left to warn her people. The Apporter's services were no longer needed and neither were Jheri's. Once their purpose had been fulfilled, they were clear of all obligations. Neither's duties included waging war with enemies after us."

"But Jheri's a Witch." I followed Ranlyn as he went to the kitchen to refill his mug.

"No. Jheri's a Summoner."

"She's still a Magic. The Raddies would have killed her without understanding the difference."

"A moot point. Her fealties lie with another coven. Her death, due to our inability to protect her, could have sparked a war. Disappearing before the Raddies got a hold of her was imperative."

"The Apporter, too?"

Donovan received a half-nod for his question.

"Super fun times. We face certain death and Jheri gets to tuck-tail and hide. Your system is broken."

"Our system," Ranlyn spoke with control, "is far more complex than you can comprehend based on one brief altercation."

"A brief altercation?"

"Yes. Brief. Short. Minimal in its duration. Before you judge the fabric of what holds this Coven together, learn it, understand it, and if you still find reason to, work to change it." He stormed off through the only closed door from the open concept room.

Ranlyn did awkward annoyance well. I drove him to it every other day, so I recognised the resulting expressions and sense of familiarity. But this anger was new. I reminded myself he was dealing with a bleak situation without the help of someone trusting to lean on. He was one of two Elders still in commission, while the other made decisions with spears instead of brains. Overwhelmed didn't cut it and my opinions were small-minded at best.

I sat back down, leaned against the arm of the couch, and closed my eyes, regretting my petty judgements.

"The Coven meeting is supposed to be tonight."

I didn't open my eyes to address Donovan. "So? Cancel it."

"Can't. Coven meetings happen no matter what." He didn't mention the missed meeting after Aunt Lacey's murder and I wasn't about to remind him. "The Coveners co-Sect Leader is unconscious and the other was almost captured by an enemy they know nothing about. The danger is ramping up, and they need to be informed their membership depends on their initiative to get their nose into the thick of it. We can't operate like a weekly book club anymore."

"Have it here. I doubt Ranlyn would care."

Anger swelled. Not my own, as I was too disengaged with the topic for anger.

"Have you bothered to look out a window?"

I sighed. "Why? Do the clouds look like a pair of clowns making dick balloons?"

His refusal to answer forced me to look up at his tight, mask-like expression. I shot him a mirrored expression, shrugged my shoulders, and closed my eyes again.

"Get off your ass and see for yourself." His voice was low and slow.

"Not into dick balloons right now, thanks."

A bash to the side of the head with a pillow forced me to pay attention. "Are you kidding me?" I threw the pillow back. He caught it with ease and tossed it onto the couch, a rise in his brow and irritation sparking across the connection.

Two small front windows were covered in dark patterned drapes. Most of the natural light came from high windows from the top floor and skylights. I pulled back the fabric to see long grass stretching out to a road off in the distance and surrounded by trees. White and yellow flowers scattered the sea of wild grass. The absence of neighbours and the yardage of greenery spoke of being up north somewhere. Other than that, no geographical indicators implied a location.

Ranlyn came back through the door and headed for the stairs.

"Where are we?"

"Jesenice." He didn't stop or look at me.

"Where the hell is Jesenice?"

"Slovenia." He reached the top of the stairs and turned right.

"Slovenia? As in Slovenia, Europe?"

"Do you know another?" He disappeared into a room, leaving me with nothing but his sarcasm.

I turned to Donovan. "Why are we in Europe?"

"It's where Ranlyn lives. Guess he figured the Raddies couldn't find us here."

Travelling was out of my budget. Northern Florida was my record for stretching beyond the borders of my Canadian city. Europe was a bucket list contender, alongside winning the lottery to fund the trip, and being discovered at a karaoke bar to one day write some timeless anthem played at every post-prom cherry-popping venture. Never something I thought I'd do on a whim—without my knowledge, no less.

I turned back to the window in hopes of drinking in every foot of scenery in case someone else crashed in and ruined our party again. Everything happened too quickly back in the Creation. Aunt Lacey was there one second, then ripped away the next. The swinging pendulum ride that scooped us up brought with it an upswing of tragedy, with never enough time to recover before the next blindsiding swing.

In hopes of bringing my world to a measurable crawl, I lost myself staring out the window at nothing of importance until Donovan and Ranlyn's footsteps on the creaky wood of the stairwell stole me away.

Ranlyn headed back through the closed door off the main room.

Donovan approached me. "He'll work out getting the Coveners here for the meeting." Relief unknotted the stress between his, and my, shoulders. He didn't deal with failure well and with Kim out of commission, he was responsible for the Sect. "He'll also work out bringing us some of our stuff so we're not conducting the meeting in blood-stained clothes. And bring Bosco."

"Ohmygod!" I clasped my hands over my mouth. "How long have we been gone?"

Donovan's expression soured enough to tell me it had been longer than I relished hearing. We had slept a long time. Add the time spent in Diluculo, and it was long enough for Bosco to have turned the house into his personal game of 'What shenanigans can I get into?' Plus, he was no doubt starving.

"He's not an infant. I'm sure he could fend for his himself."

"You're sure, huh?" I shook my head and turned back to the window.

———

When the hour came and went for the Coveners to arrive, I got antsy that no one had showed until Donovan pointed out that Slovenia was six hours ahead of home. We had a long time to wait.

Hours later, I was laying on the couch next to Kim when a high-pitched whine came from behind the door I still hadn't been through. Before I could investigate, the door whipped open and a familiar pug sprinted into the room.

"Bosco!" I scooped him up and struggled to hold onto him as he whined in odd non-canine-like noises, licking the air more than my cheeks and kicking his muscular legs.

Donovan came into the room carrying a few bags and headed upstairs and to the left. We had slept together in the same bed the night before, put there while still unconscious, but I wasn't about to make it a habit.

Europe or not, the room was capital 'C' creepy. No kid slept in there now, but they had, and it gave me the impression that this was Ranlyn's family's home. Not his weekend getaway, but a place his family had lived and maybe died. Judging his age by sight was impossible considering his strength. He could have slowed the aging process decades ago, had a wife and child who had then passed on before he looked over twenty-five. The dusty shelves and the odd way the room looked untouched painted a different picture altogether. Maybe the child died young and the room stood as a testament to their last days. Being inside was like invading a shrine, making me wonder why we were left in the room in the first place.

Face wet with enough slobber to fill a finger bowl, I went to the kitchen to grab Bosco a water dish. Warbling by the front door shifted in my peripheral. I turned to it, holding Bosco tighter. The warbling sharpened and distorted the door behind it. The air moved like heated pavement.

"Ranlyn!"

The erratic warping ebbed and shifted, and then Blake and Jared were standing in the room with shock pasted on their faces and plastic bags in their hands.

A thunder of steps came from upstairs. Donovan raced to the top of the stairs now dressed in clean clothes. Ranlyn and the Apporter emerged at a run from the doorway leading to the rest of the house.

"Oh, good. Welcome to my home. Make yourselves comfortable."

He then retreated to where he came from with the Apporter, who didn't stick around for pleasantries.

Blake and Jared did a wide-eyed survey of where they were while Donovan sauntered down each step. "Yup, you're at Ranlyn's, but you're also in a different country."

"How'd we get here?" Jared was still looking around as if trying to figure out where "here" was.

"You popped through a portal connected to my front door. When you walked through my door, a portal at the entrance sent you here. Don't expect next weeks' Coven meeting to include a free ride to Europe, but we'll give a heads up on a local change if we can. Oh, and you might want to switch your cell to airplane mode."

They swore and pulled out their phones. I never would've thought to warn them.

Before they finished making the changes, the portal began to warble again. They scrambled out of the way and watched as Gwen popped through and then laughed as her eyes widened.

Donovan left the guys to explain to Gwen what happened as he took their bags and spread out the snacks on the kitchen counter. I filled a small bowl with water and set it on the floor for Bosco, who lapped it up and panted, leaving streams of water to drool out of his mouth onto the floor.

Donovan opened the fridge and put something inside. "You gonna be okay tonight?"

The question was delivered so casually, I didn't track his meaning. He looked over his shoulder at me and opened bags of chips, spilling them into a bowl. He crunched up the empty bag and threw it into a garbage bucket under the sink.

"Why?"

He opened another bag of chips—sour cream and onion. "Caine."

I made a throaty sound. "Like I have a choice." I tried not to let the sheer thought of him mix me up inside, knowing Donovan was waiting to critique that exact reaction.

He dumped the chips into a bowl and threw out the bag. "Well, when you're done not caring about Caine, there's a shower and clean clothes upstairs. The Coveners are too busy over the hype of a portal to notice the blood crusted on your shirt and in your hair, but they will. It'll be easier to explain everything to the Sect all at once. Same with why their Coven Elder and co-Sect Leader are laid out between the couches in the laziest version of Twister ever."

"Right. Good luck waiting to explain the unconscious bodies. Maybe tell them it's an extreme version of meditation."

"You joke, but I'm using that."

"Have at 'er." I left for a shower. When I got to the top of the stairs, Gwen was asking about Kim and Miklos. I laughed before shutting the bathroom door behind me.

As I squeezed the water from my hair for the third time, I noticed it was finally clear. I touched my neck and realized something was odd. A few moments passed of turning off the water and drying off with an oversized towel before I saw myself in the mirror and saw my necklace was missing. Aunt Lacey had gifted me the silver triquetra the first time I met her and now where was it? Probably torn from my neck and laying in the destroyed Creation where she was tortured and murdered.

Fuck that puss-eating piece of shit. The thought of my necklace being anywhere close to Loring or the Puppeteer had my nails biting into my palms. The heat from my ears was so great I pressed my fists into them as I resisted the urge to scream and smash everything in the small, steam-sweating room. None of this was right. Aunt Lacey shouldn't be dead. Kim shouldn't be stuck in a husk of a body, fighting against her Elder's soul. We shouldn't be having a Coven meeting after Loring and the Puppeteer had torn the Coven's grave-yard into toothpicks.

Donovan's passive curiosity invaded the silent space in the bath-room across the thread of our connection and reminded me the house was filling with Coveners. Now wasn't the time to break down into tears and have Donovan break down with me. Freaking out on Ranlyn wouldn't get my necklace back, nor would it avenge Aunt

Lacey or Kim or any of the Magics spirits from the Woodland of Energies.

I left the bathroom wrapped in the towel and stormed down the hall and into the creepy room to focus on getting ready. Shaky hands and liquid eyeliner didn't mix. I forced a calm, pulling from a place of numbness.

After slipping on dark jeans, a grey mock vintage tee, and a teal zippy sweater, I tried and failed to stop myself from gazing around the eerie room of untouched objects. Tin toys, wooden picture frames of faces I didn't recognize, waxy dollies, and faded wallpaper with cowboys and horses in a windswept field. The pillows Donovan and I had slept on were covered in dried blood but looked no worse off as the fabric was equally unchanged as everything else.

I left the square little room as soon as I could.

Joyous voices met me before I reached the stairs and saw the light soul glows of the Coveners. The ride in, as well as their landing zone, promised the meeting was one to be remembered. Coveners perched along the steps, keeping a large zone clear around Kim and Miklos as if they were contagious.

Pushing through the group, one slow step at a time, a stuttered-step tripped me up. I grabbed onto the railing before I went tits over tea kettle, but my reflexes weren't agile enough to prevent me from banging into people and grinding my heel into someone's fingers.

I couldn't tell whose. I was too busy gaping at the blue soul among the group.

Caine's presence was expected. It wasn't as if he and Donovan were already at it, or his expression was sad or pissed off. It was simply him. Not the him I cried over in a hospital room, the him I shared my home with, or the him who broke through my walls and had me falling in love. It was the him I first met trapped in the rain drenched park, desperate and afraid to abandon his brother.

Caine cut his hair.

He stood in the crowd, talking in a small group of which I couldn't have picked out in a police line-up. I had no idea what he was wearing and couldn't hear his voice to judge the content of conversation, but I couldn't look away. The subtle difference that changed everything was a spear to the gut.

The locks that grew as he slept had been sheared to resemble the style he had sported when he was a different person than the one I knew. The sideburns remained, but the long hair and slight curls were gone. An inch of hair on his head and a half inch more in the front was all that was left. He kept the long hairstyle after the sleeping curse because I liked it. I guess that didn't matter anymore. Cutting his hair was another way of cutting me out of his life. It was already official, though we hadn't discussed terms. Somehow, a simple haircut made the fact that Caine and I were over crystal clear.

I backed up the stairs, an awkward retreat as I bumped into Rachel returning from the bathroom. I couldn't answer her when she asked if I was okay. I shot back up the stairs into the creepy little room, feeling like I might choke on my tongue, my throat was so tight. A lance of pain sliced into my rib. My heart jackhammered the shit out of my ribcage. I gritted my teeth as if I could growl at my tears to keep them from springing from my eyes.

A suffocating hot flash had me whipping off my sweater. I threw it onto the bed and paced the small space in front of the even smaller window, wishing one wasn't painted shut so I could feel fresh air against the sweat on the back of my neck.

Donovan barged into the room, slamming the door behind him, and stared at me with synched brows in a silent question.

"I don't know! Explaining myself means I possess an inkling of self-awareness, and right now, I know more about our current geographical location, which is dick-fuck all."

"You don't wig out for nothing. What happened?"

"He cut his hair!" I rushed at him and pushed him out the door, ignoring his protests.

The connection thrummed with his helplessness, ramping my anger and frustration. Donovan didn't know how to deal with me, which made sense. I didn't know how to deal with me, either. He respected my space but wasn't far. The passive support was as comforting as it was annoying.

Anxiety pitched and waned until I had no choice but to sit on the old, creepy bed and shut down the part of me fuelling the fire before I hyperventilated and passed out. When goosebumps covered my arms, I knew my blood pressure had leveled and the episode was over. A Coven meeting was in progress, so I couldn't hide away from everyone. Caine was out there, and I had to face him.

What Donovan absorbed from our connection had to be a cluster fuck of nonsense, judging by the way he leaned onto the railing overlooking the main floor below us as I joined him. Having someone emote alongside you would give the impression of a sense of empathetic camaraderie, but, in reality, it was mortifying. I didn't want to feel the way I did and I sure as hell didn't want anyone to know about it. The bloom of anger between the connection with Donovan was all me. Whatever he was going through, it was lost beneath my flurry of self-deprecation.

At the end of Donovan's line of concentrated and tense sight, I found Caine on the first floor, his blue soul glow haloing his body. Denise stood beside him, a couple inches too close, fawning for his attention by laughing louder, talking more, arranging her hair over her shoulder, and exposing her low neckline—honing every desperate skill and trick in her arsenal without so much as a glimpse from the ignorant oaf next to her.

Not that I could judge. I screwed everything up. Caine may have left that night, but the consequences of him leaving Donovan's that day far outweighed any reason for leaving in the first place. Having him see me torn-up by the mere sight of him was a dickhole move. I was happy to see he was oblivious to my freak out.

This happens when people break up and aspects of their lives remain entwined. You either persevere or one of the broken makes a further break. No amount of running would solve this and, short hair or long, his fault or mine, I needed to throw up a mask and deal with the truth of my actions when I had the time and distance to do so.

Light pressure gripped my sweater-covered arm with surprising tenderness. Donovan was looking down at me as his concern punched through my discomfort. I surprised myself by refraining from pulling away from the contact. His excitement at this was a spike in relief he hid well.

"Kim's counting on you to get through this." Donovan's reminder was supposed to evoke strength, though it pushed me closer to guilt. "You know what I mean. Kim's been plenty strong for you. Now it's your turn. And with her out of commission, I need someone to take over the huggie-feelie stuff when I tell the Coveners their Elder and co-Sect Leader might not make it and why."

A deep breath wasn't what I needed, but alcohol wouldn't help this. So, I put Caine's hair and the loss of my necklace on the back burner, not bothering to tell Donovan about the loss of Aunt Lacey's gift since saying it out loud would send us both into a spiral.

I never saw who I crushed and jostled during my retreat, so I threw out apologies like dick-shaped confetti on my way down the stairs to join the others on the first floor, hoping they didn't take it personally. We had enough to tell the Coveners and an apology was a part of it, if only for having to start the meeting off with bad news.

We started with the Ballard Family attic and Olive's restoration party. Donovan stood in front of the fireplace with Kim and Miklos at his feet, his arms crossed. I sat on the arm of the couch closest to Donovan, not wanting to stand before the group in Kim's place, even if Donovan wanted me as a replacement for his second.

We eased from the story revealing Joelly's intentions to the premonition outlined by Aunt Lacey to the Apporter's pick-up to Diluculo in the middle of the night. This led us to explain the destruction of the Woodland of Energies, the takeover of Diluculo by Loring, the Puppeteer possessing their missing Elder, Veata, and the attack by the Raddies.

It was a lot to throw at them.

Listening in but never overtaking the meeting, Ranlyn leaned against the wall by the door I had still not gone through, listening as if he was never subject to the atrocity firsthand. Maybe through the years of tragedy he had experienced, one more painful memory was unable to lessen the hollowness evil created within him? I couldn't be sure, but I figured I was close enough to assume its half-truth and wondered if one day I would look the same.

Donovan spoke of the Human Engineer's device. The warning was clear—the Raddies were everyday citizens, indistinguishable from any other Blind. The mangled radio was something even the Coveners could watch out for as long as they saw it before it was activated. The knowledge of 'see the radio, hear the noise, feel the pain, run before you die or they torture and kill you' was solid advice.

He didn't downplay the gory details of misery as our power raged out of control, our life force escaping our bodies like morbid faucets before passing out and waking up in Slovenia. We would have died without the Apporter, plus Ranlyn's home to escape to.

Caine's grey eyes were unfocused, his expression pulling to its center with thoughts I prayed to hear. When Donovan touched my clothed arm, I realized I had been trying to concentrate on grasping a single thought from Caine's head, starving for a word or phrase and coming up empty.

"I thought it'd be easier for you to explain Kim and Miklos's situation, since you can see their souls."

I switched places with him and explained what I saw and what we knew of their souls. I found reasons not to look into the eyes of the others, instead focusing on Kim's hair, Ranlyn's encouraging smile, and Donovan's hands as they lay loose on his knee.

"Someone is being brought in to help with it. A Soul Extractor. Until then, they'll be hanging out fireside. Feel free to chill and chat. They're great listeners, even if they can't hear you." The concern in my voice wasn't something I wanted to share, but the sarcasm didn't go over so well either.

For a Sect full of Chatty-Cathy's, I was surprised we weren't battered to death with questions. All were quiet. The shitstorm of information we threw at them resulted in whispered conversations in small groups rather than asking questions or doing readings like in normal meetings.

However, lowered spirits and suspicious theorizing couldn't keep the food from disappearing. As more of a comfort, all the potluck dishes lay out on the kitchen counter, emptied as normal. Worry for Kim stopped me from binging.

What if my bestie couldn't handle Miklos's soul invasion and her body shut down? Or she lost her mind in the process and didn't come out of it quite right? She was alone and was no match for an immortal.

Caine kept his distance. I wanted to talk to him, to check in, but I wasn't about to force him into a conversation in front of everyone. Chances were, I wouldn't like what he had to say or how loud he might say it. And he deserved to say it all.

I waited for Donovan to come out of the bathroom and let him in on my plan.

"Babe, come on. Why would you soul read again? Not that whatever I say will make much of a difference anyway."

I scoffed. "You're lucky I warned you." He slanted his head with silent agitation. "She needs to know we're not abandoning her."

"You mean you need her to know. You said you couldn't talk to her."

"Not, like, normal talking, but she understood."

"You know that for sure?"

"As sure as I know I'm going to read her soul and was just warning you."

He exhaled and shook his head.

"Relax. You can feel when things are about to career into the ditch. Plus, Ranlyn is here and so is Henry in case we need CPR again."

"None of that makes me feel better."

"Clearly, I'm not here to make anyone feel better. Except Kim. Hopefully."

I knelt at Kim's side, tucked my legs beneath me, and laid a hand on her chest, imagining connecting with her soul as my power came alive and began to search. Miklos was a bully and line-jumped the moment he registered my presence. It took a bit of maneuvering through the chaos of memories to shake him off as he came at me like a swarm of biblical locusts. Finding Kim's soul was harder this time— a combination of my exasperation with Miklos and the difficulty of seeing her soul glow, as it had faded since my last visit.

She was hunkered down in what was closest to the fetal position for a soul without limbs. She wasn't fighting to overtake Miklos. She had given up, like a death row inmate waiting to be led to the chair and leaving her last meal to get cold.

Fuck. Why didn't I have hands to grab her and pull her out with? Maybe a Soul Extractor had soul limbs? Like an evolved form of a soul, apart from my guppy uselessness.

Miklos buzzed by and then doubled-back. I had revealed Kim's hiding place, again, by tracking her down and he surged at me as if prepared to take us both down. Kim's soul glow quivered as if trying to make itself smaller to get away from him, but had no place to go. Bouncing him out of her body like a rowdy bar patron wasn't going to happen, but I could stop him from making things worse for Kim.

Healing her from the outside worked on the body but did shit-all for the soul. Now that I was inside, I thought it a viable option and decided I wasn't leaving without making things better for her in some way.

Without hands to focus my healing through, I hesitated. Could I touch her in the same way without her thinking I was another soul trying to hone in on her territory? Miklos surged at me again and I had no choice but to try and hope Kim understood I was a source of safety.

I crowded Kim's essence, thinking about a message of peace, and blocked the crevice she squeezed herself into from Miklos.

Come on now, girl. Find your strength. This bearded ball sack is not getting anywhere near you.

He surged again, this time hovering in front of me. His oppressive energy rolled over me with an invasive caress, as if assessing his enemy. A whip of heat and a draining zap had me curling into myself. He tried to push by me. I pushed back and retained my position to protect Kim. He lashed out again. I refused to give up my position, despite the pain, and I felt my energy wilt and fight to restore itself.

Something close to recognition flickered behind me. Yes! I've got him. Do what you need to, girl. I'm not going anywhere.

He may be an immortal, but I had the luxury of knowing what was happening to he and Kim's bodies and souls. I knew help was on the way. Another lash of his energy would have had me screaming if I had a voice here, but I held my ground and took the challenge. Changing up his attack meant all angles and intensities. I bared down and tried to connect with my power to withstand whatever he threw at me. I buffered a hit, which seemed to piss him off. His next hit was packed with more heat. I wasn't the bloody mess I should have been had his unrelenting whippings been with a literal whip against skin, but I still felt lesser every time he hit me.

Light from behind me grew. Kim was gaining strength. A slow progression, but she was brighter. If I was stronger or could explain to her what was happening and what I knew, it would make all the difference. All Kim wanted was to feel the power of a natural-born Magic. Being of the Kitchen variety never stopped her, but something was stopping her from making the leap. If she had that power now, she could protect herself.

I knew what to do.

Miklos hit me, pain lancing through my whole being. I used the break between attacks to purge some of my own energy in Kim's direction. Her light jolted awake. She became a smidge brighter.

Perfect.

I kept this up a few times, battered on one side, spreading myself thin on the other, trying to hurry things up and get it over with until a spark of energy misfired when I tried to send it Kim's way. I couldn't do this for long without depleting myself. Being at Miklos's mercy wasn't an option I was willing to explore.

Skipping a few energy doses for Kim while trying to conserve what I had left didn't seem to leave Kim wanting. She retained the strength I gave her and moved around inside the crevice instead of cowering. A nudge against me, as if muscling for more space, was the sign I was waiting for. Good. She was strong enough for the next phase of my plan.

Before Miklos could lash out at me, I leapt at Kim and latched myself onto her. Panic hit as I cocooned her light. Not my panic, but hers, bleeding through to me. She tried to buck me off, to zoom away and shake me loose, but I had a shrink-wrapped hold of her and she had nowhere to go. A slash of heat and energy-draining pain loosened my hold. Miklos wouldn't give up. I tightened my hold on Kim and braced for his next strike. I wasn't letting him break me. I wasn't letting her get away from this. Fuck them. This had to work.

Ignoring either of them was impossible, but I focused on finding the murky source of Kim's power. Nothing tangible was felt or even seen, leaving me to rely on a sense I had little practice with. When I thought I had what I needed, I pushed through another of Miklos's attacks and concentrated on the rise in my power, using it to draw out Kim's essence and to synchronize our strength.

The murkiness began to dissipate.

Pressure squeezed in around me. Power began building beyond what I had evoked. Kim's new essence was taking over and edging on eruption—the force becoming so great I was reminded of being in the back seat with Caine when he went all Hulk-like, exploded with power, and smashed all of Kim's car windows. I couldn't handle this.

I tried to detach myself, to break away from the cocoon I had created, but I no longer had control. Kim used it all and she wasn't letting me go. The bucking bull ride went haywire and the bull was now riding me.

Energy continued to build. Miklos may have continued his assault, but I couldn't tell either way. The intensity of her power drowned everything else out and held me captive in overwhelming terror of what would happen if she had a blowout of power while I was still wrapped around her.

Was this how I died in this life? Giving Kim what she always wanted and sacrificing myself in the process? Donovan wouldn't even know what took him out.

This was my fault. It was too much, too soon.

2

UNDERTAKING

Caine

Until Donovan yelled for me, I had no clue what was happening. This may have been a simple cry for help, but after everything, he wouldn't dare say my name if there wasn't a good reason, Sect Leader or not. If he hadn't sounded so desperate and then passed out, I wouldn't have given the prick a second glance.

Sophie was stuck in another Soul Reading—both she and Donovan were red-cheeked, sweating, and splayed out on the floor by Kim. I ignored my pleasure at seeing Donovan's head bounce off the hardwood and ordered someone to get Ranlyn. While Gwen took off for help, I tried to reposition Sophie, but couldn't. Her hand was stuck to Kim like it had been during other sessions, though she should have detached when she passed out.

The last time this happened, she had a seizure and her heart stopped. I pressed my fingers to her throat and felt a fluttering heartbeat. Not quite right, but beating. My fingers left swipe marks on her sweaty skin. She flinched in a whole-body twinge, then relaxed. I hovered and waited for it to turn into another seizure. When it didn't, I planted myself, took hold of Sophie's body and pulled. I dragged Kim about a foot across the floor without Sophie's hand budging.

I fumbled with her dead weight in my arms, voices from others around me hitched in concern as Sophie's head flopped back and hit my knee. When I got a better hold of her, I stuck my foot against Kim's ribs, gripped Sophie tighter, and pulled again.

"Stop!" The booming voice drowned out the worried gasps of the Coveners. A firm hand gripped my shoulder as if they might tear me off if I didn't stop pulling. "Severing the bond could kill her or produce irreversible repercussions."

"What do we do?" Ranlyn's question came from above and behind me, as he was not the one who ordered me to stop.

Another man with thin-rimmed glasses leaned over Donovan. His eyes narrowed as he grabbed Donovan's chin and moved his face to take a better look. He dropped him, leaving Donovan's head to flop back to the side. He continued looking down at him with a pinched expression before racing over to Sophie and doing the same.

"What?" Did he see something I didn't?

He held Sophie's arm and squeezed her wrist for a lingering moment. It wasn't to take her pulse, but why else would he do that?

Ranlyn knelt beside the man. "Can you separate them?"

"No." He removed his glasses and rubbed his eyes before putting them back on.

"Isn't that your job?" The Coveners jumped in with their own complaints, drowning me out. Ranlyn quieted them, saying something I was too pissed off to hear, but understood from his tone.

The man knelt again and looked over Sophie in a way that made me want to punch him. "The Soul Seer has not only read the soul of this Kitchen Witch. Unbeknownst to her, or with a wayward burden of responsibility, she has pit herself as protector over it."

Sophie flinched in my arms again. The thump of my heartbeat in my temples lessened when I clenched my teeth. "Meaning?"

The man pegged me with an unblinking glare. "An undertaking promised until the crippled soul can care for themselves. It is not always a conscious choice. Some theorize it is the damaged soul trapping the healthy as a mote of survival. A fail-safe of sorts—not always accessible when needed. Nevertheless, a most effective method."

"What happens if Kim dies while Sophie is trapped?" Henry had been standing on the edge of the crowd as if antsy to jump in and use his medical expertise.

"They both die." His tone was so indifferent my fists clenched.

Sophie taking on some promise, that would put herself in danger to save Kim, didn't surprise me, nor did the alternative of Kim locking Sophie down to protect her. "I don't care why or who triggered this failsafe. How does the lockdown end?"

"Right? This is messed up." Blake stood behind a couch and leaned into it. "What if they get brain damage while their souls are duking it out? Pull the plug or fix it."

Jared knocked him with the elbow.

"What? Oh, I'm the asshole?" He crossed his arms.

"Assurances will placate your worry, but if you wish to hear them you can leave." The man didn't bother to look at Blake while telling him off. "Once the Soul Seer's protection is no longer required, she will be relinquished of the role and the damaged soul will retake possession of their own body and awaken. Under normal circumstances, this would occur. However, since the Kitchen Witch is entwined with your Elder, there is no hope of her overtaking his power. I will have to Extract the souls while she and the Soul Seer are connected."

Ranlyn leaned in and quieted his voice. "Is that dangerous?"

"I have never made the attempt." The man made no effort to lower his voice or hide his cluelessness.

Ranlyn had to calm the Coveners again while Mr. Cardigan and Khaki's pushed his sleeves to his elbows and sat between Kim and Miklos, hovering a hand above each of them.

When the man's power engaged, it was so strong, the pressure against my chest caused my lungs to cramp. I struggled for a deep breath as everyone else did the same, many with a hand to their chest. Even the ones without that much power were struggling—or so I assumed, since I hadn't been talking with Sophie enough to know where their soul glows registered.

The guy meant business and had the power to back up his 'I know everything' attitude. Still, if a Magic know-it-all had never dealt with this situation before and was packing the kind of power he was, then who else could step in if he failed? Judging by the tenseness of Ranlyn's stance, no other Soul Extractor's were on his contact list. Great.

For a long time, nothing happened. I sat with Sophie on my lap, her hand stuck on Kim, who looked like she was sleeping. Sophie began to twitch and flinch more often. The lit fire glistened off her sweat, which got worse as time went on. Anyone would assume she was trapped in a nightmare based on her sweat and heavy breathing. Maybe she was.

The energy in the room grew and weakened as the man worked. The effort on his face ranged from stoic to questionable confusion to slight annoyance. Sophie's head jerked to the side, as did Donovan's, causing me and Henry, standing by Donovan, to flinch. Both settled back into their unconsciousness as before, but it was enough to pull me out of my thoughts. The man didn't stop or look alarmed, so I figured it was part of the process.

I felt useless, and while I wished Donovan's balls were gnawed off by some mutant form of crabs, I couldn't watch Sophie die. I wished her mutant crabs as well, but maybe the kind you can get rid of with an embarrassing trip to the ER by a med student trying not to lose their cafeteria special. I didn't want her dead, but I didn't want her to be happy. Not with Donovan. And I sure as hell didn't want Kim to die. She didn't deserve any of this.

Firelight danced off Sophie's face when I moved her hair from where it fell across her nose. An empty yearning hit me. Hating

Donovan was easy, but her? Fuck. She was Sophie. My saviour, my everything until recently. I wanted to walk away with justified hatred for a cheating bitch who river-danced permanent boot prints all over my heart. I hated how the whole dramatic mess went down, but knowing her as I thought I did, I don't think she did it on purpose.

Even if it was her fault, I was guilty for my part in it all. I made her believe we could bypass the connection, talked her into promises she wanted without understanding how impossible they were to keep. I refused to be her backup plan, but she needed to open her eyes, even if it meant cutting her hand off.

Rising again, the man's powers prickled the air around us, growing past the range he had allowed it to before and causing an ache in my chest. The man opened his eyes for the first time since he had begun and squinted in Sophie's direction. People looked at each other with questioning gazes as they shifted around the room.

Something wasn't right. My arm holding her tingled like I hit my funny bone.

Wait. It wasn't the man's power rising, it was Sophie's. Why was she doing that?

I couldn't tell if it was a good sign. She looked the same. Her forehead was slack but covered in sweat, the brim of her hair saturated. Small gasps raked against her teeth with her quick breathing becoming erratic and speeding up. Coveners shifted in their seats, looked at each other, scratched at their skin, and cleared their throats. The vibrations were spreading to my gut, making me nauseated.

The Soul Extractor closed his eyes again. His crimped expression looked like he was fighting to get a grip on the situation, but the power coming off Sophie was messing with his process. People started walking away as her power continued to build. The vibrations were transitioning from a numbness to a deep, painful burn. I groaned and squeezed her tighter, afraid I would drop her.

The man ripped his hands away from Kim and Miklos. An explosive wave of energy burst out of Sophie. I dropped her onto the wood floor. A pulse from somewhere deep in my chest caused a grunting scream that raked my throat. Shrieks from the others muffled in my ears as I keeled over, gripping my ribcage.

A deafening surge of power followed and laid me out. A high-pitched ringing in my ears had me gripping my skull while the stabbing in my chest took far too long to go away.

I blinked a few times before my night vision kicked in. Why was it so dark? I moved onto my knees and saw firelight flicker off the floor. Glass? I looked up and saw overhead lights empty of their bulbs, the skylight and windows blown out over people and furniture, glittering like snow. Lamps, pictures, and curtains had been knocked onto the floor.

Eerie quiet settled in as Ranlyn scrambled from where he had been thrown onto his back to check on Sophie. He rolled her over and searched for a heartbeat in her throat. Her hand wasn't stuck to Kim anymore.

Please be alive. Please be alive.

I rushed to her as Ranlyn was saying something. My ears popped as Ranlyn called her name. She was breathing, but still unconscious.

Water sprayed me. I looked up to see the stone of the fireplace darkening as water poured under the second-floor railing down to the first floor. Coveners were rushing around, helping each other up off the floor and over the glass. The Soul Extractor was digging his finger into his ear and shaking his head.

Blake swore and turned, water dripping off his face, as the kitchen tap was spraying water into the air like a fountain. "Where's the shut off valve?"

Ranlyn yelled something to him as I turned back to Sophie. Her eyes were now open, staring at the ceiling. Ranlyn turned back to her and pulled back with a gasp of surprise.

"Sophie?" I repositioned myself over her to look into her eyes. "Sophie? Can you hear me?"

"Donovan?" Henry was pressing his palm to a gash on his cheek as he and his wife, Louise, looked over at Donovan. He, too, had his eyes open, but wasn't saying anything.

I called her name louder, holding her hand and shaking it a bit. She blinked and focused on me. "Are you okay? Are you hurt?"

She didn't answer me. Her eyes surveyed my face with a slight crease of confusion between her brows. "Your hair is different."

3

CONTINUE WITHOUT KNOWLEDGE

Caine smiled. At me. I never thought he would smile in my direction again. The relief was such a shock I found myself staring at him.

Wait. I knew he cut his hair. Why am I on the floor? Why is it so dark?

"Keep going." Ranlyn's voice pulled my attention away from Caine. He was talking to someone I didn't know who was sitting between Kim and Miklos.

A flush of memory at what I was doing came back to me.

I tried to sit and grunted as my stomach muscles protested. Caine grabbed my arm to help me, pulling me up into a seated position too fast. Dizziness had the room spinning. I wilted to the side until something steady held me, my equilibrium not as trustworthy. My hearing cleared first. Caine was saying something in a soft tone. I couldn't tell what, but it was soothing, along with the pressure of his hand rubbing my back. As soon as my vision cleared and I saw his body was what was holding me up, I pulled back and apologized.

"No problem." His lopsided smile told me he meant it. This confused the shit out of me.

Pressure on my shoulder had me looking up into Ranlyn's concerned gaze. "Are you okay?"

"Am I ever okay, Jeeves?" I smiled at my self-deprecating jab and smoothed my hair behind my ears, finding it tangled with sweat. I tried to ignore the smell of Caine wafting nostalgia my way. If I was sweating that much, I doubted I smelled as tantalizing.

Ranlyn raised his eyebrows as if to agree, though I was pretty sure he didn't mean my body odour. I pressed my hand into his on my shoulder and he squeezed once more before standing.

Power prickled my skin. I turned towards Kim. A man with auburn hair sat with his head bowed, hands over Kim and Miklos. His eyes were closed, and he looked religious in his calm. The power he wielded was thick in the room and made my skin itch. "I'm assuming he's the Soul Extractor?"

"Yup. You sure you're okay?"

When I turned around to assure Caine I was, Donovan came to my other side and Caine was quick to get to his feet. I thanked him before he could escape. He returned a smile before he went to stand with a few others behind the couches. Expecting him to share breathing space with Donovan was far too much to expect, but I felt like an ass for not insisting Donovan wait his turn. Stupid—which is why I swallowed my guilt and left it to stew in my gut.

A mix of relief and self-righteousness crossed me and Donovan's connection.

"You can save your 'I told you so'. If you knew what happened in there, you'd be impressed."

Donovan adjusted a towel he was sitting on, the floor around it wet, though I didn't know why. He leaned back onto his palms. "No." He bumped me with his shoulder. "You were right, babe. I'm just happy we're alive for me to tell you so."

The heat in my cheeks was his. Something about the admission must have embarrassed him. I was sure as shit surprised and he knew it.

Bosco, jumping into my lap, saved Donovan from my sassy

comment. I got my fair share of pug kisses until a hitch in power had me looking back to Kim.

I gasped. "Holy shitfignewton."

The auburn-haired man's hands hovered over Kim and Miklos as feathery particles of silver light left Kim's body, travelled into the Soul Extractor's long, thin fingers, through his body, out through the other hand, and into Miklos. Neither Kim nor Miklos moved or made any protest at what the man was doing to them, but I wondered what it looked like while inside.

I passed Bosco to Donovan and moved onto my hands and knees. Not to get a better look at the Soul Extractors understated good looks, but to watch the man endure their souls using him as a waystation without a groan or twinge of pain. A man doing his job. If the soul bits floating around hadn't belonged to a person I cared about, I could have sat and watched the light show for hours.

As every piece of Miklos left Kim, her light lost its borrowed metallic tint, but didn't dim as much as it should have. Then I remembered what happened before I woke up on the floor.

Did it work? It had to.

"What's up?" Donovan leaned into me.

Hearing his question, but too captivated by watching the man work to answer, I watched the last soul piece gather within Kim and the light exchange concluded. The Soul Extractor closed his palms and rubbed his fingers together like he was ridding them of crumbs from his morning toast.

"What?" Donovan nudged me harder, his curiosity burning through the connection.

As soon as the man dropped his hands to his lap, I was at Kim's side in time to watch her eyes open.

"Whoa. Creepy Soph." Kim's voice was husky. She pushed up onto her elbows, looked at the Soul Extractor as he stood, and then at Miklos who stirred with a heavy amount of groaning as he tried to sit up. She grabbed my hand. "Don't tell me I was—No. I couldn't have. Did I?"

"Shit no." I laughed and helped her sit up. The Coveners clapped and celebrated the win as Kim made a hesitant smile. I lowered my voice. "You think I'd let the Coveners watch you floss your vagina with Miklos's beard? I mean, without charging admission, of course."

"I'd skin you alive and wear you to the movies. Now tell me what the fuck happened."

"How *Silence of the Lambs* of you," I laughed. "At least your sense of humour is intact. How do you feel?" I looked over her soul glow, wondering if she could feel the difference.

She stretched her arms over her head and twisted her neck to the side. "My head feels like it did after my nineteenth birthday. Actually, that sums it up. Should've known me then. You would've thought I was freakin' nuts."

I took her hands and sent a flash of healing magic through her.

"Whoa. Thanks."

I helped her up and saw the room in full for the first time. "I see Ranlyn redecorated while I was out. What happened?"

"No clue." Donovan stood next to us and handed me Bosco. "I wouldn't let him walk around. Glass is everywhere."

"You were out, too?" Kim put her fingers through her hair until they got stuck. "Ewww. What's in my hair?"

"Blood. I couldn't get it all out, but you look a lot better than you did."

"Blo—" She gagged and dropped her hands.

"It's your own blood, if that helps."

She retched and covered her mouth. A sheen of tears sparkled in her blue-green eyes.

"Guess not. Here." I passed her Bosco. "Sit with him and keep your heaves to yourself. He's already eaten today."

Since I wasn't ready to answer Kim's questions yet, I helped with cleanup duty instead. I managed to fix Ranlyn's car windows before, so I focused on getting the glass from the high casement windows and skylight back in place. With a dose of steady power, I ignored the blood draining from my hands and tiring my arms, causing pins and needles in my fingers, as the glitter of glass rose above us as if raining in reverse.

Ranlyn and the auburn-haired man dealt with the blown water stops and lights as we sat on the couches and gave Kim a run-down of what happened before she was knocked out while running away from the Puppeteer's Puppets in Diluculo. When we got to the point where both Donovan and I were unconscious, Caine filled in the rest.

I had no idea he was listening. When he came up behind us, Kim's eyes widened at seeing him and snuck a glance my way. She didn't have to spell it out for me to know her reaction was because of his new hairdo—a detail to gab about when we were alone.

I skipped over detailing what happened during my Soul Reading. A questioning nudge crossed Donovan and I's connection. A sense of 'shut your stupid face' was returned, one clear enough for him to refrain from calling me out.

"May I speak with you?" The professional request came from the Soul Extractor. He stood around six feet, with a slender build and square shoulders matching his sharp features. His dressy clothing and glasses gave him an uptight exterior that didn't match his incredible performance juggling Kim and Miklos's souls.

Caught in the surprise of the request, I hesitated. "Guess it depends on who I'm talking to."

His narrowed green eyes told me he expected me to fulfill his request without being questioned. Clearly, he didn't know me.

Skipping a beat, he glanced at the others and then back at me with a composed expression. "My name is Vincent. May I please have a moment of your time, Sophie?"

Hmmm. He knew my name.

His second request was more a demand than the first, though packaged as a polite question.

I scooted to the edge of the couch and made an introduction on his behalf. "Kim," I looked at her next to me on the couch, "this is Vincent. A Soul Extractor with a fancy soul glow of many years past his allotted lifespan. Vincent, this is Kim Manning. The Kitchen

Witch whose ass you saved from being swallowed by Miklos and his bully of a soul. Maybe it's an immortal thing."

"Pleasure to meet you, Vincent." Kim extended a strong hand as Vincent received it along with a gentlemanly nod. "Thanks for the ass saving."

"My pleasure." Vincent hid his impatience well. He made no effort to introduce himself to Donovan or Caine. "Sophie?"

I smirked. "Lead the way."

I followed Vincent through the door I hadn't been behind, disappointed when I found myself in nothing more than a simple room—one with the option of a formal dining space, though it held an old round table, far out of scale for the size of the room, which was the length of the house front to back. The farthest wall had a door to the backyard and the walls were lined with a few shelving units on both sides holding magic items and books—oddities I didn't have the time to inspect.

Vincent led the way to the small, beat-up table, stopping as he waited for me to sit first.

I actually laughed out loud. "Definitely from a different time."

He sat after I did, adjusted his glasses, and folded his hands on the yellowed lace tablecloth. "What did you do while you were inside?"

Making a sound between a laugh and a grunt, I crossed my arms.

"Judging by the lack of celebration, or fear, on behalf of the Kitchen Witch, I am led to believe you have neglected to inform her of the change."

I mimicked his position by folding my hands on the table. "If you knew, why'd you ask?"

"My role here was to return the souls to their appropriate vessels. Although that would seem to conclude my duties, you would be wrong to assume so."

"This is not something you need to include within your duties."

"I disagree."

"I didn't release her power so I could gain a gold star in appreciation. I did it because I knew it would save her life and knew it was something Kim would have asked for given the opportunity. Taking away her discovery of it robs her of the journey in finding it."

"You will allow her to continue without the knowledge her power has been freed?"

I nodded.

"The difference it will make when working spells or when under emotional stress is exponential."

"She's been around for a display of accidental discharge. By myself, for one. It's not pretty and yes, it can be dangerous, but I still think she should find it on her own. If she were to outright ask me, I'd admit my part, but she's worked on developing power beyond her Kitchen Witch status longer than I've even known magic existed. You don't know her, but she deserves it."

Vincent exhaled with control. "Fine."

"Fine as in 'fine' or fine as in 'I'm going to make you pay for this later' fine?"

"What about the other man?"

"Hmm. I'll take your non-answer as a possible threat of future retribution. And what man? Miklos? We aren't exactly on call-you-when-I-get-my-period-and-need-provisions terms."

He sat back in his chair, his glare gaining an edge of annoyance. "The Berisford."

"Caine? What about him?"

The slight crease between his auburn brows deepened. "The alterations did not solely affect the Kitchen Witch and this man's changes are much your own."

"Okay. And?"

A smile creased his lips. Not a happy looking one—something closer to amused superiority.

"I was unconscious for a tick. I'm assuming I missed a few things."

He nodded. "As you said, the journey is worth travelling for those it concerns. Since this is neither my journey nor my concern, I will say no more."

Standing to leave, I refused to get out of my chair and give him permission to excuse himself. "No, no, no. Using my words against me isn't cool. What happened to Caine?"

Reseating himself, Vincent leaned over the table again. "I do not know much about you, Sophie. In fact, before today, I knew you as the Soul Seer of the Mother Coven and nothing more. Stories of the last Elders' death have circulated, and I sympathize with you for the tragedies you have faced. I would think your exposure to such heinousness would cause a yearning for information, anything that would give a look at what was to come. You show great restraint on your friend's behalf, wanting to pretend you share no role in shaping their future. I would say it was commendable, but you do not stand by the same principles when it involves yourself. Your ethics propose wisdom, but your practices are flawed and denote a sense of naiveté. Living on both sides of that fence will land you ostracized, so you will need to make a choice. Either everyone knows everything, or they know nothing."

No doubt he faced the same dilemma before. "Point for you and your wise immortal knowledge." Something about this had him casting his stare down a moment as if a hint of shame leaked out before he could hide it. I didn't push to find out why. He wouldn't tell me anyway. "Your instinct was to speak to me first. If you thought Kim not knowing about her power being released was so dangerous, why didn't you tell her yourself? Why try and convince me to fess up?"

He straightened his already immaculate posture. "I suppose I sought to understand your choice not to."

"And?"

"Your heart was in your explanation, so you believe in your reasoning."

"But it's not what you would do?"

"No."

I supposed I was lucky he gave me an option. I decided to think about it. If I changed my mind, I would have Ranlyn contact Vincent for me when I couldn't stand not knowing whatever he knew about Caine.

"Can you see the soul particles you extract?"

His head tilted as if surprised by the question. "Not outside the body, no."

"Damn. You're missing out. I could see slivers of their souls as you worked. I can't imagine anything else like it."

He cracked a smile I couldn't help returning. "I hear you cannot see your own soul glow."

"Nope." My lips smacked on the "p".

"At least you can read it. Albeit no consolation. I hear the gift proves insightful."

"Huh. I've never tried to read my own soul before. How do you know I can do that?"

Vincent smiled bigger this time. "Oh, to be in a time of discovery. I've met a couple of Readers in passing—not a Soul Seer, as Readers are more common—and each one could read their own. Self-reflection is essential to well-balanced lives and I found them to exhibit these qualities more oft than others. I assumed you stumbled upon it."

"I've only read a soul a few times and every time has ended with me hurting someone or almost dying."

"Too eager is all. Your prowess will depend on your patience. Jumping into the deep end only works if you have a lifeguard on duty and leaving the Sorrel in charge will drown the both of you."

I let out a heavy breath. I hated thinking about what Donovan went through. It was gravy to put myself on the line, but he was right beside me whether he approved or not. I hated even more how Vincent separated Caine and Donovan into their family names. They meant something more to him than the guys themselves.

Vincent asked a few questions about me and Donovan's connection. Did we share abilities? How strong was it over long distances? A lot of the same ones I had heard before, but I answered anyway, feeling no reason not to. Asking a few of my own, Vincent responded with what I thought were truthful answers. His power worked on feel alone. He could feel the souls he worked with—their abilities, their strength—so I described what I saw as he reorganized them according to owner.

"Have you changed your mind?"

I didn't have to ask what Vincent meant. "Nope. Stubborn to the end." We went back through the door to the main area of the house. "I'll track you down if I do, I guarantee you that."

"I'll make it easy for you and get you my information."

He left, and I rejoined Kim and Donovan on the couch, Caine was five feet away at the kitchen breakfast bar eating a handful of chips as if uncomfortable being around Kim and Donovan without me present.

"What'd he want?" Kim passed me Bosco, who snuggled into my lap.

I shrugged. "He was asking questions about my ability, so I asked about his."

"Oh, yeah?" Donovan's suspicion bloomed in my chest.

"Yeah."

Kim sat forward and stared at me. "I don't believe you."

"Oh, really?"

"He doesn't, so I don't."

Vincent approached and handed me a folded white piece of paper. "If you change your mind."

I took it. "Thanks."

He smiled and walked away towards Ranlyn.

Kim laughed. Donovan didn't.

I slipped the paper into my jeans pocket. "Relax. It's for information, not a dick diving mission."

"Not my problem anymore." Caine laughed and shoved a few more chips into his mouth.

Youch. The twist of the knife was a literal heartache. Something I couldn't hide so I looked away from him. Kim's pursed-lipped expression was missed or ignored by Caine. The dig made not telling him something was different about him easier. Petty as it was, I wasn't feeling generous when he was taking pot shots at me.

The conversation turned casual, Kim still griping about dried blood in her hair. Caine drifted to another group of Coveners. Before, it was the four of us, all of us, uncomfortable or not. Even in awkward times, Donovan stood by, hating to see me with Caine, and now Caine couldn't handle the role reversal. The wounds were still raw. Expecting them to heal overnight instead of fester was hopeful yet selfish.

Kim pointed at me. "Where's your necklace?"

I reached for my neck and had to swallow the lump in my throat. "Lost in Diluculo during the Puppeteer's takeover."

"Shit. I'm sorry."

Shock and some brand of hurt twanged the thread of connection between Donovan and me. He didn't say anything and blubbering about it wasn't on my agenda.

I turned to Kim. "Do you remember anything from being unconscious?"

She looked up as if trying to recall something. "I remember it feeling like an intruder was in my house, but all the lights are off. You can't see them to fight back, so you hide thinking it's your only option instead of turning on the goddamn light and calling the police."

"Do you remember me being there?"

"Sort of. Not you as in you being there, but a sense that I wasn't alone in fighting whatever was coming at me and hoped it was over soon. Then it wasn't, and things got freaky."

"Freaky?" Donovan tapped my arm to get me to look at him. "What'd you do in there?"

"Nothing close to what's in your imagination, perv."

"Stronger result." Kim's brow arched.

"You poor thing." Donovan got Kim's middle finger for the comment.

"I'm fine now. Starving, but otherwise, I got lucky." She bounced up from the couch, splitting the group monopolizing the counter of food, and loaded a plate. A few Coveners wrapped her in conversation so she sat on a stool and multitasked.

Seeing her act so Kim-like made me laugh. A laugh I stifled when Donovan slid over a cushion and put his arm on the back of the couch behind me.

"What'd you do?"

4

IGNORE INSTINCTS

After a few minutes of dodging Donovan's questions, he broke me down and I explained what I did while stuck in Kim, as well as the debate with Vincent about not telling her.

His dimples caved. "Dick move."

"You think so? I wanted her to—"

"Not that. Telling me. She'll be more pissed I knew first."

"Yeah, well, I'll tell her you blackmailed me."

"Right. With what?"

My answer was cut off by Caine's laugh. We turned and saw him in the kitchen eating from a small plate and in conversation with Denise.

"Seriously?" I tried not to stare at Caine's bright smile.

"Denise can smell single a mile away. Is it really that surprising?"

"Not on her part." Thinking of Caine's girlfriend before his near four-year sleeping curse, I realized she was like Denise. It made me think maybe I was the anomaly and not the blonde. She couldn't get Donovan, so now she's going for Caine?

"You could always take him back."

I scoffed. "Right. 'Cuz that would solve everything."

"Would suck for me, but if it's what you want, then yeah, it would."

"Well, it's not." My answer was so resolved, I surprised myself. He was skeptical, but the problems Caine and I had didn't start the moment I woke up naked next to Donovan, and they sure as hell didn't end there.

"Could you call your Sect to attention?" Vincent surprised both of us. We didn't see him until he started speaking.

Donovan took a swig of his drink. "What for?"

Vincent's stare panned to mine as if I was responsible for Donovan's inability to follow orders. "For your Elders and my purpose in addressing them on matters of great importance."

I smiled and suppressed a laugh. It was ridiculous to request permission from Donovan for such a thing, but Vincent was a stickler for procedure.

Donovan put two fingers in his mouth and whistled so loud it hurt my ears. The Coveners complained, but quieted. He motioned to Vincent. "The floor is yours."

They exchanged a long glare before it seemed Vincent decided Donovan wasn't worth arguing with and he looked up at the Coveners now staring at him.

"It has been brought to my attention formal introductions have gone overlooked." He glanced at me and back to the crowd. "My name is Vincent. As witnessed, I was commissioned by Elder Ranlyn to extract the souls of Elder Miklos and your co-Sect Leader, Kim. The reason I have had your other co-Sect Leader so eloquently call your attention was to speak of the core issue that forced Miklos and Kim into such a dangerous predicament. Now, it is my understanding many of you are inexperienced in battle. I assure you the Puppeteer and the Eradicators are two enemies not to be underestimated, but this recent altercation has not been merely tragic. We have learned much concerning their motives."

"The Raddies want to kill everything and anything with a hint of magic. I didn't think their agenda was so cryptic." Caitlyn was a quiet Covener when compared to those like Blake, but looked confident speaking above the group, focusing on Vincent and calling him out in front of everyone. It made me wonder if she slipped some alcohol in her coffee mug.

Vincent looked down at Donovan as if her speaking out of turn should have resulted in punishment, but when Donovan raised a dark eyebrow, Vincent moved on.

"Under normal circumstances, I would agree, but it was explained to me that the Raddies were attempting to kidnap your co-Sect Leader and his companion, not kill them."

Snickering made its way through the crowd, the loudest from Denise. Companion? Really? I never eluded a thing to suggest usage of that word would be appropriate, though Donovan's arm behind me on the back of the couch may look cozy. Donovan ignored the crowd. If there were any Coveners that didn't know of the 'Sophie and Caine split' by the end of the meeting, Denise would make sure no one was out of the loop.

Vincent closed his eyes for a half-second. "The Puppeteer's motives are simple enough. Taking down this Coven, as a whole, has always been the objective before he secluded himself to his Creation —another like Diluculo—and with confirmation from your co-Sect Leaders sibling—" He paused and looked at Donovan who returned a one-shouldered shrug and nod. "—we have verification of this. Plus, a motive of her own, regarding powers she was led to believe she has ownership over by Loring. Who, as everyone knows, is prolonging a revenge plot he feels was left unsettled after killing your previous Elders."

The expressions of the Coveners slipped from listening to Vincent to a wash of sadness. Bringing up Aunt Lacey's death wasn't a good way to keep the group focused on moving forward.

Donovan turned to look towards Ranlyn across the room. "And we're doing what about all of that?"

Ranlyn straightened from leaning against the wall. "At the

moment, we gather our defences, see who stands with us, and fight if called for."

"So, a lot of nothing." I meant to mumble, but Donovan's increased heartrate had my blood pumping.

"Have you honed your skills sufficiently enough to fight this enemy single-handedly?" Vincent peered down at me.

Donovan stood up in front of Vincent. "You think that's helpful? Or are you volunteering to join the cause?"

"My presence establishes my intentions."

"You were hired to extract souls. Don't pretend it's anything more."

"Thanks, anyway." Kim called from the kitchen with her mouth half-full of food.

"Vincent has been a Coven affiliate for centuries." Ranlyn saying so caused some Coveners to whisper to each other. Sometimes I forget no one else could tell who was immortal. "A declaration of allegiance was unnecessary."

Hinapouri returned, coming through the door to the other room with the Apporter and a few large men—members of her Maori tribe, according to their intricate tattooing covering most of their exposed skin, including their faces. Coveners were whispering to each other again and moving to give them room. It could have been a sign of respect, but most looked shit-your-pants terrified.

"Hinapouri." Vincent nodded in what looked like a bow of respect.

"Vincent." Hinapouri responded in kind and turned to Ranlyn. "I propose an imminent incursion against our enemies." Shuffling and whispers from the Coveners grew. "One to catch Loring and his Coven Master unawares."

Ranlyn stepped close to her. "Loring is not our primary target."

"We haven't the numbers to succeed." Miklos's loud, accented voice was a shock after his continued silence upon his Extraction. "You would send your people to die? The idiocy is too much, even for you."

Power from Hinapouri's comrades flared through the room. Ranlyn attempted to smooth things over, despite Miklos continuing to berate her.

"This should not be discussed amongst the Seedlings." Vincent's voice was lost upon the other Elders, but not to us who were much closer.

"We're all a part of this Coven." The charged room revved Donovan's anger, as he was now inches from Vincent.

I shot to my feet. "Okay, okay. Let's dial it down."

Both ignored me.

"Your Sect will have no say when strategic planning comes into play. Most are no more enlightened than the Blind."

"Hey!" Blake's complaint went equally ignored.

"Blind?" Donovan's power flushed to the surface.

"Hey—" I grabbed his arm.

The flash of his visions and anger were supercharged, punching through my body with an overload of energy rushing out of me. I collapsed, catching myself on the edge of the couch and sliding to the floor as Donovan fell to the ground beside me. When I gasped for the breath I had lost, the energy that had escaped snapped back into me as if I had sucked it into my lungs, spreading within my chest like electrified needles and hunkering down. When I could exhale, another impact of power flushed back into the room.

Screams and breaking glass filled my ears and warbled when my limbs went numb.

I blinked—my equilibrium still on a tilt and making me nauseous. Did I pass out?

Vincent moved over to me, asking if I was okay, as Ranlyn called out for Blake. Blake said he "Got it" and ran for something. Water dappled across my face, falling from the top floor. I looked up and saw the jagged edge of the skylight above. Again? I thought the breaking of the glass was from Kim's release of power the last time. Was it not?

"I'm okay." My voice was husky, but Vincent nodded and blinked

—worry in his green eyes—before trying to help me sit up. The room swayed, and I swallowed back vomit for the second time that day.

Vincent scooped me up and put me on the couch, kneeling as I struggled to get my bearings. My ankle screamed. My injury or Donovan's, I didn't know, but it was safe to say it was Donovan's head wound causing the throbbing on the side of my skull.

"Babe?" He managed to get himself to all-fours.

"Sit here." Jared and Kim helped Caine onto the couch across from me. I blinked. His soul glow wasn't right, but I was seeing double and couldn't focus.

Light filled the room from behind us. I turned and saw a radiating light illuminating from someone. The light shifted enough so I could see it was Denise. She had her arms out like a doll, looking down at them as if they weren't hers. Then she started to shout and shake her body as if she could make it go away. She rushed towards her friend Jamie, who scrambled behind Gwen and a few others.

"A passive ability." Vincent was still at my side in front of the couch. "It will subside when she calms down."

Gwen was now talking to Denise, holding onto her arms and speaking in low and reassuring tones.

A wave of exhaustion washed over me as I rested my head on the couch cushion. When I opened my eyes, Donovan was doing the same. "Sorry."

"I don't know if you did anything, babe."

The room plunged into darkness as Denise got a hold of herself. Ranlyn raised his arms with the mutter of a spell and light hovered above us like a blanket of glistening tropical water beneath a midday sun.

Conversation of battle came to a halt as cleanup became the priority and Coveners complained about having to clean up again. I wanted to help, but I had nothing left and was still trying to shake the dizziness.

"Sophie." Vincent's polished voice was filled with something I couldn't pin down as he knelt in front of me. He put his hand on my arm and I realized it was regret. "I should not have ignored my instincts and enlightened you from the beginning."

"Enlightened her about what?" Donovan popped his head up, causing another bout of dizziness.

Vincent looked to Donovan, then back to me.

"Go on. I'd tell him anyway. Not the other thing." Kim was close by, but I didn't want him spilling what I did during my Soul Reading in case others were listening.

He nodded. "I know you have surpassed the stage of discovering your basic power. You are rather new, yet no longer Blind, but it seems that you have released a deeper magic than intended."

"Deeper than what?"

Donovan sat forward. "Nya?"

I sat up a bit, causing Vincent to shift back onto his heels. "Nya? Really?"

"Does Caine look different?" Vincent moved to the side to reveal Caine on the couch across from me.

Caine was bent forward, elbows to knees, his hands in his hair. Kim sat next to him. His day-to-day Persuader blue soul glow was expected. The magenta colour dancing around his body, co-existing with his natural glow was new. Gareth?

"As I understand it, you and Caine have a unique link not of your own. Vessels to formidable gifts and, until today, those gifts have not been permitted to flourish in their new bodies."

I shifted forward, mirroring Caine's position, except my fingers were over my mouth. What did this mean? Was my soul glow different?

How else would the link present itself? If it was anything like with Donovan, I would end up at the bottom of many prescription bottles trying to drown them both out. I couldn't do it. Worry from the connection with Donovan needled me. Maybe he was thinking the same thing as I was. Maybe he worried about himself, as if this would pull Caine and I back together. I didn't know, but after another glance towards Caine, I knew there was no mistaking the difference. Gareth and Nya's powers were out.

Something else occurred to me. If Nya's power was hiding until today, it meant the power I used against Loring that changed and lightened his soul glow and sent him running was mine, not Nya's. Was that the case with connecting to Caine in the park as well? No, it couldn't have been... could it?

"What's wrong?" Caine was now looking at me as I had been drawn inward into my thoughts.

"Why? Did you feel something?"

His brows synched together. "Besides the sonic boom that just exploded in my chest? No, but clearly something's wrong."

Fuck my life. "Come with me." I moved to stand. Vincent and Donovan jumped to help me. I shrugged them off and led Caine to the stairs to go to the creepy room Donovan and I were in, trying to get some physical distance from everyone on the first floor.

"That didn't take long." I overheard Denise's snide remark as she came out of the bathroom with a mop as Caine and I reached the second floor.

"What'd you say?" I moved a few steps towards her. Caine grabbed my arm and then steered me in the direction of the room.

"Seriously, Sophie? What? Were you going to fight her?"

"Would you prefer to explain things to Miss Lite-Brite yourself?"

"You'd have no right to be pissed if I did."

"Of all people though?" I huffed and struggled to calm myself.

Splaying his hands, palms up, he motioned around us. "I'm standing in a room you've slept in with the guy you screwed behind my back. The new boyfriend who happens to be downstairs and who I get to pretend I can stand as my leader. You don't get to pretend like I'm the irrational one. My shit's tight. If I want to move on to Denise, you get to shut up and enjoy the show."

"Ugh. I know. You're totally right. I'm ditch dirt for putting you through what I did. It's... just because I don't get to be with you anymore doesn't mean I'd want you to waste yourself on someone like

Denise. But if that's your game, then play it. And while, yeah, I get it's weird being in here, if you looked at the sheets a little closer, you'd see they're covered in blood. We weren't exactly having fun."

He crossed his arms. "Why'd you drag me up here?"

I exhaled. His expression was so cold it hurt. "First of all, there's been no talk of a relationship as far as me and Donovan goes. Yes, I know, you care more about a stranger's tick removal, but I care. You pretend you don't know me, but you do and you know this drama was unintentional. The situation is messed up, but we're not like that."

"Yet."

"What?"

"Don't confirm it all you like, but don't treat me like an idiot."

"Whatever. Think what you want." I pushed my hair behind my ears and took a steadying breath. "When I was stuck in Kim during her soul reading, her soul was dying. I think. Her light was dying, so I assumed she was. Anyway, it took a lot, but I released Kim's real power so she could protect herself until they got Miklos out of her. I didn't tell her. That's what me and Vincent were really talking about. He knew and thought I should tell her, but I wanted her to find out on her own."

"Why are you telling me this?"

Clenching my teeth, I exhaled out my nose. "While I was focusing on releasing her power, it affected not only Kim's true power, but Nya and Gareth's, as well."

He straightened. "So, what just happened was their power, what, freaking out?"

"I guess. The first blow out let them free and messed shit up, but the second time it must have activated them. When I looked up at you sitting on the couch, your soul glow had changed." I looked him over until he shifted in discomfort. "Sorry. It's truly awesome. Vincent only told me about releasing Nya and Gareth before I dragged you up here."

His grey eyes narrowed. "That's why you asked me if I felt anything? You thought we'd be connected like you and Donovan." I huffed and nodded. "And you don't want that." He looked at the ground and shifted his weight from one foot to the other.

"I can barely handle his emotions on top of mine. I can't imagine having three sets to juggle. I'm not strong enough for that." I swallowed and blinked away encroaching tears. "Obviously, some things are going to change for both of us. I wanted you to hear it from me and know that I didn't do it on purpose to screw with your life further than I already have."

Caine put his hands in his pockets. "We were supposed to work on that before anyway. Now I guess we don't have to."

"Guess not."

I figured he would take it well, but under the circumstances, I couldn't be sure of anything.

"Is that it?"

My throat burned in anticipation. "Are... Are we going to talk about what happened?"

His shoulders slumped. "Really?"

"Yes, really." He looked to the wall and planted his hands on his hips. "You act like I went out of my way to mess around."

"According to Donovan, you did."

"That's not what he said. While you used a desperate situation to opportunistically meddle with his free will, he told you I initiated the sex. That's technically true, but I didn't seduce him. What happened had no thought process or decision making behind it. I woke up from a dream—"

"I don't need a play by play!"

"I wasn't trying to give one!" Power flared and stuck in my stomach like I'd eaten a whole carton of ice cream. "Fuck, if I wanted to leave you, I would have."

"Bullshit. I'd been trying to pull you away from that dickwad since the first time I saw him drooling over you at my first Coven meeting. I should have known better. I'm not one to sit with a sinking ship, but I thought I could save us because we were something more, something bigger or special or whatever. It was a matter of time and we both knew it."

"I didn't know it." The churning in my stomach felt like it grew claws and sunk them in deep. I palmed my gut, trying to relieve the pain.

"You haven't once tried to make this right." He stepped toward me and pointed in my face. "You never came to find me to beg for forgiveness. Never tried to explain or promise it would never happen again. Nothing. Instead you stayed with him." He took his finger out of my face to point through the wall as if Donovan was standing behind it. "You still stay at his house."

"My apartment isn't exactly safe. I'm not about to get slaughtered to make you feel more comfortable. I was giving you space to think about what you wanted. When I realized what happened, I took off down the street with nothing but Bosco. Kim found me on the side of the road going out of my mind trying to fit the night's pieces together because I could barely remember how it all started."

"That doesn't change the fact that I'm right about the rest. You don't get to act like a victim here."

"Did you hear me call rape? Ask Kim or Donovan. I'm aware it's my fault. I fucked up everything." The overwhelming need to vomit booted me in the diaphragm as sweat pushed through my pores, soaking the back of my neck.

"Doesn't matter. It should've been him from the beginning and you let me think different." He paced in a small circle.

"I'd fallen in love with you, you asshole." The room spun as I strained to hold on. I gripped the corner of the bed and doubled over.

Caine made a cheerless laugh. "You get another dude's dick wet and I'm the asshole."

"Fuck." Another wave of energy shot out of me and drove Caine into the wall. I fell to my knees, heaving and then vomiting on the floor next to the bed so hard my back arched, sending an ache down my spine.

Caine groaned. I saw him on his knees, clutching his chest before another wave of heaving hit me and spilled onto the wood floors.

The door whipped open, Vincent and Ranlyn rushing in. Vincent stood over me. I pushed him away, not wanting him to see my puke.

"I'm fine." I covered my mouth and leaned into the mattress.

Donovan stumbled into the room and gripped the threshold, with Kim close behind as if prepared to catch him if he fell over. Caine got to his feet. Donovan stumbled towards him and grabbed a fist full of his shirt, shoving him into the wall. "You had to push her, didn't you?"

"She wanted to know!" Caine shoved Donovan away and pushed passed Kim out of the room.

Kim rushed over to me. "Shit. Are you okay?"

"Peaches and cream, baby. Can you get me something to clean up with?"

"One sec."

Donovan took a few steps towards me when she left. "Stay put, cow—" I lifted my hand at him. Energy streamed out of my palm and pinned Donovan against the wall.

I gasped and put my hand down. The power stopped when my hand snapped shut and he dropped to the floor. "Ohmygod. What the fucknuggets? I didn't—"

Kim rushed back in, saw Donovan on the floor, but continued to me, placing the garbage bucket from the bathroom next to me. "Did you do that to him?" She knelt and used a wad of paper towels on my mess.

"I can—"

She pushed my hand away. "I got it, Soph. I'm used to puke. Not so used to you attacking Donovan. What gives?"

"I think it was Nya's power. At least I hope it was."

Vincent was helping Donovan to his feet and talking below ear shot. The connection registered the pain in his lower back and my subsiding queasiness. I managed to hurt both Caine and Donovan in a matter of minutes and now Kim was cleaning up my puke. Everything Caine said was expected, but hearing it twisted the knife. Exposing the hurt instead of leaving it to linger between us was everything but cathartic—though maybe it was for him, not the injection of anger and resentment it felt like for me.

A tingle of power sifted through the connection as Donovan healed us. Physically, we were okay, but something waded beneath the surface. Maybe like Caine, he needed to get out whatever he was stifling because of fear, exhaustion, or anger. Could I handle it from him as well? Not right now, but I didn't want it to come out in a destructive purge, not with Nya's power so unpredictable.

Vincent was right. Leaving a released power to simmer and wait to boil over was as dangerous as unlocking the cages of a bear pen and throwing yummy rabbit entrails at the feet of young children.

Kim tied shut the bag of sopping wet paper towels and threw it towards Donovan, who caught it like snatching a fly out of the air, face screwing up in disgust before returning to his conversation with Vincent.

She sat next to me on the bed and I wrapped my arms around her.

She laughed. "Truly. It's no biggy, Soph. I've cleaned up enough of it when my mom was sick. Puke is easy. Blood's a different story."

"Hope you're good with the smell, because I need to tell you something and I'm sure my breath is pure ass right now."

"I'd say closer to skunk acid, but ass isn't far off."

"Perfect. You're a champ. I think Nya's power got in the mix and my body couldn't deal with it. Which, maybe you should expect and keep a handle on your emotions."

"My emotions?"

"Yeah, umm... while I was doing the Soul Reading, I tried to stop Miklos from getting to you and that meant releasing your power so you could take care of yourself."

"Releasing?" She gasped and grabbed my arms. "You released my power? Like, my real power?"

"I'm sorry. I didn't know what else to do and I wasn't—"

She pulled me into her arms and squeezed until a floating rib ached. "You're amazeballs!" I made a choked squeal, Donovan saying a passive-aggressive "Ow!" from across the small room before she let go. "You have no idea what you've done for me. No freakin' clue. I mean, I would've gotten there—"

"If anyone would've, it would have been you."

"But the time and effort you saved me? Astronomical." She squealed. "This is a momentous day. Well, except the you and Caine fighting part. Plus, the puking thing. Momentous day for me, I mean. You need an extra cuddle." She lowered her voice. "Donovan would be up for that if you're done beating him up."

"Don't stop celebrating for my drama. You'll never get to enjoy it if you're waiting for my life to cool out. You deserve this. If I could do it to the whole Sect, I would."

She grabbed my arm again. "What if you could?"

"Pump the breaks. We'll see if you have any side-effects from me forcing you into it first. We do need to toast to this at some point."

"We so do. And I need to work some spells and catalogue the differences. Ooh, and I need to get supplies."

"Go. I'm gonna wash the ass out of my mouth."

She squealed and hugged me tight again before racing out of the room.

I stood on steady ground and approached Donovan and Vincent. "I told her."

Vincent nodded with a sober stare of non-emotion I couldn't read. "In coming years, you may find yourself in the position to act, while the consequences befall on another—negative consequences, unlike your current result. Enjoy the luck of today and that your vessel was chosen for its strength. Remember, you have merely awakened this latent power of Nya's. You will need to get a handle on it before it overtakes and breaks down your body. I have seen it happen."

His saddened tone was enough to evoke a dose of fear. I needed to figure Nya's power out. My grip on my own power was baby fresh as it was.

"Keep my number. My allegiance is officially declared so I expect to see you soon and often. However, if I am needed, I will do what I can."

I thanked him, and he left the small room.

I looked at Donovan. "Do we need to talk?"

He took a deep breath and let it go. "Yes. About a lot of things. Not right now and not here. That okay?"

I nodded. "More than okay."

I couldn't tell if he didn't want to delve into the nitty-gritty or if he was saving me from another potential puking fit. Either way, I was happy. I needed a drink and some fresh air.

5

BATTLE READY

"Sooooo." Kim stood at Ranlyn's kitchen counter with a half-bitten, dripping pickle between her fingers and pointed it at Donovan. "I've decided the 'Make it Grow' test can gobble my lady berries, so you'll have to train me another way since you're the expert now." She chomped down the rest of the pickle in one bite.

I laughed and took another pull of my rum and Coke.

"That test worked for Sophie and me because it was designed by Aunt Lacey according to our abilities. Yours won't be the same."

"Either way, the 'Make it Grow' test can gobble my lady berries."

Blake slid into the stool next to her. "Walked in on that conversation at the right time."

Kim popped an olive into her mouth. "If you like lady berries."

Jared reached between them to grab an olive. "Only if it concerns his own."

Blake pulled the olive bowl out of Jared's reach. "Jealous?"

"That you have lady berries?" Jared cuffed him in the back of the head and grabbed the olive bowl, offering Kim one. She smiled and took a few.

Blake rolled his eyes. "So, our all-powerful and fearless Sect

Leaders, do we get a role in this fight or do the four of you and the Mother Coven get to play while we get benched like little leaguers?"

Donovan looked at me and then Kim. "Your math skills alone should bench you. There's only three of us."

"You three plus Caine, obviously. He may have left but he'll be back when Loring or your hot-toddy sister shuffles her sweet ass back around."

"What?!"

"Jo, Joanne, or whatever. Your totally sexy sister worth losing a nut over."

Jared nodded as if agreeing made it certain.

"Caine left?" Donovan deadpanned as he picked at a bowl of Cheezies, somehow knowing I meant Caine and not Joelly.

"The teleporter took him back."

"Apporter." Jared spoke around the olives in his mouth.

Blake scoffed. "Same diff. So, what about the fight?"

"You could fight if you knew how." Donovan chomped into a Cheezie as I fumed about Caine leaving.

Jared laughed like he expected Donovan's answer.

Blake wasn't laughing. "That's bush. Since when have you seen me in action? It's not a part of the meetings. You want us to be serious about our abilities when every week it's a shitshow for the rest of us who have nothing to do with your weekly drama with Sophie?" He focused his baby blues in my direction. "No offence."

"You're more than welcome to tap into my drama. I've had enough."

"True story, chicky."

Donovan arched an eyebrow Blake's way.

Blake cleared his throat. "We did the shielding spell and now we're not even in the house. Don't get me wrong—totally awesome-sauce, but on a scale of awesomesauce-ness, it's like being forced to ride the bus with the psycho cat lady too busy to notice she crapped her adult diapers because she's talking to her dead husband, all when you have a model girlfriend and a Ferrari in the garage. Come on, man."

Donovan wiped his cheesy fingers on a napkin and glared at Blake. "Kim and I were left this Sect for a reason, Goredema. Leading you into battle is not that reason." Donovan using Blake's Coven name changed the tone of the conversation. "If it so happens an attack is mounted in your presence, you having no choice but to engage, my priority would still be your safety and escape, not your position within an offensive strategy. That's not what this Sect was created for and I won't be responsible for turning it into that."

Blake stood, facing Donovan from the other side of the counter. "We don't know when it's coming. There might be enough time."

"To learn defensive skills, but not to get you battle ready." He leaned into his hands on the counter. "You think we enjoyed getting our asses handed to us when Loring or the Puppeteer or the Raddies decided to take advantage?" Coveners were now listening to the exchange. "I hate the fact that we've already died or almost died enough for the whole Coven. So, you can take all your romanticized visions of war and join the army, 'cuz here, training takes more than a few weeks in the mud and you're nowhere near ready."

Blake's cheeks reddened, either in anger or embarrassment, as Donovan took him down a notch in front of the Sect. Power prickled the air around us. Jared grabbed Blake's shoulder, trying to get him to back down, but Blake shrugged him off and sent a kick of crawling white and grey streaming energy through his palm across the small space at Donovan.

Donovan grabbed the shoulder of my shirt, pushing me into Kim, knocking chip bowls to the floor, and caught the stream of energy in his hands like a dodgeball. Sparks of power shot into the space between his fingers and illuminated his twisted, dark features.

He shifted the sphere to his right hand, planted his left on the counter, and, in a blurred movement, jumped over the counter and landed his worn Converse on Blake's sternum, taking him to the ground. Blake's wheeze turned into a growl as Donovan punched the sphere of power into his chest, holding it in place a lingering moment before releasing him.

When the snap of power in my palms quit, my knuckles ached as Donovan grabbed hold of the fabric of Blake's shirt and lifted him off the ground inches from Donovan's needling gaze. "Try that again and you'll be hit with more than your own pussy energy bolt." Spit flung from his lips, clenched teeth gleaming in a snarl. "Too slow, too weak, too obvious. Even Joelly could leave you busted and choking on your entrails before you ruffled her fake eyelashes."

Letting him go with a shove, Donovan let Blake rise to his feet, then addressed the shocked crowd. "Everyone wants to be involved, I get it. Put the time in. Earn your power. Build your abilities within a range that doesn't royally suck ass and I'll trust you to cover my back if the fight comes to us. Right now, you're Seedlings. Being polite about your weaknesses to spare your puppy-dog feelings does shit-all but get you killed. So, no, I'm not sorry whether you're choked about it because I refuse to be responsible for your deaths."

Turning to Blake with a brow-beating glare, he invaded his personal space. Blake's expression went stone blank as Donovan spoke low and severe. "Don't you dare insult me by apologizing. Try that again and you'll be out of this Sect and extricated from the Mother Coven completely." Over Blake's shoulder, Donovan caught sight of Ranlyn who had witnessed the outburst. Blake followed his gaze as Ranlyn gave a stiff nod, backing Donovan's threat. "Understood?"

Blake swallowed. "Understood."

Kim was at my ear. "Total overkill, but you can't deny how hot that was."

I agreed, trying to hide the flare of heat in my cheeks as Donovan's anger filtered through our bond.

Part of what made him irresistible was his unapologetic defiance, incurable passion, boundary issues, and craftiness for making his point in the most flamboyant way possible without fear. In this case, it made its mark. Blake was spanked back into line in a way Kim would never do.

Donovan came back around the counter, put my stool back where it was and sat at his own, resuming to crunch on a Cheezie. Coveners erupted in hushed excitement as Blake did everything not to hang his head.

Ranlyn came into the kitchen area and offered those around him tea.

Vincent accepted and leaned against the fridge. "What do you wish to accomplish this evening, Ranlyn?"

Ranlyn filled a mug of water and held it. After a hitch in power, steam rose from the cup and he handed it to Vincent and directed him to a selection of tea bags and sugar.

"Damn, Jeeves. Remind me not to piss you off."

He looked at me as he "heated" his own cup. "As if that would stop you."

I lifted my rum and Coke that somehow managed not to get spilled during Blake's pissing contest.

Ranlyn smiled and turned back to doctor his tea. "By the end of the night, I would love to pin down a strategic plan—one beneficial to all and reaping the least amount of consequences and causalities while ending this feud. There's been too much death already. We need to limit this to single digit fatalities."

"War is named as such for a reason. Death is inescapable." Hinapouri's attitude was too causal. She and Miklos had entered the conversation before I realized they were standing two-feet away.

I raised a hand like a grade schooler. "Well, I for one have died enough times."

"You think too much of your own mortality, Seedling. This fight goes far beyond your petty existence." Her harsh tone was as off-putting as her causal one.

Donovan's anger bloomed across the connection.

"I agree, Sophie." Ranlyn took a sip of his tea and put it down. "There's been too much death, including yours. Though I understand what you mean, Hinapouri. This has been going on for a long time. I strongly feel that it's coming to a head and I worry if we're ready for it."

"As I understand it," Vincent sipped his tea, "your sister, Joelly, has pitted herself amid all our enemies. Is this the case?"

"Joelly's been in trouble before. This time she nailed herself on all ends."

"The Ballard Family Coven helped reveal her involvement with all of them." Ranlyn couldn't have hidden his regret for how the situation leading to this 'reveal' went down if it meant cutting his eyes out. I left it alone.

"The Ballard Family? I do not believe I know of them."

"My family's newly reclaimed coven."

Vincent gave a slow nod.

"She's in it for herself," Ranlyn refocused on Joelly, "but is by all rights a devotee to the Puppeteer's coven, involved with Loring's Sect, an informant for the Raddies, and has the ability to alter herself so even our highest-level security cannot keep her out."

Donovan turned to Vincent. "If you're thinking she would be a perfect interrogation subject, you'd be right. If she wasn't released."

"We are not so ignorant to think she would not make efforts to reconnect with her Master." Miklos stroked his beard. "The Huntsman is watching."

I looked at Ranlyn for an explanation. "What's a Huntsman?"

"A Coven affiliate named Roe."

"A tracker," Hinapouri added.

"Far more than a tracker." Vincent stepped forward. "A Huntsman has the ability of a tracker with heightened senses beyond that of the gifted to include an innate sense of behaviour. Think profiler and Bloodhound in one."

"Coolio. Call me impressed."

Vincent smiled and fixed his glasses.

Ranlyn finished his tea and put the mug down. "Joelly's been squatting in empty rentals. She no longer works at the bar and is keeping contact with Loring or anyone else at a minimum. As far as Roe can tell, they're staying clear of her and not the other way around. She's become a liability, even for them."

I couldn't help feeling a heartstring twinge for Joelly.

"Don't feel sorry for her, babe. She chewed off the hand that fed her time and again. She's earned whatever she gets."

"That's like saying you should've been put down as a boy. You changed your stripes. Maybe she needs better leaders."

Donovan spun to me in his seat, his feet settling on the bottom rung of my stool, left arm on the back of my chair. "I defected once I understood what was expected of me and what that meant for others outside of the coven. This has been her since the beginning."

I gave a sly smile and leaned towards him. "You forget I've seen into your past. When she was brought to you as your shanghaied future wife, she was a terrified little girl." Donovan's brow furrowed. "She was made into this. She can get out if she wants."

"Wait." Kim raised her hands in a 'time out' gesture. "Wife? So much for sister."

"Except," Donovan rose his voice to regain my attention, "she relishes in screwing with others' lives and doesn't want to change. And I didn't forget you found that out. You neglected to share."

I shrugged. "Had no reason to bring it up before."

"Sure you didn't." His expression and connection called me a liar-lair-pants-on-fire as nips of pressure on the inside of my cheek meant he was chewing on it to stop himself from saying more.

Hinapouri called Roe and took an agonizing amount of time to find the speaker phone option so Donovan ripped it out of her hand and did it for her, quieting the Coveners so they could talk.

"Has she connected with Evaristus?" Ranlyn used the name Aunt Lacey called the Puppeteer.

"Not directly." A husky voice came across the phone. It sounded like he sucked in a drag of a cigarette before continuing. "Since everyone's spooked and freezing her out, she's constantly on the move. I followed her to Evar's coven marker. She entered but was bounced out."

"Evar's Creation?" Miklos questioned.

"Probably one of many." He took another drag.

"Where?" Ranlyn stood closer to the phone.

"Access route under Highway 406, between the Geneva Street and Fourth Avenue exits."

I laughed. "I know where that is." This gained me a look of surprise from everyone. "They call it the Thoth. In high school, a bunch of us went down with flashlights and homemade torches. You can't even stand up in most parts—just concrete walls covered in graffiti in a series of long tunnels. I still have a scar on my back from crawling through one of the shafts to an adjacent room. Well, I used to, I guess." I forget I didn't have my old scars anymore since I died and was brought back. "It's supposedly haunted."

Donovan sat back and crossed his arms. "Sounds like a guy's idea."

"Shut it."

He wasn't wrong. My childhood friend Ruby's boyfriend, Justin, and a bunch of his buddies that Serena and I went to school with came up with the ruse.

Donovan's dimples caved. "Knew I should've gone to high school."

"As far as I can tell," Roe's voice crackled in the phone speaker, "the highway was built around the coven marker since the coven's been around centuries before the 1960's, so either they came back later and uncovered it or Evar has a sheep on the city's construction payroll. Either way, it's definitely Evar's. I checked it out and the marker bears the image of the Northern Bald Ibis."

"Makes sense." Vincent pushed his glasses up higher on his nose. "The Northern Bald Ibis is a symbol of the Egyptian God Thoth. The bird of today is usually seen with shaggy oil black feathers, small beady eyes, and a long thin beak. The God was said to bear the head of the Ibis and stood for wisdom, learning, and above all, magic."

"So, there's actually a meaning behind that shithole?" I would have to remember to tell Serena. "I thought it was just some place teens went for a little harmless danger and hoping for some nookie."

"No, the place itself is just a shithole." Roe deep voice came through the phone. "A seedy dump full of rats and dirty needles, but the coven marker is in an advantageous spot since it's well hidden."

"No use to us." Miklos leaned against the counter. "Entry will not be permitted inside the Creation without proper consent."

"Joelly would know about that." Blake's hesitant voice came from behind us. His arms were crossed so tight his biceps were flexed like his skin would crack at any moment.

"She would," Donovan deadpanned.

Blake looked happy he wasn't yelled at again.

"I can bring her in," Roe offered.

"Not yet." Ranlyn picked up the phone and turned off the speaker option. "Keep tailing Joelly and see if Loring pops up anywhere. We'll look into accessing the Puppeteer's Creation." He ended the call.

Vincent leaned across the counter. "Can you speak with your sister?"

Donovan's pulse rose, teeth clenched. "Why?"

"Now that she is without aid, she may fall upon you to seek solace."

A gruff laugh bubbled up from Donovan's chest. "Man, you have no idea what you're asking."

"The information we seek ranks higher than sibling rivalry."

"Sibling rivalry would make sense if I ever aspired to be her, which if you've ever met Joelly, would be a hell of an accusation. You seem to forget that Joelly succeeded in ending me and Sophie's lives without giving a shit. And later, questioned my survival, again, without a cunt-hair of sympathy. You want to turn Joelly inside out and decrypt everything there is to know about the evil-sons-a-bitches that skank blows in her free time, ask her yourself."

Without a response from Vincent or a reprimand from the

Elders, Donovan shot to his feet with a loud scuff of his stool, storming out through the room with the round table giving a solid command. "Everyone follow me."

The Coveners looked to me. "I'm finishing my drink."

I gave a small look of apology to Henry and Louise who smiled and shook their heads, in no way thrown off by their young, willful co-Sect Leader. Donovan may have expected it, but I wasn't about to tag along. Instead, I leaned into my elbows on the counter, trying to focus on smoothing out his rough edges before he had the Coveners running laps.

"You find his actions acceptable?" Vincent sat on the stool Donovan left.

I ignored him while sitting with my eyes closed, grabbing a firm hold of Donovan through our connection and telling him to knock it off already without use of words. A release of tension in my shoulders told me he had given in to me. I was now able to bring my focus back to the room.

When I opened my eyes, Vincent hadn't moved an inch, still staring at me behind his thin rimmed glasses with a glare of intrigue instead of joining the Elders who continued in conversation.

"What?"

"Does that help?"

I shrugged. "If he walked back in this room, you'd be greeted by a different Donovan. He may have anger issues, but he's loyal and usually a good leader." I was bluffing about the leader part. I had no clue but figured if Donovan put forth the effort, he could be.

"Then why did his flock look for your direction instead of following their leader's orders without pause?"

"Her flock, too." I thumbed in Kim's direction. She waved from her spot on the other side of me.

Vincent considered his words before speaking. "You make my point. The Sect was left not only to Donovan. Though he's of some relation, Elsa herself believed his ability to lead was questionable."

"Don't you *dare* repeat that to him." It wasn't meant to sound like a threat, though it sort of was.

He turned his stool to face me. "Joelly is a viable connection to the people who want your entire Coven extinguished—she being the only one who can presumably gain access to the Creation within which that enemy hides and is connected to all others. Your companion is our link to her. Donovan will need to surpass his personal demons to defeat the ones in front of him. I do not believe he can accomplish this alone."

Vincent sat and stared at me as if I was supposed to understand what he meant. I turned and slapped my hand flat on the countertop, gaining Ranlyn's attentions from his chat with the Elders. To his credit, he barely flinched.

Kim backed up, so I had a clear view of him. "Is there an issue with the way Donovan is running this Sect?"

"I'm sorry?"

"Donovan. Is there an issue with him being co-Sect Leader or is Vincent here crossing a boundary?"

Ranlyn's lips parted, jaw slack, as he searched for Vincent over my shoulder. For whatever reason, this caused an eruption of laughter from Vincent.

"If he has you, no issue will be raised." Vincent rubbed his eye and fixed his glasses. "My apologies, Elder Ranlyn. Sophie has enlightened me about the new Sect Leader." He thumbed in my direction. "She will keep him straight."

My head twisted from the tow-headed Elder to the tears-in-laughter Soul Extractor, sensing a whole conversation I was never present for but part of. Neither man explained, but Ranlyn turned back to the others half-abashed.

"Right. Well, we have to get to whatever's happening out there. Don't we, Kim?" She stood up as I finished off my drink. "Wouldn't want to leave Donovan on his own. Who knows what kind of trouble he might get into."

When we headed into the long room with the outside exit,

Vincent followed. Kim went through the door first. Vincent called my name before I could get out. Kim stopped as well, but I exhaled in annoyance and told her to go on.

"You're keeping me from babysitting duty."

"Watch first."

I exhaled again, let the door close, and watched.

Visible beneath a clear, night sky was Donovan working with the Coveners. Training them. Each Covener stood at each other's flanks, single file, now including Kim. Not everyone could arouse their power, but from the heightened sense of energy and the slight butterfly reaction in my gut, enough of them could to create an atmospheric difference. For the ones with released powers, it meant showcasing their defensive and offensive abilities.

Blake gathered a sufficient amount of energy to create a sphere of it as Donovan had done in the kitchen. It nestled within his hands, building until he propelled it from his palms into the nothingness of the large property. The energy he created was faster and stronger than before, and Donovan was standing right next to him, encouraging him, and tweaking his technique. After throwing another shot of energy that was so bright it made everyone squint and turn away—and reached a greater distance—Donovan slapped his shoulder in congratulations. Blake was so stoked, he did a back flip.

"Like I said," Vincent leaned into his shoulder against the door, "with you around to keep him in check, your companion will excel as a leader."

6

RELUCTANT PUPIL

When I looked at Vincent, he smiled and I returned a smile of my own, confused by his insistence in calling Donovan my companion. If only he knew about Caine.

"Where is Caine?" His smirk had my smile vanishing.

"Of course, you read minds."

His tiny smirk grew. "I must admit my curiosity got the best of me. I know you care for Donovan and I know you would not allow him to misuse his power as Sect Leader, but I needed to be certain someone was taking responsibility for his actions."

"Shouldn't he be responsible for his own?"

"He should be, yes."

"Why do you need confirmation at all? You're not an Elder."

"Nor do I want to be."

His non-answers were annoying. I looked out the window again and saw Donovan speaking with Kim. I didn't know if he was instructing her, but they didn't look to be arguing and the emotions flowing from him weren't confrontational. Unlike Vincent.

Laughter erupted from him. I grabbed the door handle.

He placed a hand on mine. "Wait a moment."

"Your speculations are insulting. I'm not responsible for a damn thing Donovan does and filling in the blanks, when you know dick-all about me, is fucking rude."

"You're not as incensed as you claim."

I squared my shoulders at him.

"I happen to know you rather enjoy this power of mine because of your ability to do the same, though you have not yet figured out how to utilize it. I also know you emit a diluted pride when you see your companion out there. Diluted with guilt."

"Vincent—"

"When I mentioned Caine, you experienced remorse, culpability. When I spoke of your companion, your guilt was only due to Caine. I find this intriguing."

"Is that why you keep calling Donovan my companion?"

Vincent's expression hardened in a way I couldn't decipher. "You may not have something in the forefront of your thoughts, but still unconsciously dwell upon it."

I shifted my weight to my other foot. "So, this is supposed to be a lesson?"

"As ones of magic, we are equipped with many an ordinance. Uncovering the gifts afforded to us at birth is a feat of its own. To leave these gifts underdeveloped or to abandon them at the wayside, as one who is rather fond of his gifts, I find *that* insulting."

"Really?" I crossed my arms. "So, instead, you peer into my head and judge the fact that I haven't quite excelled at my gifts, even though I uncovered them what feels like days ago." His smug smile fueled the rest of what I had to say. "Then you presume to dissect my love life. It's pretentious, not to mention cruel, considering I haven't the time to figure it out myself as I'm too busy strategizing over saving my ass and fretting about my friends facing assholes you and the Elders have had centuries to understand. Prance your superiority complex into the other room with people of your own calibre, 'cuz I should be out there training with the rest of the Seedlings."

I walked out the door and into the field towards Kim and Donovan. Before I got to them, Donovan spun my way, his concern flitting over the connection. He stepped in my direction and stopped. I turned and saw Vincent and his smug smile close behind. I huffed and continued towards the group.

Vincent grabbed my arm and stopped me.

"What the fizz, dude?" He let me go. "Do you need a Counsellor? Because I know a few that would be glad to help."

He looked over my shoulder. I turned and saw Donovan had moved a step closer but still stood back and watched. His concern shifted to worry and confusion. Kim was looking my way as well until Rachel needed her for something.

"Why are you running to them, Sophie?"

"I don't run unless I have to. You're annoying the shit out of me, so I'm getting away from you."

"Read my mind."

"Kiss my ass."

He grabbed my arm again. "Read me. You know you can."

I ripped out from his grasp. "Did it ever occur to you that your brain is not my preferred genre?"

"That is not what I asked."

"But that's what I answered."

Half a step away from him, I was stopped dead in my tracks. I stared, wide-eyed, at Donovan who was as agitated as I was, looking from me to Vincent. Loophole. Vincent wasn't touching me. He used telekinesis to pin me down.

"Let. Me. Go."

"You can turn and work with me, or not, but avoidance with your companion is not an option."

I drew in a deep breath, wishing I could slap the bastard. I tried to convey a message to Donovan with my eyes, but the dumb-fuck kept looking at Vincent. I opened my mouth to yell at him and choked on my words. Heaving in raking coughs, I gave up and decided breathing was more important.

"You may not converse with him either."

Donovan had been choking as well and opened his arms in question but stayed where he was.

Having no other choice, I turned to Vincent. "You creepy little prick. I don't even know you. You have no right to keep me from leaving this place all together."

"Return home if you wish. However, you won't leave without him and he won't be a part of this."

My eyes narrowed. "Ranlyn wouldn't stand for it."

"My life span exceeds your eldest Elder. They would heed my instruction. Stop misbehaving like a child."

"Children do what they're told. Your age doesn't give you permission to tell me what to do."

He stepped closer. "Read my mind, Sophie."

I looked up into his mossy eyes. "Nah. Thanks anyway."

"Read my mind."

"No." I crossed my arms, happy I could move. "You watch too many movies."

"This may save your friends one day. I will make it easy and open a channel for you to access."

His eyes flickered over my shoulder again. When I tried to turn and see why, I couldn't. Whatever spell Vincent had fixed kept me from communicating with Donovan in every form.

"I don't want to access your channels. And that's not how it works." All other times I used telepathy was accidental in high-stress moments. I wasn't about to pick a fight with Denise or Loring to recreate them, though Denise would be a fun target right about now.

"Yes, it does. You know you can do this."

"I know I can pick stuff up with my toes. Handy when I drop a pen. Not so much when I drop the bass."

"Stop trying to run away from this or use humour to deflect. This could save their lives!" He invaded my personal bubble and grabbed my shoulders. "You know how. You have done it before. Do it again!"

"I don't know how!" I couldn't run. I couldn't make him listen. My power flexed at the ready.

Vincent's stare down broke to look over my shoulder. "*I ordered you to wait!*" He then moved back to me to continue the barrage.

"You ordered him? Who the fuck are you to give anyone orders?"

He straightened, his severe features softening, and rubbed one of my shoulders before letting go. "I knew you were capable."

"Back off, dick cheese!" I pushed him away from me.

He stumbled a step back and raised his hands. "Dick cheese?"

"Dick pimple, dick sneeze, dick nipple—choose your visual."

"I proved my point."

"That you're an asshole?"

"That you are lazy."

"Lazy? You want to teach me, then teach me. Don't bully me. What you did was lazy as fuck teaching."

"Okay, okay." Donovan came between us. By this point, the Coveners were in full spectator mode.

"Now you give a shit enough to go against orders?"

"I tried to calm you. He said you guys were working on something."

"Since when do you listen to what anyone else tells you to do?"

"Since when do you?"

"He used a spell against me. I didn't have a choice."

"*I didn't give him the choice either.*"

I looked over Donovan's shoulder at Vincent's smug face. "It used to not matter, choice or not."

Vincent laughed that annoying laugh again. I wanted to rip his glasses off his face and introduce them to his nasal cavity. I tried to walk around him, intent on going back to Donovan's house if I had to.

Vincent side-stepped in front of me. "I didn't speak aloud, Seer."

I huffed. "You're not getting the subtext here. Let me make it clear. Fuck. Off."

He smiled. "You said, 'It used to not matter, choice or not'. You were answering my unstated thought."

I glared at him.

"I didn't hear anything, babe."

I didn't turn around to Donovan, instead choosing to stand staring at Vincent until his smile grew enough to show perfect white teeth.

"Whoop-dee-doo. I heard you. Look what it took. You think I'm going through that every time? *Pfft.*" I tried to move around Vincent and again, he was a road block in my way.

"I happen to know you find my laugh rather endearing." His green eyes narrowed with his smile. "When you are not upset with me, of course."

A derisive snort came from Donovan behind me. I felt heat in my cheeks. Of course, he would point something like that out in front of someone Vincent considered my "companion," even if I insisted Donovan wasn't.

"Sophie." I turned to Donovan. He waved me a few steps away with him and lowered his voice. "The Coveners need a lot of work. I won't spar, but I need them to learn the basics. Are you okay with him?"

"Hmm. Rewind the last few minutes and recap when I said I'd work with him. I must've wedged that in between 'fuck' and 'you'."

His dimpled grin caused a stirring shift of déjà vu within me. It was the smile. One imprinted on my soul from a different lifetime together. What sealed it was a wash of contentment he found from somewhere within himself and sent across our bond.

"I know you hate when I do that. You have a right to be pissed, but he's helping in ways I can't."

"That's not true."

"With Nya's power released it is. I've got skills, but not with ancient power attached to an already powerful Magic."

I remained quiet.

His hands reached to either side of my head, smoothing my hair as not to graze my skin. "Come on, babe." He kissed the top of my head, a small twinge of a vision hitting him. "Think opportunistically. Use him for what he's worth and ditch." He smiled when my stubbornness drained from our connection. "I'll be out here if you need me to rip his arms clean off his body. Or I'll hold him down while you remove his eyeballs with the arms of his glasses."

I tried not to smile and lost. "You mean you'd disobey orders?"

He gave me a side-eyed smirk before returning to the Coveners.

I saw Kim at the edge of the group. She blew a sarcastic kiss my way and mouthed, "What the fuck?"

I rolled my eyes and shook my head.

Stalling a moment as Donovan crossed the field and refocused on his trainees, my brain rolled over questions all pertaining to why I would let someone like Donovan take up space in my future. I believed he would hold the bastard down if I needed him to. He may have been a fighter by nature, but he had the capacity to care, too. This aspect had me torn. The draw to him was as great as the draw screaming for me to check my brain for severe malfunction.

"We will encounter less distraction in front of the property."

I didn't comment, conceding the fact, and followed Vincent around the house towards the front yard.

He glanced at me as we walked. "Do you realize he does that on purpose?"

"Donovan does everything he does on purpose."

"True. More specifically, he could have pressed a kiss upon your lips and chose not to. You would have let him."

"Relax yourself there, Vincent."

"In an effort to prove he lusts for more than your past, he remains in the present as often as possible. Seeking forms of affectionate contact while avoiding your presumptions it is all he desires."

"Are you spear-heading a Team Donovan campaign? Is there a street team? Maybe you're hiding a t-shirt underneath your cashmere? No?" I kept walking through tall grass at the side of the property. "If I was meant to know any of what you claim, Donovan would've told me." I stopped and turned to him.

"Why would he tell you that?"

"Why would you?"

"I thought maybe you would be less difficult with him if you understood the lengths at which he strives to prove himself. It is true Donovan does as he pleases, yet he is comprised of enigmatic qualities you have difficulty accepting." I stared at him and blinked. "He is intelligent yet makes dense decisions, he is considered good-looking by his peers yet is capable of uncontested ugliness, he is full of unrivalled passion and yet can appear rather cold. You claim it does, but it does not upset you. The only thing that does, however, is the question of why not. And that is simple. You know him. Every facet, every dark corner of his brain. You understand him in ways no other can. His wish is to do the same for you and he has shared more of himself than you of yourself, this of which I am certain. By all rights, he should never have to repeat the horrors of his past as you cannot fathom the magnitude he suffers because of them."

Vincent—a stranger only hours ago—had made conclusions about Donovan that I never put together. Maybe he read things from his mind? But Donovan wouldn't be thinking about all that stuff. The fact that Vincent was right caused a bite of shame. I wanted to know everything about Donovan. Most of what he knew about me, he learned through his visions, which was unfair of me, but repeating my past left a sour taste. I didn't want to tell him. I didn't want to tell anyone. A savage truth, but still the truth. It reminded me that Caine knew the bulk of my history and now it didn't matter.

Not that I would admit any of that to Vincent. "Donovan having anything to prove is not your business. You wanna be my Yoda, then let's do this before I change my mind."

"Yoda?"

"Fine. You can be Vader, but you can't pull off wearing a cape with those khakis."

He shook his head. "Stand back." Vincent took a few steps away from me, rubbed his hands together to evoke a calm dose of power, and then turned in a circle. As he did, the waist tall grass bowed down and stuck flat to the earth in a swirl pattern.

"Holy freakin' crop circles, Batman!"

He made a small laugh. "Now, we sit."

I sat in front of him, legs crossed. "Magics are behind every conspiracy nut's theory, aren't they?"

"Not all, though some of us lack the sense of responsibility of covering our tracks. Bigfoot, for example."

I gasped and pointed at him. "Don't fuck with me, Vader." He laughed. "Are you fucking with me right now? I can't even tell."

"Focus, Sophie."

"With Bigfoot in the room? Impossible."

"Breaking down walls is more important than breaking down theories right now—walls within the mind keeping the rest of the world out."

"Mhmm. We'll circle back to Bigfoot later."

"No more staring at people hoping the words will bleed through the air. Envision the wall keeping you out. Imagine the delicate details of worn, aluminum siding, coarse stucco, or a pattern of wall-papered facade to your liking and break it down to allow the flow of words to escape. Again, the method of destruction is up to your making. You don't need to gather a word—work on creating the wall."

I brought out my power, feeling the low thrum of it move through me. Now, a wall. Build a wall. I exhaled and closed my eyes, trying to think of something wall-like.

"Remember, Sophie. It's not a wall within your mind, but within the individual you seek to read."

Right. Not my wall. A Vincent wall. What would a Vincent wall look like? I hadn't known him for long and had to think a moment. He was an immortal. I didn't know how old he was when his soul glow turned to silver, but he wasn't much older than his late thirties at the time. Rigid in his speech and mannerisms. Old world yet sturdy. A faded reddish-brown brick, mortar cracked with superfi-cial damage, the remnants of ivy having grown up the brick and torn off.

"*Interesting representation of myself.*" I heard the smile in his voice. "*Now break it down.*"

I thought of a sledgehammer and swung. The iron head bounced off with a small puff of brick dust and vibrated up my arms. I tried again with the same result.

Hmm. Much more difficult than those renovation shows, though they busted through drywall. Could I even pick up a sledgehammer? I doubted it.

The sledgehammer was gone. In its place was a regular hammer, which I knew without swinging that it was useless. A spoon? Maybe I could dig through the mortar and break him down, brick by brick.

Nothing I thought of made sense. He was too strong to break through with brute force. Mental or otherwise, I was weak. How else could I break through the wall? I created the fucking wall, why didn't I make the wall with a window?

A window appeared—a Vincent style window. Wooden frame. Wooden shutters with iron hinges, painted an earthy green and weather-worn. I opened the shutters and found single-pane glass broken up into six sections per window. The glass itself was too diffi-cult to see through. Not frosted but warped or textured. I saw through enough to see the shadow of the locking mechanism in the middle of the two panes and directed more power at it to unlock it and pull the window open.

Everything went black. The strength of my power snapped and dissipated.

"Fuckmonkeys. What happened?"

"You succeeded in getting into my mind. Gaining knowledge while inside is not a part of this exercise."

"Tease. I earned a nugget of something. What about this Bigfoot jazz? It's an experiment gone wrong, right? Or a Transmutator?"

"Your prize is the knowledge you managed to break into the mind of an immortal. In a most interesting fashion, I might add. A window. Crafty, indeed."

"You weren't exactly trying to keep me out."

"No, but I wasn't allowing you to walk in either. You should feel proud."

I didn't know what to say. I was proud, but I couldn't take a half hour to get into every brain I wanted to rummage through.

"The mind isn't a yard sale for you to peruse and discard useless trinkets." He overheard my thoughts with minimal effort. Easier than building up and breaking down a metaphysical wall. "Like all other endeavours, they prove easier with practice. This time, I will increase the difficulty. Try again."

I delved back into practice and brought my power back out. He was right. He didn't make it easier. Sometimes he deconstructed my walls or made the window disappear—every time, forcing me to inject more of my power into creating the circumstances to getting into his mind. When he ran out of obstacles, he upped the stakes and timed me. If I didn't get through the window in his allotted timeframe, I was zapped and pushed out of the sequence. Knowing Donovan was likewise zapped had me rushing to succeed. He had too much to do and didn't need to be distracted by my failings.

Once I complained about Donovan getting testy with these tactics, he moved on to thought implantation to create a conversational window, beginning with the same avenues of envisioning opening or breaking down barriers. This went back and forth for a long time, Vincent coming up with word games to keep it interesting and compelling enough for me to engage in practice.

"*Thank you.*" I meant it. His lessons were invaluable.

His eyebrows rose above his glasses. "*That was unexpected.*"

"*I'm an easy person to work with. You took the hard road in.*"

"*Pressing one to meet their potential comes easier with persistence.*"

"*You could've said you could teach me telepathy and showed me how. Manipulating me into it shut me down.*"

"*I noticed. You have developed an instinct to flee instead of fight unless coerced or given no alternatives.*"

"*Starting an interpersonal exchange with conflict causes people to fight back. You'd think after all your years, you'd know this about human behaviour.*"

"As Magics, we need to fight for our very existence. If you won't fight, someone will create a future for you."

Too many trying to do that already, the thought whispered in the back of my mind.

"I heard you." He smiled. *"Reading others underlying thoughts will come in time."* I nodded with slight embarrassment. *"Since reading souls presents a greater danger than reading minds, to yourself and others, let's work on the Soul Reading."* I inwardly cringed. *"I'll see to your safety, as well as Donovan's, and guide you through the process of reading your own soul telepathically."*

With Vincent, the Elders, and even Henry close by, those with healing abilities in the magic and medical world were around to save my ass in case I seized out before giving myself brain damage. But it was still a risk.

"A well-calculated one, Sophie. Now, I want you to find a time in your past when the power made itself known but went ignored, as happens with children."

"Right into another lesson, eh?"

"Best to maintain momentum."

"Mhmm. My powers hadn't been released until recently. How would I see anything as a kid?"

"Unless the natural powers of children are embraced or allowed the opportunity to excel, it will be buried, and the child may be so young the memory of a time when magic was a part of their lives is forgotten. I want you to find the moment that defined that path for you."

"Why? I already know my grandmother started it all when she had her sister institutionalized."

"Merely a place to begin. It will bring you deep enough into your past for you to be enveloped within your soul. Perhaps you may learn something."

Still not getting it, I stopped fighting the process and placed my hand on my chest as I had with Kim and Caine, enacting my power. I was pulled into myself without any friction, sounds and images racing by too fast to be cataloged.

"Take control of your descent, Sophie. Do not allow your soul to dictate the pace of your reading." His voice echoed around me as if he was speaking into an intercom system.

I scrambled to slow down. Memories flickered past like an old film projector. Christmases, Easters, birthdays, high school dances I spent getting drunk on vodka coolers in the bathroom with Serena, the bob haircut from Hell in the seventh grade—all passed by as I reached deeper into my past. A six-year-old's chirping voice—which, after a moment, I realized was my own—complained about Adam sitting on one side of the couch and digging his boney feet into my back. He wanted to watch *Sonic the Hedgehog*, but I was already watching *Pinky and the Brain*.

"Sift through these memories and younger, when a child's memories tend to be forgotten."

I didn't remember most of what I saw. My mother was years younger than I was now and she had two kids only ten months a part. We drove her nuts and she still managed to have more patience than I did sitting here doing nothing but watch. Like driving down a never-ending road in the dead of night while your passengers have all passed out, I was suffering from tunnel vision.

Once the novelty of seeing through my eyes as a kid wore off, it became pen-in-your-ocular-cavity boring. Not to mention frustrating, because I didn't know what to look out for.

The sound of Vincent's voice in the surrounding ether was also irritating. He kept telling me to move deeper, always deeper.

"There, Sophie. Go back."

"To where?"

"You were in a church."

"You're going to force me to relive church through the eyes of a four-year-old? You really are trying to torture me."

I found the spot to where I sat, staring at the wood backing of the pew in front of me, too short to see above the person sitting in it. My bangs were long and itched my eye. I yawned and put my feet under me. My grandmother lowered her voice and told me to sit like a "big girl".

"Were there times when your parents attended church with you and your grandmother?"

"Nope. We only went when visiting my grandmother in the summer. My parents weren't church goers unless someone got married or died."

"Interesting. Move to your first experience in Bible studies."

"Why?"

"To insert a child into a religious institution when a parent themselves has never followed that spiritual calling is suspect."

Hmmm. Finally, something made sense.

I always thought it was weird we had to attend. My Grandma Lizzie was always ready in her best-dressed for Sunday mass, but never my parents.

An early memory of being dragged out of bed and stuffed into a frilly, pink dress had a distinct level of dread surrounding it. I never wore a dress. I hated dresses and the red patent leather Mary Janes were too small. Overwhelming shyness had me sitting and reading while the younger kids were all corralled in a church basement room, away from the grownups, for Bible study. I liked stories but was bored of the one they talked about before letting us play. They wanted me to love Jesus. I didn't know Jesus and wondered why he wanted me to dress up and be awake so early.

We hopped into the back of Grandma Lizzie's green sedan, our mother driving as Adam regaled her with the morning's events. Since we behaved ourselves, we were treated to brunch. A stack of chocolate chip pancakes was put in front of me. Adam's scrambled eggs found his lap more often than his mouth, another thing for us to bicker about. My mother and Grandma Lizzie were mumbling about something my younger self had ignored and wouldn't have understood, but I knew they were talking about me.

Tossing her blonde feathered hair over her shoulder, eyes glossed with tears, Mom feigned a smile my way. "I want my kids to be normal, functioning adults. Ones who don't see fireflies." My mom handed Adam a napkin. He grabbed it but put it on the table instead of cleaning the ketchup off his nose.

"No fireflies today, mama." None of the kids who were at church looked like fireflies, but even as a kid, I could see that my grandmother was a sick firefly.

Adam shook his head. He didn't see fireflies today either.

Mom smiled. "Good, dolly."

"Of course not, Sophie dear." My grandmother leaned forward. "In God's house, there's no darkness masquerading as light."

"Relax a bit, mom. I want my kids to be safe, not confused and terrified."

My grandmother scoffed and argued about the word of God. My mother's response was lost as I couldn't listen to them anymore. She knew. My mother knew about our power. She knew we saw soul glows. She pulled away from me, pretending to be shocked when she found out, but she knew all along.

"I've had enough."

7

DOOMED FAIRY-TALE

O nce Vincent guided me out of the Soul Reading, I was up on my feet, seething with betrayal, and stomping away into the high grass lit by the moon above.

"What does this change?" Vincent remained where we sat during the reading, giving me physical space while continuing the lesson.

A few minutes passed before I could organize my thoughts enough to respond. *"She saw me heal. She knew about Olive. She met the Elders and was around when our family took oaths from new members of our coven. At no point did she sit me down and tell me she knew about our powers as children. Nothing about her mother brainwashing us to forget about it, nothing about how Adam was a Magic, too. Even if my grandmother lied about where our power came from, she still knew. She treated me like I was infectious and asked if I could stop."*

"The rational side of us will not always allow a belief of things as they are. In no way does this change—"

"I know, I know. My mother loves me. Wanted her kids to be normal. Was scared shitless of something she didn't understand. Great excuses for lying to her kids their entire life."

"Your mother may have forced herself to forget as well. Upon your declaration, it may have exposed this dark time for her, but it does not mean she was willing to believe it."

"Fancy talk for saying you don't think I should confront her about it."

"Confrontations cause the confronted to defend. The result of which will not be one of peace but may cause an irreparable rift that will outweigh the need to voice your disappointment."

"Right. So, I get to sit with this while she works out if she's still disgusted by what her children are."

"Not merely her children, but herself. She must come to terms with who she is as well. The power in your blood is as much hers as yours."

I groaned and looked up at the stars above me before closing my eyes to the slight breeze. His words struck a heartstring. I wanted to be foaming at the mouth, pissed off, but remembering my mother's young face, tortured by what could become of her kids, I couldn't retain the anger I felt after breaking the Soul Reading. Anger stewed somewhere, as did sympathy and a shit tonne of sadness.

What did my grandmother say to her to freak her out? Was it her God-fearing garbage or something more? I couldn't hold this in forever.

"You can search further back, if you like, though I recommend you ponder what you've learned. Above all, the lesson was a success."

A small laugh burst through my lips. "Success. Sure. I'll pat myself on the back later."

"As long as you do. You are a quick learner when you give in to the process. And Nya's power remained dormant. Tonight's strides are your own."

Right. Nya's power. Which means we haven't gotten to the tough stuff yet.

"Not to worry, Sophie. Rest is in order before delving into a mystery such as Nya's power. I would not want you reverting to creative expletives now that telepathy is within your arsenal."

I turned and saw him smiling, his hands in the pockets of his khakis as he stood in our crop circle practice area looking like a scholar in the wild. Why he bothered to help me at all was the biggest mystery. Maybe he knew Aunt Lacey and was helping out since Loring was on my ass? He didn't answer my thought. Instead choosing to leave the crop circle and head inside. Guess practice time was over. Or he was avoiding the question.

Inside, Coveners gushed about their practice and the cool shit they did, like in the case of Blake, who couldn't brag enough. Matt swore he could feel a stir of power near the end and thought if they practiced "ten minutes longer" he would have had it. Jared jumped on this, but I had to admit every Covener was a tad brighter than before Donovan's lessons.

Donovan was in the kitchen, mid-pour with a bottle of pop in his hand.

"You're drowning your whisky."

Donovan jolted at my telepathic intrusion and dropped the two-litre bottle, the pop spraying over the counter, and falling to the ground with a thud.

I ran and grabbed a dishrag from the counter. "Your face. Holy shit." I bent to help him clean up while in a fit of laughter.

"Consider volume next time. You scared the shit out of me." Donovan gave me a playful shove, knocking me onto my ass on the kitchen floor as I laughed harder.

"Congrats." Ranlyn stood with the Elders in the kitchen. He smiled while the others appeared indifferent.

"Thanks, Jeeves. Vincent's a pain in the ass, but he gets results. I won't send anyone running in fear, but it's something."

"Plus the Soul Reading." Vincent sat on a stool on the other side of the counter.

Donovan made an impressed sound, stood, and threw the wet cloth in the sink. "Aren't you glad I stayed out of it?"

I scrunched my nose in a mock sneer and started wiping down the counter.

Donovan laughed as he finished pouring his drink and then one for me.

"*You can do more.*" Vincent lifted a bowl for me to wipe underneath.

"*Relax and let me enjoy this for half a second.*"

"None of that." Donovan swayed his finger from me to Vincent. "It's rude."

"*Jealous.*" I sent the mental note his way and hit a wall. "Hey."

"It can't be Donovan's brain-on-the-go twenty-four-seven. My telepathy and mental defences are rusty, but still work."

"You could do it, too? Like, the whole time?"

He shrugged. "I never use it. I'd much rather have someone trust me enough to tell me something than learn it like that." The twang of dread across the connection led me to believe a horrible story accompanied his reason.

I glared at Vincent. "You didn't teach me how to block people out."

He smiled. "Now your companion can teach you."

I rolled my eyes at his meddling. Donovan didn't say anything about my internal squirming.

Donovan turned to the Elder at the end of the kitchen. "Hey, Miklos, do your hoodoo on Sophie."

"I do not practice hoodoo." Miklos's gruff and deadpan response was near comical.

"*As I said, Seer, your companion will disregard your protests in classifying your relationship, saving you with a change in conversational direction to spare you discomfort.*"

It was all I could do not to speak aloud. Instead, I tossed a pop-soaked paper towel at his face, streaking his glasses as it fell to the counted with a wet "thunk" while I spilt over in giggles.

Miklos put a tumbler of clear liquid down and met me half-way into the kitchen. He took hold of my shoulders, closing his eyes as he spoke in a foreign tongue. He released me, picked up his glass, and resumed his conversation with Hinapouri. Ranlyn smiled but didn't comment.

I turned and went back to Donovan. "Was he fucking with me? I didn't feel anything."

He laughed. "It'll help you from becoming a Puppet."

"Why didn't we do that from the beginning?" I thought back on the hours we had spent sifting through research books.

He leaned in. "Veata was supposed to."

"Oh." The reminder one of our Elders was possessed and left in the hands of evil was jarring.

As it got later, the Coveners found rooms to put themselves in for a few hours of shut-eye. The training and six hours' time difference from home left them exhausted and bleary-eyed.

I didn't realize my dilemma until the other rooms were taken. Would I stay in the same bed I had the night before with Donovan—with new bloodless bedding—or would I give a lame excuse I knew he'd swallow and saddle up on the living room's hardwood floor?

Such a small thing came coupled with such large implications.

Caine's expression stuck in my head—disgusted by the fact I spent the night with Donovan so soon since the abrupt end of our relationship. It didn't matter we were injured and unconscious.

"You figure it out yet?" Donovan leaned against the railing of the top floor in jogging pants and a plain tee as I exited the bathroom in my pyjamas.

"Umm...."

"I'm not forcing the issue, but I'm gonna pass out." He straightened and headed for the eerie room.

I looked over the railing and saw Jared and Blake stretched out, each on a couch, Bosco on his back in the crook of Jared's arms.

Going with what felt right and blocking out the berating voices telling me to do different, I headed into the creepy room and slid into bed with Donovan.

———

Boom! Boom! Boom!

I jerked awake and peered through sagging eyelids.

"Get up or I'm breaking the door down!"

Muted sunlight filtered through the small window. Early morning.

More pounding against the hardwood. Donovan whipped the blankets off, sprinted for the door, and threw it open.

"Sshiiit. Nice hair." Kim peered at me, still in bed, over Donovan's shoulder. "We're meeting. Get downstairs."

Donovan slammed the door shut, padded back to the bed, and laid out on his back in a huff. "I thought she had quality boyfriend time today?" His voice was husky with sleep as his arm was slung over his eyes.

Grunting a response I was too tired to verbalize, I pulled the blanket up to my chin in desperate need of more sleep.

Movement and the weight of Donovan's heavy arm draped over my side as he twisted his body to face mine. The comfort of his embrace caused an involuntary smile, and then triggered another not so pretty response.

"We better get down there." I pushed the blankets, and his comfort, away and slipped my feet to the floor, bending to rummage through my overnight bag for a set of clothing.

"Not so alluring in the light of day?"

"What?" *Where's my toothbrush?*

"We didn't have sex, babe. No need to freak."

"I'm not freaking."

"You are. And while it's also new territory for me, I'm not complaining. You and Caine's breakup is still fresh vulture chow." He rushed to stand between me and the door I was heading towards, hands up without touching me. "I don't have any expectations and one hook-up doesn't make you a skank, so you can stop hating yourself for it."

"You're right. A hook-up is nothing special."

"Not what I meant."

"Try weak-willed, delusional, straight-up moronic? Being a skank makes it easier to claim dick as a reason to send my life tits-up, instead of believing in some doomed fairy-tale." I side-stepped him and headed out to the bathroom.

I monopolized the small washroom, getting ready and putting my hair into a quick braid over my shoulder, all on autopilot. Once I didn't have a task to distract me, my thoughts came back to bite me.

Neither of us needed my honesty this soon after waking up. My asshole mood was too much, even for me. Did I believe what I said? It felt like it at the time. I couldn't settle with the idea my past was the single thing fuelling my present.

I stuck my pjs and bathroom stuff in a now empty room and headed downstairs.

"There she is." Blake's voice rang impatience. "Can we start already?" He huffed and mumbled something to Jared loud enough to give Denise the giggles.

"Sorry." I stood next to Kim behind one of the couches.

Caine sat across from me on a couch. Seeing him with his new hair, reflecting the man I met in his greatest nightmare, was still difficult to process. I looked away to Ranlyn, standing in front of the fire.

"If you didn't stick around last night for your co-Sect Leaders training session, meet with him after this meeting, but first see Miklos so he can perform a protection spell against possession from the Puppeteer." He motioned to Miklos who looked at his bored-with-inconvenience co-Elder. "Within hours, members of the Mother Coven and Mother Coven affiliates will arrive. Expect many and expect that they may not be aware of everything most of you already know. We need all members capable of contributing to be amongst the attendees if we hope to make a dent against the Puppeteer's plan."

"And if they won't help?" While Ranlyn may not have appreciated Denise's question, we all were thinking it.

"We do what we've always done and find a way to survive. And instead of repeating myself once the other members arrive, much can wait until later. At present, I would like to introduce you to Roe." He lifted his hand towards a man leaning against the wall in the back of the crowd.

More was going on than a simple gathering to get a tally of our numbers against the Puppeteer. His eagerness to move on was unsettling.

In his late forties or early-fifties, Roe's features were creased with that of a hard life, skin tanned like leather, ravished by the harsh sun, muddy brown hair peppered with grey and pulled into a low pony-tail. He returned a curt nod, hands pushed into his worn jeans that looked more beaten than his complexion.

"Roe is a Huntsman," Ranlyn went on. "He's been keeping a close eye on things and has come with valuable information that will be shared later this evening. Though not an official Coven member, Roe has been loyal to our previous Elders, making the choice to fight for our side. Isn't that right, Salix?"

I was focused on the yellow soul glow Roe's gift emanated—which was confusing, since yellow was reserved for Transmutators. Maybe this was what made Roe a good Huntsman. Either he had a touch of inherited genes to turn himself into something furry or could change at will and hunt his target.

"Yup, indeedy." Not the most extensive assessment of his good-side soul glow and I earned a few snickers.

Curious about what he may have to share since I knew he had been tracking Joelly, I engaged my new telepathy skills and bypassed his thin mental barriers as if I was invited. Instead of waltzing in and taking a tour, I opened a small window and peered inside like a Peeping Tom desperate to catch a glimpse of something juicy.

For the most part, Roe was listening to Ranlyn, but he soon got bored and turned reflective. I watched the reel of his thoughts and the blips of images. He suppressed a personal struggle for possessing his power—it made him a living, through his tracking and under-the-table jobs, paying for gas in his truck, and enough alcohol to with-stand the life. He yearned for more than his ambitionless family whose life goals were to procreate and make it a day without walking in the door torn to pieces or not at all. They carried a skewed sense of importance and responsibility for the gift which equalled a die-for-the-job mentality Roe hated but fell into anyway.

"At least I never dragged a woman and young into this mess", was the thought echoing through his mind.

Before he could shut down thoughts of a blonde-haired beauty, a dark sense of grief began to develop. He shifted his thoughts back to the Coven. They had become his family and allowed him to operate on his terms. He would do anything to assist in reclaiming their Creation—one that had been theirs since its inception and was now overrun by those it aimed to protect against.

A technicolor snapshot of a ravaged and infested-by-evil Diluculo popped up. Bitterness surrounded Roe's memory of sneaking into the Creation as he saw the rising smoke of fire-ravished buildings. Wandering people—Puppets or Tainted, he couldn't tell—dragged limp bodies. He was able to see a greater distance than usual. A swath of churned up earth sliced through the middle of the Creation, the remanence of the Woodland of Energies nothing but heaps of lumber.

Ohmygod!

I slammed my lips shut against a gasp, but my recoil wasn't so private. It free-flowed into the open window of Roe's mind and alarmed him of my un-stealth-like presence.

Roe stiffened and straightened, looking around the room with twitchy movements in my periphery. I focused forward at Ranlyn.

Did I close the window I made? Would it stay open or slam shut the moment I got the fuck out of there? Could Roe hear me now?

Donovan looked at me, his brows creased in question.

Shitnuggets.

The longer I focused on Ranlyn or the flickering flames of the fire beyond him, the more relaxed Roe looked. I couldn't fully see him, but he was leaning against the wall again. I got lucky.

My mind must be as open as his. No wonder Loring tap-danced into my head. I could still hear the smug satisfaction in his voice when he exposed me on calling his arm-candy a cur. And now, we assumed, he was playing as the Puppeteer's biscuit bandit back inside Diluculo, ready and willing to serve his Master. We were too busy escaping to check out what was left behind. From what I saw in Roe's head, the Puppeteer ensured he twisted everything. And the dead.... Who were all those dead people? Magics? Blind?

"Sophie?"

I snapped out of my fixation on Diluculo to find the Coveners leaving.

Ranlyn walked by me. "Please follow."

Shitballs! Did Roe rat me out?

Caine followed Ranlyn and headed into the room with the dining table. The rest of the Coveners went outside for more training, lining up side-by-side as Donovan gave instructions. I watched, wishing I was out there learning something, until Ranlyn started talking about Gareth and Nya's powers.

"So, when I tried to calm shit down with Donovan and Vincent, and the house went ape-shit spitting water everywhere, that was Gareth's power?"

Ranlyn nodded. "His strength came with the driving force of water."

"Water?" Caine sat back in his chair, arms crossed, until it tipped off its front feet.

"Don't look so unimpressed. Water is found in damn near everything, even back then. Infinite resources from streams, underground springs, the rain, even in people and animals."

"And what part of that shitstorm was mine and Nya's?"

"You created the shitstorm. Nya's power ran with it."

"Wonderful. A team effort. At least it wasn't all my fault."

Ranlyn smirked at me. "Since Nya's power is now yours, it was entirely your fault."

Caine made a throaty noise and smiled.

I gave him a wilted glare. "Slow down the smug-train, buddy. It's not like I did it on purpose."

"You didn't." Ranlyn didn't give Caine the chance to lash out at me. "Though the energy output from Vincent and Donovan was amped up. Your intervention created a chain reaction, setting off Donovan's psychometry, travelling through your past life connection, and triggering Nya's power. Since her power is rooted in energy, it created the pulse of power through the room and then activated Gareth's power in Caine."

Caine made the throaty noise again and it took effort for me to not to jump across the table and throat-kick him.

"What's 'rooted in energy' mean?"

"As a Kitchen Witch, Nya's power is less defined than Gareth's. Acting more as a catalyst. Taking existing energy around her and using it to her will. Like with Donovan—her power accelerated his psychometry and then was released into the room around you since you couldn't contain it. She could work with a lot and create a lot, but always had Kitchen Witch skills to fall back on."

A burst of cheers had me looking out the window at the Coveners. Deidra and Rachel were high-fiving about something. Whatever it was caused a spiky-haired Covener, I believed was named Aaron, to drop Caitlyn on her ass. She sat rubbing her back, as Aaron was oblivious of hurting her, too busy looking at Deidra jump for joy at whatever I had missed.

A loud thud had me turning around—the sound of Caine's chair dropping back onto four legs. "You can stare at his pretty face forever. Can we get back to learning about my power that you've forced me to deal with?"

"Forced you? What happened to being happy you didn't have to unlock it yourself?"

Caine shook his head and didn't answer. I slipped into a telepathic opening, just enough to hear his thoughts without seeing anything—quick enough to be appalled.

"Sophie!" Ranlyn's harsh tone yanked me from Caine's mind. "Hear what you expected?"

"You mean petty bullshit? Pretty much."

Caine looked between Ranlyn and I, then back at me. "Petty?"

"Real fucking petty."

"Stop it. Both of you. We don't need either of you getting so pissed you set off your new powers. They're from a primitive time without so much outside interference, which makes them unpredictable."

I exhaled and leaned against the wall.

When he was satisfied we were done, Ranlyn leaned into his hands on the back of a chair. "Advances in technology have created a dramatic change in their powers in this day. More energy, more people, indoor plumbing, vehicles, power lines, dams, you name it—a developed world equals an overdeveloped problem for the two of you. In some way or another, the world has been inundated with fabricated power sources, some driven by water itself. Pure or not, it won't make a difference."

Caine's jaw clenched. "And they're connected? To each other, I mean?"

Ranlyn straightened. "I thought that was obvious."

"That's why Aunt Lacey said we're stronger together than apart. The activation of Nya's power in me causes a reaction with his." I chinned toward Caine without looking at him.

"Another connection. Great."

"Relax. It's not like with Donovan."

"Oh, good. You can keep doing him without me knowing about it."

"Really? Go fuck yourself and see how that feels."

"Sophie, please."

I looked at Ranlyn. "Don't defend him. Apparently, you're next in line."

"What?"

"Told you—" I tapped my head and pointed at Caine "—petty bullshit. Chat later, Jeeves."

I slammed the door behind me as I headed out into the field. If anything was left for Ranlyn to tell me, he could do so later. I couldn't be around Caine right now.

In the humidity of the day, I crossed the field of Coveners to find someone I didn't want to kill.

Vincent stepped in front of me. "I know you read the Huntsman's mind."

I stopped and huffed. "Fucksucker. Really?"

"You think the invasion acceptable?"

"You'd have to have been in my head to know what I was doing."

"Of course, I was."

I made a hollow laugh. "Hypocrite much?"

"As your teacher, I have the responsibility of ensuring the ethical use of your new powers. Telepathy is not a free pass for your personal amusement. If the Huntsman's intelligence was greater and he discovered your intrusion, the consequences would have outweighed the importance of the information you gained."

I looked over his shoulder and saw Donovan instructing Kim on something. He was rushing her and she was getting pissed. With my frayed emotions, I wasn't surprised he was unable to contain his patience.

"Caine is wounded, but you are both adults—"

"Vincent, you really need to fucking shut it. I know how this will play out with Caine, at least in the short-term. I know what I need to do, including getting more training in. This second, I need a sliver of time in between each of those things to get my head together, so I don't fuck it all up. So, instead of butting heads with me, jog on and let me get some anger out by thrusting energy balls into the air or whatever the fuck they're doing before I start directing my anger at you."

A flinch overtook me. When I opened my eyes, I saw Donovan collecting himself as Denise had reached out to him—maybe for direction, I wasn't sure—but had touched him to get his attention as he was coming my way. He said something to her and continued to me. She looked towards me, a small smile on her lips.

That conniving bitch. She knew about Donovan's psychometry and what it meant to touch him. To starve Denise of the satisfaction of the attention-seeking she craved, I pulled my irritation deep within me.

I should have known our truce was short-lived. Denise couldn't be anyone but herself.

"Do you not see how unravelled a low-ranking Seedling has made you? All over the jealousy of your companion?"

"I don't need the psychoanalysis, thanks."

Donovan reached us. "What's going on?"

"More of Vincent telling me what to do."

"This is your training, Soul Seer."

"I know, Soul Extractor." Power prickled my skin enough to give me goosebumps.

He looked down at me through his thin frames. "The need to understand your vessel's responsibilities, as well as limits, is crucial. You will fail otherwise."

"Come on, man. You think she doesn't know that? I'm all for getting her ass in ge—"

"Your connection with the Berisford is through vessel to vessel and nothing more." He never looked at Donovan. "Break the ties of this time, surpass this relationship that was never meant to be, and concentrate on the one that will make the difference." Vincent took a step closer. Donovan tensed at my side. "But do not forget, when it is time to fight, Gareth and Nya need each other."

I stared. I understood the importance training would make, but I asked him to back down, to give me a break before diving in. Instead of a five-minute breather, he kept trying to convince me to respect him and his process without respecting mine. Either he didn't have as much teaching experience as he let on, or he didn't care about what I had to say.

Either way, I had had enough, choosing to step around him towards the Coveners still training. A pulse of power surged out of Blake and into the field, as well as those that were around him. A cramp in my chest had me pressing against my breastbone and fighting to calm the power within me from acting on its own.

Ranlyn said Nya's power was fuelled by energy. Well, the field was stuffed with as much energy as it could be. Erratic and untrained energy at that. Fuck. I couldn't train with the Conveners until I got a better handle on my new power.

"Babe?" I exhaled but didn't turned around. "You have to work with him."

"He thinks because he's immortal he can throw his weight around."

"I meant him as in Caine, too."

"Right. Fuck my life." I didn't want to work with anyone right now. Stick me in a bubble and let me work my magic without the possibility of killing anyone else. Perfect solution for everyone.

"Unless you kill yourself. Another possibility."

I turned and glared at Vincent. He didn't need to listen in right now, which means he knew how damaging his tactics were and was working them anyway.

Since he already had an open window into my head, I used it. *"With my current mood, you'll hit a wall and make me more volatile. I'm taking a Bosco time-out."*

"Excuse me?"

"You heard me. I need ten minutes to cuddle my dog and get my head into the right place before we do anything. You don't like that? Too fucking bad."

We stared at each other a moment before he turned back to the house.

I looked at Donovan. "I need Bosco."

8

PUSHING BOUNDARIES

The heat of the sun warmed my skin as I laid in the tall grass with Bosco at my side, he chomping at aphids as they jumped on his face or paws. The sweat on my brow was as much mine as it was Donovan's. He was busy guiding the Coveners through battle manoeuvres and hand-to-hand combat, as well as spell sequences for maximum damage. He was a proficient trainer and I didn't need to see his face to know he enjoyed the role.

Forcing a calm, alongside Donovan's drive for a successful training session, levelled us both out. Until the next darkened shadow blocking the sun didn't pass like the afternoon clouds had for the last half-hour. The scent of him in the light breeze told me it was Donovan.

I didn't want my moment of peace to end.

The crunch of grass at my side and a skittering across the connection—he knew I recognized my visitor, but I didn't acknowledge him.

A light caress trailed down my arm from elbow to wrist. A vision tensed my shoulders, gifting Donovan something I couldn't see, but was coupled with a hint of contentment, not unlike my current state, before he interrupted.

"I know you're used to chicks throwing themselves at you, but us non-attention seeking vaginas require you to ask permission to touch."

A small laugh rumbled up from his chest. "Sorry. Not quite used to non-attention seeking vaginas."

I sat up, sitting shoulder to shoulder with him—his dimples in place, as expected.

"I wish I could touch without losing sight of you." He ran his finger down my skin again.

Whatever his vision, it caused a reaction of a different sort and I was happy when he stopped before the heat of the moment had me panting.

"Do those same chicks take their pants off for a line like that? 'Cuz you don't listen very well." I could have pulled away. Really. I could have made myself break the contact. Why didn't I?

He flashed those dimples again. "You wouldn't love me any other way."

I exhaled, or maybe it was a sigh? The use of the "L" word set my teeth on edge.

"Vincent is coming." The heat in his voice was gone. He no doubt felt my guilt and figured I had enough. "He sent me to warn you. Can't say I enjoy being anyone's gopher, but he gave me a good excuse to come over here."

I groaned. He laughed.

"Another training session will do you good. Worked great for the Coveners."

"Yeah?"

He nodded. "Matt has camouflaging powers. And I don't mean his gangster wannabe camo pants." I looked to the group. The guy in his jersey and camo shorts struggled to keep himself invisible by blending into the grass until Jared tripped over him.

"Damn. We'll have to watch the sneaky bugger."

"Even Kim is kicking ass. With her Kitchen Witch abilities already pretty prime, she'll make a leap in progress."

She was working on something with Gwen and Rachel, the three stood in a triangle five-feet away from each other with their hands raised. Strikes of power and colour sparked between them until they created a steady stream of energy and a red-tailed fox appeared in the middle of them. They laughed as the manifested little critter looked up at them, pounced on something it saw in the grass, and ran after it when it took off, disappearing as it got too far from their magic.

They high-fived and started to work on it again.

"Holy shitcakes."

Donovan laughed. "I know. Like I said, kicking ass. A creation spell like that looks cute when it's a fox. Imagine it as something ferocious or as a person. You could scare the shit out of someone or create an efficient distraction."

"Maybe they can make one that looks like me and have it work with Vincent instead."

"Enough of this, Soul Seer. Time to serve your purpose."

"Asshole. You have more purpose than your powers."

Vincent must have used his telepathy on both of us, hoping to get me moving.

My teacher bypassed us a moment later, heading towards the open field away from the Coveners.

I stood and swiped grass and dirt off my ass. "How privileged of him to know my purpose when I don't."

I scooped Bosco up and handed him to Donovan, so he wouldn't follow. Both of them. Though chances were Donovan would keep his distance.

We set up a run for Bosco—essentially a hundred-foot clothesline —close to the house, so he could be outside without taking off or getting hurt while everyone trained. It helped that people loved to treat him like the Coven mascot. I didn't feel odd leaving him alone with them, which was comforting when he wasn't an in-your-purse kind of dog.

Donovan scratched Bosco's head. "Being the Bossman's fur-mommy and keeping me in line is a full-time job. Who needs a true purpose?" He winked at me, his dimples caving as I rolled my eyes. But I left them behind with a smile on my face.

My purpose all along was to figure out my shit. It didn't help that every time I thought I did, a new complication jumped on board and threatened to drown me. Starting over was exhausting. And now Nya's power was another potential shark stalking me.

Time to get above water.

———

Vincent had kept walking until he ran out of property to walk through, stopping before he disappeared into the thick woods surrounding Ranlyn's property. As I got closer, something about the trees had me edgy. I couldn't see more than ten feet into the darkness. The unknown had me picturing a slew of wild, Slovenian creatures ready to drag me in and chew my entrails while Vincent was yelling at me to fight harder.

"You fear nature more than other Magics? Not smart." Vincent stood with his back to the forest without a hint of fear.

"You made me walk out here to insult me again?" The crowd of Coveners looked like tiny action figures from here.

"Animal instincts can be vicious, but their minds are more open to us then children."

"And the translation to your passive-aggression is—?"

He smiled and put his hands in his pockets. "Your familiar lacks obedience. With minimal intrusion, you can direct and discipline him without physical intervention."

"Physical intervention? Beating him isn't a training method I'm willing to take up. He's a pug with separation anxiety."

"He holds no trust of your return. A chaotic routine and being everywhere but home leaves him fearing each time you leave is the last he will see you. Speak his language, give him the reassurance he needs, and assuage his anxiousness."

"I get it now. Your life's purpose is to soothe Earth's creatures. All but humans. The rest of us can find a way to deal or stop whining, right? How grand."

"Scoff if you wish. If you ever want to change your Seer green into a soul more evolved, then magic filling every aspect of this life will be necessary." He levelled his chin. "You have had a late start. There is a possibility you will run out of time to reach immortality, or when you do, you may be at an age you would rather not linger."

"Can learning to speak dog get me closer to immortality? If not, let's work on Nya's power. If I survive Loring and the Puppeteer, then we can talk more about an extended life."

"If you neglect to plan for your future, you will fail to experience it."

"Wow, you're a visionary. Move on, Vincent."

He took in a deep breath and exhaled. "Due to the man-made energy coursing through Ranlyn's home, and the blood-born energy flooding from the practicing Coveners, we needed a place to practice with as little contamination to the process as possible. And while Nya's power feeds off energy, the trees and earth around us will be a sufficient catalyst. First, we work through your power to find Nya's, then we bring her energy forward and tap into it."

Sounded too easy.

The process was like the other training sessions with Vincent—him telepathically guiding me, encouraging me, and annoying me until I wanted to punch him. And then I would swear and give up and he would proceed to not allow me to quit.

I found Nya's power a couple of times, but not until my own was tapped out, which meant my power reached a strangling degree before Nya's power decided to come out and play. By then, I was panting and sweating balls and didn't have the energy to hold onto Nya's power with any amount of strength.

I collapsed onto the ground, ignoring the twigs digging into my ass cheek.

"Get up." Vincent leaned over me with the stern face of a drill sergeant.

"Nope. I'm home. The Earth owns me now."

"Your power is a muscle. As is Nya's. Hers has been out of shape for centuries and yours is that of a child's. Again."

He stood and replaced his glare with an outstretched hand, lingering over my head, waiting for me to catch my breath. I pushed the image of breaking his long fingers aside and let him pull me up.

The cycle of overextending myself to the point of collapse continued until the sun was defeated by overcast. The day's end was close, not that you could tell through the clouds. Finding Nya's power, identifying it, and building it to a functional level became easier, but was still exhausting. Her power was stronger than mine and didn't fit me the same—like borrowing someone else's shoes, it never quite felt like my own. My hope was that one day my body would adapt to this new essence and gain a sense of ownership of what was now mine whether I wanted it or not. But it was going to be a bitch in the meantime.

The death grip on my knee kept me from doing a YouTube worthy face plant.

"Now that you know Nya's power, use it."

"To do what?" I straightened with effort, hands on my hips to keep me up. My cramping lungs and sweat-slick forehead was a heavy reminder I was less athletic than the fast-walking fifty-plus white hairs from the park on Sunday afternoons.

"Don't open-end coach me. Draw me a fucking diagram. I'll even take it in charades. I'm too tired to be creative and I've seen a limited amount of power used. I don't know enough about Nya's power to be free-styling it. And if you couldn't tell, I'm at the whiney stage. Save yourself and give me a goal."

Vincent looked around us, then bent to pick a leaf off the ground. "The trees are looking a little parched."

"Wha—?" I snorted. "Rain? Are you for real?"

"I am." He looked up at the cloud cover and I understood.

While science wasn't my forte, I understood the general makeup of clouds. The water wasn't ready to fall, so I would have to force it. If Vincent wanted rain, I would give him rain.

Of course, easier mentally bragged about than done.

It took twice as long to get my power to vibrate at a level without making me break apart. Injecting Nya's power into it was a pulse of energizing strength I knew wouldn't last long. Extending my arms to the sky was awkward but directed the power where I needed it to go. My novice-like progression left my arms over my head so long they drained of blood and went tingly while the powers vibrated my skin to the point of near numbness.

Something hit my cheek, making me flinch and forcing me to clamber to keep hold of my power. I opened my eyes and saw the clouds had darkened and looked to have come closer to the trees, casting a haze over the green tops.

Something else hit my head, then another down my arm, before it began to rain in earnest.

Holy fish-farts, I did it.

Vincent's booming laughter came as the rain poured with a roar and created puddles around our feet. He took off his glasses, ran his fingers through his auburn hair, and squinted against the drops.

I yelled out in excitement and let my power dissipate. The power put into the clouds remained and the rain continued to fall on its own. I jumped on Vincent and held on like a monkey. He squeezed me tight in return, still engulfed in laughter before we let go of each other.

"See? Simple direction!" He shook his hair out like a dog, shedding that hard edge he'd carried since we met.

I liked this Vincent much better.

While he was an annoying tick under my skin, he found a way to produce results. Not the rain, as I did that, but he found a way to get through to me, to get me to pay attention, even while I was cursing and complaining. All to prove to me that I was capable of something I would have laughed at hours ago. Hell, I did laugh. No way did I think I could tap into Nya's power and do something like this. Now I was soaked through and all the exhaustion was forgotten.

I hugged Vincent again. This one in thanks. I didn't know if he was still reading my mind, but if he could, he would have heard everything I couldn't find words for while I was too busy being in awe of what we accomplished.

Wind picked up as we stood, gawking at the sky. The direction of the rain shifted from falling straight to the ground to hitting us from the side. Wind from a storm is expected, but I never called for wind and my power was already switched off.

A loud clash of thunder made me cringe and gasp, then again as the sky lit up with spider veins of lightning. My first instinct was to run for cover in the blowing forest. Vincent grabbed a hold of me before I got far, holding me in place as the sky lit up in angry strikes as wind whipped our hair around in spiralled gusts.

"It's not you!" Vincent's voice was drowned out, though he yelled inches from my ear.

"Then who?"

No answer. He didn't know anything more than I did.

Although my feet steered me to the trees, Vincent pushed me back towards the house.

Gale force winds had us fighting for every step as we fought to get back to Ranlyn's. Lifting a hand in front of my face worked about as well against the beating water as an umbrella against a tsunami. That was until a break in the wind pitched me forward in an ungraceful tumble. I was stopped short in a choking hold and scalp-ripping grip before I hit face-first into the grass. Vincent had caught me by the nape of my shirt with a firm fist. The fabric didn't rip but in his hold was a chunk of my hair. I squealed and grabbed my scalp as I was retched back onto my feet.

Without apology, Vincent let my hair go, his other hand preoccupied, reaching in front of his body as a pliable force flowed from his palm—stretching threadlike fingers in front of us and forming a semi-circular barrier around us. The rain still fell on our backs, but it was the wind that caused us true struggle. The barrier was transparent, resembling the body of a jellyfish as it waved and ebbed with the wind pelting itself onto its malleable surface.

Without commenting on the shield protecting us, we made quicker ground as thunder and lightning thrashed above.

Lightning speared straight into the ground in a shower of blinding strikes. My shoes skidded across the wet ground, but this time, so did Vincent's.

When the lightning stopped, so did the thunder and the wind, leaving the rain to fall as it had when I used Nya's power to force it. Pouring, but nothing torrential.

Since the field between the wooded area and the house was Saskatchewan prairie flat, we saw everyone grouped together. When we got closer, we saw most were knelt and looking down over something.

"Move!" Ranlyn pushed through the bodies crammed together staring at what laid at their feet.

They moved like they had been scolded by their mothers, revealing Jared lying on his back, Blake fluttering about like a humming bird, hands hovering like they should be doing something.

"What happened?" Raindrops hit my lashes and blurred the people around me as makeup burned my eyes.

Before anyone answered, Caine ran up on the group. My breath caught as he looked like he had in the park in his sleeping curse, short hair and all. I fought against the tightness in my chest and impulse to run to him.

Vincent placed a hand on Jared's chest. Where it lay, Jared's jersey was torn and singed with the raging pink of burned skin. Moving through the crowd to Blake, I grabbed him by the shoulders and asked him what happened. He didn't fight me or ignore me, but he couldn't look away from Jared.

"We figured it out." His lips quivered, blond hair plastered to his head instead of in its usual spikes.

I tugged on him again to look at me. "He's not dead. His soul still glows. Tell me."

"When the rain came, it triggered something."

"And?" I touched his arm as his focus had drifted, as if he was seeing it happen again.

"The wind picked up out of nowhere, but you could tell it was from him. Then, like him, I knew I could do it. I... I just made it happen." He swallowed and wiped his face of the still-falling rain. "The lightning. I knew I could make it happen." A reserved smile tugged at his lips. "My power was right there and—Fuck. It got out of hand. When everyone started taking off inside, I looked at him, just for second, and the lightning hit him. I didn't mean to."

"Of course not."

"He's breathing." Ranlyn assured, as the crowd let go of a collective breath. Blake ran to Jared and tried to talk to him. He wasn't awake, but oxygen was a good sign.

"Sophie." Vincent was at my shoulder. He waved me to the side, away from the others. I followed. "Too many are panicked. You need to stop this before it fuels another incident."

"I didn't know it could do this." I pushed Vincent in the shoulders, making him stumble a step back. "You made me start this shit in the first place! You said we were far enough away!"

He peered down at me without his glasses on, his hair hanging in his eyes. "Now end it!"

I paced a foot away to look at the group. Jared still hadn't woken up.

"The same as it began. Find Nya within yourself and let nature reclaim the sky."

I exhaled, water spraying off my lips. "It took hours to find her power and turn it into this." I motioned to the sky. "You want to me to shut it off like a well-worn vibrator. It's not gonna happen."

I fought the urge to check on Jared, console Blake, or push Vincent around some more. I managed to force myself away from all of them, walking away to find some distance in case bringing about

Nya's power made things worse instead of better. I didn't go as far as Vincent and I had during the training session, but far enough. I hoped.

I lifted my arms up as I had before. Rainwater fell on my face while I focused on reversing what I accomplished with Nya's power.

Nothing happened.

It took a while for me to engage my power enough to find Nya, and longer to use her power for anything useful. When I could, it felt more like a desperate prayer than wielding an ancient energy. As I directed the power above me, I prayed for the clouds to hear me, for them to hold back whatever water they had left, and to move on as if I hadn't stopped them.

With my eyes closed, I couldn't see how my process affected the clouds, but I opened them when the rain turned from a downpour, to dappling my face, and then was nothing more than a dissipating sprinkle. The clouds were mere whips, reminding me of the park in Caine's sleeping curse, without the bright sun that preceded the horror of his curse. Today, I was left with a fuchsia striped sky full of a vibrant sunset.

I was in awe.

Heaving breaths behind me drew my attention. Caine was staring above us at the sky, but the breaths did not escape from his lungs. Behind him, Donovan knelt in the wet grass looking dreadful, with Kim standing next to him. Bosco shook out his coat, panting as loud and heavy as Donovan.

"What happened? Are you okay?" I moved around Caine to get to Donovan. I was breathing hard from exertion. I should have known Donovan would be as well.

Donovan was wet but not all the way through. He must have come outside at the tail end, so he didn't get the full brunt of the rain.

He struggled to get to his feet. "I'm fine." The lie in his voice betrayed him, not to mention the thread of bullshit I felt across our connection. "That was intense." The added smile didn't sell it any better when he looked like he might throw up at any second.

Why didn't I think first? My regular ol' Ballard family Soul Seeing power sent Donovan to the edge. He was enduring Nya's power stacked on top of everyday out-of-control approach to my new abilities—though he looked worse than I felt, which was rather confusing since we should feel the same.

"Get inside. I'll meet you in there."

He waved me off, looking to the crowd. "What's going on?"

"I'll tell you inside. Go."

As my power lessened, I realized Nya's power was long gone, but my own was still in a low hum as my adrenaline buzzed. His exhaustion started to seep through the connection, stronger than before, and I knew he had to lay down whether he wanted to or not. His body needed a moment to re-establish normalcy. Proof was in the fact he listened to me and headed inside, Kim following him in and taking Bosco with her.

I saw Jared sitting up in a split in the crowd. His jersey was mangled but Blake was helping him to his feet, so I assumed his skin wasn't.

"You should thank him."

I turned to look for Vincent, finding him in the crowd around Jared.

"Who?"

"Caine. With his help, it was much easier for you to stop the rain."

I had no idea Caine did anything, though it was odd to turn around and see him standing close when the rain stopped since I was further away from everyone. I didn't see him now, so a thank you would have to wait.

Since Jared was alive and healed, I went inside to find Donovan. With Mother Coven members filtering in through the portal, or however else they were arriving, winding around the crowd was damn-near impossible.

Going on pure gut-feeling, I made way for the small bedroom we shared. The space was large enough to separate himself from the crowds and was a room he had already staked claim over.

Pushing my way through the door to the main living space and up the stairwell littered with bodies was slow-moving, my patience wearing thin. I was already exhausted from training and the run-off of fatigue from Donovan was getting worse. I had reached my quota for the day and wanted to find Donovan to make sure he was all right and update him on what happened.

A few errant elbows hit their targets, opening the way for me easier than pleasantries. Sometimes it paid off to be a bitch.

Finally, I reached the door to the little room, but as I twisted the knob it didn't budge. I knocked with a heavy hand when Vincent caught up to me. Out of curiosity, I assumed.

I knocked again, this time with the side of my fist. "It's Sophie."

"Hold on. Geez." Kim's voice was muffled behind the door, though it didn't disguise her annoyance.

As the door swung open, my eyes landed on Donovan on the edge of the bed, palms on the rim of the mattress. A sheen of sweat matted his chaotic locks. It could have been runoff from the rain, but something told me it wasn't.

"He wouldn't let me get you while you were training." Kim stepped aside and crossed her arms, glaring at Donovan. "Why do you think the door was spellbound?"

Vincent nodded as if impressed, standing aside in observation.

"I'm not one for overstepping my bounds." Donovan made a sarcastic laugh. I sat next to him, Bosco stepping into my lap.

"And since that's obviously horseshit, what do you mean?"

He looked at the others before answering, as if embarrassed. "You can't do what you gotta if you're worrying about me, babe." His eyes locked with mine. "I'm not the least bit sorry I trapped Kim in here with me, even if she wouldn't shut up." Kim made a throaty noise. "You would've run and tattled, and she would have stopped." He looked back at me. "You had work to do. I made sure the Coveners had their directives and then headed in here."

"Well, shit. You didn't miss much, just Jared nearly dying after being hit by lighting Blake created, which was my fault since I made it rain. Still shaking off the dust of Nya's power."

"You made it rain?" Donovan made a light, dubious laugh.

I shrugged. "Water instead of Benjamin's, which isn't nearly as useful."

Kim giggled. "We're Canadian."

"Yeah, but I don't remember who's on our hundred-dollar bill. Do you?"

She opened her mouth and closed it, squinting in thought.

"Sir Robert Borden."

I made a sarcastic gasp at Donovan. "Dimples and brains. You lucky boy." I clucked my tongue. "You've spent lots of time at strip clubs, haven't you?"

His glare told me to stop. The connection confirmed I was right. "So, you made it rain water?"

"Yes, buzzkill. Technically, I made the clouds let the water it had built up loose. I didn't create the water itself. You know how much it took. Definitely Nya's power."

"Like an Elemental?" Kim asked.

"No, but you have two of those in the Sect." Vincent thumbed over his shoulder. "Blake and Jared will be strong once trained, if they manage to survive each other in the meantime. With Nya's power, being an Elemental is unnecessary with the correct balance of energy."

Donovan wrapped me up in a hug. "Told you it was worth it."

Interrupted by a light knock, Vincent cracked the door, then let Ranlyn and Caine in. They were both soaked, Caine's shirt sticking to the muscles beneath the thin fabric, causing an immediate stir within me. I looked at my feet before that stir triggered a hi-def memory of something more.

Turned out there was no need to look away. Once Caine saw me and Donovan sitting on the bed together, his expression soured and I no longer focused on his musculature.

"Sorry about the wet down." I forced conversation with Ranlyn.

He smiled. "Better than being swallowed by the Earth. Your vessel's counterpart found a hidden water table beneath the east quadrant of my land."

"I closed it." Caine was smug, not that he didn't deserve to be proud.

"Yes, you did. Saved me from having to fill in the area myself." He looked at Donovan. "I see you weren't left untouched."

A wrench of guilt had me shifting in my seat. He detected this and glared my way. "I'm fine. Like I said, intense, but I can handle it."

"Good. Don't want Sophie neglecting her abilities to save anyone a little discomfort."

"Of course not, Jeeves."

Ranlyn smiled at my sarcasm and turned to leave.

Caine went to follow him.

"Thanks, Caine." He stopped and turned, awkward as I had blurted it out at him. "Vincent said you helped clear the rain."

"No problem." His tone was as deadpanned as his expression.

He left, and I felt like a moron. I should have talked to him alone, but that never happens, and I didn't want to never thank him and have him think I didn't care.

Kim shut the door as Caine left it open. "If you're too whipped, we don't have to go out there. It's not like we don't know what Ranlyn's going to tell the newcomers."

"Nah." Donovan stood, keeping his back straight, though I felt the ache in his stomach muscles. "Wouldn't wanna be neglectful of your Sect duties would you, Kim?"

"My duties?" Kim pointed at herself and gawked at me. I shrugged as Donovan made for the door. "Does that mean I get to beat up Coveners or forcibly confine my co-Sect Leader? My duties. Dick." She swatted him in the back of the head as he passed her.

"Hey." I rubbed my skull.

"Shit, sorry." Kim laughed until we hit the stairway on our way to hear a speech we already knew would be filled with bad news.

9

THE PLAN

With the Sect members, Elders, and Mother Coven newcomers overflowing Ranlyn's two-story home, a hanging fog of power caught our own powers' interest. When I finished in the bathroom, using a makeup wipe to tame the black makeup running down my cheeks, we followed everyone filtering out into the backyard—now filled with so many Magics my eyes still felt like they had mascara burning them.

Bosco was left on his dog-run, so he didn't get lost among all the visitors. It made me nervous since I didn't know most of them, but Kim assured me he would be fine. I retained my worry but didn't want to stick him in that little room where someone could still steal him.

The sun receded, replacing fuchsia stripes with a hanging moon in a starlit sky above grass still wet from my training session. Since our numbers covered an expansive area, visibility of our fellow Coveners was near impossible. Ranlyn erected a blanket of light high above our heads to illuminate the crowd so not a soul would miss their Elders speaking to their flock.

Meeting Ranlyn in the speakers' position to address the Coven was Miklos and Hinapouri on his left. A few from Hinapouri's tribe stood court as well, identifiable as warriors by their extensive tattooing. Intimidating, yet beautiful, didn't begin to describe this group.

Vincent stood at Ranlyn's right, as did Roe the Huntsman, who stroked his goatee looking like he would rather be anywhere else. I wasn't about to check his mind to see where.

The faces of two others, one man and one woman, also stood before the crowd. The woman spoke to Ranlyn as the man stood with hands clasped behind him like a soldier guarding her. His short hair, squared shoulders, and scanning eyes hit this military assessment home.

On second survey, I thought I recognized the woman as a soldier from the night of Aunt Lacey's death when Donovan led us to Ranlyn to relay the horrific news, but I couldn't be sure of anything from that night.

She stood about five-foot-seven with a slender build, long neck, flawless complexion, and long wavy hair the colour of wheat, held back in place with a head band. This woman appeared to be the personification of a Bible belt princess. The chastity of a pink lacy camisole beneath a white button-down argued her innocence, though matched her rose metallic glow, accenting her natural beauty.

"Who's the blonde?"

"That would be Anne-Claire and her boy-toy Lincoln." By Kim's account, he was more than a man doing his job. "They're members of our Sister Sect up north. Exclusive. Small, but every member holds a handful of goodies up their sleeve that trumps our Sect's as a whole."

An odd stir of cagey emotions flooded me from Donovan who stood to my right.

"What can she do?"

The stir of cageyness from Donovan was becoming harder to ignore.

"Everything."

Kim gave a throaty laugh at Blake's breathless declaration. He stood in front of us without peeling his eyes from the blonde before the group. I wasn't talking as low as I thought. Although they had been through a rather charged situation, both Bake and Jared looked recovered.

"Like what?"

Jared was as mesmerized as his counterpart. "As far as I know, she doesn't possess a specific inherited ability. She's just perfect at everything she does."

"Like a multi-gold metal Olympian. No limits." Blake sounded like an infatuated teen. If she was as talented as he said, it wasn't unfounded. I suppose even Magics had their version of celebrities.

"She's especially proficient in gymnastics, I hear." Denise's antagonizing voice rang at our backs. "Deliciously limber. Isn't that right, Donovan?"

Now Donovan's cageyness made sense.

I wasn't going to say anything to Denise, but I couldn't stop myself. "At some point, this needs to end, Denise."

"Oh, does it?"

"Give it up. We get it. Donovan slept with Anne-Claire. Big fucking deal. That's like pointing out you're a bitch. Consider it public fact. He'll fuck anyone."

"Not anyone." Donovan's protest went ignored.

"Right, not you—no matter how many times you throw yourself at him."

Jared and Blake's reactions couldn't go unnoticed if they tried, which they didn't.

"And now because you have some deep-seated hate on for me, you say stupid things that make you look pathetic, which is mind-boggling because you're smarter than this." Denise's hateful expression faltered into confusion. "You're beautiful, intelligent, resourceful, and obviously talented. Aunt Lacey wouldn't have allowed any random bimbo within the Sect, which means you're important." This made the biggest impact as Denise's arms dropped to her sides. "You're a part of something huge here. Maybe the most important thing you or I will ever be involved in, and you're focusing on this same ol' trivial bullshit."

I shook my head and saw the change in Denise's expression as she dropped her tough exterior. "Not everyone likes me, I don't expect them to. And for some reason, you figure if someone's not your friend, they must be your enemy. While I may be neither, I couldn't care less until it affects my life. You feel compelled to make these comments and I can let them roll off my back—which I'm telling you from this moment on, I will—but they display a weakness far below your capabilities. So, empower yourself enough to realize you're better than that horseshit, govern more closely the type of people you keep around you—"

"Watch it twat." Jamie flashed me the finger, though I didn't look at her. Why Aunt Lacey brought her into the Sect was still a mystery to me.

"—and become a person you don't want to smack the shit out of. No one's going anywhere. Ignore me altogether if you want, but this *Mean Girls* act is played out. Move on to something else."

I ended the intervention and turned my back on Denise to face Ranlyn, who had been letting the rest of the Coven in on the condition of Diluculo and trying not to acknowledge Kim's blinding white smile stretching ear-to-ear.

"I happen to be reformed." Donovan voice was tight.

"Well, not before you had a ride from Miss Limber, thank God. You would have missed out on a woman who can do everything. Maybe I should make a go for her."

Jared and Blake laughed, their backs and shoulders shaking as they faced front.

"She's too theatrical for my tastes. It's sex, not Cirque du Soleil."

"I call bullshit."

"For real. You were way better than—"

"Okay, enough."

Jared, Blake, and even Matt, who I hadn't seen before, laughed harder.

"Waaay better." Donovan earned another round of laughter.

"Shut your face."

"It's not like they didn't already know."

Kim looked around me at Donovan. "If they didn't, they do now."

"*Pfft*. They knew." I looked back at Denise who adopted a half-way genuine smile. "With this crowd and everything we can do, nothing stays secret."

While laughter was nice, I didn't think it near as funny. I didn't want the Coven in on the complications of my life with their Sect Leader.

The tension in my shoulders tightened. "You know, what Ranlyn's saying is actually important." I pointed out to the audience. As I turned to include Denise in this, I glimpsed something I hadn't before. Caine. Standing in the row behind Denise. By the set of his jaw, he had heard everything.

Fuck a scarecrow. As if he needed this thrown in his face. The others didn't see him either, but the impact was made regardless.

Before I could say something or turn and ignore him as he ignored me, something else caught my attention.

"Why in the fuck is my brother here?"

I didn't wait for an answer before pushing through people to get to him, my eyes never meeting their disgruntled stares. Kim's apologies grew faint behind me as I closed in on what I thought had to be an illusion. My brother stood in the least likely place I could have stumbled upon him and had brought all the Ballards with him.

"Olive?" I had my palms out in question.

"Oh, hello, Firefly." Olive's voice sang as she reached for me, pulling me into a hug. I noted how ecstatic my Uncle Lewis looked as he stood behind her. Olive pulled back and held onto my arms. "Now look at you."

"What?"

Serena shushed us. "I wanna hear this."

Olive smiled and motioned for me to listen, unaware I knew everything Ranlyn had to say anyway. Turning to my Elders, Olive's arm twisted with mine as we stood in front of the crowd. I noticed Kim and Donovan followed and were now lining the outside of the Ballard group. Their presence was expected but Jared, Blake, Matt, Caitlyn, and especially Denise's was not. It didn't bother me, but I figured if she came for gossip she was going to get bored and find another group to float to.

When Ranlyn spoke of the Puppeteer's Coven marker within the Thoth, I stared at Serena, waiting for the moment she remembered our trek down into the tunnels. I laughed when the memory registered, and she raised an eyebrow in my direction.

Once the bad news escaped his tight voice, tactics changed and Ranlyn gave the reins to his blonde cohort, Anne-Claire. Before beginning, her pouty lips moved in muttered conversation to her protector, Lincoln, who nodded before her narrowed eyes darted over the crowd. Wherever her blue-eyed sights took pause, the empty space filled with an Anne-Claire clone. She duplicated herself, strategically standing to be better seen dispersed amongst the audience. People gasped and stepped back, crunching the toes of those behind them.

"I don't have the vocal projection Ranlyn possesses." She played up a sunny smile as everyone watched the Anne-Claire heading their group. "Hopefully, my Bilocation works for everyone."

As she spoke of how lucky it was to have firsthand knowledge of the two hot spots to find our enemies, Ronny—my cousin within the Ballard Coven—leaned forward to poke the image of Anne-Claire with a prodding finger. Though it would seem Kevin was the initiator of the idea, he watched as Ronny pulled back when he touched the skin of her arm. She glared in Ronny's direction. Her mouth didn't fudge a word, but her eyes held purpose and stunned Ronny to the spot before returning in synch with the original Anne-Claire.

Eerie.

Before her doppelgangers disappeared, Anne-Claire called upon Olive to take point in front of the group. After patting my arm, Olive strode to the forefront of the gathering across the uneven field as I looked to my family for answers. They didn't, instead looking as confused while the older members refused to look at me at all.

I turned to my brother. "How'd you find out about this?"

"Relax. You're acting like I crashed your sweet sixteen. Again."

"Adam."

"Serena called and said we had to meet at your boyfriend's." He moved on before I could argue the label. "When we got there, we ended up here. That's it. Where is here, by the way?" I told him. "A little far for a meeting don't'cha think? Can we even drink the water here?"

"Shut up."

I refocused my attention to the front as Olive had reached her place but caught Adam spinning around to Donovan, giving a "what the hell is her problem" glare. Donovan waved him off in warning to let it go. Conspiring already.

Olive worked a spell, so the large group could hear her better. While Ranlyn had a naturally bellowing voice, and Anne-Claire cloned herself to distribute her message to the masses, Olive's method was different. Her spoken words didn't radiate from her vocal cords. Although they originated there, once they left her lips it was like Olive was standing right next to your ear. No matter where you stood, not a syllable was lost.

"I am not one of your flock, though I do have ties to it. My family is amongst you. I refer to her as Firefly, though I am told you call her Salix." Giggles and sounds of inquiry for my nickname had my cheeks filled with heat. "It is my understanding that the Puppeteer is an adversary that has not been challenged in some time. It's not that we lack the capability to fight and win, but—as I would hope would be all your main concerns as well—in order to fight this evil, many young Magics would either parish or fall victim to become one of the Puppets the rest may end up facing. And, like your Elders, I cannot end one of my own."

Olive's sombre voice had me thinking of Veata. It was no secret our Elder had been Puppet to the Puppeteer, caused the deaths of our former Elders, and other Magics that had been in existence since before civilization was civilized.

"The devised plan is one to be executed with extreme care." Her voice evermore tenuous. "In my possession, I contain an object." By this time, Olive had the entire gathering in a silent stare of curiosity, including me who could feel Donovan's scepticism rise as Olive went on. "One that contains the ability to close the veil between this plane and that of the one where the Creation was built, as well as the Puppeteer's Creation within the Thoth."

A rise in voices spread like disease as one spoke to another and so on creating a hum. As she spoke again, Olive's voice in their ears thwarted further independent conversations, drowning them out.

"Until a better solution can be formulated, trapping the Puppeteer and his cohorts within the Creation will guarantee temporary safety of our Coven members and the Blind who he would have controlled."

"What about those already taken over?" Rang out a voice from within the crowd. "They'll be locked in the Creations with the Puppeteer!"

"This is true." Ranlyn's grave timbre reached above the simmering crowd.

"How can you guarantee the Puppeteer won't escape before he's trapped? He won't sit back and let it happen!" yelled a deep voice much closer to my group.

"For fuck's sake." Donovan didn't look at me when I turned to him in question—what circulated within him was dark and angry, but he remained focused on Ranlyn.

"Each Sect will be given a key role, though we must work together to pull off trapping the Puppeteer. Leaders will be approached to give the order to their Sect before questions may be asked. At this point, our goal as Elders is the survival of the Coven as well as the members who make it whole. The end goal is to rid the world of such evil and enlighten the Eradicators, but until this can be accomplished, snaring greater evil, even within our place of salvation, ensures no more blood spilt. And that concept, I am willing to stand behind and say to all of you, as my greatest critics, is the best anyone can presently hope for."

Having the Elders spooked was daunting. Trapping the Puppeteer within a Creation was a coward's way out to some, as I overheard from where we stood. They seemed blood thirsty to take on the Puppeteer alone—which would no doubt lead to them getting their asses kicked—but many shared the point of view.

As Ranlyn dismissed the crowd and it dispersed into smaller groups or disappeared altogether, the Sect raced to crowd around us. The foremost question was "What do we do now?" Donovan had no answers yet. He was fuming and we didn't have the privacy for me to ask him why.

Kim stepped in and reminded the Coveners they needed to be updated by Ranlyn first and until then would have to be patient.

Olive returned, with Ranlyn at her side. He looked at me, his expression unreadable. "Sophie, would you follow us to have a word?"

Donovan moved next to stand in front of Ranlyn. "Not without me, you don't."

"You can attend but know your opinion won't change things."

Donovan smiled, dimples in full flex, but there was no happiness within him. "Guess we'll see."

Since it seemed Donovan knew something, I didn't argue with him to stay away.

Donovan, Olive, Ranlyn, and I went around the house to the less populated backyard.

"'Kay, what is it?"

Olive turned to me with sad eyes at my hard expression. "This has not been brought about without extensive forethought, Firefly."

"I'm sure it was." Donovan looked down his nose at Olive. "She still needs to hear you say it."

Ranlyn crossed his arms. "Say what, exactly?"

"I've seen this tactic play out." Donovan's anger strengthened me as he spoke. "Your great plan to imprison the Puppeteer like Hannibal Lector can't be done unless you have eyes on him. On his actual form, not through one of his Puppets. Not even through Veata." No one argued. "To pull it off, you need the proper bait. Give him what he wants so he'll sit still long enough to snap the door shut."

"It worked for Tobias."

"You're taking strategic advice from my father's playbook now?" This was the first time I had heard Donovan's father's name. Why were they taking pages from books of the Tainted? "Setting Sophie up as bait to a rabid gator is less dangerous than this. The Puppeteer will kill her and you know it."

I looked to Ranlyn. "You want me to trap him?"

"It wasn't done without thorough consideration."

Donovan scoffed. "For yourselves."

"No!" Ranlyn's angered roar came with a dose of power that pricked the air. "When you're in my position, you will know the heartbreak it causes to send in one of your own instead of going yourself. If I thought I could get the job done, I would, but the curiosity the Puppeteer shows for his kin is our greatest advantage. With Nya and Gareth's presence, it brings the greater chances of Loring's entrapment to sweeten the success."

So, Olive knew the Puppeteer was related to us. I wondered how she found out. "How can you stand behind this?"

"You can do this, Firefly. I wasn't certain either but now that I see you—" She shook her head as she looked over me.

"What?"

She hesitated. "I see your Seer green so bright it pains my eyes. You have changed. Your soul now entangled with another." She smiled. "It dances with that of Nya's. I couldn't miss it."

So, I did look different. "It's Nya you want, not me." I was hurt I alone wouldn't warrant this plan, then felt stupid because I didn't want to do it in the first place.

"Not her, but with her power, you have an even greater chance to make this work."

Donovan still wasn't convinced. "How do you expect her to protect herself against what could be hundreds of evil bastards when she gets in there? Just because Nya's piggy-backing her, it doesn't mean Sophie can fight." He paced a step and came back. "Like I said, I've seen this bullshit play out, and in the end, a lot of people die, usually the bait along with them, even if the objective is completed."

"I didn't know enough about this power, or my own, to save my own ass from the rain. You expect me to run this?"

"You know more than you think." The voice came from behind us. Vincent and Caine headed our way, Vincent being the one who spoke.

"I've used it once to make it rain and set off a chain reaction that almost killed a Covener. Plus, I needed his help to shut it down." I motioned to Caine. "That wouldn't stop the Puppeteer from digging out a wedgie. This is ridiculous."

I couldn't envision myself standing within Diluculo at the mercy of the Puppeteer's minions or in Loring's grasp—two evil pricks who won't show mercy if they get the chance to take me down.

"We have to do this." Caine surprised the shit out of me. "I don't enjoy the fact I'm putting my life on the line, but hearing the full plan, I happen to think we can pull it off."

"If you wanna die, that's your issue—"

Caine cut Donovan off and looked at me. "Take offence if you want, but while living without you sucks, I'm not gonna off myself."

"I never thought you would."

"And anyway," his grey eyes fixed on Donovan, "you're not invited."

Fragile restraint drilled through Donovan as he and I searched the others who nonverbally agreed with Caine.

I looked between Caine and Ranlyn. "Did you have a brain fart and forget about the connection?"

"The connection clouds your judgement." Ranlyn's tone was soft, but the insinuation was harsh.

"And you think keeping me away when she's facing death is

happening?" Donovan made a hollow laugh. "You're fucking delusional."

"Think about this." Vincent fixed his glasses. "We need to seal both Diluculo and the Thoth. You need to lead the second team."

"No, I don't. Hinapouri is a much more skilled fighter than I am, send her. Or go yourself."

"You cannot be with Sophie." Ranlyn may as well have struck a gavel.

Before the argument could run another round on the hamster wheel, I stepped in. "I get it. You want complete focus on whatever I gotta do. Understandable. But how do you see that panning out when Donovan's miles away and, I don't know, gets taken down by a Puppet?" The slight that Donovan couldn't handle a Puppet came with quiet resentment, but I was making a point, so the implied "SHUT UP!" went without saying. "You still need me to agree to this scheme, and right now, I'm not havin' it."

"The use of Nya's power rendered him that of an invalid." Vincent didn't need to remind us.

"My problem, and one I would never allow to get in the way of what she needed to do. Distance won't make that better, which means I would be rendered useless in the concrete tunnel of the Thoth. It's not happening."

They couldn't force me to do anything and they knew it. They couldn't even knock Donovan out since it would do the same thing to me. Donovan and I were a package deal. He had to keep his distance without interceding yet be close enough to ensure a role in my safety if it came to that, which for some reason made me feel better.

Effective, yet the argument distracted me. Instead of fighting against the moronic plan pitting me as chum to a Great White, I guaranteed my place in Diluculo and dragged Donovan in with me. Yee-fucking-haw.

This frustrated me down to my core. I agreed something needed to be done, but I never thought they would offer me up as a sacrifice to do it.

A lot of pieces had to fall into place at the right time. This was why Donovan was so skeptical of the plan's success. If we failed, we could be slaughtered as soon as we landed on the other side of the veil, we could be taken over and forced to kill each other, or we could be trapped inside with our biggest enemy used as a slave or tortured—healed so many times, death would become a sought-out dream.

We made our way back to the Coveners. "Olive, how long have you known about this plan?"

She shrugged. "I'm not too sure. A day or two? Why?"

"Because I knew nothing until you started talking in front of the entire Coven. Why didn't you tell me?"

"I was told you knew of the Coven marker baring the symbol of the Ibis, the Thoth, and the condition of your Coven's Creation—"

"But I didn't know until today. Or last night." The days ran together like watercolours. "You're not only in on the plan but have some type of object that makes the plan possible?"

"My guess is your Elders wanted to guarantee the object was in my possession before moving forth. Without it, the plan was moot and there would be no sense in you knowing."

This didn't sit as well with me as Olive assumed it would.

"You're her family," Donovan butted in. "She expected loyalty from you over all others. There's enough crap behind the scenes, family playing a part of it reminds her why she doesn't trust anyone."

I could have argued, but buried beneath it all, I was surprised Donovan was bang on. Without words—since the muscles of my throat clenched, and I was unable to speak—I dredged through the grass. Olive's apology, genuine and heartfelt, didn't change anything. I couldn't talk, let alone make her understand.

10

PLAY IT DOWN

Nothing was without the intrusion of the connection, not even flossing. Donovan sent a flutter of annoyance when I flossed the corn-on-the-cob out of my teeth until my gums bled. The run-off of arguing with my brother had me working the floss too hard, but I didn't get why he wasn't pissed to hear our mother knew about our powers as kids and pretended otherwise.

Instead, he was too busy chowing down on the free food.

If everyone ate like him, Jared, and Blake, the coven would be full of belt-busters too tired to battle a pesky mosquito without a nap first. Maybe it was a ploy to keep everyone happy or a macabre gesture of a last meal. Load up now, it might be your last.

All it got me was clogged gums.

Caine was next for the bathroom. He looked to the floor and went in without saying a word. I was going to head back downstairs, but thought better of it, deciding to wait until he was done. When he tried to walk by me, I stepped in front of him.

"Sophie, come on."

"Okay look, this whole crazy bait and trap plan they've decided is best comes down on us. I know you can't stand being around me, and

I don't like this plan any more than you, but we have to make it work. I need to know that once we're in there, we've got each other's backs and can get this done."

He narrowed his eyes. "You think I'd survive for a minute if you didn't walk out of there with me? Like I wouldn't have to deal with Ranlyn or your family? I'm not a psychopath."

"My point made. We need a plan. One where both of us have the option of walking away from this alive and not mangled for life."

He gave a slow nod. We got down to the details of how we planned to give Loring and the Puppeteer what they wanted without ending up dead. Using Gareth and Nya's powers was key. Whatever it was about us that intrigued Loring and the Puppeteer, we needed to use it to stall them while quiet preparations were completed. But we knew with someone as powerful as the Puppeteer, one glimpse into our minds and our cover would be blown. We had work to do.

"We should tell Ranlyn. Be sure he didn't have something better in mind." I moved to the railing overlooking the bottom floor, hoping to see him.

Instead, I saw Adam chatting up an intrigued Denise near the far end of the kitchen. I didn't know what they were talking about, but their body language made me curious.

I rarely saw my brother show genuine interest in anyone. Interest in what they looked like naked or how they looked standing next to him, sure, but something about the way he spoke to Denise was different. He didn't scope the crowd for a better option or search for a general reaction from those around him. He watched her eyes, countered her smile, and laughed in a way that wasn't part of any game.

I never would have thought.

"Fuck."

"Perfect couple, huh?" Caine's voice made me jump as he leaned onto the railing at my side.

"More like shitshow in the making." He laughed. "He'll learn he can't play chicks here. Especially when they're stronger than him and they know it." The magical repercussions of his usual whorish ways could bring boils, sleepless nights, incontinence, impotence—the possibilities were endless.

"Nah. Adam just needs someone strong enough to put him in his place." A silent beat passed. "Now you don't have to worry about Denise setting her claws into me. Not after you put her in *her* place."

Like I suspected, he didn't miss a word of the conversation with Denise in the back field. "Sorry you overheard that."

"It's fine. Now you'll have to worry about her kissing your ass. At least you guys can double date." I side-eyed him. "What? You and Denise have things squared away and Adam and Donovan are chummy. I see a movie date with over-priced popcorn and sticky shoes in your future."

Donovan in a crowded theater was laughable. He seemed more like a drive-in guy and chances were, he missed most of the movie. "Nah, not a thing."

I watched my brother grab Denise another drink from the fridge. Practically chivalrous.

"You don't have to play it down." His serious tone caught me off guard. He leaned into the railing, then spun to sit against it and look at me. "I agreed to be a part of the Coven. No, I didn't plan for this situation to have happened so soon. I thought I had time. But I had long enough to get to know you. I see you when you're around him. You weren't like that with me."

"Now who's playing things down?"

"Your instincts fight against love because of your past. With Donovan," he shook his head, "you say it's not as serious as he claims, but come on, Sophie. You're pushing him away a hell of a lot less than your holding him close. With me, it was the complete opposite. You never shied away from his touch, even though you knew what it meant for him and his visions. You defended him at every turn. Even told him you loved him, and meant it." He shook his head again as I steeled myself from squirming from the guilt eating at my gut. "And anytime you weren't with me or Kim, or when I wasn't conveniently taking you away from him, you'd be pulled back together, and I'd see the resentment for my interference in your face."

"I'm sor—"

"It's fine. Took some time to get all that straight in my head. Even if part of me wants to push you over this railing, I do want you to be happy." He smiled a sad smile I mirrored. "This whole shitstorm turned me into a miserable, jealous asshole. Aunt Lacey warned me. Maybe she couldn't say it, maybe she hoped Gareth and Nya would find a way back to each other through us, but I think she knew your connection to Donovan was too strong for that. She knew he needed you more."

Mentioning Aunt Lacey evoked couch-sized tears I fought to blink back. I didn't know if he was right about any of that, but he seemed comforted by coming to the conclusions he did.

"He's a Class 'A' prick. Selfish, arrogant, and treats everyone like they're below him. Knowing where he came from answers some of that, though you've got a way of changing someone. He's already better with the Coveners, and certainly better off, because of you. Hopefully you're happier now without all the conflict."

I swallowed, my throat too tight. I worried Nya's ring and looked up, trying to keep the tears at bay. "I didn't want things to end like they did." I swallowed again and again, chasing a tear down my cheek.

"I know you didn't. I have no reason to think you would. I was just pissed off and in shock at how fucked up things got. The harder I tried, the worse it got. I know you didn't mean for all of this to go down like it did, but I still don't believe he didn't." He smiled large enough to get me laughing.

I swiped away a couple more tears. "Yeah, well, he is a selfish prick."

He nodded and laughed. A relief I hadn't known in a long time unknotted my shoulders. Caine didn't hate me. I could deal with the rest—whether Donovan and I were in a relationship or not and this crazy plan for Diluculo—but I didn't want Caine walking around despising the thought of our relationship or wishing he never met me. Which made me as selfish as Donovan. I knew this. But I was still happy to stand here and have an open conversation with someone I loved. He deserved love without the drama of past lives and intrusive connections.

"Did you really hate your hair that much?" I needed the levity because he didn't deserve to see me crying about something that was my fault.

He shrugged and ran a hand through the short style. "No. When losing control of everything, cutting my hair seemed like the thing to do."

I nodded. "Makes sense. Though I kinda freaked when I saw it."

"I noticed." He tried not to smile and lost.

"I promise you won't see that girl again. Playing the crazy ex isn't my thing."

"It's all good. I'd be lying if I said I didn't enjoy it. Not that I want to see you hurt."

"Oh, I know. You—"

"I promise, even if it means you returning to him, I'll make sure you make it out after we deal with the Puppeteer."

I tensed. I would have never thought anything different but hearing him say so plucked an already fragile emotional cord. I tried to speak to say thank you or something, but I lost the fight against my tears and broke down. Caine wrapped me up in a consoling arm, pulling me to his chest, saying something sweet I couldn't hear over my inward attempts to berate myself into pulling it together and making the same promise to Caine. He needed to walk out of the Creation at my side, whole and well. I wouldn't let it happen any other way.

"Your companion's patience is running thin."

Fucking Vincent.

I knew Donovan was riding the emotional roller-coaster me and Caine's conversation created—he was always there, checking in to be sure I was okay, and I was there to tell him I was or to ignore him so I could deal with whatever I needed to deal with. Right now, I didn't need Vincent butting in. Instead of answering or attempting long-distance telepathy, I held onto Caine, enjoying the moment I could never expect again.

Sucking in a breath, I steadied myself and erased the thought of Caine having to save me from possible death and fearing the opposite may also be true. After wiping away my tears and looking to his smiling grey eyes, I knew the worst between us was over. He would never forgive me, not anymore than I could forgive myself, but we could coexist and find understanding.

"You're not going to throw me over the railing now, are you?" I held on a little tighter.

His chest rumbled against my ear as he laughed. "Nah. Letting you survive to live through a double-date with Denise is punishment enough."

11

CUT-THROAT COMPANY

To pinpoint the Puppeteers location, and pray Loring was with him, someone needed to be on his tail. Roe was up for the job, but he couldn't watch Diluculo and the Thoth on his own. Unlike Anne-Claire, Bilocation was not in his repertoire, so he employed another Huntsman, Gerard. The man was another pledged to no Coven. He didn't even show up at Ranlyn's, but Roe was adamant of his worth and having another on the job would take up the slack needed to cover their asses at both cheeks.

The rest of us went back to training. Jared was getting better at his Aerokinesis—controlling the air—moulding the wind to his will and condensing it into something unexpected. Not sand or ice shards. More like crystal particles, effective if propelled through a body, Magic or other.

Deidra made sense of her Coven name Endellion. Meaning Fire Soul, it was unsurprising she connected with a heat from within. Though Matt was caught off guard when she evoked the equivalent of a flame thrower from her arms in his direction. His knee-jerk reaction was to erect a shield, saving his skin from melting off.

Other Mother Coven members participated in mock hand-to-hand combat, honing their skills or teaching less experienced Coveners what to expect and how to thwart an attack with basic defensive manoeuvres—plus a few offensive ones to fool their enemy into believing their arsenal reached beyond the basic. Without every enemy containing my ability to differentiate the strong from the weak, it would pose a great advantage.

Taking a considerable interest in the Mind Reading—specifically blocking others from reading my mind—Donovan and I made this priority one. I spoke to Caine about it instead of practicing with him. He found someone else for that. I would have liked to get more training in, but defensive strategies were more important, and I needed help with both.

———

Hours of training, mentally and physically, had me exhausted. I hadn't worked out that much in my whole life. After a shower and some food, I sat on the couch near a warm fire with Donovan quiet at my side. Olive stared into the flames across from us while Serena sat backwards in her seat, chatting with Caine. I was thankful Serena was being friendly. Overhearing Jared's name, I realized she was thinking Caine was close enough to Jared to drop a few beneficial hints in her honour.

Adam and Denise made no attempt to hide their mutual attraction, though I was happy to see Denise's leech, Jamie, kept her distance.

I wasn't a pro at keeping the soul glows around me from burning my eyes, but I could look elsewhere or only keep a select few in my line of sight. With so many at Ranlyn's, including Elders and other immortals like Vincent, I didn't have much escape. Even with borrowed sunglasses—which were pinching my nose, making the raging headache pounding in my skull worse—it wasn't helping.

Healing was an option, but with the constant stimuli, the ache hammering my temples would return before I could blink in relief. Not what I'd call worth further exhausting myself.

"Hey," Donovan was so close to my ear, the warmth of his breath hit my neck and caused a wave of goosebumps that covered both of us. "Whoa."

"Shut up."

He laughed. "Let's head to bed. I'm guessing this nut-gripping skull-pounder I have is yours."

I sighed and pressed my fingers into my temples. The hint of relief made Donovan moan. It wasn't enough and sleep was the best cure. If anyone needed me, they knew where to find me.

I leaned down with a kiss on the cheek and hug goodbye for Olive, though she was adamant she would be back the following morning, whenever that was considering the time difference. Computing the numbers wasn't going to happen right now.

Interrupting Serena and Caine's conversation came at a price. Though I was glad she had moved past hating Caine for attacking Donovan, which was an attack against me, in announcing I was headed to bed, this let Caine know as well. And, since Donovan stood behind me cradling a sleepy Bosco, it was clear I wasn't going alone. Though he had been around for one of my headaches and had to know going to bed meant going to sleep.

Once hitting the washroom and changing into pyjamas, I crawled beneath the covers in a thin, long-sleeved tee for minimal skin exposure to trap Donovan in a vision. Both of us passed out with Bosco curled at our feet snoring up a storm within minutes.

———

The farmhouse I grew up in has stood for decades without bowing to the harsh seasons. This home—one my grandfather and his two brothers constructed from the land, with their own structures close by —was surrounded by fields of wheat stretching far beyond my sight, as I would have imagined the ocean must, if one day I may set eyes upon it. The cool breeze caught the tall, swaying trees where my adventurous mother climbed and collected honey before dawn while the bees still slumbered before starting their work day.

Walking through the tall reeds of wheat that grazed my thighs, the seeds stuck to the fringe of my long dark hair and faded skirt, tugging on the dragging hem like child-like fingers sprouting from the earth beneath my bare feet.

A flash of mud-encrusted fabric was a sore spot in the sea of gold above and around me. I hesitated before moving closer, finding the fabric to be attached to a man. With no rain for over a week or pools of water anywhere but for the well, how could he be so wet?

He didn't open his eyes or move as I called him or when I shook him. Blood splattered the mud, difficult to see, and I feared he must be dead. His shirt fabric was torn, exposing tears in the flesh below. A thick, black beard matched that atop his head and was tied at the nape of his neck, tendrils of it strewn with blood and plastered across his cheeks. Another injury marred his cheek and right eye, the blood still wet as if he was injured only moments ago.

Where did he come from?

I ripped off a piece of my skirt and pressed it to the wound on his ribs. I folded the fabric and went to press it down again when the wound moved. I gasped and watched it close on its own and heal.

Was he a man? An angel? God himself?

Footsteps in the wheat crackled behind me. I spun to see another man—he, too, covered in mud.

He said something in a language I didn't understand. I stood between this new man and the fallen one, not trusting this stranger.

"English, yes?" He waited until I nodded. "Good. Excuse me, miss. Please. I must tend to my friend."

His smile was tight. His eyes were alight with eagerness instead of worry. He was lying. He knew the fallen man, yes, but they were not friends.

I remained where I was, refusing to move, waiting for him to spout more lies.

Searing pain stuck in my throat, under my jaw, like a piercing arrow. My right shoulder screamed. Pain grew deeper. When my eyes flew open against the pain, I was in darkness. Nerve strikes shot through my knees and up my thighs.

"Move and I'll decapitate the bitch!"

The lying man was gone. So was the golden wheat around me and the hot sun warming my skin. Donovan crouched in an attack position in front of me on the bed, his dark eyes filled with hate. Was it him? No. The voice was a woman's.

"Don't move, babe."

He shifted. A gleam of red on his neck and trailing down his chest caught my eye. Blood? I sprung forward. The stabbing in my neck deepened, my shoulder screaming. I hissed in pain. So did Donovan.

"Can't heal a severed head, brother, so don't tempt me."

Joelly?

The mental haze cleared. I was on my knees next to the bed, my arm forced behind my back in a breaking limb grip and something sharp at my throat. Metal shifted beneath the skin and I thought I might puke.

"You can't get Nya's power by killing her."

"Loring lied." I coughed on my already choked words and then struggled to regain control as more blood spilled down my chest.

"Meh." Joelly tightened her grip on my shoulder to keep me still, though she swayed on her feet. "Not much into believing an old crackpot's ramblings these days. They tend to bail when things get squirrely."

"Right. As if loyalty is within your vocabulary." Leave it to Donovan to not let the threat of decapitation cause a personality detour.

"Believe it or not, brother, I'm trying to help you."

"Turning the love of my life into a fucking shish kabob is not helpful."

"You woulda' killed me on sight." She leaned down, inches from my face. "It's not my fault the love of your life can't listen to simple direction!"

"You're wrong. I would've tortured you slowly." A sinister truth crossed our connection as a gaping slice in his throat gushed another stream of blood.

His fists flexed, his muscles bunching so tightly my muscles reacted. Whatever he had planned, he needed to do it and quick. My thighs were shaking. If they gave out, I would slaughter myself.

Joelly gripped my shoulder tighter until I cried out. She yelled for me to shut up and twisted the knife until I felt it puncture through something internal. I coughed as blood choked me, a gurgled wheeze amping up my panic. Donovan coughed with me and gripped his throat, his eyes widening as confusion crossed the thread of connection.

Joelly laughed. "Impotence is a good look on you. Can't have you healing too quick, now can I?"

She did something to block our abilities. No wonder my power hadn't taken over on instinct as it had in the past.

"You didn't think I'd forgive the quality time I spent with your family and filthy coven, did you? I don't overlook my grievances, no matter what bitch causes them and no matter what bastard justifies them."

I didn't get Joelly. Was she trying to help us or kill us? She needed to get it the fuck over with already, before the blood loss chose for her. A desperate heat covered me, the room around me blotchy as I wheezed and choked when the blood in my throat pooled.

"Here are your options." The pressure of the knife lessened a tad, though this allowed more room for blood to leak out of me. I coughed and drooled down my chest. "No matter your answer, I leave with my life intact or she dies before I hit the portal—or I make it my mission to see to it in the future. Not even your ghosts will know what took them out."

We couldn't answer with anything but wet gurgles and head shakes. She had the upper hand by blocking our power.

The bedroom door crashed open, bashing against the wall and recoiling against Vincent's shoulder as the top hinge let go. Joelly pulled me back into her and I felt the knife stab all the way through my throat.

Vincent, Donovan, and Joelly were screaming at each other when everything stopped. The pain of my throat being knifed hummed in a constant pain, though ceased throbbing. My heart wasn't beating. I wasn't breathing. I was frozen, but I could hear and see what was in front of me, though I couldn't move my eyes.

Donovan had rushed at Vincent and then followed him as he came over to me. My eyeline was up higher as I had been pulled backwards, so I could see them both while on my knees.

Fuck. Donovan's throat was wide open. Something in the gaping wound shone white. His breath whistled through the gash, sucking in and out of the thrashed edges of his skin. He bent over, more blood spilled out of the wound as he coughed and spit onto the floor. When he stood again and looked at me, I panicked, unable to move or help us. He grabbed his throat to cover the wound as he tried to send me reassuring vibes across the connection. I couldn't say it worked, but not seeing what was done to the both of us was a tad settling.

Donovan reached for the knife in my throat with his free hand. Vincent grabbed his arm, hitting him with a dose of visions before Donovan ripped his hand away from Vincent's hold. Whatever he saw wasn't good and the sensation of despair and a heavy sadness washed through me.

"The spell will release if you touch them, and the knife is close to her spinal cord. Now shut up and let me assess the situation."

Since Donovan couldn't talk, I imagined he was making his opinion on Vincent's tactics known telepathically, which meant Vincent managed to break whatever spell Joelly put on us.

Why Donovan wasn't frozen as well was testament to Vincent's power. I trusted he could figure this out, but the fact that he was drag-ging his heels made me squirm in helpless anticipation. Since I couldn't physically squirm, my mind was burning off energy for me by running in circles of what was happening or could happen over and over.

Vincent repositioned his glasses and looked down his long nose at me and Joelly, assessing. *"Your trust is well-placed in me, Sophie. I would keep you in this hold for years if it meant your survival. Your death is not an option."*

I believed him, but I couldn't remain like this for much longer without cracking. Pain was a constant as if when he froze me it kept every sensation and emotion I felt in that moment as it was, unchanged and unchangeable. More than a few more minutes of this was far too long.

"What the fuck?" Caine came into the room, followed by a muffled scream from Kim and stomping footsteps up the stairs and in the hall.

Donovan ran for the door. Caine and Kim were allowed in, but everyone else was forced back. Blake's and a few other's reaction to seeing Donovan's condition were much the same as Kim's. Their questions and repeating what they saw didn't lessen much when Donovan shut the door on them, since it was hanging off its top hinge and wasn't soundproof.

"Can you heal as soon as I free her?" Vincent turned to Donovan when he returned to my side.

He nodded and coughed a slew of blood again, this time hinging over hands to knees, looking pale.

Scraping of wood cut though my anxious thoughts. Caine closed the door as Ranlyn pushed through it and asked what had happened.

Donovan sat on the side of the bed and swayed enough, I would have reached out to catch him could I have moved. Vincent and Ranlyn were too busy talking to notice Donovan was too weak to manage a healing by the time they finally figured out the best way to get Joelly and I apart with my head intact. I needed to get myself out of this. Now.

Joelly had blocked my power and Vincent's spell made it impossible to engage, but what about Nya's power? It came out in my most desperate moments. I was busy trying to calm down when I should be overloading myself until Nya's power punched through. Her power was old, maybe older than Vincent's, but it was what I had to work with. Waiting for the perfect moment wasn't going to happen. Not before Donovan was too far gone.

I hyper-focused on the redness of the blood pouring down the front of Donovan's body, the torn and hanging skin of his throat, the greyish colour of his skin. He blinked and tried to soothe me again. I pushed this aside and concentrated on the horror of us dying. We had disintegrated to nothing before. In another life, we were betrayed and beheaded. I remember Millicent's panic to save her love, the panic of watching my husband slaughtered.

Something deep within me warmed. A spark of what I fought for.

I remembered the Soul Reading with Caine as I watched Nya burn to death as fire ate through her. Her scream. Her strength giving way under the fierceness of her agony.

The warmth within me grew as I recalled the torture it caused Gareth to watch his wife burn. He wanted to save her, to stop this, to take her pain, but he was trapped himself in his own hell.

Vincent turned to me, staring at me as I fuelled Nya's power. "What are you doing?"

I couldn't answer him if I wanted to and remained on course.

"Sophie, stop this."

Layers of tragedy were strong in my mind—being eaten by disintegrating pain, the anticipation of losing my husband, and watching Nya burn to death—all filled with despair, helplessness, and pain.

"You have no notion what her power will do—Fuck."

Vincent scrambled to get Ranlyn and Donovan in position, but Donovan was curled into himself on the bed, gripping the sheets. Vincent swore again and went back to instructing Ranlyn as I kept replaying the horrors of my past.

When Nya's power raged through me enough to blur my vision, I recalled the precise moment Nya's scream let loose her and Gareth's power as they burned and the true pain of their end enveloped them.

A pulse of power burst out of me like a bomb.

Vincent and Ranlyn were thrown back, and Joelly and I were thrown apart. I hit a side table and went down. I choked, blood spraying and spurting on the side table in front of me. The knife was still in my throat. Nya's power still tingled in my skin but was gone. I couldn't heal around an object, so I grabbed the blade and pulled it out.

Ranlyn screamed for me not to, but it was too late. The wound gushed and spilled between my fingers as I grasped my throat and fought for every morsel of healing power I had in me.

Ranlyn was on top of me, grasping my hands with his own. His power was a jolt that joined mine. The power running through me brought blinding pain. I couldn't scream or move or do anything but take it and hope it didn't tear me apart.

When the pressure on my throat gave way, I turned to the side and hacked up clots of blood from of my windpipe until I couldn't breathe, then collapsed back and took in a long pull of oxygen.

"You sure know how to make a bad situation worse." Ranlyn was siting against the wall, his one leg still over me. Bright red blood covered his hands and dappled his face.

"Thanks Jeeves." My voice was hoarse, but I could talk.

I gave another light cough and reached out for Donovan's pant leg. "You okay?"

He shifted to look over the side of the bed at me. "Not really."

I knew what he meant. We would live, but the process left a mark.

Ranlyn helped me sit up. I looked around the small room. "Holy frog farts. What am I seeing?"

"You tell me."

Vincent stood with his hand outstretched in front of him towards Joelly. She was laid out on the floor where Nya's power had thrown her, but her body wasn't what I was looking at. Above her, where

Vincent's hand was reaching, was another Joelly, hovering above her skinny-jean wearing body, squirming to get out of Vincent's hold. The edges of her were wispy and she was opaque without much colour.

"I guess Soul Extracting does come in handy."

"You can see her?" Vincent looked at me a moment before looking back at Joelly, who was in some type of pain over whatever Vincent was doing to her.

I nodded, wiping my mouth on my sleeve, and moved to get closer to Joelly's soul. She looked at me, connecting to the sight of me and squirmed some more. She was in pain and afraid and I couldn't help but smile. "Is she dead?"

"No. Still tethered to her vessel."

"Badass."

Vincent made a humble dip of his head and called in others to help him. With his grip tight on Joelly's soul, Jared and Blake picked her up and carried her out of the room and down the stairs with Vincent following. I didn't know what would happen if they dropped her or if Vincent lost his grip on her soul while still outside of her body, but by the intense glare on Vincent as he left the room, I gathered it wouldn't be good.

The moment the door closed on its fixed hinges, Donovan pulled me into a tight embrace. The relief and happiness across our connection held me tighter. Our tie was a weakness as well as a strength and after what happened, I needed the reminder that I wasn't alone in this. No matter what happened, he was there with me and we would find a way to get through it.

I went to have a quick shower, eager to get downstairs and see what was happening with Joelly since they had her in a chair being persuaded by Caine. I opened the bathroom door to find Bosco. He howled and danced around me. Joelly must have stuck him in here. He was no guard dog, but he would have made enough noise to wake me up and would get in Joelly's way.

I handed him over to Donovan who insisted on standing outside of the bathroom until I was done. I did the same for him. We were safe enough with Joelly under Vincent or Caine's control, but we didn't know yet what her plan was and she may not be alone.

Donovan took a handful of minutes in the shower. While he was in there, I watched as everyone surrounded Caine while he used his persuasion ability to interrogate Joelly. A lot of Mother Coven members were inside as well, though many couldn't fit in the house, so they waited and listened from outside.

Without the space to camp out on Ranlyn's floors, whole makeshift buildings were erected in the field outside to accommodate the remaining flock.

Somehow, Kim managed to save us a seat on one of the couches, which were pushed further apart so Joelly and Caine could be seated between them on wooden chairs from the table in the long room.

Donovan sat and leaned forward, elbows to knees. "She said she was here to help. What did she mean?"

Caine looked at Donovan with a side-eyed glare but seemed to shake off his annoyance and asked Joelly Donovan's question.

She was expressionless. Since she was behind me most of the time we were in the room, it was my first glimpse of her up close. Her makeup was old, as if she had been sleeping in it and then reapplying layer over layer. She looked tired and strung out, though I didn't know if what Vincent did to her was the cause of any of it.

"I want to help the Coven kill Loring and the Puppeteer."

I looked at Donovan. His eyes narrowed, strumming with suspicion. Murmurs from the surrounding onlookers rose and fell as Caine asked her why she wanted to kill them.

"They left me helpless and alone. They shunned me from all my contacts under threat of death."

It was sad. Joelly was desperate for a place in this game, whether it was to benefit herself or not, and now the ones who accepted her as the meddler and liar she was turned her away, too.

"She's lonely and desperate." Donovan gained the attention of the crowd. "It's not the first time she's pissed off the wrong people and ended up curbed when they got sick of her bullshit. Let her go and she'll try this again."

Ranlyn was standing, arms crossed, thumb nail grazing his bottom lip. He didn't answer Donovan, but he didn't look convinced of anything.

"Can you get her to show her real soul colour?" I could always see her red soul glow, but the Taint was always questionable since she had the power to alter her essence.

Caine instructed Joelly and it took a moment for her to murmur a spell and reveal her true soul glow.

"Wow. Okay."

"I feel sorry for her." Olive stood near the end of the couch. I didn't see her until she spoke. "No arguing the touch of evil, but her light still fights."

I nodded and looked at Donovan. "She's a cur. Like Loring's arm candy Malina. Like the Apporter." I looked at Ranlyn. "Less than the Apporter." He nodded and I looked back at Joelly. "Half in darkness while the rest wades in the light."

Donovan dragged a hand through his still wet hair, shaking his head. He knew Caine's power meant she couldn't lie, but he still wasn't convinced.

Ranlyn directed Caine on the next question. "How do you plan to help us?"

"I can help you get into the Puppeteer's Creation as well as Diluculo."

Donovan made a throaty noise. "Gotta do better than that. He's not exactly hiding and we already know how to get into Diluculo."

Caine shot him a look Donovan didn't acknowledge.

Caine asked her to explain further.

"Loring calls it a fish webbing. A failsafe to protect Diluculo and Pario against an outside attack, added while created, but never used until now."

Ranlyn closed his eyes for a moment too long and I knew whatever the fish webbing was, it was bad and something we weren't going to be able to moonwalk past without a problem. He didn't say what it was, didn't say anything until he prompted Caine with more questions.

We confirmed what I saw in Roe's thoughts. The Blind and Magics alike were used as Puppets to do the Puppeteer's bidding. A king among zombie slaves without the decaying flesh and insatiable diet for brains. Older Magics like Veata were harder to contain as their innate powers would struggle to regain control over themselves, so they were held separately. Captive to ensure compliance, then taken out and used like an old mop when needed.

There weren't any more questions to ask her at the moment, so instead of returning her will, Caine suggested he put her to sleep. This worked for Ranlyn, so Caine gave the command and Joelly slumped in her seat, falling forward until Caine caught her. Others helped him lay her out on a couch until they decided what to do with her next.

"What's this fish webbing?" Anne-Claire was perched on a kitchen stool, Lincoln next to her. "Can we get through it?"

Ranlyn took a moment and paced a few steps while we all waited. "In desperate times of war, Diluculo became a stronghold for Magics. A place where Magics could retreat, receive medical care, strategize—anything to get a breather out of the frontlines and make a next attack count. The webbing Joelly mentioned was added during the makings of the Creation. It acts as a magical netting that blankets the entire Creation, so no one can breach the veil if we're forced to retreat. Meaning we could remain there forever or until another solution was discovered. It's never been activated. It was meant to be a last resort option and hasn't been needed."

"Diluculo and Pario have been fought over since they learned to build worlds within the veil." Hinapouri's vague account had me envisioning her among the fighters, I assumed in the Witch Wars Olive mentioned. I didn't know much about them, but I know many died and that Aunt Lacey was a badass warrior who probably took out her fair share.

"Luring them out of Diluculo would be easier." A few nodded, agreeing with Anne-Claire, though I noticed Lincoln wasn't one of them.

"Unlikely." Vincent's tone was clipped. "Evaristus knows leaving would lead to defeat and he would never sacrifice control over Diluculo when remaining keeper of the Creation is the end goal."

Anne-Claire struggled to keep herself from looking down at her feet too long. Her usual mask of confidence was clouded by her embarrassment of being shut down.

"Agreed," Ranlyn pointed at Vincent. "We don't need a lure and we already have a plan set for when we get in. Think of breaking the netting less as fabric to cut through and more of a vault. Leave recruitment of the numbers we need to your Elders but expect to be called upon."

So, there was campaigning to do.

Ranlyn's property was bursting with Magics and yet he thought we needed more? This netting sounded worse than a vault, whatever that meant. Maybe we needed Magics with certain abilities to break into the vault? If we didn't have them in this house or outside, I wondered where they were and what happened if they didn't agree to get involved.

"And Joelly?" Donovan stepped in Ranlyn's way, stopping him from leaving. "What are we doing with her?"

Ranlyn looked over at her, still asleep on the couch, then looked at Caine. "Wake her up."

"What? You can't be serious." Donovan pointed at me. "She still wants Nya's power from Sophie. She won't stop, whether she wants revenge against Loring and the Puppeteer or not."

"Bind her." Miklos's simple solution wasn't fool proof.

I raised my hand. "FYI, she used a knife when she cut my throat upstairs."

"Thank you, babe. She doesn't need her powers to get what she wants. We don't know if she plans on bringing information she learns back to other Magics. She may be on the outs with Loring and the

Puppeteer, but it doesn't mean she won't weasel her way back in or with another coven."

The Elders won and Joelly's powers would be bound and she would be allowed to roam, though watched. If she showed a propensity for violence, even thoughts of violence, then she would be put back to sleep and tended to in small increments since her needs, like eating and using the bathroom, would still be required.

Donovan fumed as they performed the binding. Then Caine awoke her and explained the measures taken and the consequences that would follow if she neglected to comply.

"I need some air." Donovan pushed through the crowd until he disappeared altogether.

Ranlyn appointed himself for first watch of Joelly and employed Miklos and Hinapouri to start contacting other Sects to assist with any aspect of the plan, hoping more would hear their call and bear arms.

"Good." Joelly stood, fixed her tight jeans, then pointed towards the kitchen. "There food in that fridge? I'm starving."

12

A HAMSTER WHEEL

"You don't have to follow me everywhere, you know."

I stood with my hands on either side of the bathroom door, a bull-headed Donovan pulling guard duty outside the door. It was touching the first time, maybe even the third time, but it was getting old.

"I'll never forgive myself if I leave you alone and Joelly jumps for the chance to take you out. And since that also means taking me out, it's actually a form of self-preservation and not being a stalker with a shitty hide-and-seek game."

I rolled my eyes and shut the door.

After washing my hands, I found him vigilant, as expected, but he wasn't alone. Serena, Adam, and Denise were chatting him up.

Donovan and I had missed all the fun the night before. With so many Magics in one place, it had turned into a party. The reason for the get together didn't seem to have dampened the mood, as it was standard to enjoy the time while you can, knowing it could be your last when war is around the corner.

Serena hit my arm. "It reminded me of bush parties, sitting out on trap house couches, but without Jemma puking on David Kelauda."

A crush our friend had that ended with David's lap full of regurgitated blueberry vodka coolers.

"Or Ruby and Justin breaking up at least three times during the night." It was as annoying as it was entertaining at that age.

"Bush parties?" Donovan raised a questioning eyebrow. "Were your crazy days played out when you were younger?"

"More like I was a tag along, but it was fun. Where'd you get the couches and everything last night? No trap houses around here."

"Appearo? Apeario?"

"Appareo," Denise corrected my brother. I had a flash of their future, of her correcting him all the time, but he didn't look embarrassed.

"Her. She can manifest things, I guess? We had couches and a tent with tables of food and everything. It was sick."

"I didn't know Louise had that kind of power."

Denise nodded. "It was mostly from her and Henry's vacation house. She can't manifest fake things, but if she's seen it before, she can get a hold of it." Denise's personality change was whiplash worthy.

"I didn't hear anything." I looked to Donovan who shook his head.

"That's 'cuz you guys took the party upstairs before it started." The look on my brother's face was the equivalent to a high-five Donovan's way.

Donovan laughed. I didn't.

I didn't need the miscommunication.

"If by party you mean sleeping, since I passed out in about five seconds with a migraine, then sure, we *Rocked the Casbah*."

Since it was early, an enormous breakfast buffet was set up in the tents they gushed about, while picnic tables peppered the lawn. Denise followed, the previous night allotting quality time with her and Adam, which appeared the same for Serena as Jared waited in line for food, so she didn't have to.

I was piling a few pancakes onto a paper plate when the sun

warming my skin reminded me of my dream before Joelly's wakeup call. It took me a long time to rip myself away from the wheat fields. The emotions involved took longer to dissipate, even with Joelly's knife at my throat. What I saw—the injured man and the man pretending to be the guy's friend—was too close to the Ballard Family Coven origin story to be anything else, but what I couldn't decide was if it was a replay of the actual scene as it occurred or what my brain cooked up since I read the story.

Carrying my thoughts with me to the picnic table, I sat between Donovan and Olive, who was enjoying tea, eggs, and toast with strawberry jam. She was deep in conversation with Jared and Blake, who were feeding a grateful Bosco breakfast sausage.

I stabbed my plastic fork into my pancakes, shifting back to thinking about my dream. Normally, the dreamer puts themselves in place of the lead, but in this dream, I was much shorter. Without being able to catch the glimpse of a mirror, it was all I had to go by. Something didn't feel right. With Millicent, I felt a familiarity. This was like travelling beneath the skin of a stranger.

"You were."

I turned to find Vincent sitting on the bench of the picnic table behind me, seated to face me. Caine was across the table from him, involved in his plate. He stopped short mid-chew when he noticed the crowd staring toward his table.

"Care to share?" Kim questioned Vincent as she sat on the outer edge beside Olive.

He looked at me. I nodded, a signal for him to continue as everyone would have been told whatever he had to say afterwards anyway. Well, not Denise, but I wasn't about to ask her to leave.

He pushed his glasses up his nose. "Your dream was not of yourself. Not a dream at all. It was a recreation vision."

"Why would I have a vision of someone I don't know, in a time well before I was born?"

"What vision?" Donovan's coffee mug hovered in front of his mouth instead of sipping.

I explained in full. "I don't think it was me, but it felt very real."

"Visions have a way of taking you over." Donovan took the sip of coffee.

"But I don't get visions. That's your thing." I looked back at Vincent. "I get it was the Ballard origin story, but why was I seeing it?"

"It is the man in the vision that concerns me. The injured one that your ancestor fell in love with was the Puppeteer."

A chorus of "What-the-fuck?" came from those at the table.

Vincent's expression was tight. "He has changed since then— become rounder and colder—but the man was most certainly the Puppeteer."

"You're saying the Puppeteer is responsible for creating my fami- ly?" I looked at Olive, who looked lost in thought. "I know he claimed to be related but being related and creating the whole damn blood- line is a dump truck of zombie pigs different."

Vincent's posture straightened. "He is responsible for the procre- ation of it, as children were involved once he stunted his immortality long enough to procure them. His power is much your own. And in that, he has found a way to send you that vision. Either to show you proof of his claim to one of your relation or for an unknown reason."

"Spectacular." Adam spoke around the mangled food in his mouth.

"This won't somehow take away our magic or kill us if we take him out, will it?"

Kim laughed at Serena. "He's not a werewolf."

Serena gasped and turned to Vincent. "Are they real?"

"Not in the way you are envisioning."

Donovan placed his hand on my lower back. "It doesn't mean anything, babe."

I tried absorbing his calm, but it didn't get me far.

"It's okay." Olive wiped her hands on a napkin. "He may have been the start of us, but it would seem he needs to end, regardless of the outcome."

She was right. I wouldn't be the woman I was in this life if it wasn't for his intervention of my ancestor's mundane existence. Somewhere along the way, the Puppeteer lost whatever goodness my ancestor put her life on the line to protect. The story said she fell in love. I'd like to think he was worth loving back then. She would be heartbroken to see what he's become.

"He was immortal. How did they have children?" It didn't surprise me Kim wanted the details of such a thing. She was going for broke as a Magic. If her baby wheels started turning, she needed to know kids were possible.

Vincent nodded. "He somehow stunted his power's effects on his body, refusing to use it or removing it from his essence. Maybe his power allowed this process to come easier than some. He would have had to do so within a handful of years, as his wife died a mortal's death and a few of their children also died within a single lifespan. He didn't understand why they refused to take up the power he gifted them, why they declined to allow it to take them beyond the lifespan of the Blind. They harnessed the power, though not enough to live out their existence as immortals as he envisioned. Eventually, Evaristus broke ties with them."

"And then he turned into a Tainted jerkass intent on playing God in his sub-worlds where no one can touch him." I finished for him.

"How do you even know this guy?" Adam thumbed at Vincent. "No offense, but I don't know who you are. Why should we believe you?"

I felt a bit of pride for my brother not taking Vincent at face-value.

"You would be able tell yourself if you worked on your power." I may have been proud, but it didn't mean Adam was right. "I told you. You're a Soul Seer, too. I can tell by looking at Vincent that he plays for our side, which is his name since you don't pay attention. His soul glow tells me he's been around a long time. I trust he knows more than me."

"That—" Vincent scratched his neck. "—and we have met before."

"You and the Puppeteer?"

"Yes, unfortunately. Though I was referring to you and I."

Stunned silence dragged. "Ex-squeeze me?"

Clearing his throat and sanding his hands together in a clear stall tactic, he also pushed up his glasses in a nervous fashion. "Our acquaintance does not reach beyond this life with you amongst the Ballard's. None of your lives take place within the same bloodline. But I found they have consisted of Donovan in much the same capacity, though without the resistance regarding your relationship as in this life. Nevertheless, I expect the same result."

Tunnel vision had me staring at Vincent, waiting for him to either say more or take back what he already put out there. Donovan and I knew about our past lives together and we had even seen at least one or two, but to have someone in front of me state they knew me in one of those lives left me dumbfounded.

I felt the eyes of everyone at the table on me, though Caine became preoccupied with his plate.

"How many times?" Donovan's voice mirrored my listless confusion.

Vincent took in a contemplative breath. "I have befriended the two of you in fifty or so other lives. Other times, I checked in without broaching friendship."

"Holy shit." I didn't even know who said it. I couldn't concentrate.

"So, wait. Were you—Did you know Millicent and Isaac?"

The surprise in his eyes told me before his expression hardened. He nodded.

"Does it al—" My voice cracked. I put down my fork and swallowed, my throat tight as my composure slipped. "Does it always end like that?"

"I tried to help them." Vincent shook his head, his brows synched in something I thought might be regret.

"Does it?" I was too forceful and fought to reign it in. "I need to know."

Vincent's eyes wavered, swaying to and away from me in thought. He seemed to know the answer, yet unsure of how to say it. "Not always."

Confirmation wasn't something I needed from him. I could have searched my soul and read it for myself, but having him say it, having someone present to witness Millicent and Isaac's death, somehow made it more real. A flash of Isaac's face hit me, his eyes that wouldn't leave his love in his last moments, unaware of the comfort that they would see each other again. Their love so simple and pure taken because of a bunch of bigoted morons. Those people didn't deserve to know them, let alone share breathing space. Angry, sorrow-filled tears sprung to my eyes. Donovan's consoling hand on my back made them fall.

"It won't be like that this time, babe."

I looked at him, surprised by the telepathy, and saw the same tears on his cheeks. *"You don't know that."*

The seconds that passed as we looked to each other dragged. Was this all we could expect from life? A complicated love, stolen, destined to start all over again in some distant future? A hamster wheel of love and loss? How fucking depressing.

"Why would you tell them that?" Caine spoke low, using his fork to pick at his eggs without eating. Vincent turned, as if surprised he was being questioned. "You know what's expected of them. Now she knows we're facing the one who made her family. You don't think it'll be harder to pull the trigger when the time comes?"

I sniffed. "I can still do it."

"But it'll be more difficult. You might hesitate." He turned back to Vincent. "It's another string of bullshit to worry about. And you've been around them for how many years?"

"A thousand or so."

That earned a few shocked murmurs.

"Then you should know better. Like they don't worry about each other enough?"

Vincent turned away from him. "It is the truth, whether you enjoy it or not."

"I may not be a fan of this whole Sophie-Donovan destiny trip, but I'll be the one next to Sophie when we go up against her ancestor bent on burying her."

"Caine—" He looked at me, but it was more a glare as if he didn't want to. "I already knew he was family. Not how, but I knew. And worrying about Donovan is a given. I promise you, I won't fuck this up."

If the previous lives and deaths were anything like the one I peered into, then chances were this one would be no different. The image of Donovan dying as Isaac shot to the forefront again. I would offer up what's left of my sanity to stop us from reliving that outcome. As much as I kept him at arm's length, I couldn't deny the immense surge of crippling anxiety that thinking about Donovan dying caused me.

The tears wouldn't stop and the rest of me trembled.

"I could have left you in the dark." Vincent's voice was quiet. "I have before. It did no good then as it would do no good now. For either of you." He took in a deep breath. "My point in mentioning our past acquaintance was that both of you are stronger in this life than any I have been a part of in the past. You did not grow up together. Donovan grew strong under atrocious conditions, while Sophie, you were raised in ignorance and still, you have reconnected and found strength more potent that all your other lives combined."

"Nice try." I blinked away a few tears and used a tissue Olive handed me to wipe my nose. "I've seen what I was capable of as Millicent, and she far surpassed me at this point."

"Why do you think I have been pushing you? Millicent would be proud to see how far you have come, but even she could see you are capable of more."

His statement was meant to hearten confidence, I knew this, but bringing Millicent into it induced a wave of sorrow released deep within me, so strong there was a resurgence in tears that unravelled me. I couldn't help it and I couldn't fight it this time. I hated crying—despised feeling something so overwhelming it could reduce me to a blubbering mess. But there I was, sitting at a picnic table in the middle of a field filled with Magics in nowhere Slovenia, head in my hands, biting into my bottom lip to stop my sobs from coming out full throttle.

I wasn't alone. A strong soothing hand on my back from Olive and the stir of emotions it caused in the others was support I didn't want yet needed. My grief breached the small gap between myself and Donovan. He pulled me closer by the shoulders, wrapping me within his arms and burying his face in my hair, whispering soft sentiments.

It didn't last any more than a minute or two. Before long, my shaking stilled. I wiped my eyes and felt composed enough to tuck my hair behind my ear, no longer hiding, and straightened from Donovan.

Vincent leaned forward in his seat. "Your compassion for her life and death, and the knowledge of understanding your previous rise and fall, gives you an advantage in this fight, Sophie. Now you have Nya's power, another perceived thorn in your sides." He looked at Caine, whose brows were arched in an anger he didn't hide well. "You have no clue what it was like to come across the two of you again, commissioned for a job I have done an infinite amount of times. To hear of the incident with your previous Elders, to hear of the Sorrel and Soul Seer who came with no names, to find two of my oldest friends after thinking this time we would not cross paths at all. These elements have come together for a reason. I could never be persuaded to believe anything less than a divine hand plucked you for this role.

"This is no pep-talk. The events leading up to this point mean something. Whether or not our upcoming strife is the reason for the necessary anguish, or if it is to be one of a dozen or more causes you are to battle for after, this is meant to be." He reached forward and took my hand. "You will survive this."

I tried to smile at him, but I don't think I managed it. He pressed the back of my hand to his lips, got up, and left. Maybe he needed a moment to himself, but I knew I couldn't take any more if he had more to say.

As I told Adam, I trusted Vincent, and this was no different, but I didn't buy into predestined paths, whether they led to success or tragedy. With that mindset, it meant I would be in charge of making my future my own, though I had no idea what that looked like.

Looking across the way at Caine bullying his food with no intentions on finishing, I wanted to say something to him, but had nothing to give. Vincent managed to bring the others down as well, even Denise who was hard-pressed to hide her rosy nose tip and glossy eyes. The lull was heavy, as if everyone was waiting for me to say something.

"A party is definitely in order." Serena broke the aching silence for me. "What? It's gonna happen anyway. This time, you my dear—both of you—are going." She included Donovan, who raised an eyebrow in interest. "Take a nap, pound a case of energy drinks, or cast some Wake Me the Fuck Up spell, 'cuz I'll drag you into the tent by your creepy hair if I have to."

I sniffed and looked down at the chunk of strands on my shoulder. "My hair's not creepy."

"Please. It keeps growing. It's like the freakin' *Peanut Butter Solution* movie, only it doesn't make me wanna puke. You're a freak. No matter what, after all of that, you're not getting out of this tonight, so suck it up."

I remembered the 80's movie where the sticky breakfast condiment concoction grew a couple kids' hair out of control, and as Serena said, making her gag.

Donovan was in if I was. He wasn't about to leave me alone now. A dimly lit and crowded backyard, packed with bodies, was the ultimate easy-access environment for Joelly to take advantage.

Reinforcements soon began arriving. A few at a time trickled in and set up where they could, no shortage of space for the large group swelling in numbers by the hour. Once lunchtime hit, the grounds were dotted with new faces, reminding me of our time in Diluculo. Though not as festive, the resemblance was enough for a smile to tug at my lips. For some time, I watched behind dark sunglasses as glowing soul after glowing soul filtered through the portal onto Ranlyn's property. Nothing Tainted, which was most important— none except for Joelly and the Apporter.

Joelly, and whatever babysitter was appointed, floated through the crowd like she belonged, hitting on those she thought deserved a lingering double-take and watching as people demonstrated some tricks of their own. From afar, it looked like she was shopping for her next target when her powers were reinstated. Donovan tried not to pay her any attention, though I would catch him glaring at her, his pulse quickening as she paraded around the grounds among his Sect and Covenmates. Pulling his attention away from her before he sent himself into a rage was a fulltime job.

Practice was made more difficult with so many around, but we found space and worked on a few tactics with the Coveners. I kept it lowkey, so I wouldn't evoke Nya's power by accident, but I worked on the basics and more maneuvers Donovan led me through to protect myself. During a break to cool down and refuel, Ranlyn approached Kim and Donovan, asking them to follow him into the house. Donovan hesitated and looked at me.

"It's not my Sect. I'm finishing my taco salad."

"Don't worry man, I got this." Adam had a mountain-sized helping of taco salad himself, some falling from his plate onto the table where Bosco lapped it up.

Denise giggled. "You're better off protecting yourself."

Adam's face scrunched at being called out.

"True that. Point to Denise." Never thought I would be giving her props, but when the chick was right, she was right. "I can protect myself. Go be important."

Donovan looked to Kim and Ranlyn who had taken off without him, hesitating.

My power swelled with my annoyance. *"Don't pull this over-bearing shit with me, Donovan. Leave already."* I didn't look up from my food, not wanting to make a scene, but I was sick of his hovering.

Donovan leaned into his hand placed next to my plate. I stopped chewing and looked up at him.

"Would you rather I leave all together?"

"Go ahead. If Joelly kills me, you'll be the first to know." A silent laugh followed, one that left him unamused as he turned his back to me, took off, and was swallowed by the crowd.

"You know," Adam swallowed his food, "that mind reading thing makes it kinda hard to defend you if you won't fight like a normal couple."

"We're not a couple. And I don't need you to defend me against him. By the way he left, I'm pretty sure he knows it."

"Are you kidding me? He loved every second of it."

"What the fuck does that mean?"

Before he could answer, the bench next to me was occupied by Joelly.

"Well, Firefly, I say—"

Miklos slapped a hand onto Joelly's shoulder with a hit of power strong enough to make her cry out.

"Whoa!" I half-stood, about to grab his arm, but thought better of it since I didn't know if what he was doing could hurt me too. "Relax. If anyone here has dibs on hurting her, it's me."

Adam and Denise relaxed back into their seats. Adam was useless against them, even Joelly with her powers bound—though from what I saw in the field, Denise could hold her own.

Miklos let go but stood vigilant.

"Geez, caveman." Joelly rubbed her shoulder where Miklos

grabbed her. "You've clipped my wings. I'm not flying off with her anywhere."

I knew Joelly meant it figuratively, but I wondered if maybe she could fly. Caine's cousin Jet could.

I put one leg over the bench and squared my body with hers. "Why are you pushing it? You're lucky you're not dead, and what? Now you're hoping for a social visit? We're not friends."

She sucked her teeth. "Please. You're the one who's lucky they're not dead, but I digress. I didn't come for another attempt, only to explain, face-to-face, that I'm thankful to know I won't be Evar's Puppet slave. Plus—" She looked around at the open field of Magics. "—I'm having fun."

"Wow. The balls on you. We still have to fight him. Not fun. Having Elders babysit you distracts them and gratifies your need to feel important or dangerous." I rolled my eyes. "You've sabotaged your friendships or alliances or whatever you want to call them, and now you come here? You can't hide someplace else?"

Her black-lined eyes narrowed. "If you remember, this arrangement wasn't my idea. I could've chilled at the bar, but The Lush doesn't have the best security. Eddie nearly lost an arm and Drew, well, Drew could've lost the pounds they threatened to slice out of his belly and been better for it. Plus, my hide-out was ransacked."

I gasped. Fuck Drew, but Eddie was a good guy. I stayed away from the bar to save them from this shit and Joelly led the evil bitches right to them. "We didn't drag you by your thong-strings through the portal, so you're damn right it was your idea to seek us out. No way you didn't know how that ride would end. You're not an idiot, even if you make stupid decisions. You saw an opportunity and you took it. Simple as that."

She raised her pierced brow. "You're just pissed 'cuz you and Donovan are bickering like an old married couple. He wants to keep you under his thumb. Don't fall for his bullshit."

Pfft. Like I was going to take her advice. Donovan may have been panicky regarding Joelly going anywhere near me, but since she raced over to me the second he left, he did have a good reason.

Joelly leaned in toward me. Miklos moved as well, though she ignored him. I tensed and retracted my arm from the table so she wouldn't touch me. "Back in the day, I'd send him visions of gay porn to throw him off while he was teaching. You want psychological warfare?" She tapped the side of her head as if to indicate his mind was his Achilles heel.

She laughed and reached for Adam's drink. He snatched the plastic cup before she got it. Miklos grabbed her shoulder again, tugging her back a few inches to keep her in check. She dropped her hand to the wooden tabletop with a clunk of her chunky rings.

Adam sipped his drink. "No chick touches my drinks. Especially one I'm not getting any from. Even for my standards, you're too scary to put my junk on the line for."

Denise took his cup from his hand and took a sip of her own. Adam looked at me, suppressing a smile. A simultaneous "Eww" came from both Joelly and me. Adam broke down in laughter while Denise shrugged.

"Miklos, Joelly would like you to escort her to get a drink while I scrub the last few images from my head."

Adam grunted. "As if I haven't been subjected enough to you and your exploits, it's all people talk about."

Denise elbowed him and continued to confuse me by sticking up for me.

Joelly huffed. "You know, giving in to Donovan is like inviting an STI to an orgy. He's a parasite that'll destroy you from the inside out. Aren't you trying to be a shrink? You'd think you'd know better. Maybe deal with your daddy issues before you start doling out advice."

"Like you're one to judge. Though you're right, helping people as fucked up as you is the plan. Right now, it's a stretch because this whole good versus evil bullshit won't quit. And you show up here, all pathetic and begging for help, but you don't do a fucking thing to deserve it. Granted, you got a rough start and your daddy or your Coven Master or whatever, never taught you how to ask for help in a healthy, proactive manner, but you're exactly where your choices brought you. Since you're not on my couch and you've tried to kill me multiple times, go shit in the hole you made for yourself, because I've reached my maximum compassion fatigue for you and the gravy-covered horseshit you keep slopping in front of everyone."

Joelly glared as I spun back to my seat and refocused on my food. Miklos got her moving, her complaints fading under the crunch of my taco salad. Insulting Joelly didn't get me anywhere, didn't even make me feel better, but having her carted away by Miklos did.

"You really gotta work on your insults. Go shit in a hole? Who says that?"

I shot Adam the finger.

I should have been more understanding of Donovan's overprotective nature when it came to his sister. For now, I would let him stew as I didn't want him to think handling it with an ultimatum was okay but giving him a few inches of ease was common sense. Joelly was dangerous. Pretending she wasn't, even with her "wings clipped", was doing the hard work for her. I didn't plan on making killing me easy for her.

13

ACT YOUR AGE

Wanting any excuse to be around Jared, Serena dragged me to Jared's table where he, Blake, Matt, Caitlyn, Denise, and Denise's bitchy friend Jamie—who turned her nose up at our approach—were all either sitting or standing around. To my relief, Jared looked as happy to see Serena as she was to see him. A vibrant gleaming smile scrunched his cheeks as Serena slid in to stand beside him as the Coveners chatted about the "raging" party planned for that night.

"Told you!" Serena smacked me in the arm. "The Seer here thinks she's too good to chill with the rest of us."

Jamie made a snotty laugh like she expected nothing less.

"I do not. I'm a bartender. Excuse me for not wanting to hang out at another place exactly like my work for some adventurous drunken bash where you end up in the drunk-tank."

"No drunk-tank here." Matt smiled and fixed his hat to sit cock-eyed on his head.

Serena elbowed me. "Exactly, lame-ass. You can spit-shine your halo another day."

"Hey, I said I'd show."

"No, no, no. You won't just show." Jared wrapped a beefy arm around my shoulders. "You'll have an alcoholic drink in your hand at all times, you won't leave until the sun comes up, and you have to do at least one thing that embarrasses you. Then I can say, not only does our Coven have a Soul Seer, but she's boss enough to chill with, even if she is normally so straight-edged she'd give you papercuts."

"Wha—? Straight-edged my ass. And what do I get if I follow through? 'Cuz hanging out somewhere I'm already hanging out isn't a prize."

He laughed and screwed his face up in thought.

"Oh!" Blake hopped over the table and leaned in close to whisper in my ear. I laughed and had to give Blake props for the idea.

"If I win, you—" I poked Jared in the chest. "—have to serenade Serena with '*Kiss from a Rose*' by Seal."

Both Jared and Serena blushed as a chorus of laughter drowned out their complaints to both Blake and me.

Serena grabbed my arm. "I will kill you if that happens. Also—" She leaned in. "I bet he's a good singer. And if not, I'm sure he can make up for it in different ways."

I laughed. "Win-win for you."

"All right, all right." Jared raised his hands to quiet everyone. "Then, if I win, you have to sing '*Truly, Madly, Deeply*' by Savage Garden to Caine." A collective gasp from the others had him scrambling. "Or Donovan, or whoever you end up with in case it's one of those kind of nights." He managed to move past the discomfort, but it didn't make it any better for me.

"Whatever. I'll take your stupid bet."

I sealed the deal with a catcher's mitt of a handshake from Jared as Serena grabbed and shook my shoulders like a monkey shaking a tree. The Coveners lit up with laughter and applause, hyped for a party and the chance to burn off some steam after all the training and talk of battle and death.

"What's going on?" We turned to see Kim heading towards us.

"Our girl here is gonna act her age and get polluted with us tonight." Serena pointed in her face. "You in again? You better be."

"That's actually a good idea." Kim looked around us to the others. "We're meeting as a Sect. Head over to the clearing next to the house."

"Why can't we meet here?" Blake took a swig of whatever was in his cup.

"Because that's where Donovan will be meeting us. Every Sect is gathering. The Ballards will join us since Sophie is in both and they're a small branch of the Mother Coven."

"Are we?" I wasn't so sure but should have maybe asked before.

Kim shrugged, then shooed them in the direction of where it looked like Lewis and Priscilla were already waiting.

I grabbed her hand and we slowed as the others headed towards the house. "You think the party is a good idea. Really?"

"What? It is."

Stopping altogether, I tilted my head and crossed my arms. "You're not getting out of this. Spill it."

She exhaled and looked around a moment. "The fight's tomorrow." I felt my mouth drop open. "Late into the night because of the time difference outside Diluculo, but tomorrow night is when it's happening."

Tomorrow night? I knew it was coming, but tomorrow night? All this time waiting for Loring and the Puppeteer, getting beat down by the Raddies, and hiding out like a scared cottontail all ends tomorrow. Caine and I had a role to play and I had to face the Magic who created my family and another Magic who already had his try at me and lost. He wouldn't trip up this time. What if he won? Would I be recycled into the world again?

"Shit. I knew I shoulda waited for Donovan."

I had been staring at her, lost in thought. "It's fine. I didn't give you much choice."

"Still. He seemed so detached when the Elders told us. I thought maybe he was protecting you. You either did the same thing or were freaking out, but now he's tipped off."

"Yeah, well, he's probably used to it from me." I started in the direction of the Coveners. She stopped me.

"Is there something going on with you two? Other than the everyday he's an ass-wipe and fates in your way of a rockin' sex life."

"Always something." I gave a one-shouldered shrug. "Sometimes he's the asshole and sometimes I am."

"I've been saying that from the beginning, Soph."

"True that. I put him in his place when he gave me an immature ultimatum and he doesn't always like being put in his place. He's pissy. I'm stubborn. It is what it is."

"I guess. But you chose to be with him."

"Not with—"

"Yes, with. Get over your fear of labels. It's happened in previous lives, now it's happened in this one. Settle with the idea, find a way to break the silence, and get on with it. Tomorrow's happening. Love-life issues aren't as important as what you're walking into, but you'll hate yourself if you leave things as they are. Plus, you'll obsess about it instead of concentrating on the Puppeteer and Loring. You don't know what connects you two in each life. You don't want the way this one is lived or ended to negatively affect that."

"What the fizz? I never even thought about that. What the fuck, Kim?"

"I'm just saying. You don't know. I bet even Vincent, your apparent lifelong stalker, doesn't even know and apparently he knows everything."

I rubbed my hands over my face. "It's all so fucked up."

"Yes, it is." She slung her arm over my shoulders and started walking towards the Coveners. "Let's get this meeting over with, put in some more training time, and party it the fuck up. Worrying about dying can wait for tomorrow."

It could wait, but she had planted the idea of how this life's drama impacted Donovan and I's next life. If this was how we were this time around, did something happen in the previous life to create such conflict?

When we reached the others, Jared was humming the song he expected me to sing if I lost the bet. He got me laughing, but he didn't know what was coming tomorrow.

Pockets of groups scattered the property, all hearing the intel I had and learning what was expected of them, but we were stuck waiting in the beating afternoon sun for Donovan so everyone else could be made aware of what everyone else was already crowing about.

A constant dread rode the connection. I didn't blame him for not wanting to have this conversation with the Coveners, but he was good at blunt communication, so I didn't understand what the holdup was.

Everyone sighed and shifted in relief when we saw him come out of the house with Ranlyn. They must have still been talking.

Before he reached the group, I knew one of two things would happen. Donovan would give some sort of sign that all was dust under the bed or he would waltz right by me to the front of the group with intent focus on his job. I braced for either. Before he got within ten feet of me, I knew the latter choice was what he was sticking with.

His hard gaze was tight, as if it took effort for him not to look my way, but I, too, was focused on what came next.

"No wonder you were made for each other." Kim shook her head, joining Donovan at the head of the group along with Olive, who also already knew what he was about to reveal.

Donovan dropped the bomb about the fight being tomorrow. A few celebrated this until Donovan told them to shut up.

"The netting we have to get through is no spell or ritual. Many of you or other Magics with a lower skillset will be chosen to participate in the take down of the netting because your potential injury, impairment, or death will be less of a blow to the Mother Coven."

Ouch.

The Coveners shot angry glares in Donovan's direction as Kim clenched her teeth and shifted between staring at me and looking at the ground.

"I don't care about your feelings, so cut the whining. I care about your lives. The fact that you're being utilized at all is risky for everyone involved. Break down the netting so those with battle experience can do their jobs. Fail to break the netting and we may not get another chance to get inside, which means any Blind or other Magics will be locked inside with the Puppeteer and Loring."

My cousin Kevin stepped forward. "We're not even going inside?"

"No."

Again, this caused complaints, though Donovan let them go on for a minute before quieting them again. "If the netting comes down, you'll be outside the Creation, prepped and ready to join the fight if it bleeds out in the field. Otherwise, you'll do your job and be proud you were included in a historical moment for the Coven. Some of you will be joining a different group to the Puppeteers Creation. Again, most won't go inside. We don't expect him to be there, but we need to make sure he can't return to it, so it'll be closed first."

The guy had to learn to lead with the inspiring bits before telling them how much they sucked, but the point was understood. They had a role to play. Whether they were chosen because of their lacking talent or not, the success of the mission depended on getting inside the Creation. Being the one to deliver bad news was no fun. He handled it well and kept everyone's unrealistic expectations in check.

Message delivered, he was brought into conversation with Blake. I tried to get a sense of his mood beyond his role and hit a wall. Not an actual wall—he wasn't blocking me out, but his emotions were shut down. I opened a window of communication, something to peek into. Blake was talking to him, but he was checked out. Pre-chosen responses slid out like silk. He knew Blake would fight for a more important role and he had no intention of pretending he deserved it.

An idea sprang into my mind and I acted without thinking. Donovan doubled over in an unrestrained groan the moment my projected scene of us using the Coven space in his basement as our sexual playground sucker-punched him. It hit me with the same force, but I knew to expect it and braced against the wave that hit me by digging my nails into my palms and gritting my teeth.

Kim jumped to his aid as he leaned onto his hands, gripping his knees. The image I projected broke within seconds—with the sweat, skin, and panting vision surging in full colour and resulting sensations—leaving the Coveners to stare in a fog of anxious concern.

I bit down on my lip, forcing the pleasure of the vision away with the gratification of the experiment's success and the choking bubble of laughter. I received some pay-off for his discomfort, but once he composed himself, Donovan's confusion and fury boiled. I held my arms crossed like they could hold me together, fighting a battle against the giggles and refusing to catch his gaze, which was no doubt blazing in my direction like a flame thrower.

He shrugged everyone off, insisting he was fine before he stalked off toward the house.

Kim came over to me. "What did you do to him?"

"Umm, I learned to play dirty? We'll see how it plays out."

"Mhmm. Good luck with that."

———

Blaring music echoed outside. I went to a window in the hallway and saw a wedding reception-style tent lit within by coloured strobe lighting. I had no idea why strobe lighting was necessary, but I was expected to enjoy the evening and had already dragged out not attending long enough.

Kim insisted on going over the top and blowing out my hair and chose pocket-studded jean shorts, a flowy cotton tank with braded straps tied behind my neck, plus a long antique gold necklace with a tiny working hour glass filled with white sand. It was an interesting substitution to my lost Triquetra necklace from Aunt Lacey. Nothing as elaborate as Kim or Serena thought I should go with, but after pulling on a pair of strappy sandals, I considered myself done up.

Bosco was left on his line with ample food and water in an area full of toys, some automated or spelled to keep him occupied for hours. Louise thought of everything. We crossed the grass towards the tent to the fading sounds of squeaky toys to pretend we weren't about to wage war in twenty-four hours.

As soon as I walked through the plastic door of the tent, Jared was ready with a mixed drink in hand, not letting me weasel my way out of our bet. I took a sip as Kim and I made our way towards the dance floor, having already lost Serena to Jared, who got her a drink as well. Serena even worked her charm to get some of the older members on the dance floor, including Olive, Lewis, and Priscilla, who lasted at least a few songs before ducking out.

Alcohol warmed my cheeks with a pleasant headiness. Wherever Donovan was, I was sure he had at least a few of his own. Not wanting to overdo it, I found my next drink warming in my hand before I could get it down. With Kim as my dance partner, I had to admit I was having a lot of fun. It didn't surprise me that Caine hung out on the sidelines, more interested in someone with bright blue eyes and a captivating smile I had never seen before. I buried a pang of jealousy, reminding myself he wasn't mine and why, and felt genuine happiness when his grey eyes lit up in response of something blue-eyes leaned in to say to him.

After a couple of hours of dancing and moving about the crowd with Kim, I put my empty glass down on a table, hoping Jared wasn't around to see me break the deal. Kim wasn't making a move to cozy up to anyone else, so I knew she and Frog were still good, even if he was Blind and couldn't be here. I wondered where he thought she was. No way she told him about what we were facing tomorrow, but she was losing herself in the moment like everyone else—saving tomorrow's worry for tomorrow.

Most of the songs I didn't recognize, dance music not being my go-to, but a song I was familiar with mashed with another completed a mix of dance and rock landing a heavy beat had me moving.

A pair of arms moved around my shoulders from behind me.

Shock had me tensing a moment until I recognized the leather bracelet on one wrist—one Donovan never took off.

We could fight without the world ending. The booze may have helped the sudden forgiveness, or the thought of impending death, I didn't care. From what I could tell from our connection, neither did he. He was focused on me and nothing else. I joined him in that head space and lost sight of the room around us, moving in sync, managing to refrain from skin contact to ensure he remained with me and not our memories.

The alcohol and connection-induced haze took over, a prickle of power encasing my skin—stealing all tension, all worry—leaving me with nothing but him and me, peaceful in the midst of chaos.

A song change snapped me back into the room. I blinked and was looking up at Donovan as if I had been the whole time. He looked down at me as if coming to the same conclusion. A raw vulnerability crashed through the connection as we stood, winded. Not an altogether unpleasant one, but unknown to us.

"I need some air." I don't think I was loud enough, but he nodded.

I grabbed a handful of his shirt, dragging him behind me through the crowd. When it thinned, he wrapped his arms around my waist and pressed a kiss to the back of my head.

Distracted, I tripped coming out of the tent. Both of us went down and landed hard. I rolled and grabbed my shin where it was struck by his shoe, then broke down into laughter.

He stood and reached down to help me up. "So fucking graceful."

I hesitated before grabbing his hand. The vision hit him the moment of skin contact, a giddy sensation evoked from the vision raced across the connection.

I let go. He smiled, both dimples caved.

I shook my head. "So fucking obvious."

"Hey! Where's your drink?!" Jared sat in a small group including my cousin.

"Clearly, we've had enough." Donovan knew as well as I had that it wasn't the alcohol making us loopy. Plus, it was his fault I tripped anyway. The kiss threw me off.

"Nah, nah, nah." Jared took a few wobbled steps towards us. "You best be gettin' on your knees. Start singing, girl."

A flare of irritation within Donovan prickled the connection. "What's that now?"

Jared took a step back from Donovan and pointed at me. "She made the bet."

I laughed. "To have a drink in hand at all times. Nothing about getting on my knees."

"Here—" Adam reached over from where he sat with Denise. "Hold mine, wench."

Leave it to Adam to find a loophole. Though, he reclaimed his beer once Serena jumped on Jared's back, he struggling to keep them both from going tits-up.

Donovan grabbed me around the waist again and sat us on the bench of a picnic table with me on his lap. My ex, Brock, was never into PDA, and Caine was always reserved since Donovan was around, so it took me a moment to relax—a short moment, I had to admit. Refraining from skin contact was more difficult like this.

"Brokered a bet that involved you singing?"

"Nope."

"Nope?"

"You must be mistaken."

The dimple in his left cheek caved. "You realize the guy has the mental fortitude of an excited toddler?"

I fake gasped. "Bad leader. You can't pop into your Coveners head whenever you're jealous."

His laugh rumbled inside his chest and against my back. I half-turned to him and my arm grazed his. I was close enough to see his pupils pinpoint and then dilate.

"Oops. My bad."

"No complaints from me." Goosebumps trailed behind his fingertip as he ran them down my arm. Whatever vision it triggered was high on the pleasurable scale, though I didn't get to glimpse it with him.

Amongst the others in drunken debates about who had the better rack or abs or whatever inane conversations that helped avoid the horror of the next night, I would feel his touch on my exposed shoulder, arm, or thigh and would experience the resulting twinge. Testing or teasing himself, I didn't know, but I couldn't deny I enjoyed the contact.

Not that I let the others see this. He was discreet and most were too busy testing their livers to notice.

A flash of myself at Aunt Lacey's at the first coven meeting hit me, it playing from Donovan's perspective. I stuck close to Kim, eyes wide and guarded, scanning the room. He found himself checking me out instead of doing his readings, until he annoyed himself into sneaking away and grabbing a drink.

His glass disappeared, shifting to looking over me on the floor of Aunt Lacey's after I had been stabbed at work by my drunken neighbour. Confusion, curiosity, obsession, and guilt filtered through the memory. Longing was overwhelming and worsened as the memory shifted again to our first kiss in Aunt Lacey's backyard. Lust ruled, but when we snapped out of the emotional cycle, longing resumed. A deep yearning to understand why and where it came from thundered through me.

Pain in my chest spread out to my arms and the heavy emotions lifted, the memories thinning, until faint images and mumblings of the Coveners became clear. He had overwhelmed me, unable to take the burden all at once as visions weren't my norm.

The sensation of apology crossed the connection without words. I swallowed and dropped my chin, trying to settle myself as he tightened his grip around my waist, grounding me, before dropping back into my head with another set of memories. Light-hearted ones this time, ones filled with smiles and laughter, a balm to the engulfing helplessness of the last.

"Bathroom break!"

A swift yank on my arm ripped me from Donovan's grip and sent me crashing into the grass. Serena strong-armed me to my feet and dragged me along with Kim and her as I struggled to adjust to the dark backyard instead of the sunlit conversation at Aunt Lacey's. I looked back to see Donovan standing by the picnic table, his shock and disappointment railing through the connection.

"Do you suddenly require urination assistance? I'm sure there's a spell for that." We wobbled our way in the dark, heading towards the house as they didn't want to use the outdoor bathroom options, even if they were the fanciest bathrooms on wheels I've ever seen.

"No, but you were either about to cry or come. Seemed like a good moment to stop whatever was happening with you and your man." Serena hooked her arm with mine as Kim laughed. "You already broke the deal with Jared. No sense in embarrassing yourself for no reason. You're welcome."

"Relax yourself. Are we even going the right way?" The lights from the tents all over the property were confusing.

"If that ribbony light thing is going the right way, then yup." Kim pointed in front of us and to the left.

"The what?" I squinted. "I don't see anything."

"Me either." Serena's slur had me laughing.

Kim stopped, looking behind us a moment, and then looked forward again. Serena and I followed her line of sight and then looked at each other, breaking down into giggles.

"What're ya doing, girl?" Serena grabbed and shook Kim's shoulder. "I need to pee."

Moonlight shone off Kim's red hair as she looked around us. The crease between her eyes deepening. "I've got GPS."

Laughter blurted out of both Serena and I, Serena hinged over like she may piss herself right there.

Kim re-hooked our arms and pulled a hobbling Serena along. "This way, girls."

It turned out the ribbon-like light Kim was following led us right to the house. While waiting in the small line for the bathroom, she explained she had been thinking about the house, then the tent, then bonfire, to test herself. When she switched focus, so did the light. She looked around us as if following the light to where she was thinking of, testing it, and laughing to herself before blinking it away.

"You kick ass." Serena slurred again, her arm draped over Kim's shoulders. "You probably won't die tomorrow."

Kim's brow arched. "Thanks?"

"Damn, 'cuz."

"No, for real." Serena straightened, but swayed on her feet. "We could be fuckin' worm food tomorrow. You, me, our girl here, your dumb-ass brother, even your man. And your other man." I rolled my eyes at her. "Oh! Mr. Caramel, too." She dropped her head like she might sob. Kim and I laughed at her nickname for Jared. "All of us could be done tomorrow. Damn, that's messed up."

Hearing Serena's drunken epiphanies were nothing profound, but factual. I would much rather get lost in Donovan's trip down memory lane than deal with reality. I snuck into the bathroom next, closing and locking the door between myself and Serena's complaints. I was too sober for a world-is-ending conversation.

I pulled open the door when I was done. Joelly stepped in front of me. My heart squeezed before she was pulled back by a dose of Hinapouri's magic. The warrior pushed her into the bathroom behind me and followed Joelly in. Guess Hinapouri was on bathroom duty. Serena and Kim's extra loud voices came from the bottom level.

I headed towards the stairs. Before my foot hit the first step, I was launched backwards by a steeled arm around my waist lifting me off my feet.

"Shhhhh."

I spun, the grip on me loosening. Donovan was at my back, pulling me into the small kid's room.

"What are you doing?"

"I followed to make sure Hinapouri had a handle on Joelly since she made for the house soon after you did."

I grinned. "I'm pretty sure Hinapouri's more experienced at security detail."

"Not when it comes to my sister." His dimples caved.

"Ahh. Okay."

A déjà vu moment tickled with familiarity. Not surprising, given his closeness.

"Yeah, so it occurred to me the only way to ensure your safety would be to corral you in here while Joelly's distracted. Now she won't know where you are."

"Sounds like a well-formulated plan."

"Unless you wanna go play sorority sisters with Serena and Kim? I'm sure a 'Coven Girl's Gone Wild' could break out any second."

A small head tilt and smile said I wasn't leaving.

My eyes fluttered shut as a spark of power ignited in my stomach —sweat-covered skin kneading under my fingers.

I moaned and opened my eyes to see Donovan's stare darkened with a tentative eagerness. His projection had me braced against the door so my knees wouldn't give out.

"Manipulator at heart." My voice came out raspy.

With the quick visual, I couldn't tell when the vision was from. All slick skin and sensations were as disorienting as they were tempting.

"Like you can talk." He hovered inches from me. "You started it. In front of a crowd of people no less. You're lucky I've kept mine private." I giggled, remembering the result I received. "Thought you were ignoring me?"

I shrugged and dragged a fingertip down his cheek to his jawline. "Trying out a new trick."

He lifted his chin and inhaled as a vision took him over, the sensation of whatever he saw driving through us and causing him to brace a hand against the door behind me. His body pressed against mine before I broke the skin contact.

His eyes fluttered open. "See? You pretend this isn't what you want. We both know you're rebelling against nothing except yourself."

"Maybe you're not rebelling enough."

A sly smile pulled at his lips. "Why bother?"

He hesitated and then kissed me with bruising pressure. The fraction of me that screamed to take a step back and re-evaluate joined the rest of me that screamed for him. He hoisted me up against the door. I locked my legs around his waist.

He pulled away a moment. "Wait."

I panted, already out of breath. "Don't even—"

He bowed his head between us and mumbled something in a different language.

"Pillow talk?"

He shook his head. "Spell. Now we won't have interruptions."

"Smart thinkin'."

He lifted me from the door, my arms sliding around his shoulders. The old springs of the bed bounced beneath me, making me giggle as Donovan settled between my thighs and kissed me again. A vision hit him, but he reached up to cradle my head to kiss me deeper, fighting against it. I rolled my hips beneath him and was rewarded with double the sensation caused by the connection.

I dug my fingers into his back and went to pull his shirt over his head. He broke our kiss and pressed up on his hands. He looked down at me, blinking as if ridding himself of his vision.

"Hot damn, babe. You're so beautiful."

I smiled. "I know you're not seeing me. It's okay."

"It's still you—"

"I know." I sat up enough to resume the kiss and pulled him down onto me.

Whatever era he saw me in, I knew he was enveloped by me. I tore his shirt over his head and lost myself to our primal emotional loop. As with the first time, no cues or instruction were required. All that mattered was the others' needs—how they could be met using the most direct action possible yet have the pleasure stretched out until our bodies were left a sweaty, shivering mess.

14

TRIVIAL TRIUMPHS

"**S**ophie!"

Startled awake, I looked around the dark, taking a moment for the walls and furniture to come into focus.

What the fuck? Where—? Ranlyn's. Right. Wait, did I hear—?

"Yes. I am outside the room."

I looked towards the door and saw Donovan next to me, sleeping on his stomach with his face turned towards me.

Oh, shitsnacks.

"While I am thrilled you and Donovan have found your way to each other, your Elders request your presence."

Donovan stirred next to me. We had fallen asleep touching, so he was still stuck in a vision.

I sat to pull out my clothes for the day from my bag. Donovan snapped out of his vision and awoke. Slight confusion skipped across the connection. The weight of his stare at my back was difficult to ignore or concentrate on what I was trying to find.

I ran my fingers through my hair, hoping to escape the room

without looking like I got down with a leaf blower since there wasn't a mirror in the child's room.

Donovan stretched and rolled onto his back. Sleep pulled at my eyelids, telling me he was giving in to our tiredness.

He gave in while I fought against it. "No fun."

"Mhmm. I'm assuming they have a reason for waking us up. Probably one that constitutes pants."

The mattress depressed behind me. When I turned, he pulled me into a passionate kiss that broke my mood for all of thirty seconds. He pulled away before we were caught up in an emotional loop. He flashed me a dimpled grin and went about gathering clothes from the ground to put on.

I enjoyed the short-lived sight of him unclothed, then buried a flare of anxiety by pulling my shirt over my head.

"See you downstairs." He smiled and closed the door behind him.

Should I have stopped him and talked about last night? Did we need to? Ugh. Probably the adult thing to do instead of avoiding it. I overanalyzed enough shit already, why not add more? If I planned on seeing this through as I had in past lives, I had to be honest with myself and face it head on. Not now, since people were waiting, but at some point.

I exhaled and rushed to get the rest of myself ready before Vincent came back and dragged me out of here.

———

The meeting was a reiteration of our responsibilities. With it being crunch-time, Ranlyn wanted to ensure everyone had complete understanding of their roles. Many had questions about the process of breaking down the netting, but he said they wouldn't know what needed to be done until the moment came—not at all comforting.

Breakfast was next on the menu. Feed the masses, hope they don't die, or at least stop them from complaining. That's how most of the Coveners and Ballard members saw it as we ended up at the same group of picnic tables. Not that they were complaining while stuffing their mouths with high protein and greasy foods.

"So, Donovan has a nice ass." Kim made a few laugh and make kissing noises, besides my brother who groaned.

I was pretty sure Kim didn't need to see my eyes beneath my dark sunglasses to get the full effect of my glare.

"What? You wouldn't answer so I did a spell to see through the door. Not my fault his pants were off."

Another round of giggles was choked off.

"Your fault you can't take a hint." Donovan plopped down a single serving carton of lemonade in front of me.

I mumbled a startled "Thanks" taking a second to recognize what he gave me, then a moment longer to dip into surprise at him doting on me.

Donovan put down a plate full of every buffet option in front of him. "A locked door sends a clear message of being not fucking interested in answering." He tore off a piece of bacon and popped it into his mouth. "How's Toad, by the way?"

"You know his name's Frog. And he's fine. Asshole."

I held onto the lemonade. The memory of being in Diluculo in Aunt Lacey's cabin kitchen, of admitting to loving Donovan, bubbled up. My hands had been wrapped around a sweating glass of lemonade at the time, Donovan's hands around mine as he fought a vision and spoke of a future I thought would never come to fruition. Now, Donovan sat at my side instead of Caine. The prospective future Donovan spoke of come true, as Caine was now somewhere else.

Was the lemonade a sign of him remembering that conversation, too, or was it lemonade and nothing more?

Shit. What's the date? Calendar days were lost to the chaos of life in hiding. Caine had been free of Loring's sleeping curse for, what? A month or two? And still, finding any aspect of life resembling the days before the recurring nightmares of his curse was laughable. How the fuck did w—?

I jolted as something soft but wet pegged me in the cheek.

"Oy!" Adam waved his hands in front of him. "Get out of your head. You're puttin' the guy in a trance." He motioned to Donovan, who started eating again instead of questioning what I was obsessing about.

I touched my cheek, fingers coming back red and smelling of ketchup from the used napkin Adam had thrown at me.

I chucked the napkin back. It missed him by a long shot and landed in the middle of the table.

Adam shook his head at my pathetic attempt.

"Do you have the Anatolian Idol?" Donovan caught Olive and the rest of the table off guard with the question.

"What's an Anatolian Idol?" Blake looked up from laying his head in his arms.

Olive paused mid-way through spreading jam on her rye toast. "You don't need to question my preparations, Donovan. Senility has not followed me through my extra years—no more than any person who spent her adulthood in an asylum."

I felt the eyes of those who didn't know turn to me.

"I didn't mean to—"

"I know you didn't." Olive's smile was tight and filled with under-standing. "Yes, I am prepared."

Donovan nodded. "Ranlyn would like to meet with you to get your whereabouts pinned down for when it's time to use the Idol."

"That man." Olive tsked and shook her head. "Why have the conversation if you plan to have it more than once? I remember telling him the first time because I was certainly present for it."

Donovan shrugged and chewed his food, making no attempt to comment further.

Olive freed herself from the picnic bench. "I will return once I set your forgetful Elder straight, Firefly." She patted my shoulder and left across the grass to find Ranlyn.

Less time had passed since Olive was out of The Royal than when Caine was awakened from his sleeping curse, not that you could tell. If I ever needed a reminder of true survival, all I needed was to think of Olive's strength.

"I'm buying a sweet new guitar, headers, and a van big enough to haul band gear." Adam and Kevin high-fived over Denise's head, making her flinch.

I wrestled with opening my lemonade carton. "Did you start selling your underwear online?"

"I totally should. I'd be raking it in."

Denise made a throaty noise. "Gross."

Adam sent a sly smile her way.

"Why haven't you checked your bank?" Serena slurped on her straw until her cup was empty.

"Why would I?" I looked at Adam. "You didn't really get money, did you?"

"We all did," Kevin answered in place of my brother.

Serena nodded when I turned to her to confirm. "Olive paid out to all the Ballard members yesterday."

"How did you check your account? We're in the middle of nowhere."

She motioned towards Donovan. "At your man's place."

A snap of anger flared across the connection. "Why are you using my internet?"

Serena's expression screwed up. "Same reason everyone else is. What's the difference when people are staying there?"

"What?" Donovan's voice rumbled in a low growl.

"Donovan skipped the sharing is caring stage of life." I couldn't imagine him experiencing the same 'growing up in the sandbox' in his father's coven. Besides Joelly, I didn't know if he had other siblings, but he never spoke of friends. A what's-mine-is-mine mentality made sense. Though Aunt Lacey meant for the space to be utilized by others, she left it to him. Other than Coven nights and us hiding out for a bit, no one else got an invite.

"Let it go." Physically calming him was useless. No one needed him tearing through the portal and kicking everyone out of his house.

His bouncing knee shook the bench until I grabbed his thigh. We weren't the only ones on the bench.

"Either way—" Serena leaned towards me. "—with a hundred grand lining your pockets, you can afford to get some wheels of your own. Your feet will thank you."

I gasped. "A hundred grand?"

Hazard pay, protection detail, whatever Olive earmarked it as, didn't equal out to owing us so much money. For the three of us living pay-check to pay-check on dreams of careers and minimal parental purse-strings on tap, one-hundred grand was a fortune. Plus, what would I do with it in the next twelve hours? I didn't even have time to will it to someone if Caine and I didn't make it out of the Creation. How would my parents deal with it? My dad didn't even know about my mother's witchy bloodline.

"How 'bout you plan on surviving?"

The sharpness of Donovan's tone threw me off as he had responded out loud to my internal conflict. The edge of his glare was cutting.

Joelly charged into our peripheral vision. "Make them reverse it!"

Vincent was on her heels. He huffed and braced his hands on his hips, cheeks reddened with anger the colour of her lipstick and matching nails.

Donovan made a deep-chested laugh, choosing to focus on his breakfast.

I squinted at the addition of Vincent's soul. "Reverse what?"

"You were made aware of—"

Joelly spun and got in Vincent's face. "I was told the Binding was temporary!"

He didn't flinch and kept calm. "Would you have permitted the spell otherwise?"

"Like you had a choice." Donovan mumbled over the congealed pork between his teeth.

Joelly scowled at Donovan's back, snatched the knife from his hand, and thrust it down at him. A collective gasp came from those at the table.

Donovan turned with blurring speed and telekinetically drove the knife into Joelly's thigh, her fist still gripping the handle.

Breathless squeaks escaped Joelly's lips as I looked on in silent shock.

"You know better than to attack someone stronger than you." Donovan wrapped his fingers around Joelly's and yanked out the knife, then took it from her hand and tossed in the table before returning to his food.

"Heal her." I could have done it myself, but why should I? His mess, his responsibility.

Donovan looked at me, the tug on the connection giving a loud and clear, "Are you fucking kidding me?"

Babysitting was one thing. Sitting in a germ-infested emergency room was beyond the call of duty and Vincent looked content to let Joelly bleed through her jeans.

Stabbing people in open view of the Coven made Donovan a leader to be feared, not respected. He was filled with bitter rage right now, but he would regret this later when he was thinking straight.

I wasn't budging and he knew it.

He huffed and turned enough to grasp Joelly's thigh, causing her to cry out and grab onto Vincent. If not for the blood stain and her red-cheeked snarl, anyone walking by now would have kept walking. Those at the table, however, were still sitting with their mouths hung open.

Joelly's clenched fists shook at her sides. "I'll be tied down like a dog if I'm left bound when it's time to fight."

"Nah. Bosco can roam free." Donovan chewed on a piece of bacon, ignoring Joelly behind him. "You'll be penned like cattle."

"This is bullshit!"

Donovan seethed beneath the surface as he focused on his meal.

I looked at Vincent, hoping he would get the hint that this conversation was over. He did, grabbing her arm.

Joelly pulled away. "I'm on your side, Seer."

Donovan shot to his feet, placing himself in Joelly's face before I could say anything. "You're lucky Ranlyn forbade me to murder you."

The tightness in my chest from his outburst made it a struggle to inhale.

Joelly leaned in an inch. "As if your Elders know anything about you. If they did, they'd know your word was worthless."

Donovan scoffed. "Doesn't matter. I'm not hiding my kill count and you're still the fuck-up who walked into the enemy's camp and white-flagged it. Your death will come easier than you deserve." He looked around her to Vincent. "Make sure whoever's on babysitting duty keeps the traitor from coming anywhere near Sophie. And for Joelly's own safety, keep her far away from me."

Vincent grabbed Joelly's arm again, this time not letting her pull free.

"I'll be in this fight, brother! With my powers restored!"

"Keep your companion more adequately in check."

"Ha. Right. Keep your prisoner in check and I won't have to."

My "companion" had a grudge beyond any shenanigans Joelly has pulled in the last few weeks. Lecturing him about his attitude would be about as useful as trying to scrub his kill count, whatever the fuck that happened to be.

Shit. Should I be asking about his kill count?

"Set him straight, I did." Olive used my shoulder to help her get back into her seat, breaking down the images of Donovan massacring people running through my brain. "Me and the Idol will be in place without a hiccup."

"That's awesome." Adam deadpanned. "Donovan just stabbed his sister."

"Excuse me?"

Donovan nodded without making eye contact and stuck another breakfast sausage into his mouth.

"Then I'm certain she deserved it, if only for the aggravation of her presence."

Adam sucked his teeth. "Savage."

I gave my brother a withering look as Donovan inwardly celebrated with the others who laughed.

I tapped Olive on the shoulder.

"What? I'm sure she did."

"Not that. Why are you paying the Ballard members? That's your money. One-hundred grand is not compensation, it's a payoff. You've got nothing to be guilty about."

Her forehead creased. "You bet your horses there's no need for guilt. You haven't a clue the amount of dollars set aside for this family, sitting away untouched in some bank for decades. The money transferred to members' accounts amounts to pennies." She patted my hand. "Don't you worry, Firefly. This is the way of the heir and how our Coven has run since we earned the resources to do so. Any issues you encounter or questions regarding tax implications can be directed to the family accountant. Donate it to charity if you feel so inclined. The accountant can advise you of how that works as well."

"Gotta be breathing to spend it, right?" Donovan's disdainful tone matched his grin. "No shoe sales in the Afterlife."

"Shoe sales? Sophie?" Kim glared at him. "She has less than five pairs and all but one pair are functional."

"It's fine. I'll wait until after and buy some shit-kickers. Then I'll break back into the Creation and boot fuck my ancestor to death."

Donovan made a humourless chuckle. "As long you make it out. He'll have company until his Puppets break their seams, so you can skip through Diluculo in your shit-kickers."

"Break their seams?" Denise paused half way through feeding Bosco something. He snatched it from her and nipped her finger. I would have laughed if not for trying to figure out what Donovan meant. "Like, die?"

"No."

His side-eyed glance told me I was wrong.

"Really? They'll die in there?"

"Souls don't camp well with intruders. You know that." He chinned in Kim's direction. "You would've been a rotting husk by now. What'd you think was gonna happen?"

Kim made a throaty noise. "Did someone make your sausages out of your favourite pig, Charlotte?"

"I'd rather be the spider than breakfast. Pretend the Puppeteer is putting them away like action figures for when he's bored all you want. He's probably figured out a way to extend their lives, but like Charlotte—" he sneered, "—they will eventually die."

Blake gasped. "Or be wondering corpse puppets?"

Jared elbowed Blake. "Zombies, idiot. They're called zombies."

"You're the idiot."

"Jesus." Denise rolled her eyes. "You're both idiots. And both will probably end up as idiot zombie Puppets."

I heard my name called and squinted into the field of Magics in search of the voice. Caine was walking towards the tables.

What the fizz? The voice wasn't deep enough for it to be him.

Jet, Caine's cousin, popped out from behind him and waved, then ran towards me, her blonde ponytail swaying behind her.

"Jet?" I got up and hugged her. She wrapped her arms around me and squealed. "What are you doing here?"

"What'da'ya think? My parents can't keep me from this." She thumbed at Caine. "Or this guy."

Caine, Uncle Eli, and Aunt Bernadine fought their fair share alongside Caine's father, Daniel. When Caine found them, they had already folded the lifestyle and vowed to stay out of it. Caine finding them meant he got special training for his persuasion gifts, but it also looked to have stoked Jet's fire to fight.

"What about Andy?" Caine's question aligned with my own. I was happy he asked it.

Jet's smile vanished. "He's with mom and dad."

"Did you—Did you ask Andy if you had the spots?"

I looked at Caine. He stared back as if the question was over the line, then waited for Jet to answer. How could I not ask if Andy saw evidence his mother was going to die?

"Believe me, I wanted to. Before I left, I hugged him and waited for him to say something. Waited to see the look he gets when he glimpses the spots. I've seen it too many times to mistake it. But no, I couldn't ask him. I think he would have told me. After your talk with him, he feels a lot more confident letting us know when someone has the spots. A lot more."

"My bad."

"Nah, it's a good thing. Though it seems every other day he finds some poor soul with the spots in the places of future injury and I'd have to see his tortured disappointment when I stop him from telling them about it. The pinky swear thing is a right ol' pain in my ass. Thanks for teaching him that one."

"What can I say? It worked." I shrugged as Jet smiled and rolled her eyes.

15

THE PRICE WE PAY

Caine introduced Jet to those at my table, then sat with his cousin at the table behind us.

"Good to see you two are still friends." She looked between Caine and me.

We both stumbled over our shock of the observation. Were we still friends? I didn't think so, and neither did he, but we've made strides in the right direction. Still. Explaining that to Jet in front of everyone else? No thanks.

"Oh, wait—" Kim tapped the table, stealing Jet's attention. "You're the one who can fly, right?"

Kim with the save. Gotta love the woman.

"That's badass!" Of course, Blake was impressed. All the Coveners were.

I remembered seeing it for the first time in her family barn as she and Caine trained. Flying wasn't the bulk of her talent, but was nothing you could forget.

A demonstration was rallied for. Jet resisted, promising once the fists started flying, so would she. "Where will I be during this scuffle? Please tell me out front."

"What drives you to presume your talents are useful?" Everyone turned to see Vincent standing in full-on glare mode at Jet, arms crossed, expression stern.

"Why do you care?" Jet tilted her head as she questioned Vincent.

"You are unknown to this Coven and you are a Berisford. To any one of our kind, that genetic detail alone requires I make inquires."

Jet scoffed with an "Is he kidding?" expression at me.

Caine sprung to his feet. "Do you think I'd bring her in if she was like the Berisfords you're talking about?"

"I'd tell you if her soul was Tainted. Nothing to worry about. Unless you want me to read her soul for all the hidden secret revenge plots from her ancestors."

"Whoa!" Jet lifted her hands. "I'm not letting anyone read my birth certificate, let alone my soul."

"Then view her soul colour through my memories. We're telling the truth."

"Would you suggest I lie as well?" Olive's tone had a hint of challenge. "I, too, see this young woman's soul colour. Nothing about it should concern you."

Vincent exhaled. "Joelly has escaped."

"What?" A collective question from all except Donovan, who shook his head, his dimples caved in another expression holding no joy or surprise.

"How?" The question came from all sides.

"She slipped out while using the washroom. I was not permitted to enter the room, nor would I wish to. She used this opportunity to flee." He refocused on Jet. "Your sudden appearance would seem a mere coincidence."

"No shit." She thumbed toward the house. "She would've had to go back inside to get through the portal, so she's still around here or hitched a ride the old-fashioned way."

"Or my sister is getting her ass far enough away until she can make a call to her contact who can get her where she wants to go.

Joelly knows people in low places. One of them will fall for any bull-shit story."

"Message received." Vincent went to leave.

"That's it?" Donovan leaned onto his elbow, a slow angry burn filling the connection. "Joelly skips bail and that's it?"

"What else—?"

"—do I expect?" He stood and squared up with Vincent. "Joelly allowed herself to be captured. Then every one of our wise old Elders claimed she could be watched and given a chance to prove her claim to help us, one she never earned and made mid-throat slash. Don't worry, her powers will be bound, right?"

"Understood."

"You sure? Because last we checked, Joelly still wants to rip Sophie open and suck the juices out of her to get power she feels enti-tled to because she's dumb enough to believe a rumour, yet smart enough to crawl into the enemy's nest and get away without conse-quence. May as well have tattooed our battle plans across her ass and sent her on her way."

"No need for dramatics."

"This isn't drama. This is exactly what I said would happen and you chose to ignore me. You let her waltz around our flock, listen in on strategic battle conversations, and now she's AWOL. Just because she's here in Slovenia and not roaming her usual hunting grounds, doesn't mean she's not resourceful enough to hook up with someone who can break the Binding and lead our enemies straight for us."

"We are aware of this."

"And you're doing what about it?"

"Nothing."

"Nothing."

"As you highlighted, battle looms. Preparations are in process and chasing a millipede such as Joelly directs our attentions away from larger interests."

"No kidding. What do you think she was doing this whole time? Drawing away your attentions so at least one of the Elders, or yourself, was out of the picture. Slowing things down, no doubt manipulating every person she came in contact with."

"I am not arguing with you, am I?"

"No, but you're smug enough to attempt justifying your decision, like Sophie didn't have enough to worry about with her Puppeteer dickhead of an ancestor."

"Let us not rehash that, now." Though he was right on every point. Even Vincent's smug reaction.

"As messed up as all that is," Jet gave me a wide-eyed look, "and it is the highest calibre of messed up, unless you prefer I make the choice of where I should be when the big bad wolf comes to blow the whole lot of you to Hell, then—"

"You will be nowhere near your cousin." Vincent's thin patience with all of our judgements must have worn through.

"I can fight."

"You can fail." Yup. He wasn't holding back now. "Caine's success rides on rails as fragile as tracing paper. If Sophie's presence was not necessary, she would not be at his flank facing the same fate. I repeat, you are a Berisford. With your name comes weakness this Coven can ill afford. You risk the likelihood of your cousin ending your life when you become a Puppet."

"Aunt Lacey believed we could do this." The fact Caine brought this up surprised more than me.

"Elsa's premonition does not speak of success. Most have been proven accurate, true, as have others."

"Others like her?" Kim asked.

"Other premonitions foretelling many things. More recently, the forewarning Sophie received that had been tasked to me to unravel, though many lines have already been deciphered."

"Since we didn't have a choice when Sophie and I literally died and none of our enlightened leaders bothered to return a simple phone call, you're lucky most of it was already interpreted for you. Though the 'ancient cost' is still up for grabs."

Vincent fixed his glasses on his nose. "The ancient cost is paid by you every day since Sophie ensured your bond, living and dying as lovers onto forever. It has been paid for in lives lived since. You chose your fates. Future generations of your souls pay the price of that idealistic charm. Whether a short life of torturous bewilderment or one of exaltation in your past self's love, you pay it, and I am certain this is the first life you have been granted understanding of it."

Vincent's response was so crass everyone stilled as his information filtered through. I didn't want to look at Donovan or anyone else, but their stares were on us.

"Your Sect is neither the only constituency under the Elders care nor the only facing obscure circumstances. Your belief the Mother Coven was constructed to singularly protect your Sect is inflated to an absurd level. Elsa's decedent may have gifted you a squalid and damned existence with a Tainted upbringing, but Elsa is dead, and her charity ends there."

Donovan's power flushed through his blood and our connection like a bullet, ringing in my ears and stinging my skin. He pounced from the bench, gunning for Vincent. The impulse so strong I stood to attack him as well, containing the tiniest amount of rationale.

With a twitch of my hand inches from my side, my power pitched and obeyed the moment I needed it.

"Donovan—" My lips moved, but not even I heard the word.

This energy moved for me. Flowed from me and slowed everything down. I forced it to wrap itself around Donovan's arms, his waist, and tie him up where he stood mid-step to prevent his death or expulsion from the Coven—something he would consider a fate worse than death when thinking straight again.

He stopped, mere feet from Vincent, who had braced for the attack before straightening and looking Donovan over, confused at what had happened.

Donovan's expression morphed from enraged frustration to agony that threw his head back, gasping. He managed to turn his head my way, forehead creased, a plea on his lips I couldn't quite grasp.

"Let go of it, Sophie." Vincent's firm voice instructed from next to me. I hadn't seen him move.

Donovan crumpled to the ground onto his knees, crying out. I wanted him to stay put. Not to move, as Vincent had. This would make it more difficult for him to try.

"Sophie!"

Vincent's power invaded mine. Power drained from me so fast I collapsed forward. He caught me before I hit the ground.

Donovan was free. He looked at his hands and arms. Astonishment blazed across our connection.

"Donovan?"

Silence stretched as his shock twisted into hurt.

"Donovan?" I couldn't say more but had so many questions. Why did he feel as he did? What did I do? But I couldn't reach him. His emotions may have been a river driving eddies over me, but his head was closed off and I couldn't breach his mental barriers to peek inside even if I possessed the energy.

Springing to his feet, Donovan seemed lost. He stepped towards me and stopped before backing up a step. His knotted thoughts and indecision were a gripped fist in my chest, squeezing until my temples thumped.

He turned and walked away.

"What the hell was that?" Jet was helping Caine up. I didn't know why he was on the ground.

I watched Donovan disappear into the crowd. I stayed with him when I couldn't see him anymore, trying to hold onto him through our connection by following his emotions. They fluctuated at a high-intensity yet were so dark.

"Firefly?" Pressure on my arm was Olive's hand, but I couldn't concentrate on her.

"I... I don't understand."

Kim stood in my peripheral. "He'll cool off."

"He's not angry." What was he? Conflicted, for sure. Disappointed? No. This was worse. "He feels betrayed." After the perfection that was last night, maybe this hit him harder because of it?

"Snap out of it, Soph. It's just your link thing." Serena may have been right. I felt as Donovan did, but feeling as he did didn't answer any questions.

"Were you that broken up when Caine felt betrayed?" The resentment in Jet's tone snapped me out of Donovan's influence enough for me to turn to her.

Tears spilled down my cheeks as I looked at Caine next to her. "You have no idea."

My words hit Caine as I hadn't seen before—something close to acceptance mixed with shame.

"Let's go." Kim held my shoulders and directed me forward, telling someone else to come with us, though I didn't see who as I sunk back into the darkness surrounding Donovan.

Kim tugged on my shoulders to stop me as Vincent stepped in the way. "Sophie, this is an accomplishment."

"Back off, four eyes." Serena pushed me forward again. He didn't let up and stopped us again.

"Nya's power clicked like a switch." He snapped his fingers. "Did you feel it?"

"Doesn't matter. She's not me."

"With practice, she will be."

I shook my head, the sensation more a numbness. "I can't feel him when I'm her. I can't feel me."

He grasped my shoulder. "In time, you will learn to fuse the two."

I gasped.

Vincent pulled away.

"What'd you do?" Serena stepped toward Vincent enough for him to raise his hands.

"Sophie?" Kim stood in front of me, calling my name.

Others were around me now, their mumbled voices closing in around me, yet were mere echoes in the distance.

"*Sophie. What happened?*" Vincent's voice invaded the most, too close to ignore.

"He's gone."

More echoed voices raged around me as a yearning of jagged emptiness had me floating.

Donovan must have left through the portal. He was far away. Too far for the connection. The tether now stretched and thinned out.

Someone moved me. I was inside, sitting. People were talking. Less people. Their voices distracting me from the numbness taking over. Tugging at me to listen, to do things. I couldn't leave him. Not now. We had to hold on. So little was left. Did he know? Did he want to let go? Was anything left?

Yes. There, in the emptiness, the brush against the connection was light. He was there, defeat bearing down on him.

Not the darkness. Please don't do that to us.

16

SLICES OF TRUTH

Kim

We brought Sophie to her and Donovan's room, away from the others, and sat her on the edge of the bed. She didn't move, barely blinked, and didn't focus on us or comment when we talked about her. This wasn't right. Someone had to know what this was.

Not the first time since she was killed, I wished Aunt Lacey was here. She would know what to do or who to reach out to for answers.

"She looks like Joelly when you took her will." Serena chinned towards Caine.

"More like she finally cracked." Adam had Bosco in his arms.

"Or Autistic." Denise stood next to Adam behind me.

I turned so fast, she glared at me as if expecting me to punch her. I wanted to.

"What? She looks disconnected, stuck in her head." She huffed. "Everyone insists on honesty, though no one likes to hear it."

"Be helpful or shut up."

"Can this be rectified without Donovan's return?" Olive sat on the bed next to Sophie whose expression wasn't exactly lifeless—she was still there, brows pursed like she was thinking about something really hard, too distracted to listen to the world outside her head.

Vincent knelt in front of her, bracketed the sides of her face with his hands, and called her name. She blinked and searched, focusing on him. "What do you feel?"

We waited, anticipation building.

"Numb." Question answered, Sophie dipped back into the disconnected state she was in before.

Vincent let her face go and held one of her hands. Her fingers didn't grip his.

"I always thought if I could get her far enough away from him, it would negate their connection." Caine stood cross-armed and glassy-eyed. "Sophie never believed getting away or going on some type of vacation would create enough distance to reduce the connection. She thought it was a stupid idea. Clearly, it was."

"I could have confirmed as much." Vincent flexed to his feet, still staring down at Sophie. "I have seen this before." He exhaled and pushed up his glasses. "In one lifetime, it was pertinent they separate as Donovan had been requisitioned for battle—something all young men were expected to do, though he did not enlist willingly. Both experienced the same detachment."

I scoffed. "How could he fight like that? A child would be more primed to handle war."

He shook his head. "The distance was not continents away, as in this case, yet proved enough to monopolize his attentions, resulting in a quick death for both." He fixed his glasses again. "I buried her body myself."

Olive pressed a hand to her chest. "My word."

"We need to let Ranlyn know about this." My blood raced. "They need to be close to each other when we close up the Creations."

Caine made a throaty noise. "No way I'm facing the Puppeteer with her all out of it. She'd be a Puppet in a heartbeat. Probably Donovan at the same time and I don't need them coming after me."

"Here." Adam passed me Bosco. "We'll go get Donovan. He can't have zombie-walked too far on the other side of the portal. Come on." He volunteered Denise, though she didn't argue.

If Donovan wasn't as incapacitated as Sophie, I doubted anyone would know where to find him. I didn't know much about him outside the Coven, let alone picture his hang-out hot spots. Probably a bar, though which one, I had no clue. It made me wonder how much Sophie knew about his day-to-day activities. Did the kid have a life beyond the Coven?

Adam and Denise must have come across Ranlyn on their way out, because he shot through the bedroom door insisting on an explanation. Vincent answered his questions with personal experience beyond today's experience. As far as what caused Donovan to leave, our opinions were pure speculation and Ranlyn refused to try and ask Sophie to explain firsthand.

Ranlyn bent over to align his line of sight with Sophie's. She didn't react. "They've never been separated before?"

"From home to home does not cause such dissociation."

"She pushed the negative effects away when Donovan was—" I paused and looked at Ranlyn, "—in your custody." Ranlyn shifted, a bit uneasy. "She barely managed that. Clearly, this is too much. Skipping through the veil doesn't even do this, which is weird considering that's a much bigger jump than hitchin' it to Europe."

Ranlyn tilted his head. "The Creation is across the veil, but it exists in the exact spot the field lays."

Olive kissed the back of Sophie's hand. "So, when one of them slips through, they're still essentially right next to each other."

"That's the theory, though I suppose this lends credence to it." Ranlyn let out a heavy exhale. "Get her downstairs and comfortable, so there's more space to work with her if needed. I'll keep the masses outside."

The door opened as Ranlyn was headed towards it. Roe barrelled in, getting into Ranlyn's face. "You locked us down?"

"Of course not."

Adam and Denise came in behind Roe. "We tried to go through the portal, but it's gone or deactivated or something."

Ranlyn raced out of the room. I followed, stopping at the top of the stairs as Ranlyn pushed others out of the way as they crowded around where the portal entrance was. Nothing happened when he walked over the spot. Someone had closed the portal. If Ranlyn created the portal, then it should have been cancelled out by him and on this side of the portal, not the other. My portal knowledge was close to nil, but you didn't have to read Ranlyn's mind to know this wasn't right.

Vincent carried Sophie downstairs and sat her on the couch as Ranlyn cleared out the house. The few of us who already knew what Sophie was going through stuck around while the other Elders were called in. Lewis and Priscilla were in the living room already. Once they saw Sophie, they refused to leave, though Ranlyn didn't push too hard to make them. They were family.

Before we had a mutiny, Ranlyn reset the portal to ensure no one felt trapped or forced into the upcoming battle, giving them the choice to bow out. Something Miklos and Hinapouri believed was too generous and thought if they were cowards enough to run away, they should do so on foot and not with the convenience of a portal.

Witnessing a portal creation was like being at opening night of a highly anticipated movie. Ranlyn kept his voice low during the incantation, so I was unable to pick out a single word to recreate the process. Not a big deal. The power alone was exciting as hell. Sensing actual power now was overwhelming and so much more than I thought it could be. It snapped at the air around everyone in the room and gave me a rush in response. I got why it was so difficult for Sophie to adjust to. As much a shooting star to the bloodstream as it was a gun to the back of your head. A thrill either way.

The portal began to take shape, beginning like heatwaves off pavement and then condensing into something more solid, expanding, and thinning back out until you could see through to the wall behind it.

"Good to go?" Adam moved toward the portal.

Ranlyn stuck his arm out, blocking him. "Someone's coming through."

The portal destabilized again. It shifted, a pulse of power was a frenzy of energy in my chest.

Adam and Denise backed up as Veata walked through the portal.

All but Sophie jumped, either to attack or in surprise of the Elder.

Veata raised her hand, saying a strong unknown word in a language I thought might be Korean.

I was frozen on the spot, my own hands up as if I could stop an attack, but I was caught off guard and useless. I looked around me and saw everyone else frozen in place as well.

Fuck. She didn't kill us right away. Was the Puppeteer going to torture us first?

"I am the Elder I was before forced a Puppet." Veata spoke with a calm smoothness. "I no longer carry threat to my Coven. I no longer seek to destroy it. Perform any and all experiments you see fit to conciliate your mistrust."

I lost sight of her as she moved across the living room. The sound of a kitchen stool scuffed the floor behind us before we were released from her spell.

Hinapouri moved too fast for me to see, popping up in front of Veata with materialized weapons spearing down at the cloudy-eyed woman. Power was thick in the air around me, causing my chest to tighten and twitch, though none of it was from Veata. She didn't react to Hinapouri's threat. If Hinapouri looked at me with the same amount of salivating hatred, I would shit myself.

Hinapouri's weapons remained raised as threads of rope material-ized from the ether and snaked themselves around Veata, strapping her arms to her body, hands tucked beneath the rope to keep her from using them as a weapon. An incantation erased all signs of Veata's mouth and eyes, a hood added to further immobilize her senses if the incantation failed.

Ranlyn and Miklos circled Veata as well. A conversational lull took over as the Elders weren't speaking to each other. The spears hovered, the rope held tight, and Veata didn't fight against the loss of her senses.

With some of the Sect present and Donovan out of commission, it was up to me to keep things together, but I couldn't stop my hands from shaking from the adrenaline. This was so out of my league.

"This is going to be a tad one-sided if she doesn't have lips." Adam's voice made me flinch. I took in a deep breath and reminded myself I wasn't dealing with this alone.

"I will relay significant information." Vincent didn't have to offer us a telepathic peek into the process. Elder affairs weren't our business, but I was happy to keep quiet and hang around until they booted us out.

For a long time, Vincent never offered a word. I was dying to know what they were saying to her and thought the rest of it would stay a caption-less silent movie until Vincent cleared his throat and explained.

"Caine's gift was suggested by Hinapouri. Yet, if the Puppeteer is present within Veata, Caine's gift would not prove strong enough to overtake Evaristus's will. Knowing this, they thought Veata may take the baited opportunity to fake her way through his persuasion. She refused."

Denise went to say something. I shushed her before she got a syllable out. Intel was one thing, commentary was another. The fact she didn't ignore me and speak anyway was odd. What Sophie said to her made a bigger difference than I thought possible, though I doubted it would last long.

"Veata has no clue how she was taken over. She found herself losing time, not remembering letting Loring into Diluculo or how, however, Loring is one to talk too much. Once Veata was caged with other Magics too hard to control when their shells were left unused, Loring blathered on about her part in the death of her previous Leaders." Vincent turned back to the Elders and listened, intrigued. "They have Donovan."

I let out a light gasp and looked at Sophie. She didn't react to the news. Did she know what was going on? Sure didn't seem like it. Not that you could tell, since she was sitting so still, facing the fire with Bosco's head on her thigh. As the flames jumped, I saw the sheen on her skin. She was sweating and red-cheeked. A reaction to something? She wasn't close enough to the fire to be overheated.

"Veata had been growing stronger, recapturing flecks of herself when the Puppeteer took over. Not enough to regain control, yet sufficient to be present with him as he controlled her. She remembers grabbing Donovan as he exited the portal. She and the Eradicators were waiting. Since he was plunged into the same dissociative state as Sophie, his capture proved effortless. The Puppeteer was also responsible for the portal's failure. Once Donovan was given over to the devotees, Veata was released."

"Why not kill her like the other Elders?" Keeping silent was too much for Lewis.

With so many questions rattling around in my brain, I was surprised others weren't trying to talk more. Though it didn't seem like the Elders were aware we were around at all, far too busy to care.

"Evaristus did not kill the preceding Elders. Loring did." Evaristus was running the game, not Loring—like when he killed the last Elders. We couldn't expect things to be the same as when we faced Loring in Diluculo and I didn't know enough about Evaristus to anticipate his next move.

"Release with retained facilities leaves Veata with the knowledge of the blood she was forced to spill. Some would argue this psychological warfare worse than death. Senseless guilt has its pleasures for one such as Evaristus. Donovan is also of relation to Elsa and with the history they held, controlling one of her kin would be of great reward for the inconveniences she caused Evaristus over the years."

"I doubt he expected this." I placed my hand on Sophie's forehead and cheeks. "She's burning up."

Olive took off her scarf, said a quick spell, and placed it against Sophie's forehead. I didn't know the spell, but I recognized 'frigus' as the Latin word for cold. Whatever was going on with Donovan, it had to help them both.

"She's so confused." Priscilla's sad eyes looked over Sophie. It took a moment for me to remember she had the power to sense other's needs. "She's doing circles, trying to understand what's happening, but can't gather her thoughts enough to figure out why she can't be with him."

"Move!" Vincent's order came a second before Ranlyn and Miklos dragged Veata off her chair, shouldered through everyone, and forced Veata to her knees in front of the fire.

"Vincent?" He didn't answer me. He stood with his arms out, trying to get everyone to back up and stay out of the way.

Hinapouri disappeared into the room with the round table and returned a moment later with her arms full. A bowl cupped in her tattooed hands was topped with two logs of thin grey-barked wood. As Hinapouri rounded the couch, she threw the logs onto the flames. They caught fire and spit a plume of ash and embers into the room.

"Burning her is a bit much, no?" Veata may have been guilty of weakness the Puppeteer exploited but burning someone was low.

"Do not interfere." Hinapouri didn't need to tell me twice. If I changed my mind, I didn't know how the hell I was supposed to make them listen.

I looked at Vincent, hoping he would step in if things got out of control, though I didn't know if I could trust him to move against them. He wasn't an Elder and going up against one was probably not something he wanted to do.

"No need." His tone was firm. "Tests to ensure Veata has regained herself without the Puppeteer piggy-backing through our resistance are necessary. Leave if it becomes overwhelming."

Okay. Vincent wasn't my backpack. Noted.

Veata's hood was raised to uncover her chin. They altered the spell and returned her mouth, which gaped open and dragged in a desperate breath before Miklos forced her head back. The rim of the bowl was shoved to her lips without concern for her teeth. Hinapouri force-fed Veata whatever liquid was in the bowl, some spilling down the sides of her thin lips, soaking her chin and soiled clothing.

I bit my tongue. I didn't like this but didn't know how this test was supposed to go. I relaxed a bit when the bowl was empty and Veata could breathe again.

Dropping the empty bowl with a reverberating clank to the wooden floor, Hinapouri turned to the hearth. "Tinei!" The fire went out with a sucking '*whoomph*'.

Miklos removed Veata's hood, her eyes still missing as he grabbed the scruff of Veata's neck and pushed her body closer to the fireplace as the smoke billowed out, and then ordered her to breathe.

Sophie flew back into the couch cushions with a wail, knocking Bosco to the floor. She scratched at her throat.

I rushed to grab her hands, her fingernails coming away bloody. She thrashed in my arms. I yelped as Sophie was pulled from my hands and onto the floor in Hinapouri's grasp.

A flash of light zapped my vision as energy poured into the room. I covered my face and ducked into the couch, blind and bloated with my own power trying to join the fight. A loud crash and more yelling fell into the background as I fought to keep myself together. When I could open my eyes again, I blinked away dark spots as Vincent was kneeling on the ground with Sophie cradled in this lap. He was turned to keep her protected as he had held out his arm towards Hinapouri.

On the ground and twitching was not a way I ever pictured the strong Maori Warrior, but Vincent was doing something to her and she was powerless against him.

Ranlyn was reaching as well, but as a plea. "Vincent. Don't—"

"Force her compliance or she dies."

Shit. For a moment, I thought he meant Sophie dies, but he meant Hinapouri. So much for thinking he didn't have my back. No matter what, he sure as hell had Sophie's. He was like a leashed pitbull protecting it's owner.

Ranlyn took a slow step toward Vincent. "I would never let her hurt Sophie."

"She is a Sorcerer."

The room stilled. Many of us looked at each other, confused by this as Sophie writhed in Vincent's arms, still choking in small coughs.

Miklos growled. "You're protecting a traitor."

"Stop!" Ranlyn ordered Miklos and turned back to Vincent, his tone softening. "We'll figure it out. Please, let go of Hinapouri's soul."

Ohmygod. Her soul? Vincent had Hinapouri's soul? I knew he was a Soul Extractor, but damn.

Vincent didn't look like he was concerned with Ranlyn's demands. "The Ash tree smoke, that is what Sophie is reacting to. She is a Sorcerer. You are wise enough not to execute an innocent based on falsehoods. Years spent fighting one evil after the other, now the Puppeteer has you spooked enough you are turning on your own."

"We're not—"

"*They* are. While you may be the sensible one, your fellow Elders are war hungry."

Ranlyn didn't argue.

"Sophie's reaction was unlike that of someone possessed by evil. Olive, Lewis, and Caine would have suffered the same misery if they were seated closer."

Adam and Serena's powers were still caged, or they would have, too, I gathered. I don't know what would have happened to Sophie if she was left in the ash wood smoke much longer, but I had to remember to notate the reaction. What a thing to be allergic to.

"Umm, is that a normal reaction for a Sorcerer?" Adam pointed down at Sophie. Her arms were bleeding. We watched as her skin sliced open and blood ran from her elbow to her wrist as if invisible knives were cutting her up.

Vincent turned his head to look, as if fearing Miklos may take the opportunity to strike. "No, it is not."

"Fuck. Grab a towel!" Serena shoved Adam, who was closer, towards the kitchen.

He grabbed a tea towel from a basket on the counter and ran back to press it against her forearm.

"They play." Veata was still tied up and trying to balance herself on her knees. Her voice was frail as her throat, evil or not, burned from the exposure to the smoke she swallowed. The rest of her facial features were returned to her. Maybe because Hinapouri was down?

Vincent dropped his hand to help tend to Sophie.

Hinapouri sat up with a sobbing gasp, her soul returned. "You—!"

Ranlyn spun at her. "Attack and you'll regret it." He then looked at Miklos, who bent to Hinapouri's side. "Both of you."

Hinapouri shoved away Miklos' attempts to help her up, getting herself to her feet. I watched them, but Ranlyn had moved to Sophie as well, his back to them as the tension hung. I don't know why Ranlyn trusted them to listen to him, but I hoped he had some pull to keep them in line.

Caine bent to undo Veata's rope, struggling to get her untied. "They play? Who is they?"

"Devotees." Veata coughed.

Hinapouri snapped her fingers and the rope around Veata disappeared. Caine jumped at this and then helped Veata to her feet and onto the couch. Pricilla handed her a glass of water. Veata gulped it down, murmured a few words and the glass refilled itself. She gulped that down, too, and handed the empty glass back.

She wiped her mouth and took a moment. "In Diluculo, some of Evar's underlings grow weary with the monotony of servitude. To pass the time, they torture the vulnerable, those without their will intact or the ability to retaliate. Any excuse to kill if they dare try."

Serena made a throaty noise. "They're cutting up Donovan for kicks? Lovely crowd we're dealing with."

"This is no game, Seedling." Hinapouri had her arms crossed

with a military stance. "These thorn tears are equal to skipping rocks on a pond. Usual schemes by the damned are much bloodier."

Hinapouri, wizard with words, shut Serena up tight.

Since the slices occurred with sharpened blades far beyond our reach, we were helpless to stop it. The property was filled with healers, but Vincent feared healing Sophie would make the game more interesting for whoever was torturing Donovan. We couldn't leave them like this for long. They would bleed out. If it meant small doses of healing, then it would be done, but for now, the wounds were wrapped and nothing else.

Ranlyn and Caine paced around Sophie as she mewled and bled, Olive kneeling at her side. No Ballard, Berisford, or other present was strong enough to break Sophie and Donovan's bond. Relentless slicing continued every few minutes and more blood would spill to the floor.

"Anything else we Sorcerers should know to avoid besides burning Ash wood?" Serena got a shrug from Olive, who didn't know.

Ranlyn dragged his thumb across his bottom lip, half present while stuck in inward thoughts. "Under normal circumstances, this would not be of dire concern, but many herbs affect Sorcerers."

"Lovely." Serena sighed and craned her neck to the side until it cracked.

"What now? We wait for demands?" We looked at Denise, confused on what demands she meant. "To get Donovan back?"

Serena sneered. "That's too Mel Gibson, even for you, light bright."

Adam's expressed twisted. "*The Passion?*"

"It's Lior." Denise shot back at Serena, ignoring Adam.

"*Ransom*, moron." Serena swatted his arm, then looked around him to Denise. "And I don't care what you call yourself. Point is, we're not in the movies. We can't exactly call the sexy, emotionally damaged FBI guy and trace a phone call to the bad guy's secret warehouse."

Vincent swapped out a bloody towel for a clean one. "As inane the parallel you draw between this particular life-threatening situa-tion and that of the unrealistic pre-destined art form is, I am afraid you are correct. Donovan will not be returned."

"So, we're gonna play pogo, thumb deep up our asses instead?" Caine's sarcasm was new. "I don't give a fuck about Donovan, he can rot, but watching Sophie lay there like a helpless child, trapped in some silent agony, and bleeding to death while surrounded by hundreds of Magics, is fucked up. Look at her! She gets sicker and sicker, and we just keep fucking switching out the damn dish towels."

His point was made when Sophie jerked, and her other arm sliced open. Everyone in the room seemed to somehow get darker, sadder. This was bad. Caine was right. Powerful beings littered the backyard and we were sitting around watching because we didn't want the bad guys to be worse? They were already carving her and Donovan up. She was sickly looking, but her skin was burning. They were suffering while we waited for battle plans to move forward. They were the ones paying for our schedule.

Olive covered the wound and applied pressure, shaking her head. "Her light is faded. Usually, her Soul Seer green and Nya's magenta dance around her like fairies. Now it's no more than dead wood greens and wilted roses."

A flash of Sophie on her knees on the dirt floor of the barn in Diluculo came to mind. Aunt Lacey's soul glow went dark in the end. God dammit, this isn't good. "How long are we gonna wait?"

Ranlyn's brows synched. "I wouldn't let them die. If it came down to it, they would be healed in full."

"Sounds like we're there."

"There's the matter of getting inside the Creation." Veata sounded like her old self again.

"We are aware of the netting." Vincent added a bloody towel to ones soaking in the sink.

Veata nodded. "Good. However, deactivating the netting will not reactivate the Coven marker or get our forces through in one grouping."

Ranlyn took a few steps toward her. "You mention this because you have a solution?"

"Not my solution."

"Evaristus?"

Veata smiled.

I didn't like it when she smiled like that.

"An incantation. Fire. Blood. Simple."

Miklos's husky laugh made gave me goosebumps. "Never simple."

Veata winked at him.

She wasn't trying to hide the wink, but no way were we getting the whole story. "From what I know about blood or ingredients involving the body, it gives the spell an identifier, a fingerprint to see who's involved or who it's targeting. If we include blood in a spell to get into Diluculo, it means Evaristus would know who's coming in after him. He could let us all in or keep some of us out."

"Why give this guy a chance to trap us?" The fact Adam understood the danger also meant Veata knew the risks and still suggested the method.

"Impossible for you, considering you are not going in." Vincent was gruff with his reminder to Adam.

"My family and friends will be. The puppet guy could diddle their strings even if he hadn't already crawled up inside them. You could die as easily as me."

As graphic as the imagery was, Vincent didn't argue. "Yes, potential entrapment is as plausible as death. Retreating while others suffer is not an option. Unless you favour leaving your sister in this state." Adam didn't say anything. Vincent nodded. "So, we proceed."

Even with the other Elders insistence, trusting Veata was a gamble. Especially when she called for blood and Sophie had less and less to donate the longer we stood and watched. If it was Aunt Lacey telling me this plan was the best, I would slash my arms open like Sophie's to be sure I got enough to make the spell a success. Veata was nothing close to Aunt Lacey and all I had was the short time of lessons she taught me to judge by and the premonition she left for Sophie.

Right, the premonition.

It hit me and I knew. "I think she's the One."

"Like 'Neo' the one?" Adam looked at me like I had taken up crack.

"Enough with the movie references." Denise's complaint made his smirk disappear.

"We thought the last piece of Aunt Lacey's premonition was the 'ancient cost', but it's not. The line about 'trusting the untrustworthy One between man and Gods' wasn't deciphered. Clearly, Veata's untrustworthy." I looked at her. "Sorry, but right now you are." She tilted her head as if taking no offense. "I don't know any other way to look at an immortal except like a god. All-powerful, all-knowing, and sometimes all-seeing. It fits."

Ranlyn was shaking his head. "The line meant the Eradicators used the One, not the Puppeteer."

Veata rearranged her skirt as if annoyed. "Evaristus forced my work with those mongrels who were led to believe they were charged with a divine destiny while they cooperated with the evil their ancestors spat at. Their leader brainwashed enough of them into working with the Tainted, justifying that using one enemy against other mutual enemies would somehow result in their inevitable triumph. Morons."

Hinapouri readopted her military stance. "No one stands in the way of more death at the end of my spear."

Miklos chuckled. "Spear, hammer, no matter the method. The Eradicators, Evaristus, Loring, Puppets, and devotees all. They die by the hand of the Mother Coven and all that oppose it. Those who fall in the process die for the salvation of our people."

Okay. I wasn't sure how to take that.

"Then we trust her." Olive moved to stand. Jet, close by, offering her a helping hand. "We take Veata's word for what it is as the premonition called for it and trust what knowledge she brings from our enemy, continue with our plan as is, and adapt to ensure maximum survival of our members." Olive looked down at Sophie and then Lewis. "I know I want nothing more than to bring my Coven home fully intact. We've only regained our status. Losing members at this stage is unacceptable, regardless of who it's for. And diplomatic solutions are never reached when power overrides intelligence, no matter how old you are."

Whoa. Did Olive just call the Elders stupid to their faces? Judging by the side-eyed exchange between Hinapouri and Miklos, they thought so. Others did, too. A lull in conversation hit as she went to the kitchen to throw a bloody cloth into the sink and rip off a paper towel for her hands. The cold seriousness of her expression was one I had never seen on Olive before. And she wasn't done.

"Call it ideological thinking of the youth or the impatience of the old, I don't care. My family has already paid and is further paying before the first blow of war is struck. I won't bow to the Puppeteer regardless of him being family, but if you think I can't hide the Anatolian Idol and anything else on our shelves beyond all others' reach, you are quite mistaken."

Ranlyn stepped towards her. "Olive, we would never—"

"No, *you* would never." She looked over at Veata. "And I'm hoping you wouldn't either. I know where everyone's priorities lie and can count on certain outcomes. The Ballard Coven, in its entirety, are no sacrificial Seedlings and won't be treated as such without consequence." She braced her hands on the counter and looked towards Hinapouri and Miklos. "Which means you protect Sophie and you protect Donovan and you protect anyone else within my charge as well as your own instead of like inevitable bloodstains in your personal revenge plot. Do we understand each other?"

Miklos squared off with Olive, but she didn't move or back down as he leaned into the counter in front of her. "You would not be in possession of such items without the help of Evaristus. Of the evil he spawned. Years of collecting, of squirrelling away that which is not yours to keep."

"And you," Olive stood and crossed her arms, "are you not the great-grandchild of a warlord who raped and pillaged their way through most of Europe with the assistance of others with dark souls?"

"You know nothing."

"I know enough to know none of us are clean. We have taken what Evaristus has given us and made it something to fight for, be it against him or anyone else. Sophie and Donovan are already fighting in this war. You want to find glory on the front lines, you better step up and show your whole Coven you are worth the throne you were given, as those before sure as hell earned it."

Hot damn. I thought Olive was a badass before, when I found out she lived in an insane asylum and didn't lose her shit. Now she's facing Elders with power centuries older than her without trembling like a scared kitten. If I needed another strong Magic to emulate, she was it. I'd follow her into battle any day. Bet she'd make Loring eat his words before he got them out, the prick.

As one of the Seedlings it seemed Miklos and Hinapouri were happy to sacrifice to get the job done, I appreciated the leadership. It shouldn't have had to be against those who were my actual leaders, but Ranlyn was too close to the issue to do what Olive did. But he agreed with it, based on the tugging smile on his lips he tried to hide.

I had no clue where Veata stood, but I guessed she was down for making Evaristus pay for using her as he did, which did mean a revenge plot. Could be good for the rest of us, though I doubted it. I wasn't as close to the all the older Elders, but Aunt Lacey and Nitsa wouldn't have stood for letting her flock die for the bottom line. Even if, like Adam, they volunteered because they were battle hungry and naive.

While I loved this far more than I should have, we needed to get back to Veata and what she knew. "What about others?" Everyone looked at me as if I was crazy for interrupting. I looked at Veata. "You weren't the only one Evar had. Are his Puppets mostly Blind or do we have a hoard of Magics to watch out for?"

"Many Magics, including the Summoner."

Summoner? "Wait...Jheri?"

Veata inclined her head.

The last I saw of Jheri was inside Diluculo. A tiny beauty prancing through the Woodland of Energies, full of power and excited to perform a summoning for the new Elders. Did I see her running? I couldn't remember. Everything happened in a blur before I was knocked out.

Ranlyn swore under his breath. "I thought she escaped and returned to her people. I should have checked."

"She didn't get far. Using her to contact Elsa intrigued his interests and he acquired her before you escaped the field outside the Creation dragging this one," Veata flicked her hand towards Sophie, "and her dimpled lover away with the Apporter."

"He's using her to contact the dead, isn't he?"

Veata smiled. "Turning many stones in search of them."

With the Woodland of Energies being a graveyard for all high-level Magics and previous Elders of the Mother Coven, his options were infinite.

Vincent sighed and pulled his attention away from Sophie, though seemingly annoyed at having to do so. "Those taken over by the Puppeteer are not to blame. We will treat them as victims used for their gifts by an opportunistic monster and herd them like cattle to pen them down instead of killing them, if possible. If they were left with their memories intact of whatever they were made to do against their will, our sympathy will be the least of their needs."

If I was a Puppet made to kill or hurt someone, I'd be haunted by it. I didn't know what was better—to be used as a tool, without memory of what happened, or to remember everything. Knowing it wasn't my fault wouldn't matter. The act happened and an intact memory meant nightmares and psychological scars.

If Veata knew as much as she did, it meant Evaristus was happy to leave her with her memories because he's a fucked-up asshole who loves hurting people.

"Magics and the Blind alike are disappearing in droves." Ranlyn didn't get a nod from Veata, but he didn't need to. "Everyone will be in place as scheduled with no reservation concerning their roles."

And that was that. Not much else we could do but wait for the first light of morning. Fighting in the cover of darkness came with its advantages, since we needed to break the netting first. But, with the time difference, the moon would be high in the sky once we dropped in outside the Creation. Timing was everything.

While the Mother Coven had a mix-matched set of leaders, both compassionate and fierce, and the Ballard Coven had Olive, with her wisdom and fearlessness, my Sect had me. When compared to the others, I felt like a fraud. Why Aunt Lacey chose me for this was a bigger mystery than the premonition she left, and I doubted I would ever get an answer.

17

HUMAN DESIRE

Kim

Imminent danger of dying at the hand of some zombie Puppet hit me when the Elders and six members of Hinapouri's Tribe disappeared with the Apporter. Not for the attack against the Puppeteer—not yet—but heading out to scout the forest around the Creation and the netting stopping us from entering Diluculo. Enemies were likely, and a surveillance trip could still end in death for anyone in or fighting with The Mother Coven. Shit, even my Sect.

I clenched my hands into fists to fight the tremor, toying with the cuff of the jacket I took from Malina after the last fight in Diluculo. Deep breathing probably made me look like a ginger-haired bull and didn't seem to help. I needed to do something more active while I waited for the Apporter and the Elders to do their initial sweep and then bring in those in the selected groups to break down the netting. It would have been nice, but I had nothing but time and no patience.

Those going to the Thoth were already waiting for the Apporter to be done moving groups to break the netting, so they could be transported to the place under the highway. Bosco was still with Sophie, Vincent tending to her, not letting Henry get close. He and Louise let it go when Vincent started to get snappy about people needing to get going and joined us outside with the rest of our group, prepped and hanging out.

I had no desire to chat with Denise—she was complaining to Matt and Caitlyn about not having full details of how to break the netting. Our groups' Transmutator was already in the form of a wolfhound, about as edgy and impatient as I was.

Great. I have the patience of an animal.

Released powers didn't affect my personality, not in that way. Instead, it rolled around inside of me and over my skin as if it was raring to be let loose and be free.

Multiple trips to get groups moved into the precise spot of the netting meant some got to head out sooner. Before I had to watch another group be moved without me, I stood where I could watch the Apporter come through. He popped up a foot from me and stepped back with a flinch and narrowed blue eyes at my closeness.

"We're good to go."

His creepy blues looked over my shoulder and swept to the side.

I turned to find my group hadn't followed me, too busy in conversation to see me skip ahead. I put two fingers in my mouth and whistled, loud. This got their attention, and that of those around me, who sneered. I didn't care. I wanted to get a move on and now.

Disappearing and reappearing someplace else in the span of a sneeze was disorienting. So was being dropped in a dark forest until fragments of my night vision kicked in. A glitter of moonlight gleamed off of Denise's diamond earrings, enough for me to know she was behind me and to my left. Same with the gold button on Louise's blouse a few feet from Denise. The others, I assumed, were behind me, too, but seeing them was a chore until they swivelled in spot to check out our surroundings.

"We're clear." Ranlyn's voice in my head was crisp and confident, yet tense.

Matt scoffed. *"Clear? In a fucking dank-ass forest? Right."*

"Tree cover in the dead of night is about as safe as this operation gets."

"Shit. Ranlyn heard that?"

"We all did, doofus. He's using telepathy." The crunch and rustle of twigs and foliage sounded like Caitlyn gave Matt a playful shove.

"Another example of two people who need to fuck before they get us all killed." The collective gasp and Denise's evil little laugh in my head meant my wayward thought was overheard. *"Ranlyn. Cut it before we turn on each other."*

"Done."

"Shitzes!" My entire body clenched as he appeared in front of me. "Battle zone, buddy. Don't sneak up on me like that." It took a moment for the zing of my pulse to subside. Was there a dash of power in there, too? I couldn't tell. The last thing I needed was to barbeque the only trustworthy Coven Leader left.

"Mhmm. They can't hear you. I still can."

"Shut up and take the compliment."

He dipped his chin. *"Noted."*

He leaned to the side, looking around me. Snuffles in the brush and a dark shape as tall as my waist moved by us and into the woods with stealth-like grace. The wolfhound must have got a telepathic message from Ranlyn and was headed out. I had no clue who they were in human form—not that it mattered. We followed behind, the Transmutator leading the pack through the dense trees.

"How are we supposed to find the netting point when we can't see them?" Denise was nowhere as quiet as our four-legged guide. Not in her questioning or her loud traipsing through the forest to get up to the front near Ranlyn.

I looked back to Louise and Henry. Our oldest members, along with Caitlyn, ducked a branch Matt let whip back at them. His eyes too wide, scanning around him in the dark, on alert and forgetting those closest to him.

I grabbed Denise's arm. "It won't kill you to shut your face and follow, but it might kill the rest of us if you don't walk quieter."

She pulled from my grasp. "Call me bitchy, I don't care. We should've brought GPS."

"Stop." Ranlyn raised a fist in a military hand signal, his voice low as he searched to his right.

We all froze, including the wolfhound. Did we stop because the wolfhound saw something? It turned and looked at Ranlyn as if questioning what the hold-up was, so it didn't seem so. No nightlife moved in the trees. No doubt the magical energy from the Creation kept them away, but wildlife or other, I couldn't hear a damn thing.

"The Soul Seer in Veata's group can see their closest point covered by an invisible guard. Their soul is still visible to him, which means there's a chance all the points are guarded by cover spelled devotees."

"Expected." Or should have been. Though having Lewis finding the guard was good luck. It made me think of how Sophie and Donovan were. We could use her right about now. *Ugh.* Him too, I guess.

"How do we deal with them if we can't see them? There has to be a spell for that." I thought over what I knew. Plenty of spells out there for seeking out people you knew or had a personal piece of body or an item to identify the lost, but we didn't know the Magics we were looking for. They could be anyone.

"There's a spell for everything." Matt's version of whispering was hoarse and pitchy.

"Not for you, there's not." Denise turned back to Ranlyn. "How do we find the netting point without a Soul Seer?"

"You don't. Myself or another Elder does."

"Then how could the Puppeteer reactivate the netting if he's not an Elder?"

Ranlyn's inhale was slow, as was his response to my question. "Evaristus helped build the Creation, therefore he was a part of creating the netting. He wasn't always a Tainted Puppeteer." Denise opened her mouth. "No more questions as we search out a netting point. And there is a spell for that, too."

Ranlyn missed her snotty glare as he had already turned and headed out, the wolfhound still in the lead. I would have laughed if I didn't have full trust in the fact Ranlyn would shut me up, even if he agreed with my gloating.

Ten minutes of walking in silence was taxing on the nerves. Every cracking branch, every leaf rustle had me edgy to defend myself. Relaxing wasn't an option. Not only because we were smack dap in the middle of a battle ground, but because I knew if I did, my power would snake its way out of me and I didn't need a Tainted devotee sensing my Seedling energy and attacking. We all trained and had some tricks, but Ranlyn was the lone seasoned fighter in our group.

A low growl had Ranlyn stopping so quickly I stumbled in surprise. The wolfhound was alerting us of something.

We crouched as Ranlyn did, hidden by tall grass, my shoulder pressed against a tree I hoped might shield me from whatever the wolfhound sensed.

Energy swelled around me. The pressure on my chest was like an invitation for my own power to come out and play, and I had to swallow to stop it from bubbling up. It took a moment to realize the energy I felt was Ranlyn's. I bit down on the inside of my cheek to stop myself from asking him what he was doing.

Ranlyn flattened his palms and pushed what looked like a rippled haze with his hands. It shot out in front of him about fifty feet before hitting a dark-skinned, light-haired man who stumbled into view as if it cancelled out his cover spell. He spun in our direction in a defensive position, waiting for an attack.

I held my breath.

A spark of more power teased my own. A glow pulsed in my periphery. I turned to the now strobing light coming from Denise.

She was hugging a slimy tree to hide herself, her skin shining.

Shit, shit, shit. Could the enemy see her?

Ranlyn turned and swore under his breath as Denise was looking herself over and mewling as the light continued to brighten. He took off, slinking low to the ground and keeping his eye on the target who was now squinting and taking a couple of tentative steps in our direction.

Louise came up behind Denise, scaring her. "It's okay, it's okay. Get down." Louise held her hands out. A flutter of energy was added to Denise's panicked power before a blanket appeared in Loise's hands. She covered Denise, not giving her a chance to fight back.

One guy might have seen us, but this didn't mean we needed the whole damn security squad on our ass. We didn't know how many were out there and Ranlyn was gone.

Louise kept whispering calming sentiments to Denise, who looked more like a trapped racoon thrashing around in trash bag as Louise had to lean all her weight into Denise to keep her down.

Another ripple of power hit the man, this time at his flank, driving him off his feet into a spiral and into a tree. No cries of pain, no moans of half-consciousness. Nothing.

When the energy in the area subsided, Louise let Denise go by sending the blanket back to wherever she had manifested it from.

Denise popped up to her feet, hair mussed, pissed off scowl in place.

Louise stood. "A thank you will suffice."

"Thank you? For almost suffocating me?"

"For not allowing you to be the reason we die."

Louise rejoined her husband, either content to not receive any thanks from Denise or smart enough not to expect it. We moved ahead with Ranlyn as Denise wrestled leaves out of her hair.

We bypassed the dark-skinned man and I did a double-take, taking a second to realize what I was looking down at. He was broken and twisted, eyes affixed and empty, neck and body in opposite directions and twisted around the tree.

My gut lurched, and I realized how green I still was. I'd seen some shit when Loring murdered Aunt Lacey and the other Elders, but the dead devotee still hit me all the same. Was he just a dude doing a job? Sophie wasn't around to see how Tainted he was. Could he have been a Puppet and not responsible for being here at all? Goddamn it. I hated not knowing.

"Shovels?" Ranlyn's voice tore my eyes away from the mangled corpse and the thought of leaving it here to rot.

Half-a-second passed before Louise was holding long, wooden-handled metal spades. She passed me one and another to Ranlyn, then manifested a couple more.

"We're digging?" Ranlyn looked up at me as if this should be obvious. "Guess I meant, why are we digging when telekinesis would be faster?"

The wolfhound stood guard, pacing on all sides against possible threat. What could they do if multiple threats closed in on us? We should be getting shit done and moving on.

Ranlyn drove the shovel into the ground. "The anchor of the netting must be accessed beneath the earth. As it was built, is must be uncovered. You want more answers, you dig while we work."

Matt had a shovel in hand and got started around the same spot as Ranlyn. I added my shovel to the mix as Denise didn't do too much more than lean on hers.

"So, back in the day, the Elders had shovels?" I flipped a clump of dirt to the side and buried my spade again, happy to be wearing the proper shoes.

"Something like one, yes. The key for either activating or deactivating the netting is to use the sweat of man—meaning human, Magic or Blind—and the magic of an immortal."

Sparks of energy lit a patch of forest in the distance. Magics were fighting. Maybe another group came across a hidden devotee and weren't as discreet as Ranlyn at getting rid of them.

"Keep digging." We did as he continued. "Either of the elements needed to deactivate the netting require the digger to put forth more effort than the twitch of magic. It must be taxing in both forms. Once we reach what we're looking for—and no I don't know how deep it is —I'll explain more."

Fair enough.

Since Denise didn't go out of her way to help us, Henry took her shovel and added his sweat to the mix. By the time we got about four feet down, we struck something solid.

Henry knelt to sweep the dirt from the top of it.

Ranlyn snatched his arm before he could. "Touching the coffer will be your death."

Henry shrank away from the hole like it was filled with scorpions, looking to his wife in concern, covered in the sheen of sweat the netting called for.

Ranlyn dropped his shovel and, with outstretched hands, moved toward the hole. He created a cone of power like a dust devil that lifted a dirt-covered box from the earth and into the space in front of us.

"We call them Apish Coffers. Bare skin cannot touch them. Keys cannot unlock them. Incantations cannot speak to them." Ranlyn's power steadied and wrapped around the coffer, the cone morphing into a bubble-like sphere that encased the entire box in iridescent colour.

"Apish Coffers mimic human desire. It can read the beings around it, including all of you and myself, and once opened will require something from one of us. Its objective is to either receive something you desire or for the Coffer to have you understand a desire of its own. It needs my Elder blood to find it, raise it, and open it. Any Magic can be used to satiate it and there is no telling what it will require."

A brilliant line of orange and red tore through the sky from the opposite end of the forest, lighting up the clouds above like fireworks, following the line until it reached closer to our side before fading from view within the trees.

"Damn, I thought we'd break the first." Ranlyn shook his head, he still levitating the Apish Coffer in front of the group.

"That was a netting point?" Looked more like a shooting star or meteorite.

"Yup. Their coffer must have asked for someone's fire ability, hence the line of fire that broke the netting. Who do you know with the ability?"

If I pictured an actual piece of netting covering the whole Creation—based on the line of fire—it meant the Creation was enormous. There had to be many more points.

"Endellion. Deidra by her birth name. My Sect."

Ranlyn gave a respectful nod before returning to our coffer still suspended in front of us.

The small box morphed into a chest the size of a dark wooden jewellery box. The small metal clasp on the front lifted on its own, then the lid itself opened. I wanted to look inside, but after Ranlyn's warning, I also wanted to stay far away from it. From what I could see, it was empty.

Power spilled out of it like a fog machine. Dense. Stale.

Ranlyn had his eyes closed, opening them a moment later. "The sun. It's asking for the sun, unseen since it was placed in the ground."

We didn't hear the coffer speak. I guess this was why we needed an Elder. "We don't have Elementals in our group."

"No Elementals, no, but we can recreate the sun enough to fulfill its desire."

He looked at Denise, as did the rest of us. She was the last to understand what he meant.

"What?" She stepped back a step. "I don't even like this stupid power. I can't use it like that."

Another streak rocketed across the sky—another netting point. This one was odd. No fire. Heavy darkness barely discernable against the heavy clouds above it.

Ranlyn's expression soured. He telekinetically held the coffer in the air one-handed, using the other to snatch Denise by the shoulder of her pink Bench jacket, pulling her into his arms, and forcing her to face the coffer. We all uttered a few words that equalled, "What the fuck is happening?"

"Ohmygod! Let me go!"

"Veata sacrificed her eyesight. I think you can muster some harmless light."

"Dude! Her eyesight?" Matt fidgeted with the brim on his hat. "Come on, girl. Make some light again before it asks for something worse."

"I can't!"

"Just do it." Caitlyn's voice trembled.

Denise tried to get away from Ranlyn and couldn't. "I can't believe you're manhandling me like a poodle who pissed on your shoes. You're probably ruining my favourite jacket. It's not my fault Veata gave up her eyesight."

"Everyone and their baby sister have that jacket." I knew because I sold many of them. "I'll buy you another at half-price. Now, stop stalling."

She groaned and tried, again, to get out of Ranlyn's grip.

"It's called sacrifice. Veata knew breaking the netting could mean her life. Her eyesight is nothing in comparison to what the coffer could have asked for, and you don't get to choose its desires. It makes its needs known, you comply, that's it. You pledged yourself to the Mother Coven and to us as your Elders. Now prove you meant it."

Ranlyn gripped Denise tighter, pulling her into him with a growl of annoyance. Energy built. I thought from the coffer, but it was Ranlyn. Denise groaned and wobbled as his power overwhelmed her. She was now leaning against Ranlyn instead of trying to escape him.

I tried to keep my cool with this as the others were looking to me as if I should intervene. Ranlyn was right. Denise volunteered to fight in this war and was happy to be a Sect member when it made her feel cool. If she wanted to back out, she should've done it before the Apporter shipped us here, not at crunch time. Ranlyn was walking a line. It was difficult to see and hear through the capsule of magic around them, but we could, and Denise's eyes rolling around like dolls wasn't a good sign. If she passed out, I didn't know how we were going to mimic the sun without her.

Ranlyn shoved Denise closer to the coffer, he still holding onto her precious jacket, her feet slipping and scrambling at the edge of the empty hole. With the urgency of his power all around us, Denise's eyes widened at the Apish Coffer inches from her nose. Light poured from her skin, as if she switched her phasers to nuclear. Even her threads weren't enough to dam the eruption.

A pulse of power radiated out and light shot above us as if she lit the fuse of a rocket across the sky. I spun to shield my eyes and saw the streak of netting breaking above through blotchy and watery sight.

Holy shit. It worked.

A huff at my left was Denise on the ground. Henry and Louise were apologizing and pressing at their eyes as they tried to help her up. She shrugged them off and glared at Ranlyn, who was too busy closing the coffer and lowering it back into the hole. Guess once the netting was broken, magic to bury it was fair game. Though why he would bother burying it at all was something he didn't stop to explain.

He didn't further address Denise. I didn't blame him for being pissed. We had a job to do and needed to move on.

We headed out to find more anchored netting points. Ten minutes later, a stripe of light zoomed across the sky and sizzled out so fast we couldn't see anything.

"Hinapouri's celerity." If Ranlyn hadn't answered, I would have asked, but I didn't know Hinapouri had the gift of speed. It made me wonder what other gifts my Elders had.

Matt scoffed. "Nothing considering Veata's blind. Promise to take my ass out if that happens to me."

Caitlyn chuckled. "I'd have no choice but to take you out. You'd be walking in circles if I didn't."

I turned and stopped in front of them. They flinched, looking up at me. "You don't get to laugh about someone else's misfortune."

"Was just jokes—"

"Hilarious." I stepped closer to Matt and glared at him and then Caitlyn. "You decide to be a comedian again and I'll make sure you're far worse off than Blind. I'll put you on stage and make sure you get to hear just how funny everyone else thinks it is." Caitlyn looked down as Matt clenched his jaw. "No? Too mean? Until you figure out telepathy and can host your own open mic nights in your heads, keep it to yourselves or wait until your next sleepover."

Shit. Was that too harsh? I sounded far too much like Donovan for my liking.

I stalked off to catch up with Ranlyn and the others. The last thing we needed was to get caught because we were too busy fighting with each other.

"*About time.*" Ranlyn didn't look back at me. "*The coffer also took advantage of Hinapouri's power and tried to escape. Her men tried to catch it. She had to attack her own people since they forgot touching the coffer would kill them. Nothing they won't heal from but will leave a mark regardless.*"

Louise tsked and shook her head. Ranlyn had let us all know, though I was confused if the first part was for me alone. If Matt and Caitlyn didn't feel bad before, I bet they did now.

Circling to the left of the field, the wolfhound detected another guard. Ranlyn took her out before she realized we were anywhere close to her post.

Two other points were broken as we were digging—both from Miklos's fast-moving group. Another two of Hinapouri's men were working with Miklos and now one would be walking around without the sensation of touch or feeling, temporary or permanent they had no clue. The second was a secret. A literal secret. The coffer asked Miklos for a promise and he wouldn't repeat it.

What kind of a promise could Miklos keep? Were there consequences if he broke it?

The coffers had no theme to them. I didn't have much to give or I wouldn't be here in the first place, but shit, I could see and feel—everything including walking around was a luxury to a box in a hole.

Uncovered and in the grasp of Ranlyn's magic, our new coffer looked different than the first. Still a small chest, though a much older one with silver details tarnished from years of neglect.

Whoosh! Another point broken. Not ours. This one streaked the sky in audible cries of pain. Ranlyn said it called for empathy from Leon of the Ballard Coven, who was struck with years of the coffer's tragic loneliness beneath the soil. I didn't know how this would affect Leon, but Olive would be pissed. So would Sophie. He was still alive, but crippling loneliness was no joke and we had no way of knowing if it was temporary.

Ranlyn refocused on our coffer. I panted from over-exertion and waited for what the coffer wanted. Ranlyn hesitated. Fuck. This can't be good.

"The coffer has asked for the years of time taken from it. Henry's years."

Louise's eyes were so wide I saw them in the dark, shining off what moonlight we had to work with as she shook her head. "No. Can't be. It can't be."

Henry looked to take a quick second and then committed to the idea. "Louise—"

"No, Henry."

"Yes." He grabbed her hands as she fought to look anywhere but at him. "We talked about this. This is important. We have to stop the Puppeteer and we can't do it without taking down the netting. We rebelled in our youth, we stood up to the man, and gave the finger and more to those who tried to stop us. My chances of death in battle were high and may not have made any impact before being slain. This, I can do, and it will have direct impact on the plan to save our people." He took her face in his hands and made her look up at him. "It's okay, darlin'. Makes me feel young again."

When he chuckled with tears in his eyes, I clamped down on my lips and had to cover my mouth to stop myself from whimpering.

Henry dipped his head and pressed his lips against his wife's, mumbled what I thought was "I love you," then did the same to her hands before he turned to Ranlyn with a straight back and waited.

Ranlyn nodded and spoke whatever was needed to let the coffer know its desire would be fulfilled.

I didn't know what to expect and at first, nothing happened. The coffer wouldn't change its mind, would it? No. Henry's tanned skin soon turned sickly, greyish in the moonlight.

He widened his stance. Was he getting dizzy?

Louise gripped her hands together in front of her mouth, as if she was trying not to scream or reach out to touch him.

His salt and pepper hair turned white and thinned out. Age spots dappled his skin as it seemed to hang looser on his bones.

Henry stumbled. We jumped to help, but Louise caught him and helped him to a tree close by before he slid down the bark, landing too hard. He fought to keep himself propped up. Louise fought harder, holding him and repeating, "You're okay, you're okay," so many times I knew she would never be okay again.

I couldn't keep it together. Tears poured down my face as I watched Henry's slow-motion death. It was worse to watch Louise, powerless to do anything about losing her husband. Good cause or not, this was a tragedy, and my heart broke for them—so much so that I dug my finger into my breastbone, trying to hide my ragged breaths as an image of my mother in her last moments popped into my mind. I fought hard to push it aside and not to make comparisons to losing Henry, but I knew Louise's helplessness all too well.

"Tell me what you need." Louise smoothed the now wrinkled skin of her husband's cheek.

The wolfhound whined and laid down. I didn't know if they knew Henry, but this was one of those times you didn't need to know people to have your heart break for them.

Henry's next breath wheezed, and his eyelids sagged. Louse's offer of help became urgent and she repeated herself and called his name. Henry no longer responded. His head lilted to the side, his hand hanging limp in his wife's. The coffer had been buried for centuries, far more years than Henry had to give, but I wanted so many more for both him and Louise.

We flinched as the thread of the netting broke with a flash of light and rocketed across the sky with the sound of a beating heart.

"No." Louise looked back down at Henry and gripped his hand tighter, placing it against her cheek, with no reaction from Henry.

She collapsed against his still body and wailed as everyone else stood, empty of words to make this right. Willing sacrifice or not, Henry and Louise had a lifetime of memories and a future they would never get a chance to discover.

Denise, Matt, and Caitlyn looked like they had never seen anyone die before, while Ranlyn looked like he had seen too many. I had seen enough to wish it was the last time and knew I wouldn't be so lucky.

Louise manifested the same blanket she had covered Denise in, something handmade, and covered Henry in it up to his chin.

I knelt behind her and hugged her around the shoulders. "I'm so sorry, Louise. We'll get the Apporter to bring you two anywhere you want to go."

Louise took in a ragged breath. "I just want him to take me for ice cream again."

I had no idea what this meant for her, but it didn't stop my tears at the fact he could never do that.

Henry's death took him out of the fight, but it also took Louise with him. Expecting her to carry on and leave him behind was ridiculous. Not even Ranlyn pushed it. She needed to grieve, to make arrangements. Right now, she had already made her sacrifice for the cause, whether another netting point was broken or not, and I wasn't going to pressure her to stay on for any reason.

Ranlyn waved me over. I squeezed Louise's shoulders and left her with her husband. "If you're telling me we have to leave him here alone—"

"Stop. I'm not, but the Apporter is still with the other group at the Thoth. He won't be long, and we have more points to break."

In other words, let's get a move on.

Fuck. I went back to Louise, at a loss of how to tell her we were leaving her alone with her husband's dead body for an indeterminate amount of time.

"I would have given it anything." She sobbed, and I knelt behind her again. "Manifested a singing turtle. Anything. It wanted life, to take no matter the carnage it left behind. Why would the Elders create such things?"

They couldn't have expected their own Coven to be breaking the netting yet pointing this out to Louise wasn't important when her husband's body was breaking down more and more as the seconds ticked by.

I let her know the Apporter was coming as soon as he could, and that we needed to get moving. I also promised to check up on her as soon as I could, hoping I had the ability to. Louise didn't respond. I hated leaving her with Henry like this. No one could ignore her wailing cries as we left to look for another netting point.

The battle and my role as Sect-Leader felt extra real now. I didn't know if a coffer or a Puppet or tripping over my feet again might take me out.

More points broke on our search for the next one, a few asking less gruesome demands than they had of Henry. Blood was asked of a member of Hinapouri's tribe, but Ranlyn said it was nothing life threatening, and they would heal in time.

Another point was broken by a coffer's need to Soul Read as Lewis could. As far as I knew, Sophie was the only one in her family who could do this, but they all had the same family trait, so maybe it pushed Lewis into tapping into his powers' full capability. The coffer wanted to use the power to gain Lewis's knowledge of the time he was alive, a time the coffer had not yet experienced. Whether this was hard on Lewis, I had no clue, but it was no easy trick for Sophie.

After losing Henry, we were ecstatic all our next coffer wanted was to use Matt's power of camouflage and disguised itself into a perfect replica of Matt. Though it was a tad unsettling to bury it again while it still had the same likeness of the guy, at least we weren't burying another member. The coffer could have made things easier had it closed its eyes while we did it.

Unfortunately, Sophie's Aunt, Priscilla, was not left unscathed. Their coffer asked for a memory—the best one she had. It took a while for Ranlyn to let us know what the breaking netting point was. We couldn't tell by the mash of sound that came with the streak across the sky. It became clear not too long after that Priscilla had no clue who her husband was. The coffer took Lewis away from her. Not a single memory of him, but all memories of him.

Olive's threat of consequences if a Ballard Coven member was hurt sprung to mind. Priscilla was alive, but without memories of her husband she would be forever changed and Lewis along with her. Would this count for Olive? What would she do?

It also made me think of Sophie. She had no clue what was happening to us out here and, if she came out of this, would be hit with a heap of bad news.

Animal instinct was taken from the black panther Transmutator in Veata's group, creating nothing but a growling broken thread streaming across the sky. Which, as far as we could tell, would leave the Transmutator without this trait and would be quite dangerous, though time would tell how dangerous.

While digging for another coffer, Ranlyn straightened and stood back with a "Huh" as a netting point streaked across the sky, filled with the sound of a sobbing cry, not unlike the one we left behind with Louise.

"Who was it this time?" Denise heaved a shovel-full of dirt to the side and panted.

"Chelsea."

"Sophie's cousin? The coffer wanted her tears?"

Ranlyn nodded. "Showed her a lifetime of struggle and tragedy.

Orphaned by the plague, thrown-out of town in case he infected the others. Grew up a farmer's slave who had a twitchy hand for a flog."

"Wait." I stopped shovelling. "As in, the coffer has human memories?"

"As in, the coffer held a human."

"What the fuck?"

Everyone stopped shovelling.

Ranlyn raised his hand at us and images flooded into my brain. Chelsea was knocked over by a person being spat out of the coffer. The others jumped to attack, though Chelsea protected a young man who raised his hands to cover his face. Hinapouri argued they had no time to babysit, but what could they do, leave him? The Elders put an orphaned young man in a coffer for the past how many centuries? They didn't know more than that at this point, but they had lost too much already to cast him aside when they didn't know if he posed a threat.

Ranlyn dropped the view into the other group.

"A person!" Matt threw his shovel down.

"Matt." I picked up his shovel and held it out to him. "It's not something I thought our Elders could do either, but we could still have enemies out there." I backed off and looked at the others. "Let's get this shit over with and then we can have a Q and A with our new Elders, okay? And remember, they aren't the ones who created the netting, they just happen to be the ones dealing with it now."

No one else said anything, but the tension was clear. The Elders were disappointing. If this was their brand of creative battle plan, what made them any different than the enemy?

When we got to our next coffer, all it wanted was to be read its last rights, needing this to go on to the afterlife, or at least thinking it did.

Caitlyn stepped forward and recited them as if she had done so hundreds of times. When the netting point broke and flew across the sky with the sound of her voice repeating the words, she explained she had been with her father—a man of the cloth—as he gave them to dying patients at the hospital or one's going into surgery who thought they may die and insisted on the ritual.

Maybe she left before seeing the actual death, as it still looked like she was surprised at Henry's passing. I didn't know, but it begged a few questions on her decision to be in the Sect when she was from such a devout family.

A flash of light in the sky was a volcanic eruption, pushing aside clouds, and expanding out like palm branches.

Instead of stopping, the branches came our way and started dropping like a giant orange peel.

I screamed for everyone to run. We didn't get far before the brightness behind us was close enough to blind, and then it hit the ground and sent us flying.

The world around me twirled. I tried to protect my head as my body spun, but couldn't keep my arms pulled in. When I slid to a stop, I rolled onto my back and was still blinded by light. Energy filled the air with such strength, I fought to keep my power from bursting out of me. I tried to open my eyes and see what was happening, but all I got was the bright light coming from the sky, pressing down into the earth on one spot like a finger squishing a bug.

A burst of power hit, this time as if it was being sucked back into wherever it came from, throwing debris into the air and sliding me in the grass before it stopped and the whole place was eerily silent.

I blinked and waited, but nothing else happened. Was I okay? No pain. Still breathing. What about the others?

When I turned to where the light was, I saw Ranlyn struggling to get up.

Okay, our leader could still lead. I knew it may happen at some point, but I didn't relish being the only one in top spot. Getting to safety would be priority one, but where the hell was that?

A groan from my right was Denise.

I squinted through the darkness, keeping my voice low. "You okay?"

She answered with another groan I took as a no, though figured if she was really hurt she would have been screaming or complaining louder. Unless she had a head injury. Shit.

I pushed to my feet, stumbled, and caught myself as my balance was messed up.

"Ranlyn?" He didn't answer me as I got closer, though was now on his knees, finding his balance as well.

Caitlyn and Matt were stirring where they landed in the grass and someone else with long blond hair scurried off into the trees. The wolfhound? I hoped so or it was the enemy. Maybe they were retreating? A wishful thought.

I knelt by Ranlyn, who was staring at his hands. "What happened?"

Ranlyn shook his head.

"'Tis true." The voice had me jumping, finding Veata and her group coming towards us from through the trees. "Our immortality was the last of our sacrifice."

"Your immort— Can't be." If the original Elders were fighting other Magics with immortality, taking it from them would be a big freakin' deal. They couldn't have known they would be taking it from the Magics they gave it to when they created the netting, but, shit. If other Covens knew our Elders were vulnerable, this could be disastrous. Would it matter to the Coven members? I thought all Elders were immortal.

"Unfortunately, it's true." Lewis was now in the clearing as all groups had made it to us with help from the Apporter. "I don't know what your souls looked like before immortality, but I imagine Sophie could confirm if they're the same. Either way, no more immortality."

In the lull of such news, I noticed a young man off to the side with Sophie's cousin Chelsea. Judging by his tattered clothing and the suntanned skin of a labourer with sinewy arms and the need for about twenty extra meals and a five-hour bath, he was the one who popped out of the coffer. He didn't look up once at the people around him. I couldn't tell if he was scared or pissed at the Coven who put him in the coffer—maybe he didn't know who did it?—but he had been abused and eye contact for a slave was a no-no.

While the Elders argued over the next step, I wondered if the guy wasn't better off back in the coffer. I didn't know what life was like in there—if he was unconscious the whole time or had any awareness at all—but coming out in the midst of a building war surrounded by strangers in a world he knew nothing about must be terrifying. Then again, he had survived so much already, he may be the strongest of all of us.

18

THE THOTH

Caine

A duck-walk? Really? Why wasn't I outside Diluculo, dealing with the netting? Instead, I'm hunched under five feet of concrete and duck-walking through a tunnel on the way to an empty Creation.

How the Puppeteer's devotees justify crawling through this shit-hole—and don't see it as a sign of a leader who gets off on you crawling through actual shit, garbage, and whatever else stuck to or crunched under my shoes—was beyond me. I didn't care about anyone this much. Not even myself. But here I am. Fuck my life.

Vincent moved with the grace of a cat, leading in front with the Apporter, the Huntsmen Roe and Gerard, and Olive. She may be old, but Olive managed to keep moving forward.

I helped Sophie's brother, Adam, through a small connecting hole in the wall and then Jet, Serena, and Rachel. Blake and Jared helped the others of the Ballard Coven through as I went ahead. I wanted out of here ASAP and wasn't hanging around to mother everyone.

Besides, elite badasses Anne-Claire and Lincoln, as well as two others in their team, Jessabelle, a thirty-something, short-haired woman of equally short stature with small features, and Arden, a middle-aged man with hints of grey around his temples, both looked primed for war. They could manage to make sure no one got lost in a tunnel going in one direction, since they protected our backs.

Goddammit. This part was shorter than the last section. Adam was around my height and having about as much fun.

"Can't believe this dump was a high school hangout for you guys."

Serena scoffed. "One time! And it took me two hours to talk Sophie into doing it since you have to cross the highway to get down here. Chicken-shit. One of those guys owes child support to four different baby mamma's and the other is premature balding and in and out of prison, so we didn't lose out by taking off on them."

Adam scoffed. "Tease."

"Please. They wanted to ghost hunt. We wanted boyfriends. This is the place where UTI's are created, not the place to get it in."

Adam side-eyed me. "Not true."

I smiled at the guy, sure he wasn't exaggerating. As much as it hurt, I liked being around Sophie's people and hearing stories about her, though picturing her down here was a stretch.

Jet laughed. "You never know, maybe M really loved B forever."

She chinned towards the wall covered in graffiti where whoever M was wanted the other tunnel-crawlers to know they were in love. More like horny, as in Adam's case.

The bright green spray paint next to a badly planned swastika saying, "The Devil was Here and Never Leaves!" was accidently true. The Puppeteer never leaves his Creation. Not sure why he would want to when he had the power to do anything and everything he wanted within it.

As we moved along, and I could stand a bit straighter, I took notice of the walls. Graffiti was everywhere, but within it were symbols I thought I recognized in some of Aunt Lacey's research books. Theban writing for sure and maybe Nordic symbols. Animals —peacocks and boars—were painted with far too much skill for all the way under here, though I didn't know what they might mean.

Oh, an Amentia. Egyptian history was my jam and far more interesting in college than my major in IT. The Amentia was a symbol for The Land of the Dead. Not a good sign. The symbol for Ka was in there, too. Ka was a spirit or soul crafted on a potter's wheel. When the body died, the Ka lived on. Kind of reminded me of Nya and Gareth's story. Though, that would mean Sophie and I had two Ka's each jammed into our bodies.

How am I not more fucked up?

The symbols could have been put up by some college kid hooked on ancient symbolism but seeing another symbol had me stopping and staring.

"What's that?"

I didn't turn to Jet. I was stuck on what had to have been put there by a true devotee or the Puppeteer himself. A large symbol of a Northern Bald Ibis was unmistakable and looked like a harbinger of some kind of evil with its tiny eyes, shaggy feathers, and long slim beak. The dripping black spray paint didn't help, but it was an ugly bird regardless.

"I don't remember it smelling like swamp-ass down here." Adam's complaint pulled me out of the stare down with the Ibis, though the threat lingered while I tried to catch up with the others.

"Your sinuses were probably too scorched by your Axe body spray to smell anything else."

Jet's laugh at Serena's dig echoed down the tunnel. She clasped a hand over her mouth, though I didn't think she needed to.

"Shouldn't we have seen someone by now?" Gwen's question made my point for me. It didn't feel like anyone was around.

"Not likely." Anne-Claire came up behind us with her right-hand man, Lincoln, both in black tactical gear. She looked a hell of a lot better in it with her blonde pony-tail down her back. I wasn't sure if Donovan having slept with her made her less or more enticing. "The Huntsmen have been through this section multiple times without encountering others. Our expectations end there. Having never been inside, Roe couldn't speculate on the condition. Be ready when we hit the ground."

Shoe scuffs, garbage getting kicked to the side, and the light rumble of night traffic on the highway above us took over where Anne-Claire finished. If the Huntsmen were right and no one was around, then great. If the Puppeteer had other ways of surveillance, we were screwed.

A tingle of power washed over my shoulder and settled in my chest, spurring on what stirred inside me.

"Holster the energy, everyone." Vincent's directive travelled back to us, as he was still out in the lead in a hint of light used to find their way. "Save it for when we travel through."

I breathed in through my nose and clenched my jaw to fight against the block of power lodged behind my chest, begging for traction. Intended or not, Anne-Claire's warning had us all spooked. Most of us were new to our powers, but it didn't mean we were useless, not since Donovan trained many of us. But it did mean noobs getting twitchy.

The Thoth needed to be checked off the list of threats before we hit Diluculo. The last thing we needed was to deal with two Puppeteer-run Creations. They would all be lucky if Sophie and I could pull off what we needed to in the one.

Was she still out of it? Fuck, please let her be okay.

Light out front got brighter as we got closer to Vincent, Olive, the Huntsmen, and the Apporter. They were looking down at what I saw was like the coven marker outside Diluculo. This one was inset within the concrete and featuring the same Northern Bald Ibis as the one I saw spray painted onto the wall.

Olive and protection detail would stay outside the Creation.

Since she had the Anatolian Idol, and refused to let anyone else have it, she needed to stay outside and be ready to use it. The Huntsmen, plus Jessabelle and Arden from Anne-Claire's group would stay with Olive, as would everyone else from the Ballard Family Coven—except Kassie, since her Soul Seeing may prove useful. Adam and Serena weren't happy, though neither argued. From Donovan and Kim's Sect, Rachel, Gwen, and Aaron remained outside, while the rest consisting of Vincent, the Apporter, Anne-Claire, Lincoln, Kim, Blake, Jared, Jet, and myself were welcomed in.

A small group, but Vincent was more concerned with protecting Olive.

Once the two groups divided, Vincent had the Coveners staying in the tunnel step back while the nine Creation goers surrounded the coven marker, shoulder-to-shoulder. Vincent circled around the group with an old clay jug I'm sure I'd seen in old Roman documentaries. He poured out a thick, white fluid in a thin stream as he walked around us, creating a full circle.

"What is it?" Leave it to Jet to ask.

Vincent was intent on his task, his glasses slipping to the end of his nose. "Queen bees are not bred but created. A steady diet of Royal Jelly secreted by nursing bees allows a genetic alteration that develops a worker bee into a queen. This is Royal Jelly."

"Also, excellent for your complexion." Anne-Claire looked as lethal as she was beautiful, her big white smile at the comment making it plainer. I doubted Royal Jelly was the secret to her genetic jackpot.

Vincent didn't comment either way, pushing through the group to stand in this circle with the rest of us. "Under questioning, Joelly divulged this elemental key for entering. Evaristus is narcissistic enough to believe he derives of Royal Blood. Royal Jelly is not easy to come by in its natural form, especially so back when the Creation would have been constructed. It's obscure enough none would assume it the key."

The Apporter grabbed Vincent's arm, stopping him from pouring out more Royal Jelly onto the marker. The two men looked at each other as a tense moment passed.

Vincent nodded. "Go."

The Apporter disappeared, letting Jared stretch into the empty space.

"What happened?" Was something wrong with Sophie? Please say no. Since I knew Jet was okay, Sophie was my next worry. She shouldn't have been, but she was.

"Not now." Vincent ignored my question and raised the clay pot, tipping it to spill a drop of Royal Jelly on the coven marker.

High-speed acceleration spun me around and squeezed me from head-to-toe until bile hit the back of my tongue and stung my sinuses. The squeezing didn't stop. I couldn't breathe, couldn't see. My body was nothing, no bones, no limbs at all. I felt nothing but being squeezed until my skin was a husk keeping me together.

The pressure released all at once and I landed on something hard. I sucked in air and choked on something. I coughed, my ribcage aching as I wheezed, and spun onto my hands and knees.

Fuck!

A sprung to my feet and shook out my burning hands.

Sand?

Others coughed or threw up. Sun beat down on me. Jet was hinged at the waist, retching, nothing coming out. Jared did the same. Though Vincent wasn't messed up as the rest of us. That guy, I didn't get him. Immortal and knowing Sophie and Donovan before they were Sophie and Donovan? Now he's standing amongst the rest of us like jumping through the Creation was nothing? Had he done it before? If the loafer-wearing stalker was trying not to puke, you couldn't tell. Unless squinting through his glasses into the distance was a—shit.

Bodies. Hundreds of bodies. Facedown, on their backs, in twisted positions, all around us as the wind blew across the sand, blowing it like little needles into my face. I squinted and looked over where we were.

A Creation could be anything. The Puppeteer took his ancient history far too fucking seriously. Everything in Diluculo spoke of fun and celebration—of what it meant to be a Magic away from smug tourists and the Blind too ignorant to deal with the truth about us. The Thoth was nothing but sand dunes, naked trees, gnarled cacti, and a sun meant to scorch the fuck out of everything. Off in the distance was some type of monument. Another structure like something out of my Egyptian text book. He probably had Puppets pull stones on their backs like slaves, too. Something green was out there. I shielded my eyes and saw large leaves being tossed around. Palms. An oasis? Did he think he was an actual Egyptian king? Egomaniac much.

"Are they dead?" The question preceded another retching cough from Blake.

No one answered.

A body in the distance was being pecked at by vultures. Definitely dead. But the rest?

Vincent walked through the blowing sand like he was hitting the runway and knelt next to the closest body. Their face and body were half-covered by wind-whipped sand. "This one is alive."

Damn. Alive and baking under this heat and covered in sand like a seasoned chicken? So wrong. Nothing about them was identifiable. Age, race, gender, nothing. But they didn't move when Vincent touched their throat in search of a pulse.

Were more alive? Sophie would know if she were here, making me wonder what Kassie saw. She didn't say, though she looked around as if trying to figure it out herself.

"Let me buzz the area." Jet volunteering shouldn't have surprised me, but it did. "If I see anything hinky, I'll head right back."

Vincent looked at Jet, then at me, and back to my cousin. "Your gift, your risk. If something happens, we cannot retrieve you."

Jet gave a half-shrug like she expected no different, though Vincent was high if he thought I would leave Jet in this wasteland in the hands of the Puppeteer or anyone else. She must have seen this in my expression, because she walked past me, looked up and smiled while slapping a hand onto my shoulder, setting herself up to fly. The sand made for a difficult take off, rougher than I was used to seeing her do in the barn. Not that it stopped her. Jet was determined and was high above our heads in seconds.

"Damn, Caine." Blake spit onto the sand. "Your cousin single?"

I stared at him. "Yes. And has a six-year-old."

He widened his eyes and got a face-full of blowing sand.

I shielded my eyes, looking for Jet, but she was too high, and the sun was too bright to see her.

Jared swiped sweat off his forehead. "We're leaving them all here, aren't we?"

I didn't have to ask who he meant. The fact he was staring out at the bodies in the sand was all the hint I needed.

"You going to cart them out on your back, big man?" Anne-Claire giggled. "What choice do we have?"

"The choice not to leave them." Blake's tone clipped at her insensitive remark.

"Have fun helping your buddy." Lincoln agreeing with Anne-Claire was no surprise, not that it made the opinion any better.

These people could have been innocent Puppets at one time.

"Closing the Creation is our objective." Vincent rubbed his hands together, sand particles falling back to the ground. "Leaving these people does not sit well with me either, but we cannot save them all, and we have no idea what connection still remains to the Puppeteer. Leaving them may mean many deaths. Deaths we harbour no responsibility for."

No arguing followed. Not because Vincent was the boss and had the last word, but because the immortal know-it-all was right. What if we brought them back to Ranlyn's or outside Diluculo and they were still Puppets? This was war. Handing them a boat load of extra soldiers to pick us off was a shitty strategy.

"Most are dead anyway." Kassie stood with her arms crossed as if her job was done and she was ready to leave.

Her craft was new compared to Sophie's or Olive's. Lewis would have been a better choice, but we didn't expect to need a Soul Seer. Not that it mattered. Magic or Blind, the bodies in the sand would decay and be vulture food.

A blur and huff of something landed to my left. I raised my hands to defend myself. Shocked and hurried voices of others around me spiked and then settled as we realized it was Jet.

Her knees buckled, landing her ass in the sand. Her blonde ponytail was windswept, with sprigs of hair around her sweating face and reddened cheeks.

I reached down and helped her to her feet. "You okay?"

She nodded.

"See anything?"

"Nothing." She was breathing hard as she ran her hands over her hair and braced her hands on her hips. "No one's moving. Up there, they all look like dead ants."

"What about that building or whatever it is?"

"Doesn't exist. Closer I got to it, the further away it seemed."

"Wait a sec." Anne-Claire came up, moving closer to Jet than was appreciated. "An actual mirage?"

Jet looked side-eyed at me and narrowed her gaze at Anne-Claire. "Call it what you want. Nothing's there. It's probably what all these people were trying to get to. I wasn't trying to chase it down. You think you're sweatin' balls down here, try being up there."

Anne-Claire backed off and I looked out towards the building and palms swaying in the wind. It looked so real. No wonder people kept trying to get to it.

The Puppeteer was a psychopath.

Vincent walked over to the cover marker and bent to wipe the sand off.

Jet took a few steps towards him. "We're leaving?"

"We have surveyed all we can in the time allotted for this mission. Returning is essential."

"What about all these people?"

"Already tried, Fly Girl." I wasn't a fan of the way Blake looked at Jet. "Too dangerous."

She looked at me and I felt guilty all over again.

Like everyone else, I turned my back on the baking bodies and got into a circle as we had to get into this litter box. No questions this time—everyone was quiet and eager to leave.

Wind and sand made things difficult for Vincent to pour out the Royal Jelly in an actual circle. It would move and break up the line. He knelt and went over the jelly a few times before standing. All we could do was hope it was enough. The clay pot wasn't endless, so it had to be.

Vincent spilled the last drop on the marker and the dizzying, squeezing ride through the veil seemed to last an eternity.

I landed hard, much harder than on the sand. Cool air hit my lungs as I sucked in deep and choked on it. Something loud had me covering my ears, rolling onto my stomach and then my knees. My chest burned and choked me more. What the fuck? My power was like a brick with flailing spider legs in my rib cage, panicking and scratching to get out and going nowhere.

I gripped my head and dropped to my side. Grunts of fighting were mumbles as my eyes screamed in pain. I blinked through something wet and saw the Coveners we left behind on the ground, some struggling to their feet and stumbling around.

Adam's face was scrunched in, black dripping from his eyes, nose, and ears as he grabbed onto his head and pulled his hair. The light spell pulsed and turned the black red. Blood?

Fuck. The noise. It drilled through my skull. My power wanted out and couldn't. Nausea from going through the veil and from the pain had me dry heaving. I braced my hands on the cement as a gush of blood blinded me and puke suffocated me.

No air. I tried to breath in and pain sliced through my chest. I couldn't get enough in. Fuck, I can't breathe.

Choking. I'm choking. I couldn't see. Couldn't hear. Did anyone know?

I gripped my chest and held on, gasping.

I can't— Fuck, I'm passing out.

What? I thought someone said something. A man's voice calling out to me in my head.

Was I awake? I couldn't feel my body.

Wait. There. A tingle in my throat. It grew into my chest like a slithering worm. Stronger. I tried to squirm in discomfort, but I couldn't feel my limbs enough to move my body.

Spikes of pain shot through my legs and a pulse of energy surged through me. I sat up, panting and staring at a wall covered in bright spray paint.

The noise stopped.

Adam was laid out on his back, his chest heaving as he swiped at his face to clear the blood.

What happened? I panted and looked around.

Vincent was fighting a big guy in jeans. Anne-Claire and Lincoln had a few enemies of their own, all fighting like pros with a mix of power and hand-to-hand combat. Wait, there were several of Anne-Claire. She split herself up like she had when speaking to the Coven. Those they fought didn't use power. They weren't Magics, they were the Raddies. The noise must have been what Sophie went through. A flash of her and Donovan's pillows hit me, and I felt like an ass.

I saw Jet and managed to get to her, passing a few others still trying to gain their bearings. "Are you okay?"

She blinked a few times and looked around, her blood-soaked eyes wide and frantic as a scream let out. Lincoln telekinetically chucked a person into another one of the Raddies, then a wall, the ceiling, and the floor like Bosco thrashing around a chew toy. No way they were getting up.

Vincent wasn't having as much fun and looked like he was knocking them unconscious instead of killing them.

"Grab it!" I couldn't see him, but Roe's gravel-laden demand was unmistakable.

I stood and saw Roe on the ground, his fellow Huntsman wrestling someone for something. He took a punch to the head and a kick in the gut, but the guy wouldn't let go of what looked like an old radio.

The noise device?

I took off towards them, jumping over bodies of Coveners and Raddies, winding up a punch that landed a guy with a shaved head across his bearded jaw. If it was the device, I didn't want to use my power and break it. I couldn't be precise enough right now and Roe wanted it for a reason.

I grabbed the handle. Gerard let go as the guy's weight threw him down when I hit him. I let him know how it felt to get a boot to the intestines and added an extra until he gave up and cradled his gut. I passed it to Gerard and stood over the guy a moment, waiting to see if he was going to try again.

"Left him alive?" Lincoln was at my side, looking like he was hard from the adrenaline of fighting.

"Leave him." Vincent's order was unmistakable. I wasn't pushing it—not that I was going to kill the guy anyway. Lincoln looked pissed off, but fell in line, and stepped away with a glare at me on his way to Anne-Claire, who was now one person again.

Vincent helped others to their feet. I left Roe and Gerard to watch over the guy they fought with, as they were happy to do so.

Olive was curled in the fetal position, slowly moving to her feet. I reached down to help. She pulled away, clutching the idol to her chest. I raised my hands. She saw who I was and apologized. Were the Raddies trying to take it from her?

Vincent approached us and looked at me. "I am uncertain of what power you released to turn the tide of the fight. Nevertheless, it made all the difference and we procured the device in order to study it.”

“Whatever it was, it wasn’t on purpose.”

Vincent raised a brow as if it didn’t matter and turned to Olive. “Are you okay?”

Olive nodded and stood taller.

“Do you know how—?”

“Of course I know how to use the idol. Give me a breath or two and move out of my way.”

Olive wiped blood from beneath her nose and walked towards the marker. I followed and met up with Jet. Everyone seemed to be okay or were able to be healed, but the device the Raddies created was brutal and took a lot out of you regardless.

I stood to the side with Jet and watched as Olive took the Anatolian Idol in her hands, the pale marble female figure lay stoic in her palms as she held it toward the marker. “*Nemo can penetro. Nemo can dimitto. Omnis ero irretitus.*”

We waited for something to happen. It looked like nothing was going on, though an energy grew in the tunnel.

Olive pressed her lips together and shifted her weight, bringing her arms in closer to her body while staring down at the idol. Her hands lowered a bit and then more, as if the idol got heavier. Another moment passed as power built, and then she let out a gasp and dropped the idol. It landed with an echoing thud that made everyone flinch, but it didn’t break.

Olive bent and reached for the idol. Vincent leapt to pull her arm back.

The idol was pulled like dust to a vacuum toward the coven marker, crawling toward it without using its stiff marble arms. Every inch it crawled, the Idol lost its shape, bending and moulding as the marble whined like twisting metal. With our ears still ringing from the Raddies’ device, the sound was nothing, though the sight of it was enough to have us all standing and watching.

When it reached the marker, the Idol had flattened out into a white marble plate, then grew finger-like spikes around its edges, planting itself on top of the marker and melding into it. The Northern Bald Ibis was obscured beneath the immoveable object, sealing the Creation and its sun-scorched Puppets.

"Olive," Vincent's voice was low, "please tell me you possess another idol."

A beat passed. "I believe I do."

Shit. We would need another idol to close and trap the Puppeteer inside Diluculo. How did they not realize this would happen? What if she can't find one?

We wouldn't know until she got back to the Ballard attic, which would take the Apporter to get her there. Since he hadn't returned from whatever emergency happened, we left the tunnel, including the bodies of the alive and dead Raddies, using my persuasion on the live ones to make them sleep for the next hour.

We waited for the Apporter at the top of the grassy hill overlooking the highway in someone's darkened driveway. The place looked empty, but it was nighttime. We had no way to contact the Apporter, but if he was busy with Ranlyn, he would be shut off to all others while dealing with their dilemma.

Vincent gained everyone's attention. "Since we are waiting, you should be made aware of why." He paused, and it was clear whatever it was, it was bad. After speaking of the Apish Coffers themselves, Vincent told us about Henry. "Unfortunately, the coffer called for more years than Henry possessed."

Gwen gasped. "He's dead?"

Vincent nodded.

She swallowed and looked like she might say something but ended up walking away from the group.

Blake pushed through Arden and Serena. "What about everyone else?"

"I know nothing of the others."

Blake shook his head, and like Gwen, took a bit of a walk.

Vincent didn't know jack-shit. The Apish Coffers sounded

horrendous. How anyone thought of them in the first place was disgusting. What happened to Henry was awful, but I had to admit to myself that I was glad it wasn't Sophie. If she had been awake and not messed up because of being away from Donovan, it meant she would have been in either the group dealing with the netting or in our group and could have been hurt or killed by the Raddies.

She needed to stay alive. Besides not being able to trap the Puppeteer alone, I needed her.

19

THE SHADOWS

Kim

"Why is this taking so long?" The whine in Denise's voice was at high gear.

I was sick of hearing it. She had to know she was being annoying. She may not care, but she knew.

The Elders had taken turns circling the area outside Diluculo and coming up with nothing. One of our members was dead, another blind, another holding back what promise the coffer made him give— something no doubt binding. A Ballard member couldn't remember her husband of over twenty years, another was plagued with hopelessness, and we had a stranger from god-knows-what century pop out of a coffer like a snake in a can. No telling why he was in there or what his initial involvement was, but he was in Ranlyn's home with our people.

Expecting for the group in the Thoth to be successful and unscathed was laughable, but they were closing the Creation, not dealing with greedy coffers and netting points. They had to be fine, right?

Damn. Please let them be fine.

It felt like an eternity waiting for the Apporter to get back from dropping off Henry and the others and then picking up those at the Thoth. I wasn't wearing my watch and was itching to get back to Ranlyn's and get the rest of the plan going. The netting was down. We needed to close the Creation before the Puppeteer knew what was happening.

Hopefully someone would call if the Puppeteer jumped out the of Creation and zipped off to terrorize the Blind and turn everyone into Puppets.

Commotion in the trees had me hiding, peering through the dark. Was that? Yes! Caine.

I ran out to the group across the clearing and wrapped my arms around him. "You're alive!"

I squeezed Serena. Something wet smeared on my face. I pulled back, touching it with my fingers and coming away red. Blood. I fought to suppress my gag reflex. "Shit. What happened?"

"Those Raddies assholes crashed the party."

"How'd they know you were there? Or where the Thoth even was?"

"No freakin' clue. But they have the worst taste in music."

A loud whistle came from Ranlyn. "Round up! Let's move."

The plan was to head back to Ranlyn's property to regroup before dropping into Diluculo straight from there. I didn't care why, but I was happy to be moving.

Once the Apporter transported everyone back to the field outside of Ranlyn's, Denise handed over violet eyeliner she had in her pocket so Miklos could write the spell for the Apporter to bypass the Ballard Family Estate's defences on Olive's arm. Why Denise was carrying around eyeliner at all was absurd, but her vanity was handy.

"Be quick." Ranlyn looked around at the large group in the field. "We need you both and soon. I'm adding an extra group to our initial strike force into Diluculo."

"Is that needed? I thought—"

Ranlyn ignored me and looked to the Apporter. "Not anticipating the Raddies could have meant unnecessary deaths. I'll need you to move more people outside Diluculo and be mobile once inside."

The Apporter nodded and disappeared with Olive.

Sophie needed to go with us into the Creation and she needed to snap the hell out of this funk from being too far from Donovan. If it wasn't immediate, we were screwed.

I ran inside to check on her. "Still bleeding?"

Evelyn, a woman from the Mother Coven known as a healer and not a fighter, was tending to Sophie's arms. Bosco was curled up on the floor near Sophie's head. He didn't get up as I entered, though his curly tail wiggled.

"Yes, dear." Her heavy Irish accent made the situation sound extra dire. "They keep resurfacing."

"I know, we're working on it." I tried not to stare at the soaked-through bloodied bandage as it made my stomach churn. "Yeah, umm, we need to get her ready to go."

The woman looked at me like I had announced we decided to Kevorkian Sophie instead. "She cannot be moved."

"Where we're going, she won't be like this anymore."

Evelyn continued to fuss with Sophie's bandages, her back to me.

"Like, now would be awesome, but it's fine. You keep doing that. I'll wait."

Evelyn turned and glared at me. Tension built for a moment before she got up and stood in front of me. I wanted to wilt, but not a chance lady. I glared back.

"Is she ready?" Caine's frantic voice made me jump.

Evelyn didn't look away from me. "She cannot leave. She bleeds and bleeds."

"What's happening here?"

"Evelyn is being protective of Sophie's care like she took the Hippocratic Oath."

She raised her chin. "I have."

"Oh, good. I'm sure you've even paid back the enormous debt that paid for it. Now we need to take her to the cure because it sure as hell isn't in this room."

"I could cure her if—"

"Nope. You could heal her, not cure her. Kardashian-sized bootie of a difference."

A rough snuff from Bosco had us looking back at Sophie.

Caine was hoisting Sophie into a seated position. "Wanna help?"

He didn't need my help, but with Sophie's arms ripped into ribbons, it made it easier. Plus, it would take me away from Evelyn, who was busy trying to save the day instead of saving the world.

I bent and pulled Sophie to her feet with encouraging words of things being over soon, with no idea if she could hear me or not. We got her moving and Sophie managed to half-drag her feet, but it was slow going and Evelyn was on our tail, nagging us with every step.

Caine swung Sophie up into his arms. Eventually, we made it to everyone else standing in wait in the moonlit field, Bosco at our heels, the Apporter yet to return with Olive.

Ranlyn found us and looked over Sophie. "How is she?"

I clucked my tongue. "Ready for her rock-climbing lesson."

"I don't have time for your humour."

"Or the time to use your eyeballs? Or does she look better to you?"

"When we leavin'?" Caine repositioned Sophie in his arms, her head lulling to the side, her eyes half-open.

Ranlyn shifted his glare to Caine. "Rushing will kill more, not less. Let her sit."

He walked away to tend to whatever he needed to do and Caine lowered Sophie in the grass. Bosco sat next her, nudging her arm before I picked him up. I watched Caine pull most of Sophie's weight into his lap, her head on his shoulder. His fingers rubbed the dark bruising of Donovan's restraints, then smoothed her hair out of her face and behind her ear.

My heart ached. Caine loved her, was in love with her. Watching her struggle was as tough for me as it was for anyone else, but my concern touched nowhere close to Caine's. Helplessness scrawled on his every movement as he fidgeted, moving her arms in such a way to cause the least discomfort, but never moving too fast, making sure her head didn't droop, the tiniest adjustment handled as if Sophie was breakable.

"I'm sorry."

Caine's eyes flashed silver in the moonlight as he looked at me. Embarrassment seemed like a good way to die. Crawling away and losing myself in the crowd was another option.

His expression scrunched like he had no clue what I was talking about, and then softened as if he realized what I meant. "Yeah. Me, too."

He could have played dumb, but he didn't. I appreciated the fact he was real with me as I wished things had worked out between him and Sophie. Not that she and Donovan weren't made for each other, it was still messed up since someone as nice as Caine got mixed up in all this fate stuff.

Serena and Adam broke our moment to voice another round of "Why are we bringing her anyway?"

Caine let me do all the talking. He didn't look at them, comment, or ask someone to take Sophie off his hands. He seemed comfortable with his place beside her, as long as Sophie was incoherent enough not to argue or overthink the contact. Sounded kind of gross, but it was more for Sophie's sake than his. The girl had enough guilt to deal with. If she remembered anything about the last few hours and that happened to be among it, I was sure he would be okay with that as well.

Waiting for Olive and the Apporter to return with the second Anatolian Idol dragged. I was edgy yet nervous about what came after her arrival and wanted to get it all over with.

By the time they got back, Caine had checked out and Serena and Adam talked with each other more than anything, both pissy they didn't have a greater role in the battle yet complaining about the effects of the Raddies' device.

The idol was made of a female figure carved into a flat black stone—no arms, clad in a cross-hatched skirt and large holes for eyes. I didn't see it but was told the first one was white and much rounder but this one should work the same. Olive held to it to her chest like she was surrounded by a bar of cut-throat pick-pockets who had a boner for ancient art.

Timing was everything. We needed Olive outside Diluculo with the idol and ample Magics, plus Sophie and Caine had to do their thing while more of us dealt with whatever Puppets and devotees we could inside the Creation. And, no one wanted to get trapped in there, so we needed to somehow let Olive know when to close the Creation before the Puppeteer, Loring, or other evil sons-a-bitches could escape.

Olive came over when she saw us, giving us each a hug and kiss on the cheek, and then kneeling and pecking Sophie on the forehead. She squeezed Caine's shoulder before getting up and crossing the thick grass to join one of the last groups travelling to the field outside Diluculo with Serena and Adam.

Bosco wiggled until I let him down and nudged his pug nose into Sophie.

Caine pet him. "No, no. Stay down, buddy."

"He's as worried as the rest of us."

"She will be okay soon." While Vincent sounded optimistic, the crease in his forehead called him a liar. "We need to get her into position."

Guess it was time to get this battle started.

Caine stood and hoisted Sophie into his arms in one movement as we started towards where Vincent lead. Impressive manoeuvre and kind of sad he wasn't letting her go.

Vincent turned so fast with his hand out, I flinched thinking a bitch-slap was coming my way. Instead, he flattened his palm at the ground, at Bosco. The pup stopped and looked up at him, then sat as if Vincent was offering him a plate of broccoli.

Weird dog.

Bosco squirmed in place while he and Vincent stared at each other, then gave a *"boof"* and took off running towards the house.

"You speak pug, now?"

Vincent continued walking like it was the most normal part of his day. "Animals understand rooted images over words."

Caine and I side-eyed each other. "Noted."

We followed Vincent through people prepping themselves for battle. Be it ingredient packs for spell bombs or intense chats over strategic manoeuvres, the focus of the Mother Coven and friends was dialled in.

"So, you knew them before?" Caine's tone was off. He and Vincent's over six-foot tall strides had them out in front of me, but I didn't need to see his face to detect the weirdness. "Sophie and Donovan?"

"I did."

I felt like I was eavesdropping on a private conversation, though found myself walking faster to hear better instead of dropping back.

"I do not believe I have met you in any of their lifetimes."

Caine nodded, still lumbering along with Sophie in his arms. "Doesn't matter."

"It does to them."

Vincent's cool response ended the conversation. Why would Caine bother to bring it up? Talk about turning the knife.

I wondered if Sophie knew about Caine not being around before. Vincent said it mattered to Sophie and Donovan, had they talked about it before or was he talking out of turn?

Did I watch Sophie and Donovan's will-they-won't-they sex-charged drama in a different lifetime before? Shit. I hope not. No one deserved to watch soulmates struggle to get it together and be happy.

Damn immortals and their long memories.

Though it begged the question if I wanted to change my soul colour to one with a sprig of silver and live through other lifetimes, knowing what they were going through. None of that sounded fun at all.

We pushed through to the middle of the crowd, where four Magics were pouring out sand in a large area of the grass.

Ranlyn stood watch and paced until the sand dotted the field like a crop circle thirty-feet across. "When we cross into the Creation, the group will be making another crossing so we can escape and land outside the Creation instead of back here." He pointed at the Magic who laid out the sand, now drawing something in it. "They're illustrating our Coven sigil, the signature that will allow us to enter Diluculo as opposed to another Creation."

The Magics making the sigil moved in sync. Each drag through the sand with their hands erased their footprints like a live action art exhibit. The image took shape in no time and the Magics rejoined the group.

"Endellion." Ranlyn using Deidre's Coven name gave me Aunt Lacey flashbacks.

Should we be using the Coven names more? They were chosen for a reason. Damn. Dropped another Sect-Leader ball.

Deidre shouldered by Coveners with their toes kissing the circle's edge. She squeezed through as if she was afraid to inconvenience someone by making them move.

She landed between Dwayne and Priscilla, displacing Sophie's aunt, forcing her closer to Lewis. She jolted away and crossed her arms, while Lewis fought to hide how much it hurt him for his wife to be freaked out by him. The Ballards had no luck.

Deidra stared down at the sand, shifted her weight on her feet, and rubbed her fingers into her palms. Whatever Ranlyn wanted her to do had her cheeks flushed.

Power poured out of Deidra and dumped a truckload of energy out into the crowd. Enough for the shock of its potency to have us all stepping back. It took me a second to get a grip on my power, but

Deidra didn't let up. Instead, she amped up the power, closed her eyes, and dipped her head back as if consumed.

Rachel stared at Deidra, her hand at her throat, but seemed like it was out of surprise rather than taken aback by the energy affecting her. Had Deidra never used like this in front of Rachel before? Considering their relationship, it didn't make sense.

Deidra's lips moved quick like a hummingbird's wings as she looked forward with hooded lids.

I leaned in to try and see better. Fire burst from the sand circle, pushing back the crowd with flames over our heads. People stumbled over each other, making Caine drop Sophie's feet and stumbling to hold on to the rest of her.

When the fire died down a bit, flames licked at our knees, and I saw fire spilling out of Deidra's arms stretched towards the sand circle.

It wasn't the flames licking at Deidra's toes that made me stare or the shimmer of hot coals on her skin as light and dark pitched and waned, it was the ache on her face. The closed lids, lips pursed together, chin dipped to her chest—I've seen a look like that before on Sophie and Donovan, when they get stuck in an emotional loop.

Pure rapture.

Ranlyn put his hand on Deidra's shoulder. She blinked, glared at him, seemed to click back into herself, and looked back at the circle. He was the glass of cold water in her face taking her out of her trance. The image of lit coals under her skin was smothered as she pulled her arms in with side-eyed glances at those around her and then down at the ground as she sloughed off whatever had consumed her and returned to the shy woman I saw at coven meetings.

The flames receded further into the sand before they extinguished. Anyone who had sat through high school science knew sand turned to glass when ignited at high temperatures.

I knelt to touch the glass and my hand dipped into water. Cold water, dark as asphalt.

I looked up at Ranlyn. "We're swimming into the Creation?"

"Yes. Each of you will first cut yourself to give a blood offering and then will swim through the pass-way into Diluculo. We know little about this way of travel, but it's supposed to remove the pain we experience while travelling through the veil, plus we can arrive as a group."

Shit. I turned to Caine and Vincent, both bracing Sophie's weight with her arms over their shoulders. "She can't swim like this."

Vincent expression remained unfazed. "Pulling her through will suffice."

"You forget she's not immortal like you? You can't breathe for her, too."

"She's facing the Puppeteer with me, so yeah, if we have to, we'll breathe for her."

People were already diving into the water. This was happening whether Sophie could breathe or not and we didn't have time for a plan B. Ranlyn was too busy making sure people remembered to draw blood before jumping in and Vincent and Caine were too eager to get her on the other side.

Vincent pulled out a pocketknife, flicked it open, and cut his arm as Caine pulled off one of the bandages on Sophie's. She had enough wounds and blood to spare for the offering without adding to it.

I grabbed Sophie's chin between my fingers. "Close your eyes." I wasn't sure she could hear me, so was surprised when she listened. It could have been a reflex, but they stayed shut. "Can you give her a telepathic command to make her hold her breath?"

"We shall see." Vincent removed his glasses, placing them in his pocket, and passing Caine his knife, which he used to cut his palm before passing it to me.

Vincent nodded. Then both men leaped into the dark water, clutching Sophie between them.

Hoping Vincent accomplished getting Sophie to hold her breath and not wanting to be left behind, I cut my palm, passed Vincent's knife to whomever was behind me, and jumped in. The least I could do was follow in case they needed help pushing her through.

Damn. Should've worn waterproof makeup.

I hit the water and its frigidness hit back. I didn't expect the water to resemble a hot bath with my homemade lavender-mint bath bombs, but the cold struck me in the chest, forcing the breath from my lungs. With the amount of control it took for me to hold onto what I had in my lungs, Sophie had no chance in hell.

I kicked my feet as fast as I could, hoping the other side was close.

Wait. What if it wasn't a straight shot out the other side? The water was dark and gross. Could I see anything if I tried to open my eyes?

I kept kicking and swimming. Come on. This was taking forever.

My chest squeezed with the lack of oxygen. I had to peek through my eyelashes in desperate search of an escape.

Whoa!

In the cold darkness was a silvery line floating out in front of me, directing me straight ahead. Everything else was muted.

Water bubbles came from others swimming through—What the fuck?

Vincent and Caine were still swimming with Sophie a bit ahead of me, she not kicking her feet like all the others were around us.

Some people were kicking too hard. No, they were fighting something. Fighting what? Was the water making them hallucinate? Poisoning them? I had tasted a little by mistake and it was putrid.

Sophie was grabbed and pulled downward. Vincent snatched Sophie's injured arm before she got too far. She didn't wince in pain, but now Vincent was thrashing around as if being attacked.

I scrambled to get to them as Caine was dragged a few feet away and was now thrashing in a sea of air bubbles.

Shadowed fingers tugged at Sophie's bare arms, making her spasm. I punched through the water at where I saw the dark hands and hit nothing but water. The shadows were what they looked like, shadows.

Caine made it back to Sophie. She was choking. Vincent may have told her not to breath but, at some point, we all needed to, and that time was now. Caine grabbed Sophie and fought through the shadow hands trying to drown him.

Shocking pain zinged through my leg. Lightning hit the bone and ringed through my whole body like the most pissed off jellyfish I could have crossed. Shadow hands grabbed my thighs and then my arms as if desperate to capture me and drag me down. I flailed without hitting anything or getting anywhere but sinking deeper. My whole ribcage burned for oxygen and I had nothing to hit. The silver line guiding my way through the water did nothing to save me. It taunted me, showcasing my way free as I thrashed around.

Revolting water flooded my mouth. As it washed over my tongue I realized what it was. Decay, worse than rotten fruit.

The shadows, were they ghosts? Bile burned my already burning throat.

The pain worsened as the shadowed hands were winning. My vision spotted with fear-provoking blindness, fading the edges as it tunnelled. I slammed my eyes shut and flailed, kicking my hardest. Something bright came through my eyelids. The prospect of escape fuelled me to keep fighting.

Something grabbed my arm and pulled me forward in the opposite direction of the shadowed hands. I tried to shake them off, too, punching my way through the water. Whatever it was, if it was taking me down, it would have to earn it.

My neck snapped back; my body rocketed forward. I sailed out of the water into weightlessness before crashing down onto my back. I rolled over, choked, and heaved rotten water as I clutched onto grass.

Grass?

I threaded my fingers into the strands of green and sucked in deeper breaths. Echoing voices were muddled in my ears, bouncing from skull bone to skull bone like a rubber ball. A singular voice became louder. I couldn't understand it until my right ear popped and drained of water enough to hear someone apologizing.

"Soph?" I blinked, my eyes stinging. I pressed my fingers into my lids, the pressure painful yet relieving when I opened them, seeing Sophie. "Are you okay?"

My question made her laugh. "Nice Trench."

Trench? Right. Malina's short, black velvet trench coat now soaking wet.

People scrambled out of the pool of water at my side. Dark markings were all over their skin. They were grabbing at the injured areas, some crying out and rocking in pain.

Sophie helped me sit up. "You okay? They gotcha pretty good." She turned over my arm to look at the markings.

I noticed they were finger marks—like seared bruising, tender to the touch, on my face and neck as well. I couldn't see them, but they ached when I moved. My legs were far worse.

"It's all good. I can fix it." Sophie's power tingled my skin before she touched me, then burned as her healing power went to work.

I clenched my teeth and moaned as the pain struck all the nerves in me all over again.

When she finished, she was smiling. "Makes you miss drinking that orange crap, don't it?"

Between gut-wrenching stomach pains and being drowned by those shadow things, I would have taken the orange crap into Diluculo any day and bet Ranlyn was regretting the change.

20

TALK AMONGST THE DEAD

Kim spat. "I'll never get that taste out of my mouth. What were those things?"

"Everyone says something different." I shrugged. "Trapped souls in some type of purgatory, the Puppeteer's victims, watery graveyard of mutinous pirates. That's my fav. I wonder if they killed someone, if the person became a pirate, too? I'd look hella sassy in an eye patch."

A big splash and Vincent calling my name came from the water. I rushed to the edge and reached in to help Vincent, who flipped a short, blonde young woman onto her back at my feet.

I knelt next to the woman and put my palm on her chest. With a boost of my power, she choked up the dark water and was gasping to breathe.

Caine jumped in to help turn her on her side while I erased her wounds.

Vincent had waited in the water, watching to make sure the woman was breathing again. I took his forearm and pulled him out until we sat on the side of the wet grass.

"Ania!" Another woman ran to the blonde still on the ground trying to gather herself and reassure "Cheryl" she was okay.

I stood and started to pull Vincent up with me. "Your turn. Show me."

"My back." He leaned to the side and pulled his shirt up, one arm out of his sleeve so I could see deep black handprints on his skin.

"The pass-way should come with a friggin' disclaimer. Always travel with two healers since we can't use our powers down there or to take care of our own wounds."

"Those within the water were never mentioned by Veata." He grunted in discomfort as I healed the rest of him. "It is a question of if she neglected to make us aware or if Evaristus mentioned the method of travel in Veata's presence without mentioning them in order to thin the herd, as it were, before we reached him."

"Didn't know it was a spectator sport."

I turned to see Kim blushing as Caine called her out for watching me heal Vincent, he standing in his immortal glory with most of his shirt off.

Vincent pulled his arm back through his shirt sleeve and righted his wet clothing as Kim fussed with her coat and called Caine a nark.

With a small smile his way, Vincent nodded in appreciation for the healing.

I stepped towards Kim.

"*Glasses?*" His telepathic voice surprised me.

"*Oops.*" I forgot as I picked them up after they fell out of his pocket. He looked younger without them but lost his distinguished edge. "*Good luck drying them off. Everything's wet.*"

Holding them up in the air to look through the smeared lenses in the light of Diluculo, Vincent half-smiled. "*No loss. Thankfully, I no longer require their correction. Old habits.*" He smiled a fleeting moment as I laughed. "Better get ready. I need to find Ranlyn to ensure the next step runs smoother than the first."

We watched him walk away and I hooked my arm with Kim's to

head over to the group hidden behind the entrance of Diluculo by a wall of trees and tall brush.

Kim didn't move.

"What? Second thoughts? I know I wanted you here, but you don't have to be."

She swept her hand over her wet hair. "Why are you so chipper? People were inches from being plumped up floaters in some creepy cop drama. I watched you bring back another girl who looked like she was dead—"

"Not dead. Just not breathing."

Kim shook her head and stepped closer to me, "You've been a drooling idiot since the moment Donovan left, even through being carved up like a Thanksgiving turkey."

I laughed.

She glared until I stopped. "Now you're Mary-freakin'-Sunshine, saving lives, and kicking up your heels on the way to battle. I don't get it."

I sighed. "I've been gutted by my mother's fear of me, insulted by my grandmother's neglect of my family's power, unhinged by the notion I possessed the ability to hurt Caine the way I did, heart-broken by losing Aunt Lacey, and I've been utterly consumed and jaded trying to hold onto an ideal that Brock was never capable of living up to, no matter how low I set the bar." I smiled to lighten the mood as Kim was doing a pouty-lip thing. "I thought I could deal with anything. Nah-ah. I'd rather go through all that twice over with a side of hot sauce than experience the separation from Donovan ever again. I don't know what I looked like on the outside, but I was cut-off yet trapped within his longing and guilt for leaving me at Ranlyn's. Not to mention feeling everything those sadistic bastards did to him."

"You felt that?"

I felt my eyes widen as I nodded. "I can't make you understand because I've got nothing to compare it to, but I never want to feel like that again. Nor do I want Donovan's guilt to overtake his ability to fight. So," I hooked our arms again and nudged her forward, "I'm going to be Mary-freakin'-Sunshine because the relief at not being like that anymore is stronger. Plus, I'm still alive and can feel that Donovan is, too. We survived, though this won't be the case for all of us."

Kim stopped, expression crumpled.

"Reality sucks monkey balls."

Kim continued walking. "I didn't think you'd remember that much."

"About Donovan I do. I couldn't escape him."

She made a slow nod and, again, I knew she didn't quite get it. Not that she needed to. It wasn't something she needed to know to understand it was a shitty experience.

"Skipping to something less depressing before we dive in, how come you get a secret little convo with the hot professor-like immortal and I get a 'Better get ready'?" Kim's attempt at mocking Vincent's dialect had me laughing.

"No big secret. Nothing the conspiracy channel could do without." I leaned in closer. "He doesn't actually need his glasses. He just wears them out of habit."

"What? That poser."

We were laughing when we reached the others who were far from giddy and looking at us like we were doing a stand-up routine at a funeral.

The bushes were far away from the sign introducing Diluculo, and the pathway and houses didn't begin until a fair bit after that, so we had a buffer between ourselves and any of the Puppeteer's drones according to a few scouts who were sent out first.

Anne-Claire was wringing out her ponytail as her team fixed their gear. "The Puppeteer knows we're here. He has to."

"Might be a good thing." Caine earned some glares. "He's expecting us, knows we would come through here whether through water or the coven marker, and he didn't set up an attack. We could have been slaughtered like chickens the second our heads popped out of the water." A few others tilted their heads to agree. "We could be in a Hell of a worse situation at this point."

Agreeing with his statement didn't change anything. True, we could have been Puppets or dead the second we breathed Diluculo air. To me, it meant the Puppeteer had something worse planned for us and we were playing right into it.

Jet was soaked, her power enacted. "I could buzz over the—"

"Not a chance, cuz. We knew the Puppeteer wasn't in the Thoth. It's too dangerous here."

Jet rolled her eyes as if she was told to wait in the car, but she was an asset—one Evaristus would love to get his hands on. Losing her before the fight started was a stupid move.

The original plan was for Caine and me to face the Puppeteer ourselves, having the others as back-up against Puppet drones. It would all have been executed to create the illusion of war. We were going to do what we could to distract the Puppeteer, save who we could, and bail, trapping him in the Creation he stole.

When Hinapouri ordered her tribesmen to ready themselves, taking a ten-man team, Miklos, and both the Huntsman with her, my intuition prickled. Maybe not true witchy intuition. More like paranoid suspicions from years of trust issues. No one else seemed alarmed by the division in troops, so I figured it was one of many conversations I missed while Donovan and I were stuck in the Puppeteer's Hell together.

Ranlyn was quick to separate the remaining Magics into three lopsided groups. Caine and I would be out front by ourselves, as discussed. Behind us were Ranlyn, Vincent, the members of Anne-Claire's Coven, Cheryl, Ania, the five Transmutators ready in animal form, and four other members I had never met before.

The one I recognized, Ranlyn called Jeff. I didn't know him by name and it took a moment to remember him as the man who blew bubbles into balloons for his daughter the first day I visited Diluculo.

The laughter on his daughter's face when their dog—or the mother as it had the yellow soul glow of a Transmutator—would pop the bubble and he would remake another was enough to crack a smile. As much as he made children laugh, he looked like he could make a devotee or two wish they chose another target. His crew cut and tattoos pegged him as a military man or an MMA fighter.

The woman Ranlyn called Cheryl, though Ania called Cher, with high and low lights streaked through her perfect hair, looked more housewife than soldier. But, with the orange soul glow of the physically enhanced, I was confident she would be useful at my back.

Two other men, Richard and Jack, couldn't have been more different if they tried. Richard had to be in his fifties, with dyed blond hair—too blond to be natural. Jack was twenty-five at most, with dark hair tucked behind his ears and wet clothes hanging off his wiry frame. Richard's soul was bright white with no soul colour, while Jack's soul shone a pleasant blue in the initial stages of his power. Ranlyn had to have a reason for wanting both in the group within Diluculo and I wished I knew why.

The rest of the group, far larger than both Hinapouri's small group and the ones closest to me and Caine combined and multiplied, would come in when we were getting our asses kicked. Or so we hoped. Who knew what the Puppeteer had in store for us.

Ranlyn led Caine and I to the Creation's welcome sign.

"Fuck," was the totality of words that leaped to my mind. As uninventive as it was, the place Aunt Lacey once described as a "Haven"—a place for free-use magic away from societal prejudice that Diluculo was created to be—was nothing like it had once been. The innocent concept was warped into the Puppeteer's perverse universe.

I had witnessed the destruction of the Elder's cabins and the Woodland of Energies made up of trees grown from the ashes of countless Magics, but Caine hadn't.

He stood with a hand over his mouth, staring at the aftermath.

Ranlyn called his name twice before regaining his attention. "I know it looks bad, but I need you to concentrate. If we succeed, once reclaimed, we'll restore it to the how the Elders wanted it. For now, follow the outer boundary along the forest wall. Bypass as many enemies as you can. No point in engaging unless unavoidable. Leave them to the rest of us."

Too late, it occurred to me I should have said a proper good-bye to Ranlyn in case the Puppeteer saw through the ruse and killed us. Ranlyn tolerated me, maybe respected me beyond the whole call of duty thing, but he had protected me from the beginning. Knowing he was close behind was comforting, though useless since we knew he and the others would be too far away to save us if the attack was lethal.

Nitsa's shop, The Witch Hunt, had mild scorching on the exterior but was otherwise standing and secure. Odd, considering it was on fire the last time I had seen it. We crept in close and looked through a small window. In place of stocked shelves were bodies, huddled together, immoveable yet standing, unblinking. More interesting than the fact they looked like clothes hung out to dry and forgotten, was that all of them had soul glows. Most had their heads hung, dirty hair in their faces, so we couldn't see who they were.

My mind flashed with a memory of standing in front of the magazine rack with Donovan, Kim, and Caine, laughing and poking fun of Nicole, the skater-girl cashier, ogling Donovan. Two visits to Diluculo were far less than most still grieving the Creation, but it was enough to build memories. Even some good ones.

The graze of something on my fingers made me flinch, until I realized it was Caine, reaching to hold my hand. He led us away. Letting those inside free to be extra Puppets trying to slit our throats was handing the Puppeteer victory. We may be naïve, thinking we could beat the immortal or even trap him, but we didn't have a death wish.

Keeping to the plan, we didn't expect to see Ranlyn and the others or Hinapouri's small group who had taken the opposite side of

Diluculo. Nevertheless, we weren't alone. The woods around Dilu-culo used to feel like a hideout for a couple trying to sneak out for privacy. Now, every snapping branch and shuffled leaf had me twitchy.

In the hands of the Puppeteer, Diluculo's beauty was fierce, right down to its claws. A once fairy tale forest was now filled with beasts. We tiptoed past a wild dog gnawing on a bone with fleshy bits hanging off it. The bone-chomping mutt less than fifteen feet away had no soul colour so we were in no danger of exposure to the Puppeteer, Puppets, or devotees, but it was unsettling to watch.

Caine pulled me along the dark half-safety of the forest boundary.

Out of nowhere, thoughts of my childhood friends surfaced, as well as some of my mother and father. I hadn't seen any of them in too long, especially my friends. Serena hadn't mentioned them lately either. I wondered if she saw them. It would have been easier if my parents were the absent type. Would Mom tell my dad the truth? She didn't know about this plan. With her difficulty of wrapping her head around all this magic stuff, she would shit a brick if I told her the rest. Avoiding was easier, but made me a selfish daughter.

Our search for Evaristus was time consuming, giving me too many opportunities to daydream or day nightmare, if that was a thing. I remembered Kim's GPS gift and wished she had tagged along a little closer.

The maypole caught my eye, a symbol of fun right out of a cata-logue for witches, one I thought was a novelty, like the Wicked Witch of the West socks the merchants sold. The strips of coloured ribbons were now tied around the bloodied wrists of the dead. Their limp bodies swung with the breeze and were fly bait, naked or close to it, with missing eyeballs and twisted limbs.

Why off the maypole? A warning for the rest of the Puppets to fall in line like good little soldiers when they weren't possessed? The smell of their sun-blistered, putrefied flesh surfed the wind and gagged me.

Caine pulled me away, taking huge steps towards the top of a hill.

I would never forget those bodies. They were so mangled, I didn't even know if I knew them or not. The smell alone was nightmare-inducing.

Pfft. As if I needed more.

"Sophie—"

I stopped before reaching the top of the hill, Caine having pulled out in front of me. We hadn't spoken since making our way across the Creation, unless you counted me trying to wrestle my vomit back down my throat.

"I don't want to see what you're seeing, do I?"

He didn't answer. The tension in his back and the stillness of his whole body as he stared down at the bottom of the hill at whatever he was seeing was answer enough.

I took a few steps towards him unwilling to stay back. "Fuck. Please be a pit of snoring puppies, please be a pit of snoring puppies."

My knees weakened when I saw what he did. I braced my hands on my thighs before I went down. "Definitely not a pit of snoring puppies. What the shit is wrong with him?"

More bodies. A hundred? Two hundred? More? I couldn't begin to tally. Countless were pieces of people. Arms, legs, heads—chunks of meat and bone, left exposed to elements like those hanging at the Maypole. Maggots, birds, and other four-legged mutts feasted in each other's company without the need to get territorial, plenty to go around.

One thing was for sure, we were wrong about the smell coming from the bodies tethered to the maypole. Whatever odour came from them was drowned out by the wafting stench from below us.

"People are nothing to someone like a Puppeteer." Caine's listless tone was a thud in my gut.

He was right. The defiled and tortured bodies of the Elders Loring had piled, then unveiled like a game show prize was matched by the brutality of the Puppeteer who didn't get a kick out of killing them. He threw them away like a used cigarette. This was a landfill and nothing more. At least Loring had a purpose behind his killings, as psychotic as he was.

He grabbed my hand, this time pulling me to the next cluster of trees and down into a crouch behind the pile of death. The stink burned my throat, made worse by being unable to plug my nose and swat the horde of flies we stirred up.

"Shhh."

"I didn't—"

He shoved his hand over my mouth, his other on the back of my head and holding tight.

Power surged to my skin.

He shook my head once. "Stop!" His hiss sprayed me with spit.

Movement, bigger than the flies, limped across the way. A few men in soiled clothing were the closest to zombies I could imagine. They weren't right, not their colouring, their stares, their loose joints. They were Puppets, ones overworked, used, and uncared for. Whatever the Puppeteer was making them do, he was driving them to the brink of death. They didn't look our way at the heap of bodies, and I wondered if they realized they would be a top layer to this carcass pile soon.

With the separation of Diluculo and Pario erased by the destruction of the Woodland of Energies, we were out of luck with places to hide besides the flanking woods. Why we didn't see more people was a mystery. Besides all the dead ones we found, and the ones caged in the Witch's Hunt, not many Puppets or devotees were around.

I stood. "He knows we're coming."

"Get down!" Caine yanked on my arm so hard my shoulder joint screamed.

"Ow! I need that arm, buddy. Relax your shit. He already knows we're here."

His slate eyes narrowed, his forehead creasing.

I sighed, got up, and walked into the clearing before he could grab my arm again. "No reason to stick to the sidewalk when there's no cars out. Hey!" Everything went sideways as Caine scooped me up over his shoulder. "Dude. Come on." His shoulder dug into me and pulled on my belly-button ring as he headed back towards the trees.

"I'm not letting you get us killed."

I braced my hands on his back to stop myself from bouncing. "You're killing my tits. You may not want them anymore but flattening them won't help us."

"They'll survive."

"Will your balls?"

He shielded his dick as I used the misdirection and dug my elbow into his spine. He crumbled to his knees in a gasp of pain as if I had nutted him.

"I warned you, man."

"Dick move."

"Could've been. You're lucky I care if you have kids one day. It was as big a dick move as you pulling a caveman and throwing me over your shoulder like a prized womb."

His expression scrunched as he stood and stretched his back to the side.

"You're lucky all you got was an elbow-spear. Your nuts were a prime target."

"I could make a joke about size right about now, but we're mid-mission. Can we get back to it, please, or would you rather stay downwind from the rotting bodies?"

"I'm good to go." I walked a few steps backwards in the direction I was headed before Caine's caveman side took over.

He huffed and looked around but didn't follow.

"Look, I know you don't trust me. I don't trust myself, but I promise you, I know I'm right about this."

The fight drained from his features and shoulders.

"Think about it, Caine. Why is no one around when the Puppeteer's got an army at his disposal? A proven effective army with no intact conscious or change in loyalties to hesitate about. We're not special ops. I was loud as a pig giving birth when you dragged me out of the water. Our group, every person, coughing, cursing, yelling, some struggling to live and puking their guts up, and still nothing? Not a tad weird? Even you said he probably knew we came through the pass-way. He's waiting for us to find him. He's not going to let his Puppets take us out before he gets his hands on us. The pile of dead Puppets was his garbage bin. We're personal. Or I am. Either way, he wants us alive."

He looked around again, hesitating enough for me to grind my teeth. Donovan was there with me, frustrated, maybe for his own reasons.

"If you're wrong, we end up in the pile. You sure enough to have your toes be hound snacks?"

I shrugged. "I don't need all my toes. They're practically extra pets I have no use for."

He closed his eyes and rubbed his forehead.

"Relax. Stay hidden in the trees and watch my back so I can keep all my useless toes." I started walking away from him again.

"Sophie."

"What? It's sandal weather. I may not need them, but they're pretty."

Caine raced to my side so quickly I flinched before he entangled his fingers with mine. "I go where you go."

I looked down at his steadfast grip. "Okay."

Analyzing what this hand-holding business meant was too much right now, and snaking into his head felt invasive, so I let it be, leaving the overthinking for when I was equipped to deal with the guilt it would create.

"By the way—" he paused until I looked up at him, "—I do trust you."

My smile was either lackluster or maniacal, I couldn't track what he might have read on my face and I had no clue what to say. Thanking him didn't seem right. Celebrating with a "Fucking right you do!" was also wrong and rather rude. Whatever he saw, it didn't make him drop my hand, and we continued dodging firebomb potholes while my heartstrings reverberated in my chest.

Caine didn't hate me and there was a sense of relief in that, even if I knew I didn't deserve his hate.

If we were attacked after I swore the Puppeteer was content to let us find him instead of sending Puppets after us, whatever trust Caine found for me would be tested. The forests flanking us retained its sense of watchful eyes stalking our every step, begging to stick a fork in my theory. Ignoring it didn't mean we forgot about it, the invisible attention was heavy.

Caine's fingers gripped my hand as if he planned to drag me one way or the other if whoever watched us decided they were done with the voyeurism and wanted to get frisky.

He lifted our hands and I gasped, thinking someone was coming after us.

"How is he?" He was looking at the bruising around my arms.

My grasp on his fingers loosened.

He tightened his hold before I could pull away. "I'm not being an ass by bringing him up. His pain is your pain, so I was wondering."

"Better, I guess. Knows I'm safe and we're not in that limbo-state anymore. As good as he can be considering he's in enemy hands and probably wishing he was somewhere else four-fingers deep in a tumbler of whisky."

I saw Caine nod in my peripheral, yet he stayed silent for a moment. "Sorry I thought running away would solve things. Clearly, the further you're from Donovan, the worse it gets. I should've listened instead of pushing it."

I shook my head. "We're not going to die, Caine. We can leave confessions for later."

"But we won't, so I'm talking about it now."

"Riiight, because a destroyed Creation is the perfect place to talk about our destroyed relationship."

"Imploded is a good way to describe it."

I made a throaty noise. "A slow death, really. More a gut shot than a decapitation."

"Nice."

I shrugged. "Our D-Day, which could stand for Destruction Day or Donovan Day, was going to happen. Unplanned, unpredicted, but there were signs I ignored, and they led to D-Day like a wide-spread disease."

"True. I've seen your guilt. I've heard your peace and I loved seeing you in pain."

This stopped me short and I dropped his hand.

"Come on. You can't be surprised by that. I may have even said it before."

I looked around. Now whoever watched us was getting a show instead of dinner conversation.

"I've seen you close to death a few times since we split. Every time, it was instinct to save you or wish I was there to help drag you out of whatever hell you were in." He waved his hand around at our surroundings. "It couldn't happen. Kill the others, take all the rest, but never you."

I crossed my arms and looked at the ground. "I hate every moment of this." My voice was thick, but he was undeterred.

"Me, too, but I don't see a way for us to regain what we had."

I bobbed my head in a slow nod.

He stepped into my line of sight and bent to make me look at him. "I don't see an alternative. I can even admit the truth of you and Donovan being fated for each other, but I'm telling you right now, if something changes, if by some miracle you find a loophole to the connection or even want to try and deal with it without you being with him, I'm in. No matter what."

"Jesus fuck, Caine." I started fast-walking—more like stomping—away as he followed. "That's all it takes? For me to embrace you as the one, shove a slicked middle finger up the ass of the connection, and you pretend I didn't fuck Donovan? Not to mention forgive any times I may in the future if we get stuck in an emotional cycle. No prob, right? *Pfft.* I couldn't live like that and neither could you. You could barely take it for the few months you did."

"Meh. I'll even grow my hair back."

I glared at him while I kept my heavy stride.

He threw me a smile.

"Ass. Your hair looks fine short."

Caine's full lips stretched in a crinkled-eyed smile as he turned and quick-stepped in front of me, so I had to stop. "I don't need any kind of an answer. I was just making things known."

"Schoolhouse Rock can choke on *The knowledge is Power* Bill for making generations believe in honesty."

He threw his back in laughter. "You being one of this generation."

"Nah. Bury it all. I don't need—"

He grabbed my hand. "Okay, okay. Enough honesty. No more D-Day talk, whatever your definition of it is."

We resumed our walk at a steady pace towards the Puppeteer. Horrendous things were happening and more were about to happen, yet we found some odd version of peace between us. He was satisfied with himself for making sure I knew all he thought I should know, and I was—Was I happy? This whole thing was nowhere close to what I would call peace. I was happy he was happy, even if I wasn't good for him. I would hate myself later.

"I bet he's worried now."

"Hmm. Maybe, a tiny bit because he has to guess at what I'm freaking out about. Makes him nervous."

"Will you tell him?"

I shrugged, not knowing whether telling Donovan would gratify Caine's need to piss him off or my need for absolute disclosure.

Without the Woodland of Energies in our way, the perfect white sand beach was in view. It took a moment to realize why it didn't look right. The clear water was now black, more like a swamp-water cesspool than spring break drunk and dunk. Waves lapped and stained the white sand a death-like grey I wanted to stay far away from.

Another memory of fun times taken and twisted.

"If he knows we're here, why doesn't he show up already?" Caine growled and tugged at his shirt sticking to his sweat-covered skin. The beach may have lost its allure, but the Puppeteer retained the tropical temperatures, and we weren't in bathing suits.

"I'm thinking the Puppeteer doesn't move for anything unless he wants to."

I chinned out in front of me, motioning in the distance at what looked like a mirage.

21

HOW LITTLE IT TOOK

Caine shielded his eyes from the sun. "Whoa. What am I looking at?"

"A love nest? Bone tent? Maybe a genie will jump out of it."

"We could use a genie right about now."

"Yup. Bring on the harem garb. He's going to love the shit out of your pretty eyes."

Humour did nothing to smooth the edge of tension caused by looking at a four-poster cabana sitting mid-field of where the Woodland of Energies used to be.

Burgundy satin was draped poster to poster and was tied with strands of gold and laid overtop to create shade from the ruthless sun. White, gauzy draping made walls of the cozy place to escape for a macabre honeymoon couple. The middle of a desolate graveyard of tree stumps and craters, where the Puppeteer had no right existing, made it a bizarre image to stumble upon.

After my confidence in walking out into the open and waltzing up to the enemy, something inside me screamed to hide. It didn't help that outside the cabana were a handful of people—all Tainted Magics according to their soul glows. One dark-haired man clad in an expensive dark suit and deep green button down, evoked anger and panic.

Loring.

Everything about the bastard standing fifty yards away disgusted and infuriated me. The man Caine's "father" trusted with obsession so pure he murdered one son and tried to murder the other. The man who slaughtered the Elders and played it off as a favour for the Coveners to be rid of them and their perceived idolized existence. He wanted me dead or to call him Master, but I would rather chop my tongue out and wear it as a necklace than talk to him like he was a god in the flesh.

The vice grip Caine had on my hand would have cracked bones if I wasn't popping a knuckle inflicting the same on him. No doubt the Puppeteer prick was inside the cocoon of fabric, but all we saw was Loring chatting up two other Magics—two men, one balding while the other faired much younger. Neither were immortal, yet both had blackened souls corrupting the air around them. Another young Tainted man was pacing on the other side of the cabana. Guarding the Puppeteer? His soul glow was unimpressive, yet I had more experience judging unTainted souls.

I was grateful for Caine's anchoring grip. Walking at a strolling pace, we didn't want to alarm anyone of our presence, needing our approach to appear causal so Loring's first reaction wasn't to attack. Anticipating him acknowledging our presence was torturous. We closed the gap by a hundred feet before we stopped again.

The pacing man, no doubt in servitude, approached the three-man group, lips in a blur as Loring's expression morphed into a Grinchy grin, accentuating the deep lines of his skin. He left the men and stuck his head through the cabana drapes—I assumed to warn his lounging Master of their visitors before returning to the men.

A flare of cautious excitement rolled through the connection as we watched two men look at us and then called the pacing man over to follow them away.

Loring remained, looking down, and straightening the cuffs of his shirt without rushing the task, before turning to meet my gaze.

My heart hammered as I retained his stare without wilting below it, squeezing Caine's hand like it could counteract my racing blood.

"Care to join me, Seer?"

The sound of Loring's gravel-beaten voice reverberated through me with a shuddering aftermath. The last time I heard him was in my nightmare, and even that managed to soften the blow of the real thing. He was a monster. A monster with his own story I didn't give a fuck about, not now. No reason was good enough to have tortured and humiliated the Elders as he had. If he wanted them dead, he could have killed them and been done with it, but he wanted to ensure they suffered. And they had.

Would we suffer now, too? Was Loring's lust for revenge sated? Or did he have leftover resentment making his stomach gurgle for more blood?

His glib invitation came with strings, presumed Puppet strings, but also of a much simpler variety. Bridging the gap brought us closer and I found it difficult enough to keep myself from lashing out at him. We didn't stand a chance in a fair fight and Loring was no advocate for fair.

From our current vantage point, we had space to flee for the flanking woods, where our awaiting back-up crew was. Or so we hoped. I couldn't see soul colours in the forest, so they were either hidden well behind the trees, under a cover spell, or Caine and I were alone. I'm not sure which I preferred. Either way, I knew I wasn't as much of a pro-star with my powers as I should be. Uncle Lewis could see soul colours under cover spells, which meant I was a lazy shit for not making sure I prepared enough for this.

If Loring kicked my ass before we even caught a glimpse of the Puppeteer, I had no one to blame by myself.

A faint shake of Loring's head and a tight-lipped laugh was enough to get my feet moving. Caine squeezed my hand and had me checking my speed. Rushing into anything meant playing into

Loring's plan. He wanted us pissed off and reacting sloppy. I was anything but sloppy, accident prone or overthinking to a fault, but not sloppy. We came to do a job and I needed to suck it up and perform.

Caine helped me focus. His steps were as confident and controlled as if he was approaching a border cop in a tiny booth who decided if your vacation was a go or if they sent you into secondary and made you miss your flight with the addition of a cavity search. He operated as a pro on the surface and, again, I hoped my outside reflected what he portrayed. He didn't need me fucking this sideways for the both of us. Getting him killed was as unacceptable as getting Donovan killed.

His strength was contagious, so I let myself be taken by his virus.

"Mighty cozy, Firefly. The Sorrel would be heart-stricken."

Screw you, sack-puller. I didn't need his guilt. "We're here to speak to the boss. Where's Evaristus?"

His lips twitched. I was happy to see his ego was still so fragile. He wasn't the big fish here as he was back at the barn in Pario, and he didn't like it. I enjoyed this far too much.

Loring folded his hands behind his back, chin up. "En route."

We didn't comment, letting silence settle knowing he wouldn't let it remain for long.

"He's quite tickled to make your acquaintance beyond the remote viewing of his Puppets. Though I assured him neither of you were anything special—" Loring shrugged. "—his obsessions are his own."

Wow. Keep your composure, Sophie. Don't laugh, don't laugh. Think of something else. Anything else. Bumble bee butts bravely sticking out of begonias. Panda pranks a precocious pile of peacocks. A snake's eyes steely gaze on sand dunes. Clenched teeth, relaxed appearance. Fuck him, he won't get to me.

I took a breath. Steady as she goes, girl. "And Donovan? Is he among the Puppeteer's obsessions?"

A head tilt and mock pout from Loring. "Don't you fret."

I heard Caine inhale, thinking he may say something more. I

squeezed his hand to stop him. He seemed to understand and let it go.

"No pressing questions?" Cockiness set Loring's expression. When we didn't answer, he laughed. "Nothing about the man himself? About Elsa or her untimely demise?"

My insides cringed. Fucking prick.

"Your family then?" He looked to Caine and then back at me. "Or yours perhaps?"

What about my family?

Loring laughed the obscene laugh I remembered from Pario, reminding me he could read my mind. Blocking while pissed off was a chore. I tried to hold onto the tactics Vincent taught me—envision the wall, keep it in mind, and regularly reenforce as needed. Not that it mattered. Loring already got what he wanted.

"Thought that might rouse your attention. Personally, I would be more intrigued by a summary conversation of the occurrence that ended our last visit. I happen to know the power you wielded was not of your vested abilities from Nya. However, it was interesting. Old magic can control the soul beyond the person. Your bloodline or Elsa's doesn't account for your success when last we met. Something else is at play."

I had no idea what he was talking about. How could he be sure what happened wasn't Nya?

Instead of asking, I took a different route. "Joelly would love to hear you confirm that. She's under the impression I owe her something. I've told her Melina was some random skank to a second-rate Witch with heavy over-compensation issues, but Joelly insisted you knew what you were talking about."

Loring's cheeks wrinkled in a purse-lipped smirk as he stuck his hands in his pockets and glared at me.

Nothing? Hmm. I must have struck a chord to piss him off so badly he felt he needed to lockdown his reactions. We figured the Puppeteer told him to keep his hands off. It was good to see we were right. He was itching to get at me.

"Good try, by the way." I tensed, waiting to see where Caine was going with his comment. "By the time Joelly showed up looking for safety after you turfed her from your Coven, she already knew everything she needed to capture Sophie, saving you from doing it yourself and getting in trouble with your Master. You didn't plan on the Coven being smart enough to see through your plan or for Joelly to have her own motives. Your leash is short and your desperation is showing."

Loring's jaw flexed at this. Caine wasn't wrong but goading him was a dangerous game.

I got the draw to make Loring suffer by reminding him he wasn't the top of the food chain, but he would find a way to end us if his ego was slashed too deep.

With any luck, this will make him a sloppy fighter when it came time.

"Your death is his end goal, regardless of the method."

I didn't believe Loring. Caine's chuckle meant he didn't either.

"How was your swim?" Loring looked over our wet clothing with shrewd dark eyes. "The Blue Men of Minch bristled at the forceful removal from their Scottish waters for anything less than the deaths of other Magics soiling their territory. Shades hiding within shadows. You should have kept your eyes closed."

"Awww, thanks, Tips. And here I thought you wanted us dead. I doubt dear ol' grandpa-times-twenty would appreciate you giving us the warning."

A Grinchy smile darkened Loring's face. "You won't survive him to use it."

Mhmm. Asshole. He might be right, so we needed to figure out a way to let the others know for when they go back through the pass-way.

Loring sucked in a breath through flared nostrils and straightened his already arrogant posture as a new man came out of the trees behind Loring and made his way towards us. Behind him were the three men we saw as we arrived. The last shouldered an animal carcass as the other two carried what looked like bows and arrows and a musket you wouldn't see outside of an antique store or museum.

It's him. The one from my dreams about my ancestor. Evaristus. The Puppeteer. Same bushy, black hair worn tied at the nape of his neck. A scruff of a beard swathed his chin and his eyes were so dark they blended with his pupils, but as Vincent said, he was much rounder now. Not obese but overweight, like the plumped and pampered king he was.

In my vision, he took on a wistful demeanour that weakened the knees of my ancestor. A compassion now lost in the figure washing his bloodied hands in a large bowl not thirty feet from us. Whatever part of this man gifted my blood the power it wielded today was forever buried beneath centuries of resentment.

No! Stopping myself from gasping was managed by chomping down on my lip so hard Donovan reacted with a sense of "What the fuck!" across the connection. Terror and sadness for Evaristus falling so far from his roots were far from my mind. What had me freaking out inside was something I hadn't expected.

With an evil so strong they would slaughter the family they created, I expected a soul glow so dark Evaristus would look like he was on the edge of a black hole. Instead, I found nothing. Not the absence of a soul colour or any lingering good which would have been as unnerving, but as I stared at the personification of what I deemed evil, I saw no soul glow at all. To my talented eyes, he looked no more enlightened than the Blind. This sparked a memory of the premonition. 'See without colour'. This was what it meant.

"Did you sell your soul or did it keel over and die on its own?" The question was better than attacking him and I needed to know.

Caine shifted next to me.

Evaristus let a smile crack his drawn features as he dried his hands on a towel handed to him by the servant man, then turned to us for the first time. "You would be surprised by how little it took."

I expected his dialect to be foreign, considering his age and origins, but I didn't expect it to hold so much of its original strength as he rolled his "r" and elongated the "o's" in the word "took". Though the shadowy circles beneath his eyes were questionable, there was no telling if it was a feature reminiscent of his Mediterranean background or a sign of his soulless paler.

The combination of his dialect, the cool nature of its delivery, and those shadows accenting his black eyes with an extra dose of cruelty, made my power crawl out of its hiding spot and buzz to be released in full.

"What are you seeing?" Caine didn't exactly hide his question by lowering his voice, but he wasn't projecting it for anyone but me.

"Evaristus has no soul." I expected he wouldn't care if I told Caine and didn't bother to quiet my voice. Something about Evaristus gave me the impression he would never hide his soul or change it like Joelly had—as he would find it undignified, even if only a few could see it. "And judging by the devotees muzzled reactions, including Loring's, they had no clue about their Master's missing piece." I focused on Loring a moment. "Must answer a few questions, though, yeah?"

He didn't react, but I knew I was right. Evaristus wasn't about to share with his underlings, but they had to know something was different about him, even if they couldn't tell what.

"A soul accounts for so little." Evaristus passed the hand towel back to a nervous looking devotee. "Though I see you host power I had the pleasure of passing on to a lovely woman I once knew." His eyes didn't light up or budge at mentioning my ancestor. "I do not recall gifting this boon to you."

"Obviously." Cutting my sarcasm came as an afterthought.

"You are undeserving."

"Tough shit, grandpappy. What's been gifted to my blood is mine to keep. If you didn't want the power to stretch past the lifespan of your immediate family, you shouldn't have made them powerful enough to evade you when you changed your mind."

A missile of pain to the brain jellied my knees. I crumpled, gripping Caine's hand as blood splashed over my hands. Not my hands. Evaristus'.

A gush of blood poured out of the throat of a young man with long, dark hair. His nails gripped into my shoulder as I held him down and watched him die, ignoring his pleas, and waiting until his green soul glow burst from his body. Once dead, he was thrown into the cover of nearby trees and left to rot.

I was now walking down a street made of cobblestone, pedestrians passing by, none paying attention but moving aside as if out of respect. A tug stopped me from moving. I looked back to see a child gripping onto a wood post, her screams now registering as an annoyance. I yanked at the child's ponytail in my fist and tore her grip from the post, walking on in search of my temporary lodgings.

There.

I picked the child up in front of me by her hair, up off her feet as she screamed and pleaded for help. No one saw us, no one would come for help. I let the undeserving child freefall a few inches before gripping her tight again, hearing the faint snap of her thin neck, and watching the green soul glow drift from her body before throwing the limp body to the pigs.

Running. A chase. I enjoyed a chase after travelling by sea for so long. This one ran through alleys, through kitchens, farms. Mud slowed me, but my mission kept my feet moving. This one knew of his strength, knew he could not defeat me, yet had many years of experience to fight with. He would be a sound ally if not for the abomination of his existence, a power now used against me, thrown at me in wayward attacks.

Pathetic.

I struck out with power, severing the undeserving's legs at the knees, and watched them tumble. I slowed to a walk, taking my time approaching.

He gripped his thighs as blood poured into the grass—he was sweating and pale. "Whoever you be, mister, I made no transgression." He panted. "Please, tell me what I have done, let me atone."

He scrambled backward, smearing the grass as he retreated like a coward.

The cold grip of a knife handle weighted my palm as I reached out and telekinetically dragged him back towards me and thrusted the knife into the middle of his—

"Stop!"

The man in front of me disappeared. Darkness took over until I opened my eyes, adjusting to the grass under my feet, Caine's voice in my ear, and Donovan's panic joining mine in my chest.

Fuck. That man's chest would have been—I tried not to think about it, but images of the memory of what I saw wouldn't quit. Children. He killed children like snapping the head off a doll. He was a true monster.

"You okay?" Caine helped me to my feet, steadying my body while my mind was running in circles and hoping Caine's power didn't grow beyond where it prickled my skin. Not yet anyway.

Evaristus had no concerning glint in his eye for me. I was another to be erased from his bloodline and nothing else.

"I'm fine." I glimpsed at Loring and the devotees, whose fists were clenched in wait for a chance to make a move. After what I saw, Evaristus was more interested in causing death himself instead of having others do it for him.

He stared at me as if nothing affected him anymore.

Once I rode out the throbbing in my tenderized brain, I was on my feet with heavy breaths. "Papa-Evar was kind enough to give me a play by play of his fun in hacking up our family."

"This is no different than the visions many such as your mate receives. You are too weak to withstand their invasion, evidence of the essentialness of your death. Blood so diluted you can merely see souls without the aptitude of control."

If he was disappointed, I couldn't tell.

"If your whole point is to kill Sophie, then she'd already be dead. We know you kidnapped Donovan and know about their connection, so killing him would be the easiest way to make it count. Not that your minions didn't have fun carving them up." Those nameless minions behind Loring gave twin smiles. "What do you really want?"

"Is this fact?" Evaristus looked to me with stiff movements. Everything about him was inhuman to me. How could we be related? "Will you die as the Sorrel does?"

Neither of us answered. How could Evaristus not know?

Evaristus frowned, then he looked back at the cabana behind him to his right and reached towards it with a simple gesture. The cabana was telekinetically dragged through the sand as Evaristus brought it closer to him. The wood frame groaned.

I tensed, thinking he might throw it at us.

When the cabana was close, Evaristus forced it to stand up like a grizzly bear on its hind legs. As it did, stinging pain sliced my arms.

"Fuckshit." I drew in an intense gasp and held my arms out in front of me. Blood flowed from a surgical incision across both arms above my elbows.

"What's happening?"

I didn't know how to answer Caine. Nothing touched me and Evaristus wasn't concentrating on me. These weren't my injuries.

"Fuck. Donovan's in the cabana."

Evaristus' fingers twitched, and Donovan's moaning spilled out of the cabana walls. He must have spelled Donovan or the cabana to keep anyone from hearing anything including himself.

The beautiful fabric cocooning the cabana blackened in a suffocating heat that washed over my skin as pain pulsed though me. A singeing black crawled along the dark drapes—the fabric burning without actual flames or decomposing as if from sudden onset age—as it bled away all colour and fell in stringy pieces to the sand below.

Donovan.

No plush mattress rested beneath him. Hardwood dug into his spine. His legs were straight below him, arms straight out to the sides. Straps around his wrists and biceps bruised me while he was laying down. Trapping him. When upright, the straps around his biceps had blades. Gravity did the most damage as it pulled him down into the blades. His tip toes grazed the footboard of the cabana. The small piece of wood was all that was stopping him from amputating his own limbs.

Donovan squirmed and fought to keep himself from slipping. He looked up, finally seeing me. Panic and anger rushed through him, ricocheting within me, causing me to ground my teeth together to keep from lashing out. His shoes kept sliding, deepening the gashes when they did. Whatever mental fortitudes he was able to hold together while he scrambled to save our arms, he kept me out. Nothing I said would help this anyway. He needed to keep fighting to stay up.

Loring howled like he heard the joke of the century. The other men joined in without so much theatrics. Though not as plainly as the rest, Evaristus also enjoyed the scene. A small twitch of his lips showed the hint of a smile, cold smugness wading beneath.

Instinctive power began to swell within me, drowning out their voices . I didn't know who was talking. I couldn't focus enough to hear them as power pounded in my ears.

Pressure squeezed around my hand and arm. I didn't know why or where it came from until I saw Caine's hands on me. Warning was in his eyes and something else. Pain?

Power within me grew and I realized I should have given in to it sooner. As I thought this, my power switched gears and I felt Nya's power take over.

The one attached to the wooden contraption—Donovan, I had to remind myself—pitched forward, expression twisted in agony. Caine next to me did the same, fighting the takeover instead of embracing it.

Searching the edges of the shield the grey-eyed one placed before his thoughts, I found holes. Big holes to slip through. I tilted his chin up to look at me from where he fell to his knees. *"Trust me. Let him go."*

His grey-eyes widened as he strained. I overheard him try and do as I asked, to convince his body to allow Gareth's power to come out and play.

A cry from Donovan spun my attention. The oddity that was Nya's power's influence left me unfeeling towards things I would have thought important. Nya or not, I was present, though wavering between absence and keen awareness. I pushed into Nya's flank instead of letting her rule out front and felt a rush back into myself.

Shit. Donovan. Nya's power was hurting him.

Stark whiteness was bone beneath the striking red of my blood streaming down my arms. As if I willed it, the spot where the invisible blades digging into my skin prickled and tingled. It was as if my power had sent out reinforcements and prevented the hardened steel from doing further damage. The blade was still imbedded into Donovan's skin, so the wound couldn't close, but Nya's power stopped all the bleeding around the gaping wound.

I looked to Evaristus as I floated in an odd sense of disconnect, finding a genuine look of confusion cross my ancestor's features.

"Curious. She paints me a monster while inflicting pain against the men she cares for, justifying her ends."

Gareth's power finding its way to the surface distracted me from the fact Nya's power was strong enough to surpass Evaristus' mental defences.

Caine straightened to full height and stretched his shoulders. A smile passed over his face, one more akin to Gareth than Caine—both of us struggled with the effects of our gifted power taking control of us instead of the other way around. His thoughts passed to me as if they were my own. The power our vessels held brought with them strength a liquid courage couldn't match when we turned back to Evaristus.

He was observing us all in keen interest of the "unlikely dynamic", his intrigue flirting with questions he wished to ask, having never witnessed this in all his years.

Having gone without an incident of shock for some time, Evaristus was enveloped with our strange existence when I sent a cold stream of thoughts through his temples as he had to me. A dizzying effect pitched him to the side with a grunt. He stretched out his hand as if to catch himself. Loring and the men were quick at his side, inching closer in aid, waiting for him to either hit the ground, at which time they would strike against us, or for the command of attack. When he stumbled and held on to his equilibrium, eyes rolling to the sand floor and super-heated sun above him, the men waited and settled back to observe.

Instead of hitting him with the monstrous recall of death, I subjected him to the horrors of the happiness of his former life, pinched from his memories. He couldn't escape their invading emotions, even without the soul he damned to rid himself of his former wife. A hell worse than the one he forced on me since I had no connection to those he killed, except for genetics.

"Alorha chose to die." I spoke my ancestor's name—one I learned the moment I entered his mind. "Killing everything you created with her won't change her decision to leave you. Won't change the fact she refused to practice your gifts enough to live alongside you as an immortal the way you fantasized once your children were born. She forced you to watch her wither away because she begged you not to leave her in her last days. You turned your anger into a force that destroyed the person Alorha protected from death, changing you into someone no better than the Magic she protected you from."

Evaristus' expression changed from cold and unaffected to holding subdued fury. He stewed in his thoughts as he wrestled for composure.

"You think because you are all-powerful this includes you forcing other's choices. You can take all your knowledge from searching the globe for The Book of the Dead and your studies in the deserts of Egypt where your days in battle brought you, exploit your power and turn us into Puppets, make us pull off some stunt we would never do otherwise, but you are still making the choice. You would think after all the years since Alorha chose to turn her back on immortality, you would have gained the wisdom to know the difference. You were a grieving husband and you let your grief transform you into a monster."

This created a stir in the emotionless man. I saw it build as his stance shifted. He may be soulless, but I proved he could still feel, and making this apparent in front of others he deemed beneath him angered him beyond any sense of rationale. He didn't wish for me to die like the others he snuffed out like an annoying chore. He wanted me to hurt, to see the moment I wished I questioned facing him as an equal. He wanted to teach me a lesson before watching me bleed out.

A silent beat passed as Caine held my hand, now thrumming with Gareth's power and pride for my invasion against the enemy.

We lost the thread of inoffensive conversation meant to distract Evaristus long enough to get into position to close the Creation. The plan was given the boot, had its mouth stuffed with a dirty sock, and shoved into a dark car trunk. I couldn't help myself.

Evaristus lunged, arms flared out at his sides as he emitted a booming roar, displacing the air around him and coming straight for us like a lightning bolt. I shoved Caine out of the way. The hit needled for me, throwing me dozens of feet away. I bounced on the grass and rolled to a stop. Regaining my bearings, I felt too normal. I had lost my connection with Nya's power. Caine pitched forward and knelt over something. I got up, racing back to see what.

No. Impossible.

22

DEVIATING FROM THE PLAN

Caine shook my lifeless body, pleading for me to wake up, and checking for a pulse. Blood began spilling down my arms again as if the wounds were fresh.

"She remains in this life, yet not of this world." Evaristus stood with renewed calm.

Loring celebrated with boisterous giddiness.

Caine sprang to attack. I reached out to stop him, my hand going through his shoulder, unable to grab onto anything tangible.

I looked down at my hand. "Holy shit, I'm Patrick Swayze."

Evaristus made no attempt to defend himself. Loring took the opportunity to put Caine down to his knees as he had with Donovan not so long ago, thwarting his efforts before they amounted to anything worth Evaristus raising a hand against.

Evaristus looked down at Caine over his high-bridged, slender nose. "No need for that."

"What did you do to her?" Caine forced a knee up, his foot on the ground, fighting against Loring's hold.

Loring regained control and telekinetically put Caine down on all fours. The strain on Caine's face told me he kept trying but was unable to gain any ground.

Power floated all around me, but I couldn't feel any of it within me.

Did he still feel Gareth's power? He seemed too Caine-like for Gareth's power to be in there with any amount of true hold, but he was trying.

A growl came out between Caine's teeth with a slew of drool. "I won't be your Puppet."

No, no, no. Not that. Please not that. Caine knew what it was like to take someone's will. He had no control over this being his gift, but to be on the other end and at the sick creative mind of the Puppeteer meant he could be made to do anything.

He was still using Gareth's power to fight against him. Could Gareth be stronger than the Puppeteer? Nya's power made a significant move, but I used a sneak attack before he could fight against me, and then he spanked me and showed me who was boss. Now I was standing around doing fuck-all with front row seats.

"Come on, Caine!" He continued to struggle and couldn't hear me. "Fuck."

What the fuck do I do now?

Caine growled again, his face turning red with effort. The ground rumbled. A little at first, and then enough to throw my balance off.

"Whoa, doggy. What are you doing? What's happening?"

Evaristus was still focused on Caine, trying to turn him into a Puppet. Loring and the other men were looking around them and at each other. They didn't dare disturb their Master but looked lost at what was going on.

Was it Caine? He bared down and the rumbling got worse. Damn. It was him. What was he doing?

When the rumbling became violent shaking, the youngest of the men couldn't handle the anticipation and leapt at Caine. Before the man got anywhere near his target, Evaristus snatched a hold of him telekinetically, stopping him mid-attack between himself and Caine.

The growing rumble hit my ears with a resounding crash. The ground cracked and sludge-like water, like the stuff from the beach, filled up the fissure, forcing the Creation in two. Swampy water spilled over the edges, saturating the grass, the smell still hitting me in this fucked up realm Evaristus sent me to. The crevice grew until a seventy-foot ditch of swampy, churning water stood between us and our enemies, creating a wide buffer.

This was Gareth's power. Caine did it once by accident at Ranlyn's, this time he did it with purpose. No hidden water source this time, but one close by did the trick. Quick thinking.

Caine shifted back onto his ankles as Evaristus lifted the man off the ground. Loring's attention must have been too divided to concentrate on taking over Caine.

Evaristus held up the man who squirmed and flailed and threw him into the water. When the man bobbed back up to the surface, he gasped and cried out for Loring, for his comrades, for anyone to help him. They didn't try and get to him. They stood by and watched as he panicked and was pulled under the surface of the rough water and didn't come back up.

Did Caine do something to the water to make sure anyone who went in never came back out? Or did Evaristus hold him under? I couldn't ask them and wasn't sure which I preferred.

When I looked back at Caine, he was now over my body again, trying to clamp down on my bloody arm wounds.

Shit. Donovan. What was I thinking? Apparently about nothing but kicking ass, not considering what it meant if I lost. Was he dead? He was on the other side of the cracked earth with Evaristus and Loring and I couldn't tell from here. I didn't have my Soul Seeing intact and all I saw was Donovan slumped over, blood dripping down his arms and off his fingers.

An itch at my back took me back to my dreams of the park again, before all this started, before Caine and I met—when he was a terrifying dark figure I chose to run from. Someone had heavy eyes on me, watching me. I may no longer be in the park Caine was stuck in during his sleeping curse, but I was still in Diluculo, even if I couldn't interact with anything else in it. The same tense muscles pinched in my back and the distinct urge to take off danced in my feet.

I curled my shaking hands into fists. Turn or run? Turn or run?

How much did I want to know? What if I was dead? If this was God or some type of other god or goddess or angel, I wanted nothing of it. No way in hell was I leaving yet. Not when I didn't know if Donovan was alive or dead and Caine still needed me. Maybe this was my brand of Hell. Forced to watch Caine die, guilt-ridden with the knowledge my recklessness caused Donovan's death. Then to have Donovan taken away from me in the afterlife as well.

I couldn't stand the thought and contemplated running and trying to jump over the water-filled crevice to get to him instead. I couldn't drown as a ghost, could I?

I tensed to step forward, away from the itch. A voice steeled my step.

"I should be offended you were about to abandon me."

I didn't move, didn't turn around. I would have known the voice anywhere, but it had to be a trick.

"No trick. No god or angel. Only me."

Turning was slow-motion torture. When I saw her, all I could think was how different she looked than when summoned by Jheri.

Aunt Lacey smiled, big enough to see it in her eyes, and clasped her hands in front of her. "More real?"

Did I say it out loud? "Yeah."

She leaned forward with a sly expression. "Because I am."

She gave a small laugh and raised her arms in invitation. I rushed forward to wrap my arms around her. She laughed while I sobbed. I couldn't help myself. Seeing her summoned figure or witnessing her incorporeal soul take off to wherever it was going when she died, was nothing to seeing and feeling her squeeze me until breathing was a chore. If I was dead, I wanted Aunt Lacey there in the end. As much as I wanted to live and be part of the plan Caine and I set out to do, Aunt Lacey's embrace was everywhere I wanted to be.

"You're not coming with me, Salix."

I pulled back. "I'm not?" Aunt Lacey shook her head. "Oh, good. Donovan too, right?" When she laughed and shook her head again, a hit of relief soared through my veins and I hugged her with renewed excitement. "So, where is he?"

"There." She looked to where his body hung from the cabana, still bleeding. "Do not worry about him, Salix. No need at present." She smoothed my hair and focused my attention on her. "We must be quick. My presence is only allotted company at your last breath to guide you and Donovan onto the next step. This is not that moment. I refuse to recommence with my Soul Shepherd duties just yet."

"Are you supposed to?"

"Debatable. One day you will possess more power than even me, given the opportunity. Although I'm over-encumbered with pride for your progress, right now, Salix, you cannot defeat Evaristus."

"We were only trying to—"

Aunt Lacey's eyes closed, head tilted in a painful struggle.

"Aunt Lacey?"

She righted herself and blinked a couple of times. "I'm okay."

"What happened?"

"I'm not allowed to say or learn so much."

"Says who?"

"Since I am best suited to ensure you and Donovan receive the smoothest transition in death, I was sent to gather you up and bring you over. However—" She raised an eyebrow without finishing. I read this as her indicating she had no plan to follow through regardless of who ordered her to. "You need to know you cannot beat the man. Not yet. Nevertheless, you can reduce him to less than whole."

"Reduce him? Like, attack his manhood? Break him down psychologically? That's how I ended up like this."

Aunt Lacey was shaking her head.

"I'm sorry, I don't get it!" I grabbed onto her arms. "Don't leave before I figure it out. If it's anything like your premonition, I'm so screwed."

"Salix stop." She grabbed mine back and stopped me from bouncing. "You can do this. Think back to your first lesson and use Nya's power to bring nature's energy forth as your ally." Another squeamish reaction came from Aunt Lacey as she fought against whatever she was being chastised for. She recovered fast. "Her powers are yours now. Treat them as such and they will respond."

Aunt Lacey bowed over and fought against whatever she warred with. Her fingers dug into my shoulders. "Wend is strong yet cannot aid you in dispatching Evaristus. Soon, you will need him to match your strength." She fought against what pulled at her, again. "Make him stronger!"

She grabbed both sides of my face. A vision flooded me and disappeared in a flash as Aunt Lacey was ripped away from me like she was tethered to a leash the whole time, disappearing in the faded forest behind her as I was torn back in the opposite direction.

"Sophie?"

I opened my eyes. Caine was leaning over me.

"You can't win that easily, boy!" Loring's voice bellowed over the rush of water.

I sat up and looked in the direction I last saw Aunt Lacey—the spot empty—and then looked back at Caine, who wrapped his arms around me for a fleeting moment, but I felt him. I was back in my body.

"I don't know what happened, but I'm so glad you're awake."

"I'll tell you later." I hoped later would come.

I got to my feet, looking to where Donovan hung from the cabana. He managed to regain his footing on the cabana's edge, but by this point, I couldn't feel my arms.

I saw his lips moving but felt him louder than whatever he said.

Evaristus was calm, standing still, hands out to his sides.

Loring had a thumb grazing his bottom lip and looked far too amused. Jutting his chin out and looking beyond us, we followed his line of sight and saw a gathering of people heading our way. Puppets. Calling on his Puppets was a tactic I figured Evaristus didn't do without consideration. He wanted us for himself, so what was he doing?

"Shit. What now?"

Caine closed his eyes and called his and Gareth's power back in force. He must have let them go when he caused the split. Nya's power surged in curiosity, but I didn't let her out yet, waiting to see what Caine was about to do so I didn't somehow screw that up as well.

He faced the horde of Puppets. None of them were familiar, which was a bonus. He drew his arms out behind him and crouched down, energy flowing out of him in droves. I didn't know what he was doing until drops on my head had me looking up at a sheet of swampy water like a protective blanket, providing a wide berth between us and the edge of the dripping water barrier. Visibility was greater than I expected. He kept the barrier thin and we watched as Puppets smacked into it like bugs on a windshield.

I was in awe.

Holding this in place looked easy. As if Caine had done this before and was currently doing it with little effort, which I suppose he was. The beach gave him a constant flow of sludge to fuel the wall, and once the water had spread beneath the feet of the Puppets, he worked it like a conveyer belt spinning beneath the Puppet's feet. Every droned footstep turned into a run to keep up.

When they became too much, he flicked the floor of water like a table cloth and sent them all flying off their feet and into each other while the water threatened to drown them.

Caine's laugh was unlike him. Gareth's power had taken over and he was having fun.

Water rained down on us as I watched. Nya's power continued to push at me, warring for attention until it became uncomfortable and then painful. I smoothed my hair of the water, switching Nya's power on in the same swipe. It became easier and easier when it was already begging to be released.

Caine looked back at me, Gareth's power in him recognizing Nya's power in me and vice versa.

I looked up at our bubble of protection. "I need to get to Evaristus."

The cocky smile told me he had it covered without him verbalizing how. "Stand back."

I did and watched as he reared back like he was about to pitch a pumpkin, grunting with the effort. He forced a direct blast of water at the Puppets, catapulting them away in all directions, giving me time to get away before they could get back to their feet.

We exchanged a smile and I turned towards Evaristus.

My ancestor stood, eyes closed, concentrating on controlling his Puppets. How sweet it was for this all-mighty power of his to work in my advantage. If ever I was an opportunist, this was the time.

Loring and the other man, plus the servant, darted across my vision behind Evaristus, sprinting in Donovan's direction. He was awake and struggling in pain from the blades in his arms and from Nya's power. As before, I pushed myself forward—so Nya wasn't ruling the decisions—to take care of Donovan. With Nya's help, I didn't have to think twice when I lifted a hand toward Donovan and watched my energy visible to my eyes, spring across the river between us, freeing Donovan from the bladed straps. He fell to the ground and crouched there, unable to lift his arms as he watched the men coming for him.

I healed our wounded arms and surrounded the part within Donovan that ached from Nya's power, wrapping it in the same healing power.

He stood and looked down at his arms, then across the water at me before ducking at the hits from Loring and the other man. They missed him. He wheeled around and put the standing cabana between him and the other men. With a dose of magic, he shoved the cabana at the enemy. Loring dodged the gambit by jumping two stories above it. The lesser Magics with slower reflexes weren't as lucky. They crashed onto the ground along with the splintered wood of the cabana.

Donovan relished the opportunity to have his bout with Loring. I knew this without delving into his brain. He wanted revenge for Aunt Lacey's death and he was salivating for the chance to do what he wanted the first time they met in the barn, when I wasn't strong enough to allow him operate at full strength.

When Loring landed, he didn't have a chance to defend himself. Donovan took advantage by sending a blast of power at Loring's chest, launching him like a rag doll. The other man started to get to his feet and the servant man never got up.

I knelt, focusing on my target across the water and laid my hand on the grass, sending my power out through the earth and using the energy of the water Caine used Gareth's power to create. The grass beneath Evaristus' feet began to move.

Pride filled my chest, Donovan's pride, as he watched what I was doing before turning back to his targets.

Nya's power surged through my hands and across the greenery on Evaristus's side. The tactic Aunt Lacey was talking about—I needed to let Nya's energy reunify with nature to use hers and my power as one. Growing things was part of my power, the first trick Donovan had taught me. With Nya's boost, it was much more than a trick and I had a plan to make Evaristus "less than whole," as Aunt Lacey had advised.

With his attention still on his Puppet's, Evaristus didn't feel it when I edged growing blades of grass over his sandaled feet. I didn't want to spook him. I made slow progress, careful not to rush it, even with every impulse within me calling for the opposite.

Donovan fought Loring and the expression on his face told me he wasn't holding back this time. His arms were still covered in the blood that had run down to his fingertips, as were mine, mixing with sweat as he fought beneath the baking sun.

Battling it out with Loring may have been a mission for Donovan, but as my eyes lingered a moment in his direction, I noticed he wasn't always winning. When he incurred a hit, I didn't feel it. It was hard for me to care at all in this state, but when Loring got close enough to throw a fuelled punch that had enough power to snap a neck, Donovan pitched his body backward and away from Loring's fist in a blurred movement, disappearing and reappearing a few feet from where he had been standing.

I never saw him do that before. It was like the Apporter, but he only moved a short distance and was a blur instead of invisible. Being strapped down had to have meant he couldn't go through solid objects, but he was familiar with the trick as he did it again and again, nimble as a squirrel, evading everything Loring threw his way.

Refocusing on Evaristus, the slithering grass grew like sticky weeds, inching to encircle his feet like a hunter's snare, without applying pressure until it surrounded. Salivating for my moment, I calmed my breath like a sniper.

Movement on my left drew my attention. Hinapouri's group charged in my direction. Caine needed the reinforcements—he was holding his own, but an extra group of Magics could never be discounted as helpful. About to turn my attentions back to Evaristus before he caught sight of Hinapouri's group, another crash from over my head to the right was a distracting hit.

Ranlyn's team was attacking Hinapouri's group.

The tattooed warrior glared in my direction. Was she coming after me? Did Evaristus have a hold of both groups as Puppets and were bringing them down on me?

Evaristus opened his eyes and his Puppets slumped to the ground. Hinapouri and Ranlyn's groups kept running at me. They weren't Puppets.

I lost my chance to attack Evaristus and now everyone on Evaristus' side of the split, including Donovan, stopped to look at the two groups.

Vincent was running full tilt towards me. He screamed my name, but I didn't understand his warning.

Hinapouri was headed for me, but Miklos was headed for Caine, the group divided to take on each of us while the leftovers went for Ranlyn's team.

"Down!" I ducked as Vincent slid to my side.

A sting of power grazed my back as Vincent threw a hit of power at Hinapouri and then encapsulated our bodies before Hinapouri could throw a spear through my chest. It hit and deflected off of Vincent's barrier and disappeared back into the ether.

Devotees came from somewhere, clashing with our back-up. Hinapouri and her tribal members, Miklos, and both Huntsman, couldn't get to Caine and fought against Ranlyn, Anne-Claire, her Sect members, Ania, Cheryl, Kim, and the five Transmutators. Varying degrees of ferociousness growled and shredded the enemy. No longer galloping, carefree beings, a black panther, cougar, wolf, lynx, and giant brown bear were moving faster than I thought possible, holding their own and terrifying those who tried attacking them.

Evaristus mobilized his Puppets again, taking on anyone he could while Caine snapped back into using the water as a weapon.

"Why are they fighting against us?"

Vincent glared down at me. I didn't understand his surprise until I heard his thoughts of astonishment that I had surpassed his mental fortitudes. *"Concentrate on Evaristus. The plan is unchanged. Do as you can. We may have to leave at any moment, so make it worth it."* He hit Hinapouri with a blast of magic that pelted her before grabbing hold of her soul and partially extracting it. Her body fell, but her floating soul was thrashing around as if it could still fight him.

I did as Vincent instructed and left him to his job so I could do mine.

Behind Evaristus, Donovan was back at Loring, the other man no longer there. I didn't see him and had no idea if Donovan killed him or if he bolted, but it was Donovan and Loring squaring off. I shrugged Nya's power back into full gear, kneeling back to the ground since Evaristus returned to commanding his Puppets. This time, I moved to make the biggest impact.

Growing grass wasn't enough. The vision Aunt Lacey left me

with reminded me of the dandelion growing technique, but I had forgotten another tactic used against me after meeting the Puppeteer for the first time as he possessed Veata. With the slight alteration, I didn't need to pause. As was desired, so it occurred—an addictive aspect of Nya's power I adored.

I grew the threads of grass out, a foot in length, adding my extra fortifications before slapping them into Evaristus skin and wrapping them around his legs. He cried out in pain. His Puppets collapsed to the ground, leaving Caine and the back-up group tensed to fight without targets.

Evaristus tried to tear the grass off of him. I fortified it with Nya's power. The barbs stuck into his skin and wouldn't let go as I squeezed his thigh to dig the barbs in deeper. His white linen pants were blotched with red stains growing bigger the tighter I squeezed.

I was thrown onto my back, careening into Vincent's legs, and taking him down with me as he had been hovering behind me. Donovan had taken a hit—a big one. Big enough to counter Nya's strength. As I gathered my wherewithal and spun to him in concern, he had already regained his footing, blocked a hit, and made his own. He must have let go of Hinapouri's soul a crucial moment before I accidently took him down, or her soul would be lost.

I reached out and into Donovan's mind to check on him. He thought he was sloppy and was tightening up his tactics. He wanted every ounce of contact to count.

Filtering all his power into pockets of energy, Donovan filled those pockets with one of two additions. With his power of growth, he would propel a hit containing this power at Loring, so when it crashed into his rival, Loring would feel the damage, but Donovan's magic would also expand a section of Loring's flesh with agonizing pain, stretching with bubbled misery for as long as it took for Loring to heal. When Donovan started adding attacks containing a dose of the antithesis of growing, it would drain that part of Loring, leaving a patch of decayed skin that broke down his defences even further, distracting him while he fought to heal either form as Donovan struck Loring with blow after blow.

I raced for Vincent, shielding him as Hinapouri tried to take advantage of Vincent being down. I caught Hinapouri's spear mid-air before it sliced Vincent's throat open and used it like a slashing blade.

Using the fight around me and my desperate need to get Hinapouri away from Vincent, I siphoned a gulp of energy to fuel Nya's power. I laid a hand on Vincent's chest, encasing him in an extra skin of protection and expelling this energy around the both of us like an expanding Hoberman Sphere in a snapping pulse. The spheres shocking energy hit Hinapouri and any others that posed a threat to me or my allies, sending them to the ground, seizing in convulsions.

Hinapouri fought against it better than some, with a seasoned warrior's strength. A temporary fix until Vincent got to his feet.

I redirected my efforts to Evaristus.

Since I was no longer leading the growing threads of grass, they were left to slump like Evaristus' Puppets. They didn't retreat or fall off him, but hung in place by their barbs. This was enough for Evaristus to pull a section off one leg. It crumbled in his hand like cigarette ash. As soon as I got back to it, like the Puppets, the threading was back in action. Since a living section of it was still in his other hand, its barbs bit into his palm, twisting and encircling his wrist, snaking up his arm as it stretched along the length of his legs.

Evaristus sent hits of power my way, his positioning awkward as he hunched over his right leg and bent at the waist. I was able to either wheel out of the way, skittering to the side on my hands and knees like a primate, or parry the blow with simple shields akin to what Donovan taught me. Much easier than if Evaristus had full control over himself.

I noticed his lips begin to move with a spell or incantation. I was sure the result would be catastrophic since he had lifetimes of spells memorized. I stretched the weeds up to clasp onto Evaristus' chest and then his throat and face, shooting up like a rock climber grasping for higher ground. The bladed grass sliced into his face as he clawed at it. The grass stretched to encircle his mouth, shutting away whatever spell he had hanging on his tongue. For good measure, I covered his eyes, leaving him in total darkness.

Considering his strength, I figured he didn't try these casting tactics earlier because he underestimated my ability to put him in a position where he had the slightest trouble escaping. Now it was too late. I had him.

Before they were lost beneath nature's weapons, I saw the flash of panic in his black eyes as the threads of grass held tighter. He still had an arm loose, but it was like he had forgotten about it, too busy trying to get his other limbs free. Fingers scraped and ripped, trying to free his body parts but every place it ripped, a flinch of power had me squeezing tighter, ensuring no matter how hard he pulled, he wouldn't gain ground.

Piercing pain slashed through my skull. Bloodied faces of people in the grips of death whipped in front of my eyes and disappeared as quick as a sneeze. Pain hit me again. Blood, screams, green soul glows being snuffed out, flashes of what Evaristus did to our family.

Diluculo came back into view as Evaristus gained a small amount of control or thought he did. He thought he could blind me, intimidate me.

A wall around my mind snapped up with a dose of Nya's power, blocking his desperate attempts.

I pushed ahead, this time with psychological warfare of my own, and watched as he bucked and thrashed around in the bonds of the grass, muffled protests barely heard above the sounds of battle around us.

Puppets who had fallen were now regaining consciousness—the ones who weren't already dead. They either ran for the trees to escape the battle, were immovable with shock, or were joining the fight. Not all knew what side they were fighting for and, in the confusion, were going after everyone.

I ripped open a telepathic window with Donovan to let him in on how I planned to deal with Evaristus. *"Remember, we may have to leave at any moment. Kill Loring or dispatch him the same as I plan to do with Evaristus."*

He didn't answer me, but I didn't expect him to. I knew what he was thinking—his frustration clear at the reminder he may not get to take Loring out the way he wanted to or make him pay in the equivalent manner with which Loring murdered Aunt Lacey. He needed to end Loring on his own time, in his own way, but he didn't have the luxury and wouldn't be allowed to drag Loring out of the Creation to exact his revenge on home territory. My way could still settle his score, so he needed to choose.

The grass was now taking Evaristus over. He couldn't fight back as it grabbed hold of his loose hand flailing about. Loring was too busy and too selfish to come to his Master's aid, concentrating on his own survival as Donovan tested his strength and patience.

Once Evaristus was doused in his own blood, unable to heal or escape as the threads thickened, the barbs began tunnelling through his body, snaking further inside and scraping his internal organs, escaping out through burrowed holes like panicked rats. I knew the time was coming and called for Caine.

I sensed him fighting no more than fifteen feet away, Gareth's power made me aware without looking. As I had with Donovan, I called to him, told him my plan, and a moment later when he rid himself of Roe—who was a great tracker but didn't live up to his physical prowess and fell at Caine's hands for his laziness—he came to my side.

I looked up at him from my squatted position. "Start to close it."

The ground began to tremble. Caine held onto my shoulder so we both weren't pitched into the water as we were near the edge. Not everyone was present for when Caine cracked open the Creation, so many were knocked onto their backs, stumbling off course from their opponents. The Transmutators became skittish as they fought their animal instincts to flee into the trees.

Now that Caine was doing his part, I had to finish mine. Even in misery, Evaristus refused to surrender, still fighting back with what little he could. When I began to take those threads and use them to tear away and separate sections of his body, he fought harder.

As Joelly claimed, killing Evaristus wouldn't be easy. Detaching the arm I got my first real hold on, proved wasteful. As soon as I felt the shoulder joint separate and his skin give way, he somehow managed to pull himself back together. I couldn't casually tear him apart. I had to rip him apart in quick movements and keep the parts away from his body and each other to prevent them from reattaching.

I took in a steady breath to begin again.

The ground still trembled as Caine closed the crevice, steady but not too quick. It needed to remain open until I could reduce Evaristus to pieces or else the whole plan was spoiled. I wasn't making enough ground and Caine was making too much.

Caine knelt by my side and laid a hand atop mine. "I'm not positive this will work. Let Nya take the wheel a bit more and I'll let Gareth have his fun. We need to give Evaristus a good fight."

I managed to do as he said by shifting Nya's power a bit more out front and sensed it as Caine allowed Gareth's power to do the same. He found a way to join his power with mine as we both dipped into Evaristus' thoughts. Caine started filtering water into the blades of grass and through Evaristus' body. Pain occupied my ancestor's thoughts and now the panic and hopelessness of drowning, lessening his fight against what I had begun to accomplish.

I felt his arm separate. This time, I pulled it far from his body, using the weeds like an extra appendage, then unravelling the limb from its bindings and tossing it the few feet it needed to plunk into the surging water. Then, to ensure it wouldn't bob to the surface to somehow crawl its way back to Evaristus, Caine used his power to drag the arm under like a hungry shark.

Caine kept closing the gap. Everyone trying to fight had a hard time of it as the ground trembled. This included Donovan, who was attempting to end Loring, adopting a wide and low fighting stance.

Pieces of Evaristus were torn into chunks with the gruesome

fleshy sounds of splattering blood and ripping muscles, the limbs then thrown into the crevice while Caine held them under. Neither of us knew if closing Evaristus and his body parts up in the crevice would kill him for good or if he could somehow regenerate. For now, it granted us enough time to attempt escape and close the Creation.

Evaristus was missing an arm and flanks of flesh from random parts of his body. When his right calf was torn off, he collapsed to the ground and wriggled around in failed attempts to overpower the bonds that tore at him.

Caine and I continued without remorse for breaking down this immortal piece by piece. We couldn't be certain the soulless immortal felt the loss of his limbs, but we were positive Evaristus knew what it meant for him as lipless sounds of fury tried to escape his throat. Still bucking, his body as he lay on the ground, fighting to gain footing without his feet and losing inches of flesh as he did, he never gave up, never surrendered, never pleaded, or bargained for his life.

My mind was closed to him now, but he must have known this was one task I intended to see through. If this stubbornness made me more alike my ancestor, then so be it. I refused surrender or gifting him opportunity return to his personal mission, no matter what Coven backed me or what combinations of powers I had within me.

The crack at our toes drew nearer. "We've got to hurry!"

Swamp water dappled my face and sprayed into the air as the earth moved too fast for how much was still left to accomplish.

I shoved a lasting memory into Evaristus' mind—the first glimpse of Alorha and Evaristus meeting. To before I knew their names, before I learned Alorha's entire bloodline was doomed to Evaristus' murderous grief, to when they too were strangers and Alorha's intuition saved his life. Then I ripped Evaristus' head off his shoulders in hopes he would be stuck with the memory until we came back for him or into his afterlife, if this was his true end.

When his neck was a headless geyser of blood, water, and grass tentacles wriggling around like worms, his body thrashed like a dying fish. Caine tossed Evaristis's head into the water as I cracked his chest and torso down the middle like a wishbone. His ribs protruded at all angles as they, too, were tossed into the crevice now a couple of body length's wide.

Caine directed the water to hold all his parts under and moved to zip up the remaining gap before Evaristus could try and escape.

"Wait." I put my hand on Caine's arm and looked at him, thinking of Donovan and Loring, knowing he heard me.

He shook his head. "No time."

"Make time."

Caine stood and dug into his power, continuing on task.

I flexed to my feet to see Donovan still exchanging attacks with Loring across the water. "*Donovan.*" He didn't look to me. "*Make the deathblow or fight another day.*"

The edge of his lips moved in a grimace at being rushed. He resolved to bury Loring with his Master, forcing him to share the grave he dug by killing Aunt Lacey.

I left his thoughts to himself, lessening the distraction of my invasion. I kept watch in hopes he would alter his tactics, though constantly aware of the crevice at my feet now less than twenty feet wide and closing fast.

A dodging blur rushed by Loring as he struck out at empty air. Donovan blurred a second time, and then a third, landing a blow to Loring's back and knocking him onto his face. Loring spun over in time for Donovan to shoot some type of trap over him, pinning him to the ground. Donovan wailed a fist into Loring's jaw. It broke the trap and Loring rolled toward me enough for me to see blood and drool drip from bloated lips as Donovan's power swelled the whole side of his face and closed his eye.

Loring popped up quicker than I thought possible, but Donovan shot at him with a football tackle to the gut, thrusting both their bodies into the path of the closing crevice.

"No!"

Nya's power drained from me in a panicked heartbeat as Donovan and Loring, struggling mid-air, headed for the crevice.

In blind fear, I rushed forward in a muscle-ripping sprint to stop Donovan from sacrificing himself just to get rid of Loring. He and Loring had flown from the opposite side of the crevice in a tumble of limbs.

Donovan was hit with a blast to the shoulder. I skidded to a stop at the edge, falling and scrambling to get my feet out of the way before the crevice chomped them off.

Splashing water stung my eyes. Something plowed into me while I was blinded and threw me down. I sucked in oxygen, chest burning, head pounding, wind was knocked out of me.

When I could open my eyes, still struggling to breathe properly, the crevice was inches from closing. Loring's hand and fancy cufflink were the last I saw before the split in the earth was nothing but a scar and the ground stopped trembling.

Prickling pain crossed my shoulders and back. Power. Donovan's?

"Babe?"

I spun and found Donovan sitting on the ground, knees up, leaning back on his hands. "You fucker!"

His one dimple caved. "As if I would let him take me down."

"*Pfft.*" Kim stood over Donovan, blood-splattered and smiling. "Saved your life, punk."

"Thanks. I'll buy you a cookie basket if we get out of here."

I rushed to Kim and threw my arms around her. "That was you?"

The cocky laugh from her said, "Damn straight it was."

I turned on Donovan and shoved him. "What the fairy-fuck is your problem?" He cocked an eyebrow in response. "You weren't supposed to dive in with the jackhole. You dying wasn't a part of the plan."

He glowered at me. "Neither was telling off your grandpappy and you two going all ancient power on his ass, Miss Hypocrite Princess of the Year. Bitch later. We're not finished."

Caine may have pushed Gareth's power back a bit, but he still had him out of the box. The look of disconnect in his eyes was enough to make someone think twice about who they were talking to. It made me wonder if I looked different when I took on Nya's power as more than a side piece.

The battle raged on. Bodies were laid out on the ground, strewn amongst the others in varying degrees of dead and injured. Exchanges of magic raged across the field in flashes of light and peaks of energy, making my power itch to get out and take someone on. Watching good and evil soul glows alike rise from their battle beaten bodies and disappear in one form or another was painful to watch—to see how much death we had accrued and contributed to. This was supposed to be the safe option, the one to save more lives than if Evaristus had gotten out of the Creation.

If not for Donovan's combat-focused adrenaline, I would've crumbled when the despair of so many lost souls hit me.

We still needed to escape so Olive could use the Anatolian Idol to lock Evaristus and Loring in for good, meaning more potential deaths before this was over.

Donovan blurred around bodies before striking out against a devotee. The impact on my fists and releasing pressure of power from my hands didn't quit as he moved from one target to another. He needed more healing, immediate healing, so I brought out my power and then Nya's while still retaining the majority of my control, being sure to protect the part of me connected to Donovan.

Caine was still close and Gareth's power greeted Nya's with a smile.

I scanned the field and found Vincent still battling Hinapouri. *"Evaristus and Loring are no longer a threat. Commence with the next step."*

"Understood." His internal voice was strained yet satisfied.

"Sixty seconds. Make sure you're behind me." Ranlyn's telepathic voice gave the directive instead of Vincent's. He sent it to the Coven and allies as Vincent must have warned him of our success.

"This way." Kim went running to the right of the Creation, following her location gift to Ranlyn in the fray. The thread of silver was strong through her eyes, stronger than before we entered the Creation.

The transmutated bear took out a devotee who got too close to Ranlyn, giving Ranlyn the opportunity to stand and survey the shift in his flock. But not all were in position.

I looked at Caine. He understood our need.

We shared thoughts to allow him to see the souls who needed safety, then plucked them from the fight like daisies and dropped them on the safe side of the battle.

"*Now.*"

Ranlyn side-eyed us, refocused, and put his arms out to his side as if awaiting a strong embrace. Energy built from the Elder until he brought his arms straight out in front of him. An invisible force reached across the field and shot the enemy into the trees on the other side of the Creation in a continual blast of energy.

Our people started disappearing.

The Apporter was collecting the Coven in sizable groups as Ranlyn shielded the horde from the enemy. Everyone standing was taken to the pass-way before devotees could get to their feet.

23

DESTINED FOR DESTRUCTION

Caine and I informed the flock to keep their eyes closed to avoid drowning by The Blue Men of Minch. Splashes told us jumpers hit the black liquid before hearing the warning.

"Sophie!" Donovan yelled over the breaking waves of the Coveners taking to the veil, drawing my attention while I was still consumed by Nya's power. He refused to take the leap until I did.

After closing my eyes, I glided through the cold waters, enveloped in the old and familiar power of The Blue Men of Minch. I knew them. Understood their suffering. How or when was a distant memory I couldn't grasp. I opened my eyes to glimpse them surrounding the flock with opportunistic eagerness. Of the few who missed the warning, many of The Blue Men were on them, attempting to take their prize for the transgression of invasion within their waters.

A pulse of power their way was a call out in mercy, not warning. My magic didn't hurt them. They turned to see who called to them and swam up to me, abandoning their targets, too overcome with curiosity to continue the hunt.

Shadows of men were what the Magics of today saw. Through

Nya's power, I saw The Blue Men as they were—human-like kelpies of the water. Storm bringers. Protectors of their realm.

One swam around me as I floated, enduring the assessment, before they returned to face me. *"Freagairt beò—"*

I lifted my hand. *"Chan eil geamannan ann an-diugh. No games, no riddles. You will let us pass without death and we will send you home."*

The Blue Man hesitated, confusion in it's mind at how I knew it's language, how they understood mine, and if I meant to trick them.

"The one who meant for us to use this pass-way tricked us into disturbing you and your kin. He is now unable to return you to your waters. Grant us passage and I will grant you yours. If not, death will follow." I looked to the right. In the shadows of other men was Caine, Gareth's power out front, ready to take on the men if needed. *"Attack and you risk entrapment in this empty well attached to a world with no sky, no souls, and no way out."*

The Blue Man interrupted his comrade, who attempted to speak out of turn. The Man growled in protest and the comrade slunk back with the others, more shadow than man in their fear.

"A bheil thu a 'gealltainn?"

"Yes, you have my promise. If we fail, I know you will find us in any waters we dip ourselves into, sea or bath, and we will expect the greatest of revenge."

The Blue Man drifted back to join his comrades and nodded at me.

I looked again to Caine, who swam to me. We joined hands, growing our power together and out into the water to send The Blue Men of Minch home to the sound of crashing waves and thunderous clouds.

When I opened my eyes again, the waters were still dark, still tasted of rot, and still remained a pass-way to and from the Creation, but it lay empty of the danger of death it once held.

I surfaced, braced my arms on the edge of the pass-way, and took a deep breath, though I hadn't needed to underwater. How Nya knew The Blue Men of Minch, I didn't have a moment to figure out as the glowing souls of Magics blinded me. They flitted around like the fireflies of my childhood. When they came into focus, I realized they were trying to kill each other.

Caine hadn't picked a target yet, but he was up out of the water and walking into the battle with the confidence of Gareth's power still leading the way.

Pockets of people had no soul glows at all. Humans? The Eradicators had joined the mix.

Ranlyn's backup outside Diluculo, meant to protect Olive and the lesser Magics of our Coveners, were taking on a force championing for Evaristus. Predicting his enemies would have forces waiting outside the Creation, the Puppeteer must have dispatched devotees. Now these Tainted souls were fighting in the name of a Master they had no clue was left in pieces, drowned between earth and water.

Nya's power's influence drained from me as I looked around for anyone I cared about within the chaos, more myself without the ancient power clouding my thinking. My family was out there among the fighting Magics. I needed to find them.

Something punched into my line of sight. I wheeled back into the water.

Donovan had his hand out, reaching for me, dark water dripping over his face from tendrils of hair stuck to his forehead. "Where's Olive?"

I reached back and let him pull me out of the water. "No fucking clue."

"We need her to close the Creation."

"No shit. Go look for her. I need to find the Ballards. She might be with them."

A flash blinded me, the field never dark for long with all the exchanges of power. Donovan took off into the fray as if chasing after a lost puppy and not into spurting blood and pissed off Magics. His panicked search pounded with urgency across our connection to find

Olive and the idol. This was his element and he was confident within it.

A redheaded Magic threw a hit of energy from a grounded position and popped up onto her feet.

Kim? Holy fuck! Who was she—? Oh shit.

I sprung forward as Kim's hit landed. Now Joelly was making her strike. People were running everywhere. Flashes of power zapped my night vision and I lost sight of Kim and Joelly.

When everything came back, Joelly took advantage of the chaos, screening Kim's sight and forcing her down again.

Nya's power surged within me, pitching the field to the side. I jumped and took Joelly down, her shot at Kim going wild. I wobbled to my feet, losing sight of Joelly and Kim as vertigo took me back down to my knees.

Someone grabbed my arm. I pulled but didn't shake them. A voice ordering me to stand echoed in my ears. I was on my feet and didn't remember how I got there.

When I refocused, Olive was talking. "Olive?"

A crease between her eyes deepened. "What's wrong?"

"I'm fine."

I looked around for Kim. Unsteady, but standing off with Joelly a few yards away, Donovan had joined Kim. He was pitched over, hands on his knees to keep himself steady, and glaring at Joelly.

Nya's power must have taken over to keep me steady. I sidestepped her strength to feel a tad more myself and Donovan stretched to a standing position. The ache in my gut told me he still felt the effect of Nya's power. Manageable, yet uncomfortable.

Knowing I needed it, I let Nya's power takeover more again and felt it as it fed off the energy around me.

Donovan grunted and fell to all-fours as Joelly took off into the crowd. I cradled our connection with power, allowing Donovan to rise and be of use.

"Firefly, why is Veata fighting Hinapouri? Is she a Puppet again?"

My strength fought with Nya's for understanding of what she

meant. I spun to find Veata, cane in hand, fighting against the snarling Maori warrior.

"Did you close Diluculo?"

"I couldn't. Joelly stole the Idol."

It made sense why Kim was fighting her and why Donovan showed up but didn't take Joelly out. He must not have known where it was.

"Hinapouri and Miklos tried to kill Caine and I inside the Creation. They can't be trusted. Check on the Ballards. We'll get the Idol." I looked at Kim. "Which way did she go?"

Kim looked into the crowd, then pointed. "That way." I was running before her last word left her lips.

I made a wide circle, planning to sneak up behind Joelly. A plume of purple light came at me. I dodged it, Nya's power erecting a shield, the shot glancing off into the crowd somewhere. The dead and injured were obstacles to hop over. No time to heal or assess everyone, though healers were making the rounds.

Joelly was weaving through Magics, ducking hits and taking those out in her path. I pushed through people in my way and headed in her direction, elbowing through Magics and getting knocked around.

"Soul Seer."

The heavy accented voice came from around me, but I couldn't see from whom when I stopped. Stabbing pain crippled my left foot. Bones separated as if an invisible spike drove through the top of my foot. My hands came away red after I grabbed at my Converse covered foot, now throbbing and filling with blood. Nothing was in it and Nya's power was lost as I screamed.

Shocking jolts of pain shot through my arms, forcing me to let go of my foot. When I let go, the pain in my arms stopped. I stood and tried to leave. My foot was stuck in place and tugging wasn't helping.

Miklos stepped in front of me. He was the one who called me and made me stop.

I tried to flee but couldn't scramble out of whatever was holding me down. Blinding pain hit as something spiked through my right foot, pinning me in place as it had with the left. When I looked up at Miklos, he backhanded me and knocked me flat on my back.

Whatever he was trying to say to me was swallowed by my rocked brain and the noise around us. Anger filled his strong, accented voice and I had no clue why he was doing this to me.

When my eyes fluttered open, my body was upright, my shirt bunched in Miklos's fist as his immortal glow seared my retinas and bleached out everything else.

Pain. Blackness.

I was on the ground again. What happened? Fuck! My feet, I couldn't move them.

Was Donovan okay? My hands burned as if using power, yet I wasn't. Who was he fighting?

What will hurt? Someone told me it would hurt, but they didn't say what, or did they?

Strong arms cradled me close, the warmth of body heat seeping through my shell-shocked, death-like numbness. My body jerked.

Pain. Blackness.

The voice who told me something would hurt was now asking me if I could heal. How? My thoughts lagged like a glitchy computer, lost to spiralling focus as I screamed, then squeaked when my breath was used up.

When the pain from my feet faded, I found myself in Vincent's grasp, his face and neck bloody.

"What happened?"

"Miklos used a rooting spell to pin your feet down. I ripped you free and healed you. Can you stand?"

The battle around us continued without me. Vincent glared at anyone close enough to do damage.

I nodded.

Vincent helped me to my feet, then pulled me towards Donovan who had been close by yet taken out along with me through our connection.

Joelly was standing in spot, unblinking, unmoving.

"The Kitchen Witch froze her in place. Rather accidental."

"Don't call her that." I told Vincent.

Donovan and Kim stood and waited as we approached.

"Why don't they grab the Idol, now while she can't move?"

"The spell will break if they touch her and neither knows where Joelly is concealing it. I believe it was your companion's idea to hold off, thinking a face-off while his sister is in an incapacitated state was of no fun to him."

"Great." I knew Donovan wanted Joelly dead, but not taking advantage of the situation was stupid. *"Screw this, I'm getting it."*

Vincent didn't argue.

Alarm flooded Donovan's eyes as I got to Joelly and looked her over. "Don't touch—"

"I know, I know."

"Let me suspend her soul in a state of extraction while you search. The spell could break at any moment or may be broken by someone else."

Battle still raged around us. If a wayward shot hit Joelly, she would be loose, and no one knew what abilities she had absorbed before showing up to the field if she was able to get herself free of the binding laid on her by the Elders.

Vincent lifted a hand out between he and Joelly's frozen form, his power building. He yanked back his arm as fast as a striking cobra and cursed. I didn't think I had heard him swear before. It felt more unnerving than why he pulled back in the first place.

"You booby-trapped her?" Donovan turned to Kim.

"What? No!" She looked at Vincent, who was now shaking out his hand. "I didn't mean to do—" She waved at Joelly. "—whatever that is. How the hell do I know what it did?"

Donovan sighed, his irritation running through me when he turned from her.

Even if it complicated things and took our focus from the battle around us, Kim should be proud. I didn't tell her that, but I would have to remember to do so later.

Vincent rubbed his arm like a heart attack victim.

"You okay?"

He nodded and looked Joelly over as if looking for a way to bypass Kim's failsafe.

Clouds rolled in as if the shock Vincent endured had created a chain reaction.

"Use it."

We looked from Vincent to each other, though Donovan still had his eyes on the battle. I sensed his drive to get into the thick of it coupled with resentful restraint at being forced to deal with Joelly instead.

"The atmospheric response is likely the result of the Seedling in your Sect as it was before."

Kim scoffed, eyes on the building dark clouds and flinching thunder. "Blake is doing this?"

"Rain may be a bit much, but the energy might short circuit our problem."

"You want me to use Nya's energy to shockify Joelly? Seriously?"

His stare from behind his thin-rimmed glasses said he was serious without the need to spell out why. We had limited time. Olive needed to close the Creation and the idol in Joelly's possession was the way to do it. Kim could undo the spell as it was done, if she knew how. Since she didn't, we were shit out of luck. I had to try, and now, before Blake stopped whatever it was he was doing.

I called on my power and then Nya's. The energy in the field made this easy—too easy—and Nya's power was in more control than I anticipated. It washed over me, buffering the world outside my mind with cotton-like numbness. Present, yet disconnected, I opened my eyes to the field to siphon what my Covener had conjured in the sky.

Donovan backed away from me as if distance could take away the wrench that was growing within him. It hit me before Nya's power took over and stopped me from feeling the pain he now tried to combat by pressing his hand into his chest. Nya's power was a numbing force to the concern of others around me. Though I tried to care, I found it difficult to do anything but focus on the sky as Donovan fell.

Reaching overhead, I allowed the energy to explore my body before collecting it within my arms and hands and each of my fingers. I rubbed them together as if sprinkling salt and reached above to pinch the clouds into a solid mass to filter its power through me, accelerating the strength of the Seedling, who will one day be strong enough to make the sky bow to them. For now, I needed a little of their gift to ensure the Creation was closed.

A ruckus at my side was Vincent and Miklos in combat, joining the others in bloodshed for their cause or for their Master's cause. Why Miklos made the spineless move against Vincent while his back was turned was not my concern. I closed my eyes to them and the brutality of my surroundings. Energy saturated the field like a sticky fog before gathering to me like silk, cocooning me and the brazen force still building.

"*Remember your companion, Sophie. His pain is your own.*"

My pain? No pain existed. Freedom was a driving force so strong I had to open my eyes to understand Vincent's message.

Donovan was on his knees, gripping the earth, biting down onto his lips through grunts of profanity. Kim was bent over him, trying to help, yet unable as he pushed her away.

Flashes of power shone from her blue-green eyes, showing something further perplexing me.

They were in danger because of me, this was clear in her thoughts. I terrified her.

I pulled excess energy gathered from the overcast down and around me and Joelly, pushing the others away to give myself a large birth to test Joelly's defences. Donovan and Kim were knocked down and shoved aside, as were others mid-fight, none appreciative of my need to protect them at Vincent's insistence. Kim yelled and pulled Donovan under the arms, dragging him away and crashing into others as my crowding power expanded and covered us like a loose wool blanket.

Shimmering snaps of opaque power covered Joelly and I, leaving enough room to see the field through small windows of the shield. Kim mouthed something to Donovan, who struggled to his knees and wobbled to his side, clutching his chest and wheezing though pale lips.

Kim spoke again, yet I couldn't hear her.

I slipped into her mind, her thoughts a mash of chaos now focused on my eyes, a golden brown instead of deep brown as normal.

What Kim felt emanating from me was unsettling. Fear. A warning to stay away from me, away from the shield.

Good. Safety was far from me. She needed to remain clear or reap consequences greater than the concentration of power from myself as a Soul Seer without Nya's power's influence.

I turned back to Joelly, the mission for the idol more important than the others' discomfort with who I was or what power I used.

Testing the electrified field of protection Kim added to her spell meant running my fingers around Joelly's body. I planted my feet and further teased the edges of the failsafe. Strong, built in desperation, yet not stronger than me.

One hand above and one in front of Joelly was meant to channel the power needed. I lifted my face to the still gathered clouds and closed my eyes with intent. A surge of light and charged power forced itself from the ether down into my loose shimmering sphere of protection. A ripple across the surface and a deafening boom of bright white, blue, and magenta lit up the field.

Power streamed through me, filling me with the energy of nature on course to Joelly. A pure, uncluttered force I somehow missed, yet knew I had never experienced. But something within me had and desired more. Holding onto it longer than needed, and nowhere near as long as that part of me craved, I let go for fear of destroying Joelly and the idol along with her.

A choking wail pierced the outer edges of my awareness. The brilliant light of power subsided, though my shield remained.

Joelly was now on the ground. I knelt and laid a hand on her shoulder as the crying out of those in battle and of another, more piercing moan niggled my interest. I ignored it and read Joelly's soul, diving into the last moments before Kim froze her. Feeling the idol as Joelly felt it instead of seeing it.

I pulled back and reached into Joelly's boot, finding the small black figure, and turning it over in my hand. Such a beautiful piece destined for destruction.

More screaming included my name, calling from outside the shield, a nagging I found disruptive and ignored it.

I ran my fingers over the craftsmanship of the Anatolian Idol, a figure representing the creation of human beings and fertility. Ancients carved the figure into marble. Now the idol was to be used to do the opposite of its intent by closing a womb within the veil, aborting its people and preventing further creation. All on the field should be shamed for ruining such a piece.

I looked around and did not see shame on the faces of those in the field. So much anger, revenge. No ambition to create or bear witness to anything but death.

All those but Caine. Gareth's power was a beacon in the crowd—Caine out of view, off to my right, always on my radar as he searched through the collective Magics for Jet, frantic to find her, yet unable to. Drawing every drop of sweat, dew, and water in the soil to weaponize his search with brutal efficiency. Fear spilled out of him, for he knew she wasn't among the others in the field.

Waving arms caught my attention. What was this? The redhead. I searched for a name and had to pull myself out of Nya's power clouding my thoughts.

Kim. She was screaming at me. What was she—?

"Take down the shield!" Kim looked over at Donovan who was on the ground, his legs kicking out from under him like he was being shocked, his neck muscles straining, red-faced with dimples caved by nothing close to a smile. Vincent had Miklos on the ground, his fist in the air as if holding something, Miklos's soul within his grasp.

I looked down at Joelly, neutralized and unconscious, her Tainted soul dwindling. Little would be needed to end her. She threatened my life in the name of acquiring that which was not hers to take. I understood this.

"Sophie, stop!"

Vincent. He didn't want me to end the cur's life. He held the life force of my Elder in his fist, but insisted I not do the same to Joelly.

"Focus beyond Nya's power, Sophie. Remember your objective. Think of the Puppeteer, of Loring, of the Mother Coven. Diluculo must be closed. You have the idol."

I did possess the idol. The screen around me dropped. I did as Vincent wanted and refocused on Donovan. I surged towards him, seeing him in pain. Everything flushed back to me and I knew it was my fault.

"Don't let Nya's power drop!" I spun to Vincent to see him sprinting in my direction.

"If you allow Nya's power to leave you, you will feel the effects of Donovan's electrocution. Heal him first."

A harsh gasp hit my lungs like I swallowed ice water and Nya's power stretched like an elastic band and threatened to snap as I fought to keep control. My fear for Donovan pushed to override it all.

Others could heal Donovan, but this was my fault. I needed to make it right.

I gripped the remnants of Nya's power as if dangling from a cliff edge with sweaty palms and no lifeline. Prickles of pain creeped into my gut like faint cramps and built in heartbeats, twitching in my muscles, and making me faint as I rushed to Donovan and put my hand on his chest. Seeing Donovan semi-conscious, eyes fluttering and rolling in their sockets, was enough to shock Nya's power out of me, but I held on.

Healing power drove through me, into him. He grabbed my arm and held on, body arched, and rigid.

Nya's power drained from me. I couldn't hold on any longer, couldn't keep a hold of anything, including my strength to remain upright.

I looked up into the sky with fresh eyes, repossessing myself as reality forced a wave of guilt. "I'm so sorry."

I didn't even know who I was apologizing to. Everyone deserved it.

Donovan's exhaustion kept me down another moment. An ache overtook his relief. He was happy not to have Nya's power enacted, but I felt steamrolled. I couldn't fully heal us before Nya's power retreated. Without her ancient energy, I would never have pulled off getting back the idol from Joelly. She would have spanked my ass and given me the finger all the way back to her Master's hideout and we would've spent forever chasing her down while Evaristus and Loring crawled out of the Creation before it could be closed. I doubt Olive had a third idol.

Vincent stood over my line of sight, where I sucked in oxygen along with Donovan. "Sophie! Where is the idol?"

I raised my hand still clutching the small black figure. Vincent grabbed it from my hand and took off.

"Is Joelly dead?"

I rolled onto my side and saw Donovan looking at me. "No."

He sat up and looked to where Joelly was. "Did you check?"

I pushed to sit up, Kim helping me. "She's hurt, but alive. Maybe not for long."

Shouting broke out. I recognized Caine's voice. I had heard this volume from him once before, in the park when he was screaming for Cole before he was awakened from his sleeping curse. Racing to him, Kim and I found Caine in a wrestler's lock, his hands on Ranlyn's shoulders and Ranlyn's on his. Vincent, Blake, and Jared were all attempting to make Caine back down without magical intervention. Gareth's power was nowhere now. Caine lost hold of his power, too upset to keep it.

"Did you see her? Did you see her come out? Let go of me! You know I can make you!" Caine tried to shake off Blake, his threats getting him nowhere.

Others still fought around us or helped the injured. They couldn't babysit him or guard the pass-way, though they were trying to stop anyone who popped out of the water, not knowing if they were Puppets or devotees.

Caine had no choice but to back off. He pushed away from them, stopping from trying to get by them and stalked off, kicking a dead body and screaming in frustration. When that wasn't enough, he took on a devotee another Magic was fighting and laid them out in a single punch, leaving the Magic fighting the guy pissed off he didn't get to do so himself. I didn't think any power was behind it. He was pissed off enough that he didn't need it.

He ended up approaching Blake and Jared, his hands up as if in surrender. I didn't know what they spoke of, but it looked to be half-apology half-instruction as he pointed out into the field of Magics.

I found Ranlyn ensuring Olive's safety. He and others used a mix of shields and hits of magic against devotees who were seething to take her out. How they knew she had the idol was a mystery, but they knew, and forced the others to work overtime to keep them from getting it. I ran to help, throwing hits of magic into the chaos. I didn't feel it did much damage but it distracted them enough for Ranlyn and the others to keep them from being pushed over or worked around.

"Caine! No!"

Ranlyn let go of his shield. Others pressed in to take over as he sprinted a few steps towards Caine, who was making another go for the pass-way. Jared and Blake barrelled into Ranlyn and grabbed hold of him. He screamed at them and tried to get around them, but they wouldn't allow it, going as far as putting Ranlyn down onto the ground as Caine dove into the water of the pass-way.

"What the fuck! Wha—" I couldn't believe Caine did that and didn't have time to go after Blake and Jared to figure out why they thought attacking their Elder was a good idea. Flashes of light, spirals of power, and a lightning shower had us all hitting the ground to duck and cover with nothing to hide under.

I searched above us and saw spears of lines around what had to be the edge of the Creation, high up in the sky like a bomb without the mushroom cloud.

A blinding force stung my skin as a blast flew our bodies across the ground before sucking back a few yards in a vacuum recoil that left the field in eerie silence.

Olive had closed Diluculo.

"No. No, no, no." I scrambled to my feet in search of the passway. How far were we tossed? I looked around us in the darkness, trying to see a ripple of water in the moonlight.

Nothing was there but Magics—those moaning in pain, the dying, and the dead. Their soul colours were all I could see, not their bodies or their injuries.

And no water.

"Caine!" He couldn't have gone in. He couldn't have. I called his name again, again with no answer. I knew he wasn't in the field. He knew we were closing it. Why would Caine go back in?

Tears clouded my already compromised sight.

I saw Blake on the ground and grabbed him. "What did you do? How could you let him go back in?"

His purple soul glow assaulted my eyes. "He made us! He used his power and persuaded us to stop anyone who tried to stop him."

I sunk back on my heels.

"I'm sorry. The guy is strong. I didn't want to do it."

"It's fine." I sobbed. "It's not—You couldn't help it."

I shouldn't have been surprised Caine wanted to go after Jet, but he didn't know for sure she wasn't in the field. Now he was stuck in there with devotees, and Loring and Evaristus if they got out of the crevice and got themselves back together. If we thought crushing them in the earth would kill them, we wouldn't have bothered to seal the Creation.

I looked around the field in a deaf numbness. Scuttling Magics on both sides disappeared or took off into the trees. The Creation was closed, the fight over. They had nothing more to fight for and scattered.

Kim sat at my side. "We'll get him out. He's trapped, not dead. He'll get his cousin, we'll reopen the Creation, and he'll be fine, Soph."

I wanted to believe her, but in her exhaustion, even her optimism was limp.

What did that look like? Not unlike the sleeping curse, but with true enemies going after him and not Loring's mind games. He won't be okay if they get him. He'll be tortured, twisted, used for his persuasion gift. Horrors of what would happen to him filled the spaces of my brain. Jesus fuck. No. He wouldn't be fine.

"Sophie." Kim tugged at my arm again and pointed off in the distance.

Was it Caine? Maybe I saw wrong and Caine didn't go through the pass-way or maybe Jet was in the field. No. She was pointing at Donovan, walking off towards something. Joelly.

"He won't listen to anyone else. You know he won't." She stood and pulled on my arm, muscling me to my feet. "Come on."

She was right, but it didn't mean I wanted to be Donovan's babysitter right now.

I came up to his side and looked down at Joelly, still unconscious.

He stood up and crossed his arms, not looking away from his sister. "I wouldn't kill her like this. Her eyes would be opened before wasting the bitch. She doesn't get off that easy."

If my concern for Caine overwhelmed him, he didn't mention it—too focused on Joelly, who was still a tousled, silent heap on the ground.

"Or she does. Will they let her go again?" How could she be walking around while Caine wasn't?

Donovan took a deep breath, filled with emotional turbulence. "No clue. She's at the bottom of a huge list of priorities right now."

More was within his concern, yet I noticed he held back.

"I'll ask Vincent." I turned to try and find him, needing to feel useful.

"You know Vincent's not an Elder, right?" He called after me.

I didn't stop or turn around. "I know."

Leaving Donovan with Joelly may have solved the problem for me. Right now, I didn't care what condition she was in when I returned.

24

———

CLEAN UP

Vincent and Ranlyn were with Jared and Blake, who wouldn't quit apologizing for attacking their Elder. Ranlyn tried to get them to stop, to say he understood, but they were freaked out and rambling.

The Ballards were off to their right. I was ecstatic to see my brother and cousin still alive but wasn't ready to make a full body count yet.

Jared's eyes widened. He stepped through the group to get to me. "Sophie! I'm so sorry."

"Save it for church. Blake already explained. Go round up the Coveners and see who's still alive." Telling them to shove off gave them a mission to prove they were still needed and stopped me from bashing their heads together.

"Wait." I looked over Ranlyn's pink frilly soul glow. I didn't notice until now, since Nya's power took over most my thinking for me.

"I know."

"How—"

"A consequence of removing the netting."

"Damn. Steep punishment."

"Yeah, well, we weren't supposed to be the ones to break it. It crippled us in other ways, too. You'll have to talk with someone about it once we get everything settled. Until then, my soul colour?"

"Cotton candy sprinkles."

"Same as when we met?"

"Yup."

He exhaled. "Okay, I can handle that." He went to walk away.

"Wait up, Jeeves. What about Joelly? Give Donovan the chance to kill her and he will. Might have already, though Kim will try and stop him."

Ranlyn nodded and somehow looked years older, covered in a generous sampling of blood from head to toe. "We'll bind her and let the law handle her."

"Righto. Sure. The law. Being responsible for some Blind flatfoot's death by vengeful bitch is a superb way to cap off the night. Feel like slitting a puppy's throat, too? Maybe set a guinea pig on fire for kicks?"

Ranlyn huffed. "Not Blind law. Our law." He walked off, ordering others around and calling for healers.

I looked to Vincent, baffled.

"You thought us so unorganized?" He laughed when I didn't answer. "Yes, we have our own officials. Politics are a large necessity in keeping our world hidden and left untouched by modern society." He started walking back towards where I left Donovan.

I followed. "Is that why you're not an Elder? Politics not your bag?"

"Many reasons prevent me from becoming an Elder."

I stopped him mid-step.

"Sophie—"

"Good, you know it's coming. Maybe I've tried this before, I don't know, but Ranlyn and Veata are the only two Elders left. You're older and more experienced than all of them. Plus, now they're not even immortal."

"True."

"And, no offence to them, but I trust your judgment over theirs any day."

His smile hit his eyes before his lips moved. "Thank you."

"Be as humble as you like, but you need to step up."

A moment passed. "I know."

We started walking again.

"We have had that conversation before." Vincent looked at me side-eyed.

"I thought so."

We stepped over a few bodies without soul glows. "You always believed I should be more involved, become one amongst the regents that ruled Coven society. It is natural for me to resist, so I have."

"I'm clueless about whatever I said before. It didn't work and now we need you. If that doesn't get you on Team Elder, nothing will."

Kim and Donovan looked at us as we approached, hearing the end of the conversation neither of us were going to repeat.

Vincent focused on playing messenger, telling Donovan what Ranlyn decided.

"Fine by me. Let the Sovereignty have her. As long as when the trial happens, I'm there to lobby for her execution. They can have their fun for as long as they want."

"The Sovereignty?" I looked at Kim, but she didn't know anything more than I did.

"The Sovereignty is no different than the Blind's system of law. Happens within the same buildings of power, though you will find the ruling Sovereigns through doors leading to small examples of Creations. Even your criminal housing system is the same. Our prison cells are found down different wings, guarded by Magics, but all-in-all, quite similar."

"So, wait. You're both telling us there's a law that can handle the Tainted or whoever else steps out of line, but that they weren't called when the last Elders were butchered? They let shit-sprinkles like Loring and Evaristus run around playing with the Blind like skin-Muppets, but they'll put the hammer down on Joelly who, yes, has tried to kill me more than once, but amounts to an ass-pimple in comparison to the festering hemorrhoids we trapped in the Creation. *Pfft.* Guess the criminal system isn't too different than the Blind's after all."

"Covens deal with their own affairs as they see fit. Bringing in the Sovereignty to deal with Loring meant there was proof Loring had no cause to end the Elders."

"No cause?" Kim's voice was raspy and too high. "You're implying he did have cause?"

"No, I'm saying that if Elsa's transgressions were examined next to Loring's, it would be up to the Sovereignty to decide what was done about it. And while Elsa may not have been Tainted, she ended her fair share of lives and a death by death count may have proved against the Mother Coven's favour and the new Elders would have their hands tied without the ability to deal with Loring as they pleased. Leaving the Sovereignty out of it means they can enact revenge without consequence."

"Unless someone like Loring decides to take it to the Sovereignty." Donovan was still looking down at Joelly. "They wouldn't, but why leave it to chance?"

"Precisely." Vincent fixed his glasses as if punctuating the point. "Running to a court room for every nicked bumper and overgrown rosebush is for the Blind. We are capable of settling our own scores. A nuisance like Joelly is an easy case and one she will not win as she infiltrated our Coven under false pretenses and caused harm against family."

"Something she doesn't have on me."

My head was pounding from the abundance of information as well as the overall shitstorm that was our night. I had so many questions, yet no energy to ask them or to process the answers.

Donovan bent to Joelly and I felt his power awaken. I thought he may have killed her right there, but he healed her, so she could wake up.

She jolted upright and looked up at us and then the field.

Vincent raised his hand. "Due to constant attempts against members of this Coven, including that of your own kin, it is decided by the Mother Coven Elders to have you taken to the Sovereignty to be charged and punished as they see fit."

Joelly's eyes widened. She got to her feet in jerky movements.

"While you are being transferred into Sovereignty custody, if you so much as endeavour to escape or do harm to any other, we will be forced to execute you on spot without trial. Do you understand?"

Joelly looked around again, as if trying to find an ally and coming up empty. She nodded.

Vincent turned to Donovan. "Will you stand guard?"

Donovan smiled in response and Vincent left.

I ran after Vincent. "Are you going to?"

"I am undecided." He didn't ask what I meant. He knew.

"Did I get that answer from you before?" When he didn't respond, I knew I hadn't and was wearing him down. I headed in the Ballard's direction. "Don't make me go to Ranlyn." I would make good on my threat. Not now, but Vincent would be an Elder and soon.

The distance and dark of night couldn't hide his expression. I was eighty percent sure he would lobby for the position, but I believed he would fulfill the duty whether under official capacity or not.

Coming up on the small crowd of Ballards, my stomach dropped when they circled something I couldn't see. Was someone injured? Was someone dead?

I pushed into the crowd. It was Leon. He was covered in someone else's oversized sweater as his wife, Tapi, fussed with trying to dress him. His front leg—now his right arm in human form—had been severed. The healing powers of a Magic can do miraculous things, but they can't re-grow limbs. Leon was left with a stump of an arm that ended above his right elbow, the skin smooth and perfect in every way, but he would never be the same, human or animal.

Everyone turned their backs so he could change, our bodies his dressing room as Tapi fussed over his every movement while he insisted on doing things himself.

I reached around Ronnie to tap my Uncle Lewis, then moved to him once Leon was standing and dressed. "How's everyone else?"

"Technically, we didn't lose anyone." When I was confused, he told me about Priscilla and her memory loss. "It's flattering to think the Coffer asked for her most precious of memories and have them be about me, but—"

"We'll help her remember. A spell, something has to work."

Lewis nodded, but I knew he had to know I had no clue if such a spell existed.

"Adam will adjust in no time, I'm sure."

"Adjust?" I gasped. "Can he Soul See?"

He chuckled and nodded.

Leaving Lewis with a blood-flecked Dwayne, who without his cowboy hat looked like a stranger, I went to find my brother. He wasn't standing with the group. He, Serena, and Denise were off to the side. No doubt to get away from the soul glows. Serena's was a low burn. Denise stood with her arms crossed. Adam had his back to her and he was now covered in a seer green soul glow.

"Hey bro. I hear you need some dark sunglasses."

He turned to me, screeched, and covered his eyes. "I can't even look at you. Your soul is ridiculous. How can you stand it? This can't be what you see all the time."

I laughed. "You'll get used to it. At least you didn't get your ass killed."

"This little bitch helped." Serena chinned in Denise's direction. "When those Raddie jokers showed up, Adam thought he was Jason Statham and nearly got his head lopped off."

"Did not!" Adam kept his hand across his eyes.

"Did so, boot licker. Her light might not do anything but blind you, but they didn't know that and started screaming like she set them on fire."

"I could'a handled it."

"Doubts." I looked at Denise. "Thank you. For real."

She nodded. "No prob. He's being a baby about it now, but he's alive to complain about it."

"He'll learn. Or keep being a baby. Prepare for that, too."

She rolled her eyes. "Wonderful."

As Lewis said, the rest of the Ballards were alive. They didn't fight in the frontlines, but they stood firm when the enemy came at them and was present for breaking the netting. I could see a change in the eyes of even the most confident, something facing enemies for the first time and surviving created. A healthy respect for the power, a lust for more, and the fear it could have been their first and last chance of doing so.

I pulled Olive aside and told her about Caine.

"Oh, Firefly. How could he do such a thing?"

"Believe me, I know. Though it's family. Something he has none of. Of course, he went after her. What I need now is to reopen the Creation to get him out."

"I...." Her mouth opened and closed. "A hug can't fix this. Though I'm afraid it amounts to all I can give right now."

"There has to be a way. Something on the Ballard shelves. Something to counteract the idol."

"I'll look. I'll scour the shelves and research all I can."

The "but" hung between us. She didn't know of an item like that, which meant it wasn't on the attic shelves.

"Fuck." I tried to hold myself together and lost it to angry tears. Anger directed at Evaristus and Loring, but also anger at Caine.

Olive put her hand on my shoulder and I pulled away. "You have no idea what it's like in there. Heaps of dead bodies—" I shook my head, remembering the overwhelming smell. "Caine being trapped is everything but okay."

"I know. I won't give up." She reached up and wiped away a tear. "We'll find a way."

I sniffed and tried to ignore Donovan's concern through the connection.

"Go, Firefly. We've got them. You do what you need to. The Apporter will bring us home." She kissed me on the check and wiped away more of my tears before I headed back to Donovan and Kim. I wanted to talk to her about Evaristus and Alorha, but this wasn't the time for family history.

Others began erasing the evidence of the battle as I got to Kim. Donovan joined us, his eyes red-rimmed as he would have been crying with me.

The bodies of the dead wouldn't be stumbled upon by the Blind, as they wouldn't get this far into the field with its location hidden to those without the knowledge of its existence, but it wasn't the Coven's way to leave them to rot in the next day's sun.

The dead belonging to Evaristus or Loring's Coven would be buried in a mass grave, but those of our own would be readied and returned to their families or brought to morgues with allies willing to stage a plausible cause of death for those who hid their power.

Clean up helped as no one wanted to discuss the events. We focused on the work without conversation. Exhaustion, emotional or otherwise, didn't seem to play a part. We kept moving to keep our heads clear and, with minimal amount of physical exertion, used whatever ability we had at our disposal to move, bury, or wrap the bodies. It still took a few hours. Considering the death toll, this was a quick operation.

For those present in other wars, as stated by Veata, this was a skirmish in comparison. Although the Apish Coffers took her sight, Veata still gave Hinapouri a good fight before the Maori warrior and Miklos took off without sticking around to finish it. Veata claimed her other senses were at their most heightened in all her life.

She left behind three of her fellow warriors within Diluculo as they tried to kill Caine and me. Same with Roe, the Huntsman.

Cheryl, the Suburban housewife look-a-like, was struck down by a female tribe member who escaped with their leader.

To my surprise, Anne-Claire was amongst the dead, a teary-eyed pissed-off Lincoln prepared her body to be taken back to where their Sect buried their fallen.

Rachael from my Sect was killed as well. Deidra was beside herself. No tears fell in her shock, unbelieving the horrific reality, that her girlfriend could be gone.

Aaron, like Leon, didn't die but would be changed forever. His chest, neck, and left side of his face were marred by some type of magic. They healed it the best they could, but sometimes magic makes marks that cannot be erased, and these Aaron would wear forever in the form of burnt flesh. Without knowing different, it would look as if he had obtained the burn years ago, the skin wrinkled and drawn like that of a melting candle, pulling the corner of his mouth down with his cheek.

More members from the Mother Coven had also fallen victim to devotees, but I didn't know most of them. None except Jeff, the bubble blowing father his small daughter would hopefully remember as bringing her happiness with his antics.

Of course, many of the Raddies who stood and fought lost their lives as they had no chance without their favourite makeshift machine available to mow down the competition.

The knife-happy men in Diluculo were dead, but the same couldn't be said of Loring and Evaristus. With any luck, they would be, but considering luck was a tractor trailer full of rabbit's feet delivered to the wrong place, we had to assume they were alive and would be until the Creation was reopened.

I stayed behind and helped with the dead and the battle scene. Last time, with Aunt Lacey, we all left the travesty to be dealt with by someone else. This time, I assisted where I could.

The sun had been up for at least an hour when we finished. The field was wiped clean. The flattened Anatolian Idol over the Coven Sigil was the lone evidence of change.

"Are you coming back to Ranlyn's?" Donovan covered the last body in a layer of earth with a telekinetic push and then regrew the grass around it.

"Umm." I hesitated as Vincent brought Joelly over, with Kim following. Donovan didn't address her and waited for me to finish. "Yeah, Bosco's there."

"Olson is ready to return you to Ranlyn's, once he drops us off at the Sovereignty." When we looked confused, Vincent explained Olson was the Apporter's birth name. "I will escort Joelly to the Sovereignty and meet you back at Ranlyn's."

Joelly shrugged Vincent off her and stepped back. "Come on now, really? The Sovereignty? I don't stand a chance."

Donovan laughed a humourless laugh.

"You have been given hours to reconcile your fate. We have an appointment to make."

"Bind me forever! Shove me in a storage locker! I don't care. Don't turn me over to them!"

"Come now." Vincent grabbed her arm and tried to drag her off.

Joelly bucked him off and booted him in the gut, then turned and kneed Donovan in the crotch as he sprung at her. Kim yelped in pain but I didn't see how as I crumbled with Donovan. A throbbing cramp gripped a set of balls I didn't have and needled up my stomach.

Joelly straddled atop of me as I lay winded with phantom pains. Before I could defend myself, she pulled on her ring. The jewel slipped out to become the tiny handle of a garrotte chocking wire she pressed into my throat. I swung my arms at Joelly's face as I tried not to move my head and take myself out for her. The wire was so sharp I knew without seeing it that if Joelly had the proper leverage, she could end me.

While Joelly's face twisted in hatred above me, I saw hands grab the sides of her head and wretch it to the side. She made a gurgled squeak as her neck cracked, and then she was tossed to the side. Donovan stood over me, blood trickling down his throat from a slice across it. Joelly laid in the grass, unmoving, her eyes still open.

I rolled away from Joelly to get as far from her body as I could. Donovan coughed, twisted his neck to the side, and pushed some healing power into the wound before wiping off the blood with his hand.

Kim and Vincent, plus the gathering Mother Coven and Sect members that had converged to get ready to be sent back to Ranlyn's, stood in shock and stared in stunned silence.

Yes, Joelly was warned. Yes, she had been given a million second-chances, but I didn't think, when it came down to it, that Donovan could be so heartless. And now, I received nothing but relief emanating from him for the righteous kill.

Vincent walked into Donovan's personal space. "You dispose of the body."

"My pleasure."

And it was. Burying Joelly didn't take long and the sense of relief from Donovan doubled when he covered Joelly in the shallow grave. She wasn't getting up this time.

Kim didn't ask me how I felt about it but kept looking at me as if expecting me to complain or comment in some way. I didn't. With him high on the satisfaction he felt for getting rid of Joelly, I couldn't muster the disgust I think I would have if disconnected from Donovan.

Back at Ranlyn's, everyone took turns showering. The tent that had been our place to party as we let loose before the fight was now temporary housing for the dead until they could be returned to their families. A few lingering Coveners recapped the whole fight, still jacked with adrenaline. Not all had the zeal for it as Blake did, but they still sat and talked, staying clear of speaking of those who were no longer around, and concentrating on using their powers and the cool things they saw Magics do.

Using the room with the dining room table behind the closed door, we made do for the Elders, Vincent, Donovan, Kim, and myself to gather with questions as Bosco snored on my lap.

I let them know what happened with Evaristus and Loring before they joined the fight. Talking about Caine made it difficult not to break down, but I managed, finding my emotions reeling back when I explained how Evaristus pushed my soul from my body and how Aunt Lacey found me.

A whole new set of questions pelted my way about Aunt Lacey—what she said, and her role as the one to shepherd Donovan and I into our afterlife.

"She's the one Caine and I saw after Joelly disintegrated you?"

I nodded. Kim was in awe.

I didn't tell them about her saying Donovan needed more power. I didn't know what she meant and didn't know how to go about getting it, even if I did.

"When are we going back in?" I broke their amusement at me seeing Aunt Lacey. Images of her were lost as thoughts of Caine and Jet in a nest of Tainted took over.

Ranlyn looked to me and tilted his head. "Many are either trapped or dead within Diluculo. At least twenty that we are aware of on our side alone and that doesn't count the endless amount of the Blind and Magics that had been missing since before we went in. I'm truly sorry Caine and Jet may be alive and trapped. When a plan is formulated, you'll know, but don't expect any progress for months. Maybe years."

"Years? With all the power you have, 'maybe years' is all you have to give me and anyone else who has someone they care about stuck in there?"

Ranlyn leaned towards me, elbows on the table.

"Don't bother. I get it. Priorities. And Caine and Jet aren't it. It doesn't mean I have to be happy about it."

He sat back. "Fair enough."

Fair enough? Fucking dickhole. I bet if it was someone close to him or another Elder, a plan would be issued the following week. But no, it's fine. Caine and Jet can wait years.

I wasn't worried. I'd have them out before then. Olive had to have something in the attic. My answers were with her, not at this table.

Ranlyn exhaled with something close to a sigh. "Miklos and Hinapouri are no longer welcome in this Coven. If you see either of them, contact myself or Veata with the info, but don't approach them. We'll warn the others of this as well."

Kim shifted in her chair. "Why were they attacking their own Coven members in the first place?"

"They weren't." Veata grinned, white pupils shining with a mischievousness. "They were attacking the Soul Seer and her grey-eyed lover."

"Excuse me?" Donovan's irritation twanged our connection enough to make me swallow in discomfort.

Veata's head crooked to the side. "My mistake. Things changed while I was in use as a Puppet. That'll earn you a reputation of another sort, Soul Seer."

Kim made a throaty laugh while Donovan's irritation grew claws I felt, though he kept control of.

"There have been many premonitions and prophecies over time." Vincent moved on and saved me more embarrassment. "Called forth by gifted Magics and many-a-time, they ring true."

"Saying what, exactly?" I wasn't letting him out of telling us.

Vincent took a breath. Ranlyn took over. "Hinapouri and Miklos were acting upon a foretelling, believing they were saving themselves and others from a future that can never come true."

"Spill it, Jeeves."

A heavy sigh, now from Vincent as his eyes shifted around the room. "As prophecies or premonitions go, this one in particular is frustratingly cryptic. I won't bore you with every word, but once it was sifted through and deliberated upon, its main thesis illustrates a future where you," he looked to me, "and Caine dismantle the Sovereignty."

Glancing at Donovan, who was looking in front of him, eyes far away and pensive, I couldn't help but answer with, "Does it need dismantling?"

Vincent actually laughed. Not a chuckle, but a full-out belly jiggler.

"I don't fucking know!" Bosco awoke with a snort. I ran my hand down his back to try and soothe him. "I learned about it two seconds ago and now you're saying Caine and I are taking it down like turncoating the Mafia!"

"Or Donovan." Ranlyn earned him multiple sets of glares. "That was one place where we stood undecided."

"Premonitions rarely spell out names." Kim sat up in her chair. "Why did they assume it talked about Caine? And how did you know it was Sophie? No one questioned that part?"

Veata leaned into her cane. "It spoke of a Soul Seer."

"I'm not the only Soul Seer out there."

"No." Vincent exchanged a shifty look with Ranlyn. "You are, however, the only Soul Seer in this Coven and the only Soul Seer we know of that has survived the Death Trials more than once. Now that you have explained further, you have also received intervention from your Soul Shepherd to incapacitate Evaristus. All outlined within the foretelling in its own way."

"And why the debate of Caine or my involvement?"

Ranlyn folded his hands on the table. "It spoke of a union."

"What?" Donovan's tone was flat, though his blood pressure jumped. Or maybe it was mine as my eyes went wide with the fear of impending wedding dress shopping.

"Not that type of union."

"We don't know that." Veata's grin was far too amused.

"Please—" Ranlyn's patience was thin, but Veata continued to smile, amused. "It was more like a union of hearts, described as one that had spanned years beyond Sophie's life. The assumption was as vessels to Gareth and Nya. Hinapouri and Miklos were convinced it was the only explanation."

"I tried to make them see otherwise. I told them I had played a discerning role in those years Donovan and Sophie lived and died and reconnected. They were beyond reason. If they were wrong and

Donovan was truly the culprit, killing Sophie and Caine would cover all bases."

"Though," Veata shooed Kim out of her seat and sunk into the chair, "the Berisford's urgent need to reopen the Creation to save their family would lend credence to their suspicion."

Ranlyn shook his head. "It won't happen."

"Umm, ex-squeeze me? If you mean reopening the Creation, damn right it will."

Veata splayed her hand out in a 'I told you so' gesture.

Ranlyn closed his eyes and pressed his fingertips into his lids. "Diluculo, according to the prophecy, will be reopened, evil from inside will be released, and the Creation will be destroyed. The one's responsible will harbour evil and educate the Blind, all creating a split within the Coven and one within the Elders."

"But the Elders are already split." Kim leaned against the wall. "And that had nothing to do with what Sophie and Caine or Donovan did or didn't do. The Elders got there on their own."

"True." Vincent made a single nod.

Ranlyn huffed. "At the risk of destroying the Sovereignty and starting a civil war, they insisted a more proactive approach was appropriate and called for the three of you to die now instead of later. They didn't even consider other possibilities and went straight to ones that might still gain the Sovereignty's attention. And we don't need that."

"Wait a second! Instead of later? You make it sound like down the line it's still a possible consideration for you to kill us. Should I mark my calendar or is this the world's worst surprise party theme?"

Kim leaned forward to the back of my chair. "Why would it start a civil war?"

"That would mean part of the Coven would be on our side." Donovan half-shrugged as if he found the silver lining.

"Fine, but is there reason for the Sovereignty to be investigated?" I looked at Vincent. "You laughed and didn't answer when I asked."

Vincent continued to stare at me until a small crack of a smile was too much for him to hold back.

"We don't know anything for sure."

I scoffed at Ranlyn. "How diplomatic of you."

Donovan's anger rose. He slapped his hand down on the table. "You knew this was what Hinapouri and Miklos believed, and apparently Roe and Gerard as well, and you still brought them to Diluculo, knowing they may use it as their opportunity to handle the situation 'proactively'. If it sounds like I'm being judgemental, it's because I am. You put our lives in danger and didn't even give us the courtesy of a heads up. So much for diplomacy."

"The Huntsmen were led by lies and fear. They didn't hear the prophecy to decipher it themselves. They trusted the Elders they were with and thought it was sanctioned by all. Hinapouri and Miklos had given their word to hold out for concrete proof."

"Please." Donovan rolled his eyes. "You know how spear-happy Hinapouri is. You actually believed her?"

"This isn't helping." Ranlyn looked around the table at all of us. "Take all the time you want to read the prophecy. I'll make it available. But for now, relish in the fact that we managed to trap two of the Coven's greatest enemies. Save the rest for another day. We're not going to solve anything else right now."

Closing the Creation was no small bucket of potatoes and before we were lost in cryptic prophecies that would spin our heads in exorcist circles, we deserved a nap and to soak in the small triumph while we could. We had no guarantee that Evaristus or Loring's devotees wouldn't forge another attack or use weaker Magics to kill or torture their way back into Diluculo. Because of this, Diluculo's seal would be guarded around the clock for when the time came when we made the attempt to get inside. Not that they could stop me from getting Caine out. I won't give up on him.

The sun was up, but we were all losing steam. The banter surrounding the less touchy subjects of the battle had been told and everyone was crashing wherever they could. Jared sprawled out, making the four-person couch look like an intimate loveseat when we came out of the small dining space.

After having the quickest possible shower, as I had no hope of hot water after everyone got to it first, then reliving the muscle clenching experience as Donovan hurried through the process in half the time I had, I scooted into clean clothing until the shivering subsided.

Sleep was a must. But as I lay under the covers of the small bed next to Donovan, I couldn't relax. So much had happened and I was running on fumes, but as sleep began to pull me under, images of the dead heaping bodies in Diluculo, with Caine being amongst them, stopped sleep from taking over.

Then I was thinking of myself. Of the past me and what it was that made my past-self think of using a spell as I had on Donovan and mine's souls. Of course, it was love, but without thinking of the repercussions, this cost we paid since seemed too steep to weigh out.

Donovan was overthinking as much as I was, keeping the Sandman away when I thought I might be able to pass out.

"What's the matter?" I couldn't take it anymore.

His lids flipped open but closed as he shrugged and put an arm around me, staying atop the blankets to avoid skin contact, pulling my body to his body.

"No. Something's bothering you, so it's bothering me. What is it?"

His lids opened again and looked to me with harsh bloodshot eyes, then rolled to his back. "Are you going home tomorrow?"

"Why wouldn't I?"

"I like having you around."

"Aw, shucks, Donovan. I like having you around, too."

"Shut up." He fought to hide his dimpled smile and lost. A hint of regret hit the connection. He wished he hadn't said anything, and of course I mocked him for it because I'm an awkward asshole like that.

He settled for wrapping me up in covers to my chin and pulling me close. I didn't know what was on his mind or causing him stress in the first place. With so many topics to choose from, I could guess, though I didn't know if I could handle his answer at this point. I was too exhausted.

He seemed to have come to some type of a breaking point where he shut down and let whatever it was go.

After that, sleep came easy.

25

POST-CRISIS

W e awoke to dark skies and Bosco jumping between us and licking my face.

"Sorry guys." Kim leaned against the door we forgot to lock. "I've been entertaining him all day, but he's impatient. Everyone's leaving or has left already. Time to get going."

She closed the door behind her, giving us some privacy. Donovan took the opportunity to hold me a moment longer. He was awake but laid there as if struggling to wake up.

I didn't want to let myself enjoy the moment, but I would be lying if I said I didn't crave the comfort. Instead of fighting it, I moved Bosco out from in between us and let myself be held. I forgot about Caine, prophecies, and civil wars. I wanted something painless, something real. And while this may result in pain later and was developed from a connection that was fabricated centuries ago, it was what I needed right now. We spent immeasurable moments existing together in a bubble of intimacy far more than I had experienced previously.

The backyard had been cleared of its temporary housing tents and dance hall, as well as the makeshift morgue. Peering through the window between our small room and the hallway to the washroom, I realized how lonely it must be for Ranlyn to live here. The oppressive blackness of the back field had lost all hint of joy in the absence of the Coveners and our allies. A fair trek to escape population, which meant something bigger was holding Ranlyn to this place. Something nostalgic.

Ranlyn's home was ours while we sought safety and now we were the only ones left. Vincent hadn't said goodbye before leaving. After knowing us for centuries, you would think he would stick around for a while or return with us for a cup of coffee or bottle of rum and to talk about all he knew about us. Maybe it was too hard for him. I didn't even know where home was for the Soul Extractor, but with the rising issues, I figured I would see him soon. Reopening the Creation would happen whether they assisted or not, but I hoped Vincent would be by my side when it happened.

One place I could count on him being beside me—along with Kim—was when I went to speak with Eli and Bernadine about Caine and Jet being trapped. Definitely not something Donovan could be present for, but something Vincent could explain when my words failed me. They didn't know Kim, but it was important to me for Eli and Bernadine to understand that no one was leaving their daughter and nephew in the Creation to rot.

The next Coven meeting would bring us Coveners back together if Henry's funeral hadn't first, though we didn't have the chance to speak to Louise about that either. She may not want us there. She may want out of Coven-living all together. Not that I could blame her if she did. The way Kim explained Henry's end, I would be a constant mess in Louise's position.

With everything packed and ready—and Bosco leashed and panting in excitement for wherever we were going—I gave Ranlyn a hug, promising to meet soon, and then we went through the portal to

Aunt Lacey's. Donovan and I stepped through together to avoid the dissociative zombie effect.

We didn't talk about what led to the initial separation and Zombie situation or why he had left Ranlyn's in the first place. The consequence of doing so was unknown to both of us at the time, so I didn't expect he would do it again. Nor did we speak of our connection or the price we now paid for a love felt in a time neither of us understood. The complications of that, plus much else, could wait a few days and maybe not even then.

Having to work the next night, Kim drove home to St. Catharines, but Donovan insisted on driving me home. It would take him out of town unnecessarily, but he wanted extra time together and me staying for dinner was the first of his stall tactics. Nothing fancy, since we ordered pizza and wings to get that extra hour or two in. When Bosco finished gnawing on some pizza crust, it was time to go, and he was out of excuses.

As far as dealing with the post-crisis depression stage, it was staying at arm's length as we doused it with greasy foods. Avoidance was our greatest tactic for the moment.

Donovan stuck the keys into his ignition.

"How old are you?"

He paused and cracked a hesitant smile. "Twenty-three. How old are you?"

"Twenty-three. Guess that makes sense since we come back in each life together."

He nodded. "Any reason you're asking?"

I shrugged. "Just wondering."

Donovan felt my awkward deception across the connection without calling me out. I was glad, since responding with the true reason—that since we had already slept together, and spent centuries following each other around time, that it was probably something I should know.

Pulling up to the front parking lot of my building, I could see the cast of anxiety in Donovan's pinched expression in the dim light of his Z24.

"Coven night's soon. It's not like I'm never going to see you again."

"Oh, I know." Donovan masked his worry by smiling, showing off both dimples, but I felt his insides squirm. He wasn't sure of anything but was too afraid to say so.

Donovan wanted to help me upstairs, but I could manage my bag tossed over my shoulder and Caine's over the other shoulder, since Bosco was on a leash.

We said goodbye with nothing but the words, Donovan's longing following me all the way out to the entrance of my building and the whole elevator ride up to the sixth floor. I knew he remained close by, but I needed some space within my own apartment to recalibrate after everything we went through.

My building wasn't the classiest, but this run-down apartment was mine and when I opened my door, the familiarity comforted me like a child's favourite blankie, calling me to a cookie log and a mindless *Supernatural* rerun.

"Nice place."

My voice caught in my throat as I spun towards my small darkened hallway, since I hadn't the chance to turn on the lights yet. Vincent leaned against the wall like he had been waiting a while.

"Thanks." My heart hammered in my chest, along with Donovan's panic. "I have a phone and a buzzer. I would've let you in without the breaking and entering. Or should I be worried?" Vincent laughed, yet not in a creepy or red-flag type of way, so I worked to calm my shakes before Donovan burst into the room.

Vincent's tongue grazed his lips as if he was thinking about how to proceed, then straightened his already straight glasses. "I want to help you take down the Sovereignty."

Speechless, I stood staring at him.

He didn't have to repeat himself. I understood. As far as I knew, taking down our world's version of the law would start a chain reaction other Magics would never stand for and would cause a civil war. He knew this and was opting to forge ahead, at my side no less.

I poured us both a few fingers of whisky and we sat on the couch. Vincent talked and I listened.

———

Sign-up and stay current on book cover reveals, sales, giveaways, and more with S.J.'s newsletter! http://www. sjcairns.com/newsletter-sign-up/

———

Read on for a teaser of the never before released DEPTH, SOUL SEER CHRONICLES, BOOK 5.

DEPTH TEASER

Depth, Soul Seer Chronicles, Book 5

We thought we hatched the perfect plan. Instead of perfection, Caine was trapped with the enemy and months later I'm no closer to knowing if he or anyone else survived.

One life-altering mission is, apparently, not enough.

Tearing down the Sovereignty is also on the docket. This is Vincent's priority, but when Donovan's dark-souled mother proposes a truce to save her son and reveals Vincent's dirty little secrets, everyone questions Vincent's.

Distracting me from continued failure to reopen the Creation is my all-consuming connection with Donovan. One dampened by a nagging conscious as not even he knows my most dangerous plans.

Of all the victims in this growing war, a little boy has lost everything. And since I can't save everyone, I have to save what I can of his innocence.

ABOUT THE AUTHOR

S.J. Cairns creates paranormal romance fantasy from her hometown in Southern Ontario, Canada. When S.J is not plugging away at her laptop on her comfy couch, you can find her chasing around her two-year-old daughter alongside her husband of twenty-one years or working in true chaos at the local women and family's homeless shelters and an anti-human trafficking safe house.

Website: www.sjcairns.com
Facebook: www.facebook.com/SJCairnsauthor
Twitter: www.twitter.com/SamiJoCairns
Email: samijocairns@gmail.com